Leaving a disjointed education at fifteen, Keith found employment and a successful career in the construction business. Two years of conscription with an infantry regiment in Cyprus during the Eoka terrorist campaign was the only disruption to his long work career. Keith and his wife, Gill Mott, have lived in Sri Lanka, Thailand, India, Vietnam and Spain.

# Dedication

To my wife Gill Mott with gratitude for her patience and support

Keith Wallace

# ORGAN EXPRESS

AUSTIN MACAULEY PUBLISHERS™

LONDON ∗ CAMBRIDGE ∗ NEW YORK ∗ SHARJAH

A CIP catalogue record for this title is available from the British Library.

The book is a work of fiction and any similarity to people or actual events is purely coincidental.

ISBN 9781786122957 (Paperback)
ISBN 9781786122964 (E-Book)

www.austinmacauley.com

First Published (2018)
Austin Macauley Publishers Ltd.
25 Canada Square
Canary Wharf
London
E14 5LQ

# Acknowledgments

To Jean Kavanagh and Susie Pearce, who were invaluable during my early attempts at writing, and also Diane Morgan plus Tony Redstone who wrote very helpful critiques. Finally without Andrew the computer man's services, I would have been floundering.

# Chapter One

Luc Tun was just able to see the swirling waters of the Tonle Sap as it flowed gently south to a point where it would meet the mighty Mekong. All around him people stirred. Their mood was distinctly apprehensive and he sensed this particularly so in Lai Mee, his young sister-in-law, who was huddled close to him for protection.

The group had been assembled there the evening before when a blanket of darkness shielded their arrival from the unwanted attention of prying eyes. Sleep had been difficult as, other than the sparse shrub growth which had survived a regular cycle of flood and drought, there was nowhere for them to shelter. Confusion and uncertainty occupied their thoughts during the day which followed and until less than an hour before there had been little to reassure them of the progress being made by people who had promised them a better life.

It was growing dark again and the only sounds came from muffled breathing, an occasional low cough and the gurgle of water as the river ran relentlessly on. Some of the group were fortunate as they had carried food and drinking water with them, others among them were less so. Both Luc and Lai Mee had been part of the enforced agricultural resettlement plan when Pol Pot and the Khmer Rouge seized power in Cambodia. Both had learned from that experience and understood the importance of not being without food and clean drinking water.

Lai had persuaded Luc twice during the day to share a little of their meagre provisions with the people around them and they had been offered bundles of the new paper currency in exchange for their generosity. Both, however, knew the value of money when there was little or nothing to buy.

A chill wind stirred through leaves of the banana trees in the plantation where the group had been hidden for a day and two nights. Luc felt Lai's small hand steal inside his shirt for warmth. Despite the press of people around them, he was aroused by the intimacy of this, although he realised she was merely seeking comfort.

It was almost five years since the pair had scraped a pit with their bare hands just deep enough to take his wife's dead body and this was not the first such grave that they had dug together. His wife's parents had lasted less than a year of enforced labour and both his children had died from malnutrition, despite attempts by the adults to ensure they were given a larger share of any food.

In the years leading up to repatriation by the Vietnamese army Luc had little time for physical comforts, as starvation inhibits sexual need. When they were allowed to resettle in Pnom Penh, the old family home had seemed to carry too many ghosts for Lai Mee. As a young girl she had shown great courage throughout their ordeal in the paddy fields and jungle; back home, however, she demonstrated a timidity which was out of character. When Lai Mee asked to share his sleeping mattress, Luc had realised that she sought nothing other than his protection. A sensuous body pressed against a man dulls reason and it had been three nights before he allowed temptation to dim both his sense of decency and responsibility. Now as he felt the small familiar breast pressing against his torso he remembered how willingly she had given herself on that first occasion. They had been happy in the three years which followed and gradually Lai came to accept the presence of imagined ghosts in the old homestead as those of protective ancestors. Their lives took on some semblance of normality and after regaining possession of the family home they found the means to purchase small luxuries which had previously been denied them.

The urn was exactly where his father had said it would be and when Luc recovered it, from the tangled roots beneath an old acacia tree, it still contained the entire wealth of four thrifty generations. His father had always been astute and the pot was buried by him many years before.

Pol Pot's policy for Cambodia was based on a monetary free system of self-sufficiency where people would survive on what could be provided by an entire population working in agriculture.

On retrieving his father's nest egg Luc realised that caution was necessary as, despite liberation, any sign of affluence might draw unwanted attention.

It had been essential to bargain hard when purchasing second-hand dental instruments. This had been the first step taken to re-establish the dental practice which was abandoned when the Khmer Rouge drove all residents from the city. To keep their new-found fortune intact and to protect it from the attention of others, Luc negotiated a loan through an unscrupulous moneylender at an exorbitant rate.

The couple then lived simple and happy lives together, regularly offering gifts at a temple where they both worshipped. Luc and Lai Mee were aware that they were extremely fortunate to survive the genocide which had so violently been enforced by a brutal and harsh regime.

Lai Mee was much smaller than her sister, but despite lacking her sister's stature she had proved tough and resourceful throughout the whole of that terrible ordeal. Unlike many of her contemporaries, Lai had not succumbed to deprivation and had somehow retained her fine good looks.

As Luc and Lai Mee rebuilt lives together their happiness was marred by the loss of a complete family and the fact that they were unable to replace the two children and heirs that had been left behind in damp paddy field graves. Eventually the couple felt the strain of Lai's failure to conceive, a failure which they attributed to years of poor diet. Had Luc not come across an article on IVF treatment in an out-of-date medical journal, they might have accepted that they would be unable to further perpetuate the family name. The fact that this treatment was available only to childless couples in more affluent Western societies did nothing to deter Luc and he decided that they would attempt to travel to a country where treatment might be available to them.

He was pondering the wisdom of this decision when movement among the people alerted him to the fact that something was at last happening and the murmur of voices was eventually overshadowed by a single quiet voice of authority.

"I want you to collect all your belongings and then make your way to the water's edge. Once there you will find a number of small boats waiting to take you to a ship which is anchored out in the deep." Luc was reassured by the fact that this instruction was repeated in a number of languages and also impressed by an indication of professionalism when the voice continued.

"Please be careful where you tread. It is important that we keep noise levels to a minimum and for obvious reasons we are unable to light your path to the river."

Patience is a gift which most Asian people learn during their formative years. Luc and Lai watched as fragile craft ferried people off into the darkness and their very large group slowly diminished in size.

When Lai Mee expressed anxiety that there might not be room for them, Luc placed a consoling arm around her shoulder. An ability to survive in extreme circumstances generates a certain cunning. When the foreigner had asked him to pay both fares in full, Luc offered a percentage by way of deposit and promised to pay the rest when the ship reached international waters. The man had simply shrugged before taking the deposit and nodding his head in acceptance.

Luc was aware that many of their fellow travellers had been less cautious and the fact that money was still owed to the organisers convinced him that he and Lai Mee would not be left behind. Their turn to be transported across came at last and as he felt river gravel beneath his feet, Luc wondered if this might be his last contact with the country of his birth. If this was to be so, he had few regrets. Cambodia had not been kind to him in recent years. He had lost both his wife and children, together with his wife's parents and other relatives.

When Lai Mee and he had eventually returned home, they had waited in vain to be reunited with other members of their respective families who were sent to different locations at the start of the resettlement programme.

In the absence of his father Luc assumed ownership of the family's hidden valuables. As a firstborn son the inheritance would in any event have become his and he therefore suffered no feelings of guilt over using an asset which was unavailable to many of his fellow countrymen.

An old woman squatting in the prow of the fragile craft was screeching instructions to someone who appeared to be little more than a child and who was handling the steering pole while standing astride in the stern. The old woman's dialect was barely understandable and Lai Mee thought it was intermingled with a smattering of Thai, a language which she had briefly studied while at the Phumi Ta Krei College in the north of their country and close to the Thai border.

The current became stronger as signs of the bank where they had been moments before faded rapidly into the gloom of night.

Luc felt reassured by the child's obvious competence when backwash from some larger vessel ploughing its way upstream threatened to swamp them. He was unable to determine if the youth was a boy or a girl although with deft strokes the boat was turned into the oncoming wave.

While the article explaining IVF treatment had interested them, it had created little more than a glimmer of hope. There were, so far as they were aware, no hospitals or medical centres in Cambodia which offered that particular treatment. The whole of the country's somewhat limited welfare system had totally collapsed during the rule of Pol Pot and was now hard-pressed to cope with the immediate task of getting back onto its feet and healing the genuine sick.

Luc believed that if his country's population was to be restored to former levels there would in time be a demand for IVF treatment. This would, if and when it came, benefit the younger generation although it would be too late to overcome problems for those who were now of childbearing age.

Through generosity to a patient who was unable to pay for dental treatment, Luc learned that there was an illegal organisation offering passages to Europe for those who could afford the substantial fee. To demonstrate his appreciation of Luc's sympathetic attitude, the patient suggested that they share a bottle of rice wine. As the hour was late and there was no one waiting in the surgery, Luc agreed. The warming spirit helped loosen his patient's tongue and once he became talkative, he explained that his present financial dilemma had resulted from helping a younger brother find money to pay for an illegal passage.

Luc was unable to conceal his interest and the patient eventually offered to arrange a meeting with the people trafficking organisation.

Two weeks after sharing the bottle of saki, Luc was taken by his new talkative friend to an interview room behind a district police station. The boldness of choosing such a location struck Luc as cavalier and he felt doubt dampen his enthusiasm. When the interviewer asked searching and personal questions, it occurred to him that the man's chief concern was what Luc and Lai Mee's family would be told if a contract was agreed.

When explaining that he and Lai were without family, the interviewer became noticeably more relaxed and his accent more pronounced. This was quickly identified as French and Luc assumed the man to have stayed behind following colonial rule. The interviewer's caution and air of professionalism eventually helped ease Luc's earlier concerns. When his turn came to ask questions, he was encouraged by discovering that their initial destination was to be Algiers. He was also told that after a stopover in North Africa the group would then be taken across the Mediterranean to Marseilles for entry into France. The trafficker smiled when Luc explained that he spoke a little French and that his wife was quite fluent in that language.

Luc's recollections were distracted by the shadowing bulk of a much larger vessel as their small craft passed beneath an anchor chain.

On one side of the darkened ship a lopsided gangway was suspended and the youth at the helm had little difficulty in bringing the sampan alongside this rickety structure. With surprising agility the old woman stepped across onto the bottom step and, with a deftness which belied her apparent age, she quickly made the craft fast alongside.

Having been the last to board the sampan, Luc and Lai were amongst the first to make it to the upper deck of the larger vessel. With his night vision accustomed to gloom, Luc was able to see that people who had made the earlier crossings were now assembled in an orderly manner on the open deck. While suggesting to Lai that they move across to join this group, someone that he thought might be crew gruffly ordered him to be quiet.

"Your voice will carry over open water and if we are to make it safely through border control it is important that no one suspects what is happening out here."

A while later the sound of a gentle thump from the bottom of the companionway indicated that yet another frail craft was alongside. With the last of the late arrivals assembled on deck, a man then appeared to be taking a headcount and Luc assumed this indicated that everyone was now safely aboard.

Eventually appearing satisfied, the individual with the clipboard then quietly addressed them.

"One of the crew will shortly take you below to the hold, where you will spend most of your time throughout the coming journey. It is important that you stay concealed during the hours of daylight as we will pass other shipping and your presence should not be revealed. When nightfall arrives you will be allowed on deck for exercise and fresh air." He paused briefly while another crew member appeared to be prompting him.

"You will also be served food twice a day and it will be brought to you in the hold. Now, so that you all know what to expect, we will shortly be getting under way and in roughly five hours' time we will be stopping to allow the customs and immigration launch to come alongside. When officials have checked the ship's papers we hope that we will then be free to travel the short distance downstream to where Vietnamese authorities will repeat the same procedure." A long pause followed and Luc wrongly assumed they were about to be shown below.

"It is important that complete silence is maintained while our manifest is being examined," the spokesman continued.

"Those of you who wished to bring babies and young children along will perhaps now understand the reason for our refusal. Any indication that we have people below will activate a search of the ship and your discovery will result in both it and the crew being impounded. All of you would then of course be returned to Phnom Penh where you would face the consequences of attempting to leave the country without permission."

When the man spoke next it was to ask if there were any questions before they were taken to the hold. Although the briefing had seemed sufficiently explicit, Luc was surprised that not one question was raised.

Climbing steadily down the vertical steel ladder into the hold's black abyss, Luc realised it was as well that small children and elderly people had been refused permission to join the group. Lai had proved her fitness and agility many times in the years since they were together, yet he feared for her safety during the seemingly bottomless descent.

Darkness increased as a rumbling noise overhead indicated that the hatch covers were being closed. Mercifully there were only minutes to wait before the cavernous hold was illuminated by a series of weak lights, lights not unlike those used over emergency exits in cinemas and other poorly-lit places.

Vibration and the squealing sound of winch clutches next indicated that the crew was making ready to get under way. This was confirmed by the sound of heavy chain and a deeper throbbing noise from the ship's engines as the anchor came up.

Luc had believed their pickup point to have been somewhere upstream above Phnom Penh; this was partially confirmed by the time estimated for them to reach the border crossing.

As his eyes became accustomed to the gloom, Luc noticed that a number of thin mattresses and coarse blankets were scattered at random on the steel plate floor of the hold. Collecting two mattresses and sufficient blankets for their needs, Lai quickly secured a vacant space in a corner between the ship's side and a bulkhead.

"This should allow us a little privacy on at least two sides," she declared, while placing their belongings on the deck plating and covering them with blankets.

Both border checks seemed to take an incredibly long time and they were able to see, from the expressions on the faces of their fellow travellers, that they were not alone in their fear of discovery. A murmur of relief travelled around the echoing hold when the ship finally got under way. From that point the journey progressed much as they had been told to expect, spoiled only by the fact that latrines and washing facilities were limited. Because of this, their short time spent on the open deck each night was eagerly awaited. If inadequate latrines caused disgruntled feelings, an abundance of food was met with approval. The rationing quota was in all probability much greater than the people had been accustomed to for many years. Through the contentment of satisfied appetites, most passengers lost count of the days that passed. The journey became boringly monotonous until eventually they met open sea and the ship's motion indicated a more turbulent passage. This in turn brought seasickness to many of their group.

Throughout the voyage the majority of passengers had in the main isolated themselves. Luc and Lai were content to remain within this anonymity as they assumed that on reaching their destination there would be no further contact with fellow travellers.

Luc was surprised when the engines slowed and an unusual amount of vibration indicated that the ship was going astern. He immediately assumed they were either about to drop anchor or manoeuvre alongside a quay. Confirmation of this came when a jarring bump had most of them staggering to stay on their feet.

As the heavy hatch cover was rolled back and the brightness of daylight streamed down, there were murmurs of surprise.

Someone with a loudhailer next summoned them to fetch their belongings and meet him up on deck. While Luc had also lost count of the days spent below, he felt sure that they had as yet not reached Algiers.

Their long period spent in subterranean gloom made focussing difficult, although Luc was eventually able to see that the ship was tied up alongside a wharf inside a bustling port. Derricks on a ship astern were discharging cargo, while on the quayside stevedores scurried about their work. Indicating the stevedores, both men and women, Lai Mee observed, "Those people appear to be Chinese. Where do you think we are?" Luc's response was cut short by a further announcement.

"Please pay attention, everyone." This instruction was issued by the same man who had told them what to expect at the start of their journey.

"You will now go ashore, where transport will be waiting to take you on to a medical centre. Once there, you will be examined by a medical team prior to the recommencement of your journey. For what will then become obvious, men will be separated from the women and you will have an opportunity to freshen up and take showers. I feel confident that this will be welcome after the poor facilities which you have experienced here on board." A faint smile played over the man's features as he announced this and it seemed to meet with welcome relief from the gathered assembly.

It occurred to Luc that there was no mention of a medical examination during his initial interview or during their pre-departure briefing. Luc also speculated on what might happen to any of the party who were found to be medically unfit. Keeping these thoughts to himself, Luc thought there seemed little point in adding to the unusual episode of events by further worrying Lai Mee.

# Chapter Two

The calm expression on Kate Savage's face was misleading and her mind was in turmoil. She was waiting in the reception area of a suite of offices which had obviously seen better days. Kate realised that there were many such office suites in Saigon which was in the process of recovering from the aftermath of war. She also understood that a meeting here might result in an enterprise more significant than anything that she had previously undertaken.

Glancing across at the elderly Chinese who had accompanied her, Kate was relieved that she had taken her grandfather's advice and asked his accountant friend for support and assistance.

Lung Chen's professional help had proved invaluable to Bob Savage while running an airfreight company and since making his acquaintance, Kate had also gleaned a great deal of important information about businesses in the region and the Mekong Express Company in particular.

Despite being semi-retired, the Chinese accountant maintained contact with many people throughout South East Asia and had learned that the owner of the company which Kate was hoping to purchase no longer had sons. There had been two; one was killed by regular North Vietnamese troops when patrolling the Mekong Delta with an American marine force. The second son was fatally wounded by a landmine in the Quang Tri Province. Both heirs had been lost during the American-aided war between North and South Vietnam.

Lung Chen had also established that there were two surviving daughters, an unmarried woman who was past childbearing age and one who had recently been through a difficult divorce in which her ex-husband was given custody of their children. The elderly Chinese accountant had concluded this information by telling Kate,

"My understanding is that the elderly owner has no close relatives that are in a position to take on his company. The business has experienced fierce competition from two other companies which are also operating from the Bang Dang jetty. It is unlikely that either of these would be interested, or indeed, be in a position to make, a counter offer for the Mekong Express Company".

Lung Chen's distaste and lack of enthusiasm for the proposed deal was obvious. From the outset he had counselled against it. In fact the elderly accountant suggested that if Kate wished to invest in business, there were many opportunities available where the risk was considerably less than one where sole income was derived from operating a ferry service.

What Lung Chen did not know was that, in addition to money in a trust fund which she had gained access to on her twenty-fifth birthday, there was an additional bequest from her grandfather.

Savage Air Freight Services owned a hydrofoil which was surplus to requirement and unbeknown to Kate, Bob Savage saw the vessel as a means of guiding his granddaughter into commerce.

Kate had initially been overwhelmed when offered the hydrofoil on long term charter, although she had then impressed her family by negotiating advantageous terms subject to finding suitable work for the somewhat unusual craft.

Startled by a ringing from the receptionist's telephone, Lung Chen all but fell from his high-backed chair. Realising that the accountant had briefly dozed off, Kate stifled a grin and they were then shown to an inner office.

Pleasantries were exchanged and Lung Chen formally introduced Kate to the ferry company's principal. This man's searching scrutiny then bordered on a form of rudeness.

The slightly-built Vietnamese owner was unaware that the young woman sitting opposite had access to one of the unique craft which his company operated for carrying passengers throughout the vast waterway network of the Mekong Delta. The principal might also have been forgiven for assuming he was dealing with a rich innocent who was simply indulging a passing whim. Certainly Kate's appearance suggested that she might be better suited to the catwalks of the fashion trade.

Kate was a strikingly beautiful young woman of medium height with attractive olive-coloured skin and lustrous black hair. The ferry owner immediately assumed that there was mixed blood somewhere in the young woman's background.

"Portuguese, perhaps?" the old man mused. His suspicion of mixed breeding was unerringly accurate. Kate's father had been of mixed race. His father, Bill MacDougal, was a Scot by birth and his mother Ajuna was from a wealthy Tamil family who had established themselves in the old Sri Lankan capital of Kandy.

The man's suspicions regarding Kate's lineage may have been correct, although what he could not possibly know was that, having been raised in the world of freight handling, she had gained access to and a great deal of knowledge of one particular hydrofoil and its complexities.

When Kate Savage had acquired a first class honours degree from an Oxbridge university, there was pressure from within the family for her to join the airfreight business. Reluctantly succumbing to pressure, Kate had then spent many hours alongside her mother at the controls of one of the company's Cessna Caravan amphibian aircraft. On the completion of prolonged periods of instruction it became all too obvious that Kate had neither the aptitude nor an inclination to become a commercial pilot. Eventually accepting this, her mother then suggested that she should shadow the company's commercial director, with a view to taking on some of her responsibilities.

In being less than enthusiastic, Kate realised that she possessed an independent streak which had probably been inherited from both her parents. Because of this, she believed that joining the family-run business would result in heated clashes with her mother. At around this time unexpected help arrived in the form of an honorary aunt who was visiting from England.

Ruby Pardoe had been a close friend and colleague of Kate's late father when they had both worked for Sri Lanka's head of state security. From an early age Kate was allowed to visit and stay with Ruby in England and when she attended first school and then university in that country, they became firm friends. Ruby was a shrewd business woman who had inherited a small seaside hotel, initially building on that business; she had then expanded into becoming the owner of a chain of hotels and motels. In all probability Ruby's business involvement would have remained at a high level had not one of the larger multinational hotel chains made a much overvalued takeover bid. The eventual sale then resulted in Ruby having more spare time than she had previously been used to, much of which was then spent in Sri Lanka with her friend Lorna Savage, Kate's mother.

When Ruby learned that Kate was being pressured into joining the family business, she had intervened, arguing strongly that Savage Air would have difficulty in accommodating two forceful and strong-willed women. Lorna Savage and her father eventually accepted the wisdom of this and the only other two board members breathed sighs of relief.

"Let the girl find her feet," Ruby had counselled. "She is not going to drift around doing nothing. Her brain is far too active for such idleness. If she works at something entirely different she may eventually wish to join the company and bring fresh ideas in with her. You will not want to go on forever and your brother Richard is not getting any younger."

This remark was addressed to Lorna, who was not at all impressed or pleased by being reminded of her age. What Lorna had not been told was that Ruby was about to gift Kate nineteen thousand English pounds a year for ten years as a means of avoiding inheritance tax. For the same reason Kate had also been given a valuable city centre office block by her aunt from which a further substantial income was derived.

It would have been entirely possible for Kate to invest the capital sum from her grandfather's trust fund and live a life of considerable luxury although, as her aunt had predicted, Kate Savage derived little pleasure from inactivity.

When Ruby eventually got round to asking what she was going to do with the Flying Dolphin hydrofoil, Kate said she would find work for it. There then came a prolonged period of silent contemplation as Ruby digested this response, until eventually suggesting,

"It is possible you do not realise that when your grandfather acquired the Flying Dolphin, it was his intention to use it for ferrying passengers from Jaffna across the Palk Straits to Kodikkarai. This was of course dependent on a cessation of troubles with the Tamil Tigers. Sadly we are all still waiting for that conflict to be resolved."

A distant expression then clouded Ruby's features and Kate thought the older woman's thoughts had returned to her involvement with the island's conflict.

"It wouldn't have worked anyway," Ruby continued. "Your grandfather is a freight man and didn't understand that operating a passenger service needs reliability. It also requires backup. If your only craft has mechanical problems, operating schedules fail and your passengers quickly find alternative means of travel." Ruby paused and Kate took the opportunity to suggest,

"I'm not sure that I understand the point you're making." Her aunt nodded before continuing.

"A good reliable service is essential in business and although I realise you have always shared your grandfather's enthusiasm for the hydrofoil, over-enthusiasm can be both risky and dangerous. If you are serious about this, I would suggest that you need additional craft and certainly so if you intend carrying passengers. More importantly is to find an existing route which requires an injection of cash or where the operating company is ripe for takeover."

Realising the wisdom of this last remark and the enormity of such an undertaking, Kate understood that Ruby had quickly arrived at an accurate appraisal.

"I don't think you should rush things. You are fortunate in so much as you don't have to immediately concern yourself with generating personal income. If you seriously think, however, that you would like to make use of the Dolphin to start a business, you should certainly consider acquiring an existing company. When and if you succeed, I would be prepared to buy in if it's something that you would like me to do. I would also then take an active role. Say as finance director. That way I would be able to keep an eye on my investment and if I thought things were not working, pull you out before it was too late." Kate had then thought long and hard on Ruby's offer before responding.

"Are you sure that you would want to be involved? Selling the hotels has freed you from all kinds of problems and I think you should now be enjoying a relaxed life without business worries."

"I'm not ready to be turned out to grass just yet, girl, I have had months of inactivity and it's not sitting well with me. Maybe that's why I'm suggesting a business involvement with you. Perhaps I'm just being selfish."

Following the conclusion of that conversation some eighteen months had passed until Kate had reached this stage of serious negotiation. There had been numerous wasted journeys, she had considered several down at the heel businesses and looked at any number of hydrofoils in various stages of dilapidation. Kate had taken Ruby's advice seriously from the outset and realised that she should acquire not only additional craft but also routes and the necessary licence to operate.

"Uncle Lung Chen, will you please ask the honourable gentleman if the licence he holds allows him to operate on routes other than to Vung Tau?" A negative head shake in response to the accountant's question prompted Kate to continue,

"Will you also ask if there is a possibility of the existing operating routes being extended?" Kate had known the answer to both questions before they were asked and so the principal's further negative response came as no surprise.

"Will you please say our offer is 995,000 US dollars for the business together with its complete stock and operating licences?" There was a brief moment of hesitation before translating this; Lung Chen had previously estimated the business to be worth in excess of one point nine million dollars.

The ferry company owner's manner then changed from solicitous to one of outrage and considerable irritation. Kate, however, forestalled the principal's response by asking Lung Chen to point out that the company's present ratio of profit to turnover was far from flattering.

Kate then detected a defensive expression cloud the Vietnamese man's otherwise impassive features. It did not, however, prevent a tirade of what seemed to be abuse.

Some while later, and after further protracted wrangling, Kate felt confident that the owner's attitude was weakening and with Lung Chen's interpretations she continued to whittle away at the principal's resistance.

Pots of tea served in delicate porcelain cups came and went as the discussion continued and Kate believed that if anything was to be gained, they were in for long and protracted negotiations. She was surprised therefore when Lung Chen unexpectedly announced,

"The principal has asked me to inform you that he will accept one point five million US dollars, Miss Savage."

Kate had been prepared for the horse trading to go on for much longer and to cover her surprise she made pretence at using a pocket calculator before responding.

In the intervening months prior to this meeting she had travelled to Canada, Scandinavia, Greece and Italy in search of a suitable company, all to no avail. Realising that their bargaining power now owed much to the poor state of the Vietnamese economy, Kate was also aware that a business undertaking in Vietnam would be reflected by its income.

"One point three million US dollars is my final offer," Kate announced, as she rose and began returning papers and other miscellaneous items to her briefcase.

Both Kate and Lung Chen had reached the door to the outer office when a guttural harangue reached their ears. Kate then ran into the elderly accountant's back as first he stopped and then turned.

Lung Chen was not given to expressing signs of pleasure or excitement; now he actually smiled as he held out his hand.

"Congratulations, Miss Savage. I believe that you are now the new owner of the Mekong Express Company. And by the way, the previous owner wishes me to say that he believes you to have Chinese blood in your veins. I am not sure if that is meant as a compliment to you, or as an insult to my forebears."

While attempting to absorb the shock which had resulted from their achievement Kate moved back into the principal's office, bowed deeply, smiled and then offered the Vietnamese man her hand.

"Uncle Lung Chen, would you please ask the honourable gentleman if he would consider working as a consultant for our new holding company? I would want him to agree to a minimum six month contract together with relevant clauses covering confidentiality and suggest if he is agreeable that you negotiate a suitable remuneration."

This proposal was accepted almost as quickly as it was offered and Kate was pleased that she had entrusted her grandfather's accountant to negotiate this final detail. She was also very aware that she had dominated negotiations and was shrewd enough to know that she would have need of Lung Chen's experience in the months ahead. Kate also supposed that oriental men were not comfortable with being upstaged by younger people and certainly not by younger women.

"Before we leave will you also arrange for the available staff to be present in the Bang Dang offices on the first morning of the takeover? I realise that some of the operating crews will be unable to attend, although we will get round to meeting them as and when they are free."

It had been a long day and as Kate crossed the busy road into Dong Khoi Street she felt exhausted.

"A stiff gin and tonic should put things right," Kate decided, while hoping that Ruby might anticipate her need and be waiting at the bar.

As the Continental Hotel came into view through a throng of people emerging from offices and shops, Kate felt pleased that the day had produced a satisfactory outcome and that she would now be able to confirm to her aunt that the journey she'd made from the UK two days before was worthwhile.

Ruby Pardoe watched her niece's approach with a strong feeling of pride; she had been sitting beneath trees on the Continental's terrace for some time hoping for Kate's return.

It was interesting for Ruby to watch people at the other tables turn and follow her niece with their eyes as she threaded her way through them. There was undoubtedly an air of innocence about the young woman and she seemed unaware of the impression her very presence created.

"Phew, it's still hot! Is that a gin and tonic you have? Lovely, it's just what I was thinking of as I made my way here." A drinks waiter quickly appeared and Ruby realised that he had also been aware of her niece's approach.

"Now, tell me, how did it go? From the expression on your face I would say that you have had an interesting afternoon."

"Better than interesting, Ruby. You and I now own a ferry company, or at least in theory we do. Obviously contracts have to be drawn up for signature and arrangements made for the first stage payment." A raised eyebrow in response to this remark indicated that further explanation was required.

"I persuaded the owner to accept payment in four instalments spread over two years as I felt sure disposal was more important to him than liquidity. We eventually settled at four percent interest on the outstanding balance. I hope you agree that it's cheap money and will keep funds in our operating account while we generate income."

"Umh, that's an interesting ploy," Ruby murmured. "It certainly is cheap money and I think you were shrewd to have concluded such an agreement."

It seemed obvious that Kate now wished to move the conversation on in an attempt to hide the pleasure she had derived from a successful outcome.

"The owner was probably fortunate to hold on to his business when the South ceded victory to Ho Chi Min's forces at the end of the war. Not many of the free enterprise operations were allowed to continue. My guess is that he, along with other businesses on the Bang Dang Jetty, has since made some good contacts within the party system."

A moment later Ruby whistled appreciatively when Kate responded to her asking what final figure had been agreed.

"You certainly have excelled. I rather think this calls for a celebration and I'll order a bottle of Moet while you go off to freshen up."

"Steady on, Ruby. There's a long night ahead and I thought we might eat out at a really good restaurant that I've found. It's tucked away in a back street where mostly only local people eat and the authentic South Vietnamese food can be mouth-wateringly delicious."

# Chapter Three

The illegal refugees had barely time to disembark before they were being herded onto an assortment of buses, which then travelled from the quayside in a convoy that snaked out through the busy streets of a small town.

"It seems strange that the organiser's previous concern for secrecy is not much in evidence here," Lai Mee observed.

Peering out through the rear view window of their coach, Luc caught one last glimpse of the ship. The vessel appeared unusually smart and out of place amongst the other cargo vessels in the dock. Black smoke was billowing from its funnel and this caused Luc to have some feelings of unease.

"It's probably that the generators are supplying power to the ventilation system," he silently tried to self reassure.

"I imagine there will be a need for lots of fresh air to circulate through those smelly holds now that our poorly-washed groups have left."

Somewhat consoled by coming to this conclusion, Luc then concentrated on taking in their surroundings. The sprawl of township suburbia quickly merged with open scrub countryside as the convoy sped along in billowing clouds of dust. They passed an assortment of farm carts which were drawn by lumbering water buffalo and Luc decided that this was an area of poor peasant farming.

Some twenty minutes had passed before the convoy slowed and then turned onto a dirt track. The ride now became less comfortable and their vehicles bounced along an uneven surface. Fortunately this discomfort was short-lived and eventually they drove in through the high wooden gates of a complex that consisted of low buildings which were surrounded by high security fencing.

Luc thought units within the complex appeared to be industrial and reassured himself once more with thoughts of the organisers' astuteness in choosing such an ordinary-looking facility.

"Please make sure that you remove all your belongings from the buses. Vehicles other than these may transport you back to the ship," the same authoritative voice instructed as they began climbing from the coaches.

"We will split our things and carry half each," Luc told Lai, when they were informed that they must now separate. Both had learned the hard way that it is essential to guard one's possessions and reasoned that by dividing them, they would be halving the risk of theft.

It came as something of a surprise when, instead of shower cubicles, the men were first taken into what appeared to be a very well-equipped and clinically clean medical centre.

Some time was then absorbed with the tedious task of form filling and when this was complete they were each given a thorough examination by male doctors. Once this process had been dealt with adhesive bands were attached to an ankle of each man. Luc had seen similar arrangements used in the Phnom Penh hospital when he was there to carry out dental treatment. He understood the bands were used for identification during surgery although it occurred to him as strange that the same procedure was being used for routine medicals.

Bending to examine the tag on his own leg more closely, he was further surprised by the fact that a series of identification numbers and codes were being used instead of his name.

Once the doctors had finished with their examinations the men were instructed to pass through a series of elaborate x-ray and scanning machines. While awaiting his turn Luc took the opportunity of looking round and felt sure that an apparatus in a small side ward was a life support machine. He was still more surprised when he spotted a well-stocked drug dispensary in another annexe.

After being x-rayed and scanned, each of the men was required to give blood samples and their identity number was then written on the sample bottle labels. With the completion of this exercise the two white-coated doctors were joined by the same man who had made all previous announcements.

"You may now put your clothes back on. Or if you wish you can carry them. It is only a short distance to the men's showers, although some of you might wish to wear shoes. There is no need for you to concern yourselves with modesty as it is unlikely that you will encounter womenfolk on the way."

As the group filed out it was noticeable that some young men were being held back and Luc supposed it was because of some medical defect which had been found.

On entering another low building through a pair of sliding doors, Luc immediately realised that a primitive arrangement of shower heads had been erected above concrete sluice channels. Once more he felt some admiration for the organisers' efficiency and forethought in providing an alternative to the poor ablution facilities on their ship.

Some out of character jostling for the nearest cubicles then took place and this determined Luc that he would not give way to bad manners.

When a spray of hot water began to flow he mentally relaxed and would have remained longer had some of the men not begun drifting back to their clothes. Feeling clean and refreshed from an abundance of hot water and soap, he was relieved to find his belongings intact and on the bench where he had left them. Had Luc then been less concerned with possessions he may have felt some alarm when realising that the shower block doors had been closed. It might also have occurred to him to question the sound of a heavy diesel engine which filtered in through the ablution block walls.

Wiping soap from his eyes, Luc was searching for a towel to dry himself on when he realised that his heart was racing and that he was also struggling to breathe.

"Surely life cannot be this cruel, when I have already been through so much?" With racing thoughts Luc was convinced that he was now having a heart attack, while with some desperation he next tried to think of anything which might reduce the pain. Breathing difficulties and fear clouded his thoughts and the pain in his chest grew stronger. Weakened by this, he slumped to the floor while attempting to suck a greater volume of air into his lungs.

Luc was on the point of giving in to the inevitable when he realised that there were other men in the shower block who were experiencing similar difficulties.

Having survived some of the worst atrocities that the Khmer Rouge had inflicted on the Cambodian people, a mental and physical toughness had helped him to survive then and he now crawled to the entrance doors with the last of his remaining strength.

With final moments of desperation driving him on, Luc's fingers probed at a seal at the bottom of the doors until with a gasp of relief he felt a flaw in the rubberised material. With some difficulty and the last of his remaining willpower he managed to prise the seal up and was immediately rewarded by an inrush of cool air against his knuckles. Jamming his fingers deeper into the gap he rolled onto his belly and placed his mouth to the tiny vent. Clean air had never tasted sweeter and he breathed deeply and then exhaled into the vast airless ablution block.

While lying in this position for some time Luc felt the pain in his chest recede and with some great relief his strength slowly returned. Further precious minutes passed by until he began to feel more comfortable and his mind then began to question what was happening.

"Surely the people who brought us to this place are more than just robbers? If that was their only motive they need not have gone to such elaborate lengths."

Luc reasoned that it would have been simpler to have executed the group prior to embarkation or at the eleventh hour while they were still in the hold of the ship. Lateral thinking had helped him survive the Pol Pot years and now as his head cleared he began to think of ways in which to escape this latest catastrophe.

On eventually concluding that the people responsible for his near asphyxiation would at some time return to open the doors, if for no better reason than to collect their victims' belongings. Luc planned that when that happened, he would attempt to sneak out and then find Lai Mee.

Reaching across with his free hand he was able to grasp a bundle of belongings which had been left close to the doors. Struggling to search inside the valise with one hand he was vaguely aware that the sound of the noisy diesel engine had stopped almost as suddenly as it had begun. Had Luc realised the significance of this he may have felt less afraid; instead he fumbled through the bundle with one hand while continuing to prise open the lower door seal with the other. The discovery of a small notebook seemed ideal for the purpose he had in mind. When he had wedged this into the tiny aperture he tentatively withdrew his hand and was relieved to find that a small amount of air was still filtering through. It next occurred to Luc that he should attempt to increase the size of the door seal gap so that a greater volume of air might flow in.

His search was made easier now by having both hands free to explore the array of belongings which were scattered around him. Coming across a large metal spoon, which he thought could be used as a lever if he was also able to find something to weigh the handle down, seemed useful. A broken piece of ductile iron piping, that had probably been discarded when repairs to the plumbing system were made, appeared ideal for purpose.

With fresh oxygen steadily filtering through into the airless chamber Luc's breathing improved dramatically and he was now able to move amongst the bodies strewn around him. His failure to find anyone alive finally decided him that survival and escape was what he should concentrate on next.

Thinking ahead and realising that he and Lai Mee would need both clothes and money if they were to survive in an environment which he presumed was completely hostile, he moved his pack closer to the entrance.

At this juncture it had not occurred to him that he would be unable to find Lai Mee, or that they would fail to escape.

Briefly he thought of putting his clothes back on and then dismissed the idea, when realising that he would need to feign death and that his clothed body would be conspicuous.

At regular intervals he placed an ear to the gap beneath the seal to check for sounds of movement. On one of those occasions he heard voices, although they quickly faded and moved farther away.

To give an impression that he was not the only one who had crawled to the doors in an attempt to escape, Luc pulled three more corpses close to the entrance and intended lying amongst them when someone came.

Feeling there was little more preparation that he could now make, he next decided to search through the discarded baggage to see if there might be something useful which would further aid his escape.

An assortment of scattered bags and cheap suitcases contained little and Luc was saddened by how ill-equipped his fellow travellers had been to start out for a new life in another country.

Looking round he made a silent resolution that he would attempt to avenge this unwarranted act of cruelty. He had experienced similar feelings when his family were destroyed by the Pol Pot regime, although in his struggle to return to a life of normality he, like so many others, quickly forgot this resolve.

Discovering a cold steel object in one of the better quality travelling bags drove thoughts of the past from his mind and his hopes soared when realising the value of his find. Cautiously extracting a heavy revolver from amongst an assortment of quality clothing, Luc read the name Webley stamped in the machined metal above the pistol grip. He had never so much as held a weapon before although he had seen enough films at cinemas to know that a weapon would need to be loaded and that the safety catch should be off if it was to be of any use.

Searching deeper into the valise, Luc next discovered a box of shells for the revolver amongst some expensive toiletries. A pigskin wallet came next and it contained an unbelievable amount of American greenback dollars together with English pounds and French francs.

Encouraged by his find, Luc swiftly searched through other discarded belongings and next discovered a small cache of diamonds in an old military style backpack. Having now been through absolutely everything, there was further time for thought and Luc concluded that using the pistol would alert people in the complex that someone had survived their mass assassination. With this in mind he placed the weapon in his bag along with the paper currency and diamonds for possible future use.

More than an hour had passed when his patience was rewarded by the sound of a metallic rasp indicating that someone was about to enter the shower block. Luc quickly lay down amongst the spread-eagled bodies which he had earlier arranged close to the entrance. For good measure he draped the limp arm of a corpse across his face and then remembered that he had not removed the spoon and notebook from beneath the door seal. Frantically scrambling to disentangle himself, he had barely seconds to spare when daylight next streamed in.

Some words which he did not understand were spoken in what he supposed to be a Chinese dialect and then the sound of retreating footsteps indicated that the building had not been entered. Despite assuming that this was for the need to vent the airless shower block, he remained quite still.

Luc had learnt caution during his years of enforced labour and decided to show further patience and restraint. It was as well that he did as after a little more than five minutes he heard the sound of a soft padded footfall and realised that someone had returned.

Cautiously peering out from beneath an entanglement of limbs, Luc watched as a shadowy figure began searching through the scattered belongings which surrounded him. It then occurred to Luc that the man had returned alone to have first pickings of whatever was worth taking.

Having ruled out using the revolver, his attention was drawn to the one item which might be useful as a weapon. The heavy iron piping, which had been used to weigh down the spoon, was within easy reach and he knew that if he was to make good his escape, this might be his only opportunity.

Searching through discarded belongings appeared to absorb the other man's whole attention and when Luc tripped against the drainage step and almost fell, the man was so absorbed with his underhand task that Luc's off-balanced stagger went unnoticed.

The downward blow was delivered with a force generated from hatred and contempt. As the pipe struck bone Luc told himself that his victim had been one of the people who had been instrumental in mass murder and he felt neither remorse nor guilt for killing another human being.

A hollow ringing sound caused by the impact reverberated throughout the shower block and Luc was concerned that the noise might attract further attention from outside.

Cautiously peering through the now open doors he waited until satisfied that no one had been alerted to the noise and then returned to the prostrate body and checked for a pulse. This was cause for further alarm as it was obvious that the thief was still alive and breathing.

Luc then realised that for his vague plan to work, it would now be necessary to complete his recent act of violence. He had killed twice before. On the first occasion it had been a Khmer official who had been responsible for the death of an elderly woman friend of his mother-in-law in one of the labour camps. His second victim was guilty of attempting to steal food from their group at one of the jungle encampments and had offered resistance when discovered.

Luc's upbringing had until then reflected the privileges of his early life. He had attended a good school before going on to university where he had studied medicine first before moving to dentistry. Certainly nothing that had happened before the upheaval which so dramatically changed the lives of Cambodian people had prepared him for the hardships which followed. He had learned quickly though and, although small in stature, Luc developed a steely toughness which helped him survive where many others perished.

Unthreading a belt from a pair of somewhat ragged and discarded pants, he wrapped the sturdy leather strap around the robber's neck before threading it through the belts buckle to form a tourniquet.

A sound of breaking wind at first startled him until he realised that by standing on the victim's back he had released some flatulence. Applying strength to the noose, Luc maintained a firm hold until finally judging that at least one of the killers had suffered a similar fate to that of the many other dead people scattered on the cold stone floor all around him.

Emitting a sigh of relief when he discovered that there was no longer a pulse, Luc then swiftly stripped the clothes from his victim's body. Fearing that the trickle of blood from an ear and the heavy swelling at the base of the man's skull might draw closer inspection, he re-positioned his victim's now naked body against one of the shower cubicle supports and hoped this would indicate that the man had fallen and banged his head when starved of oxygen.

A yellow sash which had been worn over the robber's outer clothes attracted Luc's attention next and after donning his own garments he slipped the band over his shoulder, hoping that it might provide some form of identity when he stepped out from the shower block.

Casting a last look around, Luc was once more shocked by the wanton carnage which had so recently taken place.

"For no better reason than to renege on an agreement to transport these poor devils to a better life," Luc thought, with feelings of anger and hatred slowly building.

"Now I must attempt to locate Lai Mee and we will then need to find some way of escaping from this detestable place." While thinking this, Luc also realised that it would be no easy task. Collecting his valise from where he had left it by the doors he then casually strolled out from the shower block, hoping to project an image of someone who belonged.

Luc had walked only a little way when he came across the open doors of what was so obviously a second shower block. Cautiously peering in to first ensure that he was alone, he then quickly took in a scene of identical carnage to the one which he had just left. Naked corpses were strewn around on the concrete floor and it took much longer than he would have wished to determine that Lai Mee's body was not amongst them. Though greatly relieved by his inability to find her, he was also at a loss to understand her absence.

With overwhelming dread clouding his hitherto fertile thoughts, Luc made a further search and would have continued had it not been for the sound of people approaching. Sinking thoughts of utter despair all but rendered him incapable of taking the further steps of self-preservation until a strong urge to find Lai Mee galvanised him back into action and he realised that there was little or no time to lose.

With tears streaming from his eyes he resignedly picked up the old valise and cautiously made his exit from the lifeless shower room. Grief was an emotion he had thought to never experience again. Now too late, he realised that Lai Mee had become a very important part of his life. Luc had never made comparisons between his sister in-law and his late wife, yet with more tears blurring his vision he now understood the strength of Lai Mee's love and loyalty to him.

Moving cautiously from the protection of one building to the next he silently vowed that somehow, someone was going to wish that they had never included Luc Tun in this inhuman act which had deprived him of his only true friend.

A stretch of open ground some fifteen metres wide was all that now separated him from the perimeter fence. He was about to cross this strip when he caught sight of a small group approaching.

Realising that he should take cover if he was to avoid being seen, Luc then watched from a place of concealment and saw the group approach one of the smaller buildings. It was also with more than passing interest he noticed that without exception each of the men was wearing distinctive yellow sashes similar to the one which he had taken from the robber's body in the shower block. Oblivious of being observed, the group stopped beside a hut with barred windows and peered in. Both the tone of their voices and the lewd gestures which followed suggested they were either intoxicated or high on drugs. Eventually they appeared to tire of their self-made amusement and walked off in the direction of the shower blocks.

Luc might have been at the perimeter fence and under it had it not been for the sound of a woman crying. Curiosity and a feeling of hope had him then stealing across to where the group had stood only moments before.

The barred windows were without glass and as Luc peered into the gloom, he saw four young women and three adolescent boys, all with looks of bewilderment on their troubled faces.

Instantly recognising Lai Mee, Luc experienced feelings of euphoria which then rendered him incapable of action. Tears of relief and joy flooded his eyes, his knees weakened and it was necessary for him to clutch at the wall for support. His brain seemed unable to grasp that his wildest hopes had been realised and that some divine intervention had guided him to Lai Mee.

Precious seconds were then wasted while he pondered on what to do next. Glancing down he saw that the door was not locked and had simply been secured by just one strong sliding metal bolt. Clutching this with a trembling hand he discovered that it slid back easily and he quickly gained access to Lai Mee's hut.

"I am so relieved to see you, Luc!" Lai Mee exclaimed, her eyes mirroring the joy and happiness that he was now feeling.

"We think that a group of men who were here a moment ago were being very rude and they frightened us. They also seemed rather stupid and quite rough." This explanation was then quickly followed by a question.

"Have you had your shower yet?" It then occurred to Luc that none of this group was aware of the danger that they were in. His immediate concern was to escape with Lai Mee although he realised that he could not abandon Lai Mee's fellow prisoners to face what he felt was certain death.

With an arm around Lai Mee's small waist, Luc raised his voice to gain attention.

"There is no easy way of telling you this. Please listen and try to understand what I have to say." He paused a moment to give emphasis to the warning he was about to issue.

"You are in grave danger and it is probable that you will all die unless you escape from this place. I don't know how many of you came here with family and friends, although I can tell you that without exception they are all now dead."

A gasp of incredulity greeted this statement and Luc had to raise his voice to regain their attention.

"If you are unable to believe me you will only need to visit the shower blocks to verify the truth. Any time spent doing so, however, would be better used in escaping." It was clear from the bemused expressions that none of them, including Lai Mee, believed what they were being told.

"My wife and I are leaving now. If you follow our example, I think your best chance will be to split up. There are open paddy fields beyond this compound and if you stay together in a group, you will be easily spotted when our captors send out search parties looking for us." At this point one of the adolescent boys found his voice.

"We have a madman in our midst. He describes the organisers as our captors and claims that the people who came here with us are all dead. He is a fool. Take no notice of him. I am not going anywhere. There is nothing to be gained by wandering around outside. All that will achieve is to alienate the people who are trying to help us. My family scraped together just enough money to pay for my passage from Laos to the free world and I'm not about to squander their sacrifice on what this idiot tells us."

Despite this interjection Luc could see that at least two of the others were looking anxious and when one suggested it would do no harm to take a look at the shower blocks, he knew it was time to leave.

# Chapter Four

"Would you like your usual bacon roll this morning Mr. Greenwood?" Charlie was engrossed with a newspaper and in particular with an article covering a group of African refugees who had been picked up from a sinking boat in the Mediterranean. He was in fact so absorbed with the newspaper that he had not heard the tea lady's noisy trolley.

"Yes please, Margaret, although Heaven knows I shouldn't. If my midriff expands any further, I will have to think of buying a corset."

"Oh, get away with you! You've been saying that for months and I can't see as how you have put weight on." Charlie was not displeased to hear this although he realised that the chirpy little tea lady was erring on the side of flattery and that selling mid-morning rolls was how she earned a little extra cash.

It wasn't that personal appearances bothered him. Vanity certainly was not a part of his makeup. Weight, however, had been a matter with which he'd had to contend for most of his adult life.

Charlie was, or rather had been, an amateur steeplechase jockey for more years than intended and, had it not been for a crashing fall which left him with a badly broken femur, he may still have been racing. The bone had not knitted back as it should, leaving Charlie with a slight although noticeable limp.

"Thank you, Margaret." Charlie winced as he rose from his chair and made to go round the desk to take the coffee and roll from her.

"Bloody screws in my old leg are playing up this morning. It's the cold weather, I suppose."

The greatest influence in Charlie's life had been his grandmother Lizzie. In fact when his mother had remarried and gone off to America with her new husband, Lizzie assumed the maternal role with a smooth and almost imperceptible change to their relationship.

In the last letter which Charlie had received from Lizzie before she died, she warned that he should not go on racing for too long. On rare occasions he wished that he had taken heed of her advice; on others when he looked back over the good times, he understood why he had not. Charlie had been seduced by a life which provided him with a great deal more excitement than most people could hope for.

Moving gingerly back to his chair, Charlie noticed the large beech tree with its branches threatening to penetrate his window. There had been an early hoar frost and the beech's leaves were curled and glistened white against the glass.

"Winter really is setting in now," he mumbled. While he was still racing he had always looked forward to this time of year as it created riding opportunities. Now, with so many arthritic aches and pains, his discomfort had brought a change of heart.

Taking one last glimpse at the scene outside before settling back to read his newspaper, Charlie looked across at the cricket field and noticed that the square had been fenced off and abandoned until next season. Midweek evening cricket matches were some compensation for his life at head office. In the past three years he had spent more time here than he would normally have liked.

The building had been converted to offices from a stately home and it was rumoured that during the Second World War it had housed important German prisoners. Hitler's deputy Rudolph Hess was supposed to have been kept in a heavily guarded room on the top floor after he had landed in Scotland to negotiate a peace with Winston Churchill. Charlie, for one, doubted the authenticity of this, although he often thought prisoners who had been kept at the house were more fortunate than most. Although loss of freedom was a condition he did not wish to experience, the view from barred windows out across the splendid English setting of a country park was, he thought, preferable to some barbed wire enclosure.

"God, I don't know how much longer I can take this inactivity," Charlie thought. His bad mood was next exacerbated by spilling coffee down his shirt and he realised that he would have to visit a launderette in the coming days. His distraction was then once more directed to the article on the plight of the refugees.

"Poor buggers, they must be desperate to attempt a crossing in that bloody awful boat." There was a picture of the boat in question and Charlie doubted that he would feel safe crossing the River Ouse on it. Turning the page he contemplated making a start on the crossword although quickly decided against the idea and to save it for an afternoon of further inactivity.

In folding the broadsheet his focus was drawn to an article describing a wealthy oil magnate's escape from kidnap and ransom. Charlie might not have bothered to read on had the photograph of a man which accompanied the article not looked familiar.

Mustapha Al Hameed was credited with the oil magnate's rescue. Charlie had not known the chief inspector's first name; he had, however, known the man well enough as he had served under him for the better part of two years while completing national service in Cyprus.

"So that's what's happened to the Chief Inspector," Charlie mused as he read on. It transpired that the former head of the mobile reserve was regarded as one of the more effective anti-terrorist operators in the private sector.

Through an increase in hijackings and kidnaps there was sufficient publicity regarding these people for Charlie to assume that large sums of money were to be made by offering a protection service to the world's rich and famous.

"Ah well, good luck to the old devil. I suppose I benefited from being seconded to his outfit," Charlie grudgingly conceded. He had not given much thought to that particular period of his life for a number of years.

"God, I have done nothing more than laze around all morning. It's lucky that I am no longer responsible to some of the old time site agents, as I wouldn't last long on the strength of what I have achieved today!"

Charlie had been made director of engineering services some eighteen months before and the position was not sitting well with him. Throughout the earlier part of his career, he had definitely been a hands on person.

There were certain responsibilities which came with his new position although very little which stretched him in a way that he would have preferred. He was accountable for his section's group of competent engineers and was required to ensure that they worked within financial constraints. He was also expected to attend frequent meetings which under normal circumstances he would have found tedious. In recent months he had actually found himself looking forward to these moments of respite from what was becoming a wearisome lengthy period of inactivity.

Charlie's early life was one of hard graft and he had been brought up to believe that work should take precedence over leisure and pleasure. Both his grandparents had seen to it that he understood you got from life no more than what you were prepared to put in.

On completing a degree course at Birmingham University Charlie then joined the construction company which had sponsored him through his final years of education. It was never his intent to bind himself to just one employer although he had been required to repay the cost of their sponsorship through a contract of employment. Once this period of commitment had been served Charlie was so embroiled with company activities and the camaraderie which existed amongst its staff that he was content to remain within the company framework.

When the morning post arrived Charlie seized it eagerly, hoping that it would give him some respite from boredom, although what he found was nothing other than the usual round of circulars on health and safety and the availability of staff training courses. When he had consigned this array of paper to his waste basket he then drifted into a state of semi-consciousness, a situation which was becoming ever more frequent.

Eventually a gust of wind caused the branch of the beech tree to scrape against his window and the noise woke him from his comatose state of lethargy.

Glancing down at his watch he breathed a sigh of relief on realising that it was lunchtime. Charlie had spent an entire morning either half asleep or feeling sorry for himself; a state of mind which he decided should not be allowed to continue. Lunch at the office was one of the highlights of a typical day for Charlie, simply because it provided an interlude from the tedium of inactivity.

The directors' dining room was used only when clients or important dignitaries were being entertained and at other times both staff and directors ate together in the cafeteria.

"Don't you dare take that last portion of steak pie," a voice from behind called out.

"And why not? At least you will have someone to cook for you when you eventually tear yourself away from the pub this evening."

"I thought my waistline was bad, although you really should take a look in the mirror," Bill Arthurs grinned back. Over the years Bill and Charlie had worked on numerous contracts, sometimes in inhospitable countries where creature comfort was not always a consideration.

Bill had been promoted through the company system from a junior plant manager to his current position of managing director for the company's mechanical plant division.

"You've had your chances. If you hadn't been such a philanderer during your misspent youth, you could also have someone at home looking out for you."

This brief exchange brought grins to the faces of other staff in the canteen queue, all of whom were familiar with this regular banter.

Charlie's first contract as a junior engineer was on a major bypass project where Bill had been the plant manager. When Charlie suggested to a section foreman that the lower tolerance levels on the sub base was costing the company additional blacktop material imports, he was told that if he thought he could improve on what the experienced grader operator was achieving, he was welcome to try. What the section foreman had been unaware of was that during holidays from both sixth form and university,

Charlie had spent all his time working for an earth-moving contractor where he had learned the skills of operating heavy machinery.

When the section of sub base which Charlie levelled was checked, it was found to be plus a quarter of an inch which was just inside the maximum tolerance allowed. Stories about this and the section foreman's embarrassment quickly spread and it was eventually heard by Bill, who sought Charlie's company in the pub on a day when the site was rained off. Since then the pair had become firm friends.

"So, how have you been amusing yourself this morning?" Charlie asked, as the pair found an unoccupied table.

"Trying to finalise my budget before going off to Papua New Guinea," Bill groaned.

"I'd forgotten you were going, lucky sod. Wouldn't care to swap and let me go in your place?" Charlie retorted with genuine envy.

"Sure, you can go. Bit of a wild and woolly place from what I hear. It won't be a picnic and I'm pleased it's only going to be a short trip. If I really decided to swap, you would soon be withdrawing your offer and you know it."

"You might be surprised then. God, Bill, I would give anything to get away from this place for a few months, even a few days if that was all that was on offer. In fact if we don't land that power station contract down on the Severn, I think I'll quit." Something in Charlie's tone made his friend look up and pause before suggesting.

"I really think you're serious?" Bill's tone had changed from joviality to one of concern.

"What's brought this on, Charlie? It's unlike you. You're not a quitter. Everyone here thinks that you have the company name running through you like a stick of seaside rock."

"I wish I'd never taken this appointment. It's doing my head in. There just isn't enough to keep me occupied, Bill. The engineers in my section are competent people and rarely require input from me. Sure, I have a responsibility for the end product and believe me I go through everything with a fine toothcomb."

"I am sorry. I hadn't realised you were finding the job difficult. Is there anything I can do?"

"You misunderstand. Work isn't the problem. It's the lack of it which is driving me nuts. I have never in all my life known time to drag the way it does here. Since the completion of Sullom Voe I have felt completely wasted."

Following this unexpected observation a gloomy silence descended over the table and Bill appeared to lose interest in the food which he had previously been tackling with gusto.

"Please Bill, don't take this to heart. It's no big deal. It's just me. I can't stand doing nothing and if something doesn't break soon I am going to reassess what I'm doing with my life. I am still only in my fifties and I have never been one to subscribe to the theory that you can't teach an old dog new tricks. Although thanks for the offer of help. I really do appreciate your concern."

"You bloody old confirmed bachelors are all the same. If you'd had a wife and kids to bring up you would need to think about responsibilities and wouldn't be considering kicking over the traces." Charlie's friend paused to look out of the window at two rabbits which were grazing on the lawn.

"What you need is a holiday. I don't recall you taking one at all last year. If things are slack, why don't you take off for a couple of weeks to freshen up?"

Charlie's shrug was difficult to interpret and Bill was not sure if it indicated a lack of enthusiasm or simply that his suggestion was not being considered.

"I reckon if you spoke to the old man he'd not object to you taking as much as three weeks' holiday in one go. Worst thing that happened to you was that last riding accident. While you were still racing everything was tackled with enthusiasm. I've noticed recently that you seem lethargic and your old zest for life appears to have deserted you."

Bill paused to pour more water from a jug into his glass and while doing so he wondered if he had gone too far with both his observation and advice. Quickly deciding that this was what real friendship was all about, he decided to continue.

"Why don't you do something out of the ordinary, say, like taking that horse of yours over to Ireland and riding her round the West coast? I imagine if you researched such a project in advance there would be stabling en route and good digs where you might sample some real Irish hospitality."

Whenever possible Bill had followed Charlie's amateur racing career with more than passing interest. He had learned something of the horse world and knew that Charlie still owned a retired chasing mare which he kept stabled at livery.

"That might be a good idea, although at the end of it I would still need to come back here. It's all right for you, you have Pauline to go away with, someone with whom you can share the pleasure of a holiday."

Charlie had not wished to sound self-pitying and so thought that he should add to this.

"I realise, and you have reminded me often enough, that I have made my bed and so I should accept that I now have to lie on it. Normally I'm okay at putting up with my own company, although holidays are different."

"Well, why don't you give one of those singles holidays another go?"

"Not likely. I had barely stowed my bag last time when some old divorcee was trying to get into my bunk. Not my scene at all, I'm afraid."

Three summers before Charlie had taken himself off to Greece on a sailing holiday which catered for single people. He was one of only two men in the group and the other male was well past pensionable age.

"I have to say though, that your suggestion of Ireland appeals. I did a spell on secondment over there when they brought natural gas in from Bantry Bay and I fell in love with Cork and the South."

As people began leaving the dining room, Charlie promised his friend that he would give the idea of an Irish holiday further consideration.

The afternoon was monotonous and passed equally as slowly as the morning. Eventually noise of staff leaving the building filtered up to him and after a reasonable gap which he deemed fitting to his position, Charlie followed in their wake.

Parking in a convenient spot close to his house, he then strode through an alleyway on a short route to "The Three Cups" public house in Newham Street. A familiar early evening crowd appeared to be in good form and a pint of real ale was placed in Charlie's hand before he'd barely time to catch his breath.

The warm atmosphere and humorous conversation proved a pleasant interlude to his very unexciting day and it was not long before his glass was empty and he had set up another round of drinks. A third pint appeared in front of him before he had finished the second and Charlie realised he would become embroiled in a heavy drinking session unless he then called it a day.

Making his way back home, he noticed a hacking saddle on display in Peacock's auction rooms. On impulse he tried the door and was surprised to find it was still not locked. Charlie made his way across to where the saddle had been placed for viewing and then judged it to be a sixteen inch Eldonian in good condition.

"Can I help?" a voice from behind inquired. Turning, Charlie saw a man who he recognised as one of the auctioneers.

"Sorry, I spotted this saddle and on impulse tried the door."

"Bloody boy. That's the second time this month he's gone home without locking up. I'll put a flea in his ear tomorrow. Are you interested then? I think it carries a reserve of twenty-five quid. Belonged to some farmer out at Pavenham. He's passed away and his widow is not interested in horses."

"It's certainly been looked after and the one I have needs to go in for repair. I believe the auction takes place on Wednesday?" The auctioneer nodded to confirm this and added that he thought the saddle would come under the hammer at around midday.

On Wednesday morning Charlie asked one of his staff to hold the fort while he drove back into Bedford. He had become familiar with the town while working for a friend's husband during school vacations. On eventually concluding that living in the company's bachelor quarters was not for him, he decided that buying a house in the town was a sensible alternative.

Arriving at the sale room, Charlie encountered an individual, who he thought might be a dealer, who was attempting to acquire the saddle at a knock-down price. Charlie topped his bid of twenty-six pounds with a further twenty and the man walked away with a resigned shrug.

Delighted with his purchase, Charlie decided to drop it in at the house before going back to work. As he opened the front door his telephone was ringing and on picking it up he heard a voice which he instantly recognised.

"Charlie? Your secretary said you'd popped into town. I took a chance on catching you at home. Skiving, I suppose?" Charlie laughed.

"I'm on my way back, Bill. I've just bought a second-hand saddle in Peacock's sale and dropped it off."

"Well, I hope that doesn't mean you have already booked the Irish holiday. I've been talking to the boss and he's come up with something. Anyway can you get yourself back here sharpish? He wants to see you at four; will you be able to make it?"

"Of course, I'll be there, don't worry. It sounds mysterious, what's it all about?"

"He will explain. It's a little complicated and I honestly haven't time to go into detail. I have to get off home now and start packing for my trip. My flight time is early evening and I'm cutting things fine. Good luck, I hope you approve of what he has lined up for you!"

Charlie heard the receiver click at the other end and cursed loudly. He was intrigued although knew he would have to curb his curiosity for a while longer.

At four o' clock he was shown into the chief executive's office.

"Afternoon, Charlie. Sit yourself down. Bill has been telling me that you're getting restless." The bearded man paused for a reaction to this typically blunt opening remark, although when Charlie failed to respond, he continued.

"To be frank, I wouldn't want to lose you. Because we value your input, I have come up with a couple of things which you might like to get your teeth into. There is a small job which I would like you to take care of and when you've sorted that out, I would then like you to take on a management role for a harbour contract in Sri Lanka."

Charlie was about to ask if this meant demotion although his question was anticipated.

"You will not be losing your directorship and when the harbour project has been completed, I would like you to return to head office. Will you do this for me, Charlie? We're desperately short of people capable of heading up a project of that complexity. It's an overseas grant-aid contract. I want it completed on schedule and without any cock-ups. What do you think?"

"Yes, of course. That sounds great! Although you mentioned something you want me to do first. What would that be?"

"There are some engineering problems on the mass transit railway project in Hong Kong. Alistair Meckown has asked if we can supply some engineering assistance from this end. He wants someone to convince the client that one of their proposals is wrong. It shouldn't take more than a week and then it might be an idea for you to take some leave before going to Sri Lanka. There won't be much opportunity for holidays once that project starts." Charlie knew that Alistair Meckown was the project manager on the mass railway contract in Hong Kong.

"When do you want me to leave?"

"Wednesday morning from Heathrow. You will have Martin Mansfield for company as he is taking charge of temporary piling on the Ma-On-Shan contract."

"That's good, I like Martin. I worked with him in Kenya. It will be nice to have someone to share a tedious flight with and more so as some of his stories can be quite amusing."

The flight was scheduled for late afternoon and as previously arranged, Charlie found Martin Mansfield waiting for him at the Thai Air check in desk. Martin enjoyed a reputation for being an extremely good works manager with a particular skill for marine work and piling. He was also a fine singer and Charlie had spent many evenings in expat bars listening to Martin's renditions of the Irish songs he had learned in his youth. He also knew other songs which had their roots in the construction industry and was word perfect when he sang the McAlpine fusiliers.

"Word has it that you are going to run the new job in Sri Lanka, Charlie," Martin probed as they were about to separate in the arrivals lounge at Kai Tak airport.

"Is there any chance you might find a place for an old piling hand on the Sri Lanka contract?"

"I dunno, Martin. I've not picked up on it yet and I'm surprised that you would know anything about it."

"Och, I have known this past two weeks or more. You better than anyone should know how the grapevine works in our company, Charlie."

"Fair enough," Charlie replied with some resignation. "If I think there is a place for you, I will certainly try to get you out. Although why in the hell would you want to go there anyway? The island has been torn apart by civil conflict for the last dozen years or more. No one in their right mind would normally want to work there."

"Ah right enough, although the tax situation is a big incentive and besides you will need someone to watch your back if things get rough."

It transpired that the engineering problem which Charlie had been asked to resolve was simple and he doubted that there was really a need for his input. The one consolation of his stay was that he was able to spend an evening watching horse racing at the Happy Valley racecourse. Although his real interest was in steeple chasing and not flat racing, he was intrigued by the atmosphere and the frantic betting frenzy of the Chinese race goers.

# Chapter Five

Luc Tun and Lai Mee were moving cautiously towards the perimeter fence while making full use of every available building to shield their approach. They had reached a point where just one building remained between them and the boundary when they saw a solitary figure moving purposefully towards them.

Pressing Lai back into shadow, Luc took the pistol from his valise. As the figure strode round the corner he was startled to see it was a woman and that she was also wearing the now familiar yellow sash. Had he not moved quickly to clamp her mouth she would have called out and betrayed their presence. On next realising that the muzzle of a revolver was being jammed into her eye any urge by the sash wearing woman to resist quickly disappeared.

Rapidly considering what he should do next, Luc summed up the situation and instructed Lai Mee to remove the sash from the woman's shoulder and also the coarse denim skirt that she was wearing.

"Tear the skirt into strips. We will need something to bind her hands and feet and also something to keep her quiet until we can make good our escape," Luc urged.

"What about this yellow band; would it not be easier to secure her with that?" Luc then very quietly told her that they would probably have a more important use for the sash although with all that was happening, there was no time to explain in detail.

When Lai Mee found difficulty in tearing the very tough material that the skirt was made from, Luc impatiently thrust the revolver into her hand and instructed.

"If she moves so much as a muscle, shoot her." The utter look of horror that this instruction prompted fortunately went unnoticed by the woman and Luc quickly followed his instruction with what he hoped was both persuasion and reassurance.

"It will be no more difficult than the Khmer guard that you killed when we last fled for our lives."

There was no way of knowing if the woman understood Khmer although Luc hoped so, as in reality he knew that Lai never had, and was most unlikely to, ever kill anyone.

The material tested his strength; despite this he eventually produced sufficient strips with which to bind the woman's wrists and ankles. For additional security Luc also shredded the coarse cotton slip the woman was wearing beneath her skirt to be used as a gag.

"I believe it will help us to avoid unwanted attention if you now put this sash over your shoulder." Luc indicated the yellow band which Lai had proposed using to secure the woman and once she had complied, he asked,

"Will you now please give me a hand to roll her between the foundation supports of this building?" With the tightly bound and gagged woman safely deposited and out of sight, Luc suggested,

"I hope that those bindings will prevent her from wriggling free as we will in all probability require all the time there is to make good our escape."

Emboldened by the fact that they were now both wearing distinctive yellow sashes, Luc decided that they should try to relax and act as though they had every right to be strolling through the complex.

On stepping out onto open ground between the fence and buildings, they had covered no great distance when a group of people ahead of them appeared to be heading towards a small picket gate which had previously been obscured from view.

"Let's keep our distance. We don't want to get close enough for them to engage us in conversation, although it might be useful to follow them."

When the leading group had passed through the wicket gate, Luc and Lai watched with interest as they entered a small shed beyond the perimeter fence and seconds later emerged wheeling bicycles.

"Our fortunes may have taken a turn for the better!" Luc exclaimed when they found an assortment of unattended machines propped on stands inside the lean-to cycle shelter.

The group that they had followed through the perimeter fencing was now some distance away and appeared quite small as they pedalled up a rise on the dirt road.

Paddy fields stretched away toward the horizon on either side of Luc and Lai Mee and occasionally they caught glimpses of brightly-coloured kingfishers diving from fishing perches for small fry in the shallows. The road was both dry and dusty, although the scene around them was idyllic and Luc found difficulty in comprehending the carnage which they had so recently left behind.

Because Lai Mee had followed him from the medical centre unquestioningly he would have demonstrated an affection rarely displayed had they not been mounted on bicycles. Luc's relief that Lai Mee had not perished in the shower block still threatened to overwhelm him. On numerous occasions in their past Lai had demonstrated an unflinching loyalty to him and whilst she had not asked, he now believed that she was entitled to further explanation.

Lai's eyes widened with horror as Luc next described how he had managed to survive and the terrible scenes of death which he had witnessed. Lai Mee was neither shocked nor surprised when Luc told her of how he had dealt with the baggage robber as she had acted as his decoy when years before he had killed the Khmer official. Lai also understood that injustice and abuse of the weak was one of the few things which might prompt the man she loved to take violent measures.

"When I searched the women's shower block looking for you and drew a blank I gave up all hope of ever finding you alive and my feelings of despair were utterly indescribable."

Despite their present circumstances, Lai Mee felt a warm glow of pleasure at this completely out of character pronouncement.

"It seemed all too obvious that you had perished along with the others although I was unable to understand why your body was not in the shower block," Luc continued.

"I don't think I will ever be able to describe my feelings of relief and joy when I found you in that cell." Lai would have felt overwhelming happiness in other circumstances. Now, however, she was struggling to grasp the enormity of all that was happening.

"I wonder why your group was spared?" Luc's next question then helped to re-focus her thoughts.

"Perhaps they had other use for us. Maybe they were planning to sell us off into a life of slavery? I read an article before we left home which suggested that slavery is still very much practised in many African, Indian and Middle Eastern countries." A pothole in the road next caused Lai Mee to lurch to one side before continuing.

"It may have been that we were going to be sold to some rich Arab potentate. The people in my cell all appeared to be young and fit. They were also not unattractive, probably quite valuable in fact." Luc's response was no more than a nod and might easily have indicated agreement.

With her slowly clearing thought train, Lai Mee next decided to broach another subject.

"If we are able reach that town where we left the ship, will you report what has happened out here today to someone in authority?"

In the time that they had spent together since his wife's death, Lai Mee had slipped into the familiar role of female subservience and Luc was therefore not surprised that she was content to leave the important decision making to him.

Had Lai not asked and drawn his attention to what they should do next, it is probable that Luc would have considered attempting to make contact with the local police. Now as he pondered their present dilemma he remembered how they had disembarked from the ship with little sign of the previous secrecy which they had been subjected to. Luc also thought of how openly the convoy of buses transporting their group through the town had travelled with little or no attempt at concealing what was happening. In addition to this, there was also the group of cyclists ahead who he presumed were heading into town.

As Luc considered these facts it seemed probable that the medical centre's activity was known to many of the town's inhabitants. If that was the case, he decided that they should exercise caution before making contact with the authorities or people in general.

"I think first we will try to lie low somewhere. In fact, I have a strong feeling that we should avoid the town altogether. The group in front appears to be heading in that direction and if it's where they all live, there will be a greater risk of our being recaptured."

"I realise you saw things back there which were horrific but do you really think that the medical centre people would risk coming into town for us? Surely they wouldn't dare do such a thing."

"When they discover that you are missing they will want to recapture you as quickly as possible as they will be all too aware that there is a danger of you getting word to some authority which will ultimately deal with them. The mere fact that you are missing will indicate the possibility that you wandered around the compound and they will assume that you may have seen the carnage which existed in both shower blocks."

Luc paused to regain his breath; moments before they had started on the rise over which the group in front had now disappeared.

"If I were in their shoes the town would be the first place that I would start looking even if it meant raising suspicion amongst the local people." Lai appeared satisfied by this conclusion, as she next asked,

"Can we stop soon? I realise we should press on and that I am being a nuisance, but there were no toilet facilities in our hut and I now badly need a pee."

Looking ahead, Luc could see the familiar skeletal structure of a wind pump straddling a pump house.

"We can stop there," he pointed. "You should be able to find some privacy and it will be good for us to leave this roadway for a while."

Some minutes later they arrived at the site which had obviously been constructed to pump water for irrigation purposes and Luc concealed their bicycles in a small copse of willow beside an irrigation pond. When he had inspected the area to ensure that they were alone, he squatted down in the shade provided by a somewhat dilapidated pump house building. This in turn allowed him a vantage point from where he had a clear view of the dirt road along which they had just travelled.

The sensation of his chin falling to his chest roused him from a deep urge to sleep and he struggled to shake away his now extreme feelings of fatigue. Luc's limited understanding of medicine through dentistry convinced him that this drowsiness was a reaction to the events which he had earlier experienced.

Splashing sounds from behind the pump house brought an amused smile to his face. Throughout the harshest years of their experiences under the Khmer regime, Lai Mee's obsession with cleanliness had been legendary and it had often been suggested by her friends that she would willingly forfeit food if the alternative was for her to be able to bathe.

As Luc fought off the urge to sleep it occurred to him that unlike the rest of their group, Lai and the people in her cell had not been given the opportunity of taking a shower.

Somewhere overhead the unbroken song of a lark intensified and the peaceful atmosphere once more brought Luc's chin to his chest. Vigilance was one more discipline which Luc had taught himself under the punishing years of Pol Pot's regime and some instinct compelled his tired brain to stay alert.

Shaking off his drowsiness, Luc now made a conscious effort to focus on the dirt road along which they had travelled. With some alarm he next realised that a speck in the distance was travelling steadily towards them. Moving swiftly but cautiously to the rear of the building, he was relieved to find Lai Mee already dressed and in the process of combing her long black hair.

"Come quickly, Lai. There is someone travelling from the direction of the medical centre and we will need to find a place where it is safe for us to hide. My guess is that they are looking for you and they will almost certainly stop and search here. The pump house will probably be the first place they will look and we should give it a wide berth."

Grasping Lai's hand while searching for a suitable place, Luc's eyes travelled to the base of the structure which supported the wind pump. Looking up he immediately saw that a small cabin had been erected just below the vane gearbox housing and that a steel access ladder was leading up to it through the supporting framework. It occurred to him that this had been erected to provide access for maintaining the mechanism.

"Will you be able to climb up there?" A hesitant nod from Lai's head sent loose hair cascading over her face and he knew that she would attempt anything he asked of her. He was also further convinced of her ability when remembering the numerous times that she had descended into and climbed from the ship's hold.

"Place your arms through the handles of your valise and wear it like a haversack. It will free your hands for climbing. Whatever you do don't look down and remember the many times you climbed from the ship's hold. Now go and just keep climbing until you reach the cabin. You will then probably find a trapdoor which will lift up and through which we will gain access. You start climbing now while I attempt to find a more secure hiding place for our bicycles. If they are discovered we will almost certainly be found."

Lai was struggling with the weight of the trapdoor when Luc reached the point where she was perched perilously on the metal rungs of the ladder.

"Don't be afraid," Luc encouraged. "I will come up behind you to help. Just hold on tight with one hand."

With additional support the trap door yielded and Lai quickly scrambled up into the small enclosure. There was barely room for the pair of them to stand, although when squeezed tight to the outer uprights there was just sufficient space for them to lower the trapdoor back into its recess.

The small cabin contained nothing other than a pot of grease, a grease gun and a large adjustable wrench. It was also obvious that the structure had been built some while before as the corrugated steel cladding was pockmarked with rust holes. Through these holes the pair was afforded a panoramic view of the surrounding countryside and the road along which they had recently travelled.

Peering out, it quickly became apparent that the figure Luc had seen was riding a bicycle and, as it drew closer, Lai Mee quietly explained,

"It's one of the youths who was with me in the hut, back at the medical centre. He must have discovered the shed and decided that the bicycles offered him a means of escape. He has obviously been pedalling hard as his face is very red from exertion." Luc was not surprised by this observation as he knew Lai's eyesight was much stronger than his own.

Further speculation about her former companion's intentions was interrupted by the sound of an engine coming from the same direction that they had all travelled. The youth at first seemed unaware of this, although Luc instantly recognised it as being a fast-moving motorcycle. When the youth increased speed quite dramatically, it seemed certain that he was now also aware of the danger.

Luc rarely used profanities although he swore expressively as they watched the youth swing off the dirt track and onto the pump house hard standing area.

"If those people from the centre are chasing him the poor devil will have no time to hide before that motorcycle reaches us. We can only hope it will pass by and doesn't stop."

Luc and Lai Mee watched from their somewhat precarious position as the young man dropped his bicycle and desperately searched for somewhere to hide. Finally with a gesture of despair he threw himself down amongst the willows in the copse which barely offered some form of light screening.

Unerringly the engine note changed and from the peering inspection of the rider it seemed certain that the wind pump site interested him. The motorcycle slowed perceptibly as the rider braked and it then slewed off the road in something resembling a broadside before coming to a halt on the pump house forecourt.

Watching from the closeness of their vantage point, it was noticeable that Lai Mee trembled as the rider first pulled his machine up onto its stand, lifted goggles from his eyes and then removed an ominous-looking revolver from a holster at his waist.

Inspecting the pump house took the man little more than seconds and it then seemed inevitable that he would search the copse of willow. The motorcyclist had taken barely two paces into this thicket when the youth lost his nerve and broke cover.

The first random pistol shot appeared to find some part of the young man's right leg. His stride faltered and he then gamely carried on out into open paddy. Lai Mee and Luc then watched in horror as the gunman next took careful aim and shot the young man through his left leg.

A grim look of satisfaction spread over thuggish features as the motorcyclist then strode towards the fallen figure. His voice next clearly carried up to them as he asked, in badly pronounced English,

"Where others go?" It seemed obvious that the youth was now in some extreme pain and his response was barely discernible. It was then that the assailant showed a streak of cruelty which was beyond belief. There was little more than a moment's hesitation before he simply placed the muzzle of the revolver into the palm of the young man's hand and fired. Luc was then hard-pressed to stifle Lai Mee's sob of horror as the victim screamed in absolute agony.

While Luc was trying to calm Lai Mee, the brutish motorcyclist asked the same question again. Despite distortion in words which was obviously caused by sheer agony, the youth's response was now clearly audible.

"They stay together. Go into fields. I no go with them when find bicycle." A grunt of satisfaction seemed to indicate that the vicious brute would remount his motorcycle and continue searching for the other escapees; instead he forced the muzzle of the pistol into the young man's mouth and fired once more.

Yet again it was necessary for Luc to exert pressure to stifle Lai Mee's own piercing scream. Desperately trying to calm her so that she would not give away their precarious position, Luc whispered reassurances.

"Perhaps he will leave now, although we should remain very still and keep quiet. This structure is most unstable and any movement up here will be transferred down to the base."

Luc's attempt to comfort and reassure Lai Mee was short-lived. The killer did not remount his motorcycle and leave as they had hoped; instead he searched both the copse and building once more.

Lai was the first to detect movement in the wind vane pump structure and somehow she managed to strangle a whimper of fear. The sound of a heavy boot on a rung of the ladder was their next indication that the killer was slowly climbing up to them.

Luc knew for a certainty that if he attempted to take the pistol from his valise it would cause further movement and alert the man below to their presence. In fact the tower structure was moving quite considerably with each faltering step as the assailant came on up. There was also a hesitancy which gave the impression that the person climbing was bothered by both height and the instability of the tower.

Lai Mee's expression was now one of abject fear. Luc gently pressed her back against the outer cladding of the cabin and cautiously reached down for the heavy wrench. A grunt of exertion from beneath their feet warned them next that the trapdoor was about to be raised.

As the trapdoor cover came up, Luc swung the wrench down with considerable force. In that one fleeting moment Lai Mee realised with some hope that the man was holding on with both hands and was in no position to use his weapon. The fact that he had used his head to open the trapdoor was further indication that he was afraid of heights. She then momentarily and with some satisfaction saw fear register in the man's eyes in that all too brief second before the wrench crunched into the bone of his skull.

As the body fell it collided with some cross members which were in place to stabilise the flimsy structure. This ricocheting impact caused the tower to lurch alarmingly. Eventually the wildly gyrating movement subsided and Luc then eased himself down through the trap door.

During their nerve-racking descent Luc coaxed and encouraged Lai Mee. This most recent of their terrifying ordeals had left her badly shaken and she was barely able to control her trembling limbs.

A strong sense of relief came when Luc at last felt his foot make contact with the body of the killer, which was lying at the base of the steps. While lifting Lai Mee clear of this obstacle to spare her further horror, Luc thought it likely that the man's neck had been broken during the fall as his head was twisted at an awkward angle.

Valuable time was then lost as the pair clung to one another, sobbing with a sense of both relief and disbelief that somehow they had come through yet another ordeal unscathed. They stayed locked in one another's arms for far too long until Luc finally disentangled himself and bent to examine the still form at his feet. There was no sign of a pulse although this did not surprise him as he thought his blow with the wrench would have been sufficient to kill most men.

"People from the medical centre are bound to come looking for him. I think we should make a move and try to put some distance between ourselves and this place," Luc next suggested.

There was then one brief moment while he toyed with the idea of taking the motorcycle, although on reflection he dismissed the idea as he thought it might be recognised and also indicate that at least one of the fugitives had managed to elude the ensuing search parties.

"We will leave him and everything as it is. When his friends find him they will assume that after catching the youth, he then continued searching for the other escapees and fell to his death from the tower."

Lai, who was still badly shaken, seemed unable to take in what had happened and as Luc was considering this he remembered searching the victims' baggage in the men's shower block. For some inexplicable reason this recollection aroused thoughts for their immediate future and an urge for him to act.

"I am going to search both him and the youth before we leave; they may have things which are worth taking." The ruthlessness of this suggestion further disturbed Lai Mee's already troubled thoughts and she asked,

"Do you feel no remorse? Are you completely insensitive? You have now killed twice and yet you seem unmoved." Luc understood that she was in shock although his sympathy was not sufficient to prevent him from retorting angrily,

"Make no mistake, Lai Mee. Had I not done what was necessary, you would either be back in that cell with the others or lying here dead with me and that young man." He indicated to where the youth had been brutally murdered only a short distance from them.

"If my searching troubles you, I suggest you turn your back or move away and ignore what I am doing. My guess is that we are far from out of the woods and I will use everything available to prevent our recapture."

Still visibly shaken, Lai slowly accepted the wisdom of this. She blew her nose in an attempt to console herself and then apologised for questioning his judgement. Only partially mollified, Luc chose not to respond.

"I would like to take his pistol, but if it's missing when he's found they will know that there were others here and it will encourage them to intensify their search of the area."

A moment later he grunted with satisfaction. The killer's cheap plastic wallet contained some twelve hundred yuan in bank notes of various denominations.

"Your assumption when we came ashore appears to be correct. It now seems obvious that we are in China. We will take most of his money and if we can avoid recapture we will at some stage have need of food and shelter. This money will be easier to use than our foreign currency and it should not attract unwanted attention."

Luc's optimism helped raise Lai Mee's flagging spirits and, while she did not altogether share his confidence, she decided that she would try to shake herself free from pessimism.

"It will look suspicious if his pockets are completely empty when they find him and to overcome that possibility I will leave a few of the notes, together with some coins."

Searching the murdered youth's body was a far more gruesome task and despite the experiences of previous forced labour, Lai had difficulty in suppressing an overwhelming urge to vomit.

The bullet which had been fired into the young man's mouth had blown the top of his head away and exposed a mess of brain matter together with other cranial tissue.

Luc retrieved a small quantity of American dollars from a rear pocket of the youth's jeans, although the heavy clasp knife which he discovered in the inside pocket of the young man's coat seemed of greater value.

From feelings of decency and respect Luc would have covered the young man's body had he not realised the consequences of doing so. With a shrug of resignation he was about to move away from the macabre scene when he noticed a well-worn path leading off at right angles from where the body lay. Motioning to attract Lai Mee's attention, he next suggested,

"I think we should retrieve the bicycles and then see where this path takes us. It has the appearance of being used frequently and may lead us to somewhere where we can hide up for a few days." To emphasise his reasoning Luc indicated the hard-packed soil which was free from weeds and other vegetation.

"I think that brute who killed the youth from your cell is the forerunner of a much larger search party. They will probably assume that you and the other escapees are heading for the port area to alert the authorities. If that is the case, we are going to disappoint them."

"How clever!" Lai Mee approved, as Luc retrieved their two bicycles from the irrigation pond.

"It's as well I took that precaution. If two additional machines had been discovered, the assassin would have shown much more caution when climbing the wind vane."

As Lai was mounting her machine Luc hesitated and then changed his bicycle for the one which the youth had been riding. He then explained that he thought it had better tyres and was also sturdier than the one he had first chosen.

"You lead and I will follow, although watch out for potholes. It would be quite serious for one of us to fall and sustain an injury now," Luc quietly reasoned.

# Chapter Six

Sightseeing was a pastime which neither Kate nor Ruby had any interest in; there had been little else for them, however. Their days of waiting with a high degree of frustration were occasionally enlivened when the two women's presence was required by lawyers working on the sales contract for the Mekong Express Company.

"Good news, Miss Savage. I am relieved to be able to tell you that at last your notary is satisfied with the contract and it is now awaiting signatures."

Kate had been dawdling over a late morning croissant on the terrace when Lung Chen surprised her. She was slowly becoming accustomed to the accountant's direct approach and was not at all taken back by the lack of any form of greeting.

"Thank you, Uncle Lung Chen. I feel sure that my aunt will be delighted, as she is rather anxious to finalise things before going on to complete some other business back in England. Would it be possible for you to arrange for us to sign the contract later this afternoon and then possibly meet the staff tomorrow morning?"

The elderly accountant politely refused an offer of coffee before agreeing that Kate's request should be possible. Kate thought she detected irritation in his manner as he bowed formally before leaving and she supposed this reflected his distaste for haste.

When Kate bounded into her bedroom, Ruby was struggling to complete a Daily Telegraph crossword which an airline steward had passed on to her earlier in the week.

"I think things are moving at last. Lung Chen has just been and he is going to try and arrange for us to sign the contract this afternoon. If he is successful the bad news is that you and I will have to be up early tomorrow morning as I have also asked him to arrange for us to meet the staff at Bang Dang jetty. I know they all arrive early and I would like to catch them before they become involved with other things."

"Don't worry about me getting up. I am so bored with crosswords and trying to amuse myself that I would be happy for the meeting to be held in the middle of the night."

True to her word, Ruby was waiting for Kate in the hotel lobby at five thirty the following morning.

A noisy hubbub greeted them as they arrived outside the small jetty offices which were used by the operational wing of the Mekong Express Company. Kate was relieved to see that both the former owner and Lung Chen were already there and waiting for them.

Following her niece's example, Ruby bowed deeply. She appreciated both good manners and signs of respect, although when this performance was to be repeated on numerous occasions, her approval of social niceties began to slowly waver.

Moving in response to a nod from Lung Chen, Kate held her hands up to indicate that she wished to address the already assembled people in the somewhat packed room. She had considered carefully what she should say and out of deference to the Vietnamese appreciation of etiquette, she hoped a formal approach would meet with her future employees' approval.

"We, that is, my aunt and I, are honoured to be here with you this morning. I imagine, however, that what I have to say next will come as a shock to most of you. There is no easy way of telling you this and so I will not waste words." Kate paused to allow Lung Chen sufficient time to interpret.

"Your company has been sold and is now under new ownership. I am, however, both honoured and pleased to tell you that my aunt and I are the new owners."

The murmuring response to this created the need for a further pause until Kate once more held her hands up to regain attention.

"The first thing I would like you to know is that we intend operating the company as a going concern and that we have not purchased to simply asset strip."

A state of nervous tension caused her throat to go dry and Kate was grateful that the pause, which was necessary because of noisy discussion, allowed her to take some water from a small bottle which she'd had the foresight to bring to the meeting. Moments rolled by until finally the noise died to a level where she was able to make herself heard once more.

"There will be changes, although providing I have your full support all staff positions within the company are secure. In fact, I believe that in due course we shall be recruiting as I have plans to expand on the services which were being operated under former ownership."

This announcement brought murmurs of interest from one small group and Kate then realised that Lung Chen's translation was only partially necessary.

"From the comments I am now hearing I believe that many of you understand English. Given time I also hope to have some grasp of your language."

Kate noticed that this announcement appeared to meet with some approval and so she continued,

"Our future plans for the company are at a delicate point of negotiation. When these have been concluded I will call a further meeting to inform you of any changes which may occur. Your former employer has agreed to stay on in an advisory capacity to help through the transitional period and Mr. Chen will also be around for the foreseeable future." Kate indicated the Chinese accountant, who was still interpreting.

"This, by the way, is my aunt, who is also my business partner." Kate drew Ruby to a more prominent position by her side.

"My aunt's name is Ruby Pardoe and I am Kate Savage." There was a moment of silence while both women were being seriously scrutinised. When this appeared to have satisfied general curiosity Kate continued,

"Is there anything that you would like to add at this point, Ruby?" This brought the focus of attention back to the more mature of the group's new employers.

"Briefly, yes. I realise that we have only just met, but I would ask that you are not deceived by my niece's youthful appearance. She has had a deep involvement with business and with your cooperation she will steer this company to success and a prosperity which we can all share. Unfortunately I have to return to London for a short visit once this meeting is over, although when I return my door will always be open to anyone who has a problem. Thank you Kate, that is all I have to say for now."

With the people's attention refocusing on her, Kate continued,

"I have taken the liberty of arranging for caterers to bring food in for us this morning as I thought sharing a celebratory breakfast might be a good way for us to begin. I hope you have not already eaten as good food is better enjoyed with a good appetite."

A further murmur of surprise greeted this announcement and Kate was pleased she had learned, since considering South East Asia as a potential trading area, that without exception the people all enjoyed good food. Almost as an afterthought it then occurred to her that she was missing something which was also important.

"Please, before we eat, are there any questions?"

Most of the concerns which followed were about changes to their work patterns and responsibilities. It was also obvious that any alteration to their pay structure was of immediate concern.

"There will be no change to your conditions of employment, nor will there be pay increases for at least six months, although I feel sure you would all like me tell you that the latter was not so. Initially we are going to feel our way cautiously forward. For long-term stability I believe that is essential. When we deem it right to do so, I would like to introduce a bonus scheme which will be linked to profitability, although I feel sure we have a long way to go before we reach that situation. Now is there anything more before we eat?"

Most of the staff were moving to where caterers had left food containers on tables and Kate thought she had come through the first staff meeting unscathed. As she and her aunt were about to join the gathering staff crowd a hand was raised from amongst a group who had as yet not moved. Mentally Kate chided herself for being complacent.

"Please, yes please. If you have a question, go ahead." Kate thought the man might be in his early thirties although she wasn't sure. He was wearing a seaman's cap and a navy sweater, which probably indicated that he was a crew member. In addition to his clothing, he also wore an insolent and over-confident grin.

"Miss Savage, will you tell us what experience you have of running passenger-carrying ferry services?" The man's eyes were boring into hers and Kate sensed that the grin concealed a very mean streak. She also realised that if she showed signs of either hesitation or weakness she would not only lose face but also much of what she had thus far achieved.

"I have no experience of operating passenger ferries. My background is in the airfreight business. My family, I should explain, own "Savage Air Freight Services. With one exception that company specialises in hauling freight on amphibian aircraft. The exception is a Hercules C130 bulk carrier which I feel sure many of you will be familiar with. Your previous owner has agreed to stay on in a consultancy capacity for an indefinite period and initially I will be contributing new ideas and injecting fresh management skills. I also hope that I will be able to rely on you and other experienced staff for assistance."

A murmur of what sounded like approval greeted this statement although the man who had asked the question continued to stare fixedly at her. Kate was satisfied she had not weakened and returned his gaze with similar intensity. A moment of silent impasse followed until the seaman shrugged, turned and then walked towards the food containers.

"I think you handled that rather well," Ruby told her niece as she rootled around in the steaming containers of hot food for more of the prawn dim sum which had so obviously taken her fancy.

"We will have an opportunity to talk once we are back at the hotel, Ruby. Now though, I would rather circulate amongst the staff while we still have them all in one place." Kate had barely finished saying this when they were approached by a female staff member that both women had noticed earlier.

"Miss Pardoe, Miss Savage, my name is Xia De-Hong, although everyone around here calls me Molly and I am the company's reservations manager."

This hesitant introduction then produced an amused chuckle from the young woman until she continued,

"That's the fancy title I was given awhile back. What it really means is that I am a senior booking clerk. I have worked here for going on fifteen years, which I guess makes me one of the longer serving staff members. Because of that, some of the others thought I should act as their spokesperson."

The young woman hesitated, seemingly in an attempt to determine if she had Kate and Ruby's full attention.

"We appreciated your frankness this morning. Obviously the fact that the company has changed hands has come as a complete shock. We were given no indication that such a move was on the cards and I reckon it will take some time for us to get used to the idea, although if you continue to be as upfront with us as you were this morning we will certainly give you a go."

Molly's spoken English with a pronounced American accent was excellent.

"Thank you, Molly. I can and do assure you that we will also give you a go." Kate's smile was an indication of her approval for Molly's straightforward approach.

"My family has always been in transport and it is my hope to continue in the same business. Strange as it may seem, it has always been a passion of mine." A waiter offering them more food caused Kate to pause.

"When my aunt and I began looking for an investment Mr Chen initially suggested other involvements which would carry less risk. My heart, however, would never be in owning some hosiery factory where sweated labour is the order of the day. I want to enjoy what I am doing. I also want to step out from this office and smell the sea, feel fresh air blowing in my face and get a buzz from solving problems. That's why I'm here, Molly, and yes, I'm sure as hell going to give it a go." This brought a smile of approval from Molly and the three women then chatted on for a while until, as the young woman was about to leave, Kate asked,

"Who was the man that asked the late question regarding my experience at the end of our briefing session, Molly?"

"Oh, that's Tommy Jung. He is one of the younger ferry pilots. He is from China, in fact. He came to us around three years ago with good references. He had previously worked on the Yangtze in a similar capacity, although you don't want to take any heed of his smart-assed questioning, Miss Savage. He likes to swank in front of the others and maybe listen to the sound of his own voice some."

"Do we keep detailed files on company employees?" Kate next asked. Molly told her that personnel would have full and complete dossiers on all the staff.

When Kate asked her to point out the head of personnel, the young woman grinned.

"I guess that's me, Miss Savage. Are you looking for anything in particular?"

"Yes, I would like to take a look at the files for all the operations people and in particular the one that has details of the company's longest serving and most experienced skipper. That is, of course, if the two things are one and the same."

"That will be Captain Wang," Molly replied without hesitation. "Would you like me to fetch those files over to head office?"

"No Molly. That will not be necessary as I shall not be using the head office facility. I am going to move in here where I can be at the centre of things. My aunt and Mr. Chen will probably work from the old building, although eventually I would like all of us to be here on the quayside. I am not in favour of split locations." Kate paused, expecting there to be some objection. When there was none, she continued,

"There seems sufficient space to accommodate me here in the interim and if we find that moving admin people across creates a crush, we can install some more portakabin's." A thought then occurred to Kate and she asked,

"Do you happen to know if we own the freehold on the head office suite?"

"I think so, Miss Savage, although I'm not at all sure. Your Mr Chen is probably better qualified than me to answer that question." The young woman's smile registered uncertainty.

"There is an unused office through here and if I can find a desk and chair, together with some filing cabinets, will that be okay for now?"

"It will be fine, Molly, and I won't need those staff files until this afternoon. I am going back to the hotel with my aunt to help her pack. She is flying off to Bangkok and then to London later this evening."

"That Molly girl certainly seems to have her finger on the pulse. I think she is someone we will have to look out for," Ruby told her niece as they walked back to the hotel, having turned down an offer by Molly to have one of the staff drive them over.

"Were you thinking what I was thinking when you asked about the head office suite?" Kate's puzzled expression prompted her aunt to elaborate.

"That we dispose of the place. It's a bloody old mausoleum and I can tell you, without consulting Lung Chen, that we own the lease. Not the freehold. Although the possible good news is that the lease still has some eighteen years to run, so I reckon we might raise a little money on the remaining time."

"Well that would be something, as every little bit helps and I imagine service charges on places like that are high," Kate responded.

"I thought your idea of providing breakfast for everyone was brilliant. It went down very well and certainly created a good atmosphere."

"Let's have some coffee out here on the terrace before we go in to pack as there is something that I want to talk about." They found a table in the shade and were quickly served.

"Okay, this is great. Now, what is it that you want to discuss?" Ruby asked. "You made it sound quite ominous."

"No, it's certainly not. It's just that as we are going to be working closely with the staff, would you mind if we dropped some of the formality? I understand the need for a little distance, although I think all this Miss Pardoe, Miss Savage stuff is far too formal. How would you feel if I let it be known that we like being referred to as Miss Ruby and Miss Kate?"

"Great and I rather think you will quickly get the hang of managing people. It was certainly a quality which was lacking in my old business," Ruby suggested, after nodding her approval.

For a while both women were content to savour good coffee and enjoy sheltering from the sun. The dining room waiters and kitchen staff were taking advantage of the lull between breakfast and lunch and Kate smiled as she watched two cooks having a smoke behind the seclusion of a rattan screen.

Not for the first time she reflected on her own good fortune. Kate realised that, but for a quirk of fate, she might also have been born to an underprivileged family with little opportunity of education or advancement.

Kate also knew that she was lucky and had few regrets with the hand that had been dealt her. There was only one thing which ever troubled her and that was that she had never known her father.

Rory, Kate's dad, was killed by Sri Lankan terrorist's just months before she was born. Both her grandfathers, together with an uncle, had attempted to fill this void, with a modicum of success. Despite their best efforts, however, she had always badly missed having a father around.

Kate next thought about Molly and the South Vietnamese people with whom she would be working. She had previously spent time researching the background of the country where she hoped to operate and knew that when the Americans abandoned their southern allies, the North Vietnamese had exacted harsh reprisals against the vanquished peoples of the South. She also learned that it became difficult for qualified people to work at their former professions and that it was not unusual to find lawyers, doctors and other skilled people performing menial tasks to support their families.

Lost in these thoughts Kate was startled by her aunt requesting another pot of coffee from a passing waiter. As the man disappeared, Ruby asked,

"So you are going back to the office this afternoon?" Before Kate could reply, Ruby continued,

"There will be no need for you to come to the airport with me this evening. You will in all probability become involved and worrying about me will be a distraction. I can arrange for the people on reception here to arrange for a taxi."

"No, I want to come. I also have to arrange some plane tickets for myself. One of the first things I now need to do is go back to Hanoi to see Admiral Tanaka. I promised that I would let him know the moment that ownership formalities had been dealt with and he in turn has suggested that it will only then take a matter of days to issue an operating licence for the new route. When that has been dealt with I would like to go on to Koggala and talk to Grandpa Bob about shipping the Flying Dolphin over from Galle. Then when you return, we can get down to work and concentrate on our business."

"I still think it's unnecessary for you to waste time going out to the airport. The hotel can surely arrange for a travel agent to stop by with some tickets. Let's talk to them now before I go on up to finish packing."

Kate's flight reservations were made as easily as her aunt had predicted. The travel agent arrived with debit card and credit card forms and from his schedules and timetables suitable flights were selected.

"If you have a little free time when you get back from Koggala, you might try renting a house or an apartment for us," Ruby suggested. "Hotels are okay in the short-term although I would prefer some real home comforts."

Kate spent the afternoon familiarising herself with the files covering both operational crews and shore-based staff. Early the following morning, she found Molly already waiting for her in the office.

"Good morning, Miss Kate. Captain Wang will be tying up alongside at around nine thirty. We radioed him last night and told him that you wished to see him. He will come right on up as soon as his craft has been made fast alongside." Following this Molly then asked, "Can I get you some coffee?"

Kate found that there was much to absorb during the morning while waiting for Captain Wang and at nine forty a knock on her office door announced his arrival.

"You wished to see me, Miss Kate?" The man's English, like Molly's, was flawless and as she held out her hand in greeting she was satisfied that she was looking at someone who was dependable.

"Captain Wang. Thank you for coming so promptly. Will you take a seat? I'm afraid our selection of chairs is not up to much although we will, I hope, eventually find some that are more comfortable. Would you like coffee? Please say yes as I would like to take some of your time this morning, although if you prefer tea, I am fairly confident that can also be arranged?"

"Coffee's fine. I acquired the habit while the Americans were here." Kate thought that the man's tone indicated approval of the Americans more than for coffee.

"I will come straight to the point, Captain. I would like you to prepare a craft for a trip which will take at least two weeks. You will need to select a crew, arrange for additional barrels of fuel to be carried on board and also an auxiliary pump to discharge oil into the fuel tanks. We will be living and sleeping aboard so cooking facilities and food should be included. Oh, and also some bedding for everyone." Kate's pause was unnecessary as it was obvious that the thoughtful-looking captain had absorbed all that had been requested of him.

"I am travelling north tomorrow and from there I will then be flying home to Sri Lanka, where there are some loose ends which require finalising. I imagine I will be back here in around ten days. Can you arrange things in that time?"

"No problem. Everything will be ready for your return. You suggested that we would be living aboard. Does that imply that you will be travelling with us?" Her smile and nod confirmed this and Kate expected him to then question their destination. When this was not the case, she found herself warming to Captain Wang's quiet air of competence.

# Chapter Seven

The track surface over which Lai Mee and Luc cycled was relatively smooth and they had travelled a long way before coming across the first signs of habitation. It was in fact little more than a rough shack with a noisy dog chained to a post. Despite the animal's barking, no one came to investigate and the pair pedalled on by.

Light was failing as night approached and they were both relieved when coming across what appeared to be a disused animal byre.

"I think it should be safe for us to spend the night here," Luc suggested.

"If we continue one of us might easily blunder into something in the dark and injure ourselves."

To prevent the bicycles from betraying their presence, Luc wheeled them some way off and deposited them out of sight in one of the drainage channels which abounded in the area. While he was doing this, Lai Mee made a comfortable bed from some rice straw which had obviously been stored in the byre for some time.

Fatigue is a good sedative and despite their earlier experiences, together with growing hunger, the couple spent a comfortable night. Luc was outside surveying open country as a dawn sun crept over the eastern horizon, and when Lai Mee joined him, she asked,

"Is there something to drink?"

"There is rainwater in a tank which has been collected from the roof and also dirty water in the irrigation channels, although I don't think we should drink from either source."

Despite being thirsty Lai Mee could see the wisdom of this. She understood that they would need to be careful with what they ate and drank in the days ahead if they were to survive.

"I think we should risk going back to the dwelling that we passed late yesterday afternoon. My guess is that it belongs to some peasant farmers and we can only hope that they have no contact with the medical centre," Luc suggested.

"Yes, I agree. Survival without food for some while will be difficult although not impossible. Becoming dehydrated through not having clean water to drink is another matter though, and something we should try to avoid. I drank from the irrigation pond beside the pump house where we almost perished yesterday. That was foolish of me and I can only hope the water there was not contaminated, as my going down sick is certainly not going to help our situation," Lai Mee observed.

Luc Tun had retrieved both bicycles and they took a long hard look around before setting off back in the direction that they had travelled the previous afternoon. Smoke spiralling upward was the first sighting they had of the well-concealed dwelling.

"If there is anyone around we will try to barter for some food and something to drink. Whatever we do we shouldn't let them see that we have lots of money. One thing that really bothers me is the aggressive-looking dog that we saw as we passed yesterday, although if it does attack us, I have the revolver and as a last resort I will shoot it."

This observation brought some frowning concern to Lai Mee's features and she hoped that nothing so extreme would be necessary.

The dog was not tied to its tethering pole and contrary to Luc's fear it approached them with its tail wagging. An elderly man with grizzled features and a permanent lopsided grin then followed close on the animal's heels.

A gatepost which appeared to have seen better days seemed ideal for Luc to rest his bicycle against and when free from this encumbrance, he bowed formally and then offered the old man his hand in greeting. An expression of uncertainty came to the lopsided features which seemed to indicate that the man was unsure of how to react. His odd expression, however, suggested that he was harmless and Luc was encouraged to ask in poorly-spoken Cantonese,

"Can you sell us some food and let us have some water to drink?" The man's response to this came in the form of some expert mimicry. First he pointed to his ears and then to his mouth, after which he made what appeared to be exaggerated and negative movement with his hands. With only a moment of hesitation Lai Mee understood what this meant.

"I think he is telling us that he is both deaf and dumb." This observation brought a further moment of consideration until she suggested that she would attempt to communicate their needs through mime. In this she was successful and although his expression remained fixed, a glint appeared in the old man's bloodshot eyes and the strange-looking individual responded to Lai Mee's mimicry by rubbing his forefinger and thumb together, indicating that he would supply sustenance at a price.

Responding, Lai Mee then showed him one of the yuan notes which they had taken from the motorcyclist's wallet. A cunning expression briefly replaced the old man's grin and he held up two fingers. Lai Mee nodded her acceptance and the old peasant farmer motioned for them to follow him into the shack.

A quantity of rice, together with fried eggs, was quickly produced and also a very welcome pitcher of crystal clear drinking water. With their thirst slaked and appetites satisfied, a jug of rice wine was produced and it quickly became clear that their host took more pleasure from this than the food, which he had barely touched.

With a sigh of contentment Luc indicated that they were both now replete and their host then motioned for them to follow him outside where he led them along a short path to a further cluster of dilapidated buildings.

Proudly, it seemed, the deaf mute showed them henhouses containing healthy-looking fowl and sties which housed an assortment of sows and their litters of piglets, all evidently well cared for.

"I think he is telling us that this all belongs to him," Luc suggested. The man seemed to understand and nodded his head in agreement. When he next mimed sleep with the back of his hands pressed to his cheeks, Lai's interpretation was that they were being offered somewhere to stay for the night.

Although surprised by this, Luc quickly came to a decision.

"Maybe we should. We seem a long way from other signs of habitation and we are also a good distance from the medical centre road. Ask him how much. There's bound to be a price, although don't agree to his first figure."

Following their initial contact Lai Mee had now assumed the role of both mimic and communicator and the old man immediately held up the fingers and thumbs of both hands in response to her question.

"He is obviously asking ten yuan. Offer him five and try telling him that we would like to stay for longer than one night." When Lai Mee quickly reached an agreement to pay six yuan for each night's stay, the old man appeared satisfied.

"It seems obvious that we are paying him too much although if it also includes food you will have concluded a good deal." Luc praised Lai Mee's negotiating skills.

A morning exploring their newfound host's property and inspecting his other animals was eventually interrupted when billowing clouds of dust alerted them to the fact that they would shortly be having company. Fearing that it might be a search party from the medical centre, a moment of panic settled over them and the dog's changing behaviour indicated trouble of some kind. The large animal's ruff stood erect from his collar and he now continued to utter a series of deep rumbling growls.

"That animal seems to sense unwelcome company and I think we should find somewhere safe to hide," Luc responded, the urgency of the situation clearly etched on his features.

Despite having the appearance of a simpleton the old man immediately sensed their fear and beckoned that they should follow him. He took them to an enlarged corner of an irrigation channel on which a large flock of ducks was swimming and without preamble he cut down two hollow reeds before motioning that Luc and Lai Mee should enter the pond. Hesitating as he remembered their bicycles, Luc was about to return for them and drop them into deep water when their new friend tugged at his arm and mimed a pedalling action indicating that he realised the danger and would take care of things. Lai Mee immediately understood and motioned Luc to join her as she stepped into the water and then moved beneath the shelter of some bulrushe's while experimenting with the improvised breathing tube.

Buoyancy proved troublesome until they managed to grasp some of the bulrushe's to hold themselves down. When satisfied that this would work they both came to the surface and then watched the homestead buildings with trembling anticipation. Their wait was short-lived and they realised that had more time been taken in finding a place to hide, it might have been disastrous.

An increased intensity to the dog's barking now signalled that the unwanted visitors had arrived.

From their place amongst the water reeds, Luc and Lai Mee watched as three men and a woman searched first the old man's home and then the assortment of scattered buildings. This intrusion appeared to cause alarm amongst the livestock as a series of shrill squeals from the piggery could clearly be heard. When the newcomers' search failed to produce any positive result, two of the men then roughly manhandled the old man who, despite his seeming frailty, managed to accept this treatment without signs of fear.

"He's brave and not as stupid as he looks," Lai Mee whispered, as they watched the now familiar display of mimicry. In the next instant Luc felt Lai Mee's growing alarm as the searchers turned in their direction and moved towards their hiding place. Luc placed a reassuring arm about her waist and this gesture in all probability saved them from being discovered as Luc then noticed a fresh stain of soil rising from the bottom and realised that Lai Mee's bulrushe's were being slowly uprooted. But for Luc's forceful restraint, Lai Mee's natural buoyancy would have carried her to the surface in full view of the searching group. Silently Luc prayed that his own reeds would hold fast and he then lent further strength to holding Lai Mee down.

The brief sensation of seeing hostile faces through a tangle of reed stems and murky water was terrifying enough, although they were thankfully spared a prolonged period of this as the searchers moved away from their limited field of vision.

When the same search was repeated the following day the submerged couple were assisted by the fact that they carried sacks of building bricks to act as ballast with which to negate their natural buoyancy. In addition to this they were quickly surrounded by the flock of ducks which had become accustomed to their presence and now took full advantage of the dislodged vegetable matter which the submerged couple stirred up from the bottom.

Despite this added form of protection, Luc prayed that they would not have to undergo the ordeal too frequently as he realised that Lai Mee's courage was being stretched to its limit.

The third day of their stay went undisturbed although but for the dog's alertness they would have been caught napping when the searchers arrived again on the fourth afternoon. A further attempt was made at questioning their host although when this proved unsuccessful, the medical centre group left without a further search.

In addition to pork and chicken there was also duck, vegetables, eggs and rice to eat. By comparison to former periods in their lives, the abundance of food made it feel as though they had found some kind of paradise.

They had been living with the deaf mute for several days when he conveyed with a little difficulty that he would be taking surplus produce to the local market. When he was sure that he had made himself understood, the old farmer produced an ancient bicycle from one of the buildings and attached a small two-wheeled cart to its rear. On this conveyance their host then loaded an assortment of trussed chickens and pigs together with baskets of eggs. When every scrap of space was filled on the rickety vehicle, yet more fowl were suspended from the handlebars of his bicycle. In addition to this there was also one small piglet strapped to the bicycle's rear carrier while lying on its back. Lai Mee chuckled with amusement at the sight of this comical menagerie although any amusement which Luc might have felt was clouded by concern.

"I realise that the old man has displayed a willingness to conceal us from the medical centre people. I am concerned, however, that his going to town alone might cause problems. You know how he has a fondness for rice wine and who knows what might happen if he has too much. Perhaps I should go along to make sure he doesn't let anything slip if and when he becomes inebriated. Will you try telling him that I would like to go with him and that the load will be made lighter if it is shared between two of us?"

Lai Mee's mimed suggestion was instantly understood and readily agreed to; in fact the old man took advantage of Luc's offer by fetching sacks of rice which he placed over the crossbar of a second sturdy bicycle. When this had been wheeled out Luc was relieved to see that it was not one of the machines which they had stolen from the medical centre and which were still submerged in the duck pond. He thought further use of those two bicycles should be avoided as there was always risk of them being recognised by one of the medical centre staff.

"Please take care, Luc. It is more than likely that those people will still be looking for us and if anything were to happen to you, I would rather have stayed in that place and been put to death with the others." This was said with such conviction that there was no doubting Lai Mee's concern.

"Don't be afraid. I certainly will be careful. I have the revolver concealed beneath this smock which the old man has loaned me and there is no way that anyone is going to take me without paying the ultimate price." Lai's look of uncertainty prompted Luc's further reassurance.

"Travelling with all this farm produce should in itself be enough of a disguise and I have also tried to take on the appearance of belonging."

Glancing at him with some amusement, Lai Mee felt a little reassured by his changed appearance and she thought the coolie's straw hat and smock would assist in his attempt at producing anonymity.

Watching with some apprehension as the old man and Luc pedalled out of sight, Lai Mee next busied herself with tidying the shack and washing the few dishes that their host possessed. When satisfied that the old homestead's cleanliness had now been greatly improved, she prepared food for their evening meal.

Lai Mee then began to feel the loneliness of the deserted holding and, once all her chores had been dealt with, she decided that it should be safe for her to walk out and explore the surrounding paddy. As she was passing one of the barns a whimpering sound halted her in her tracks and she retraced her footsteps to where the big dog was tethered. Motioning for the animal to accompany her once he had been untied, the dog dutifully bounded along by her side and Lai Mee realised how much she had come to enjoy the animal's company. A relationship had developed between them and she was wise enough to understand that the titbits she fed him and the petting he received was a contributory factor.

Both Lai Mee and the dog had travelled no great distance from the homestead when they spotted two wild rabbits grazing on green shoots of the vegetation which was growing on the flower-strewn bank of an irrigation ditch. The dog immediately set off in pursuit and while one of the rabbits escaped down a burrow, the second was killed instantly. Then, next demonstrating how well he was trained, the dog brought the dead rabbit to her and dropped it at her feet.

"Good dog!" Lai Mee patted him enthusiastically. The animal, seemingly pleased by this praise, wagged his tail vigorously and then bounded off to continue a further hunting foray.

Lai Mee's enjoyment on her first real day without fear since escaping from the medical centre was such that she lost all track of time and it was almost dark when she arrived back at the settlement carrying two plump rabbits. Luc and their host had also returned from market and were both anxiously waiting for her in the gloom.

Some time passed while Luc gradually cleared his thoughts of the apprehension he had experienced and eventually he told her that the old man had successfully sold all the produce they had taken to market. He also described the scenes of activity and bartering which took place. What was of particular concern and interest to Lai Mee was the fact that there were a number of people in town wearing the distinctive yellow shoulder bands.

"There was certainly an air of alertness about them and I felt sure they were still looking for someone, presumably you or the other escapees."

"I think we should stay away from that town when we move on, although to be frank I am not looking forward to the uncertainty of leaving this place. It was so peaceful and relaxing out on the marshes today that I actually felt quite envious of the old man and his life here." Luc's look of understanding then prompted Lai Mee to ask the question which she had been pondering for most of the afternoon.

"I wonder how safe we are here. Do you think those people from the medical centre visit regularly?"

"I don't know; it might be worth asking the old man before he gets too far into that flask of wine."

Had he not now become accustomed to the mimicry which was necessary when Lai Mee communicated with their host, Luc would have been amused by her gesturing antics. Eventually, however, she concluded that the old man had indicated that few people ever ventured out to the holding, mostly because of tidal flooding and a fear of the quicksand's, which were known to exist on the marshes.

"He certainly knows of the medical centre and understands that the people involved there are often cruel and not to be trusted, although he seemed surprised that I should think anyone from that place would ever visit him other than on the occasions when they were looking for us. Apparently there are a few inshore fishermen who know that he is here, although most local people believe the area is too unstable and prone to flooding for it to be suitable for habitation. I also think, now that he has described some of the dangers which exist, we should both take care. It would be the worst possible tragedy for one of us to wander into one of those quicksand's."

"We will keep an open mind for the moment and if there has been no sign of anyone coming here in say a week or so, you might ask the old man about our staying on for an extended period."

"I have a strong feeling that will not present a problem, as he always seems happy when I pay our weekly lodgings in advance." It then seemed as though, in response to what had just been said, the deaf mute reacted by passing a fresh flask of rice wine for Luc to refill his cup.

"It's uncanny although sometimes I think he understands a lot more than we give him credit for," Luc suggested. "Perhaps he lip-reads?"

"Yes, I agree. In fact he is probably more aware than either of us. I suppose he could have powers of telepathy or maybe he is psychic." Lai Mee realised that Luc would not agree with this latter suggestion and not unsurprisingly he conveniently changed the subject.

"I would give a lot to know what really happens out at that medical centre and why they killed so many people for so little. It would be incredible if their only motive was robbery or indeed a deliberate intention to renege on the obligation that we had all paid for. I searched through the belongings of the other men in my shower block and with two exceptions there was absolutely nothing of value. In fact those poor devils that travelled with us were mostly destitute."

Lai Mee understood the silence which followed was an attempt to allow the anger Luc Tun felt to subside. She was then about to clear away the remnants of supper when he surprised her by continuing.

"We lost both our families to the Khmer Rouge and I did nothing to avenge those deaths. When I overcame fear of asphyxiation in that shower block, I vowed that if I was able to escape and find you, I would then do everything in my power to really hurt those people for their inhuman crime and I am not going to walk away from my moral obligation a second time." This was said with such conviction that there was no doubting Luc's sincerity.

Had Lai Mee seen the full extent of the cruelty which Luc had witnessed, it is possible that she may have been more sympathetic and possibly shared his concern for justice. Now though, her worry was for his safety and being able to continue with the unexpectedly peaceful life which they had stumbled across.

"If our host allows us stay on longer, I shall be pleased. There is plenty of food for us and if I accompany him to market regularly I might learn the reason for what happens back there." Lai Mee understood that her man was still referring to the medical centre.

Apart from an unusually high tide which brought sea water very close to the buildings, there were no alarms in the weeks that followed. Their host, the old man, was able to convey to Lai Mee that he had lived on the holding all his life and that the sea had never once encroached or caused concern for the homestead's safety. Both she and Luc were reassured by this and Lai was encouraged to ask if they might stay on for an indefinite period. The old man immediately showed his delight and approval. His agreement to their request was also sealed by his producing yet another flask of wine.

Days ran into weeks and the weeks into months. If the routine was sometimes monotonous, it seemed as nothing when compared to the time they had spent in the forced labour camps of the Khmer Rouge. A feeling of trust was also developing between them and their host, so much so, that increasingly he would indicate that he wished Luc to take produce to the market alone. This often occurred when he had consumed more wine than was probably good for him. The fact that Luc almost always returned from those sorties with improved payment for their goods and which was way over and above what their host was expecting, strengthened the bond between them. By eventually refusing to take further money for their lodgings, Luc and Lai Mee understood that their help and companionship was now important to him.

During one of their regular but somewhat difficult communications Lai Mee established that the old man's parents had owned the holding and that it had passed to him when the last of them had died some twenty years before.

Lai Mee was content with their lives, although secretly she wished that Luc would give up on his vendetta against the people who had come so close to murdering them.

Through regular visits to market, Luc slowly became proficient in the local language and his invariable mistakes appeared to go unnoticed. This was partially understandable as, in addition to the native population, there was a large number of Vietnamese who had settled on the island as refugees following conflict in their own country. It was also obvious that many of the refugees still struggled with the local dialect and language.

From his early visits to town Luc learned that they had been landed on the island of Hainan in the South China Sea and that it was only a short distance from the Chinese mainland.

When Luc one day revealed that he had actually been back inside the medical centre, Lai Mee's earlier concern turned to horror. Brushing this aside he told her that he had donned one of the yellow sashes which they had taken during their escape and then simply walked around the complex as though he belonged. Despite this incredibly dangerous risk, Luc's visit proved disappointing. There had been little or no activity at the centre and both the main reception area and shower blocks were empty. Had it not been for the odd sash-wearing flunky going about some menial task, Luc might have thought that the establishment had been abandoned.

One particularly hot day, while the couple were bathing from a bucket which was placed out of sight behind the house, Luc noticed that Lai Mee's body had thickened during the months that they had been living on the marshes. Her waist was no longer as slim as it once was and her small breasts had filled to a proportion which now excited him.

"I think this life and the abundance of good food has been beneficial for both of us," Luc murmured huskily, as he slowly caressed Lai Mee's all too enticing body.

"Do you think we should go inside?" Lai responded with a noticeable tremor to her voice. "The old man might return from the fields at any time."

"I can't wait. I need you now, sweet woman." Lai Mee smiled happily and bent to place a towel for them to lie on. This proved unnecessary as the temptation of the darkened space between her upper thighs was too great. So strong was Luc's unexpected ardour that when his first need was satisfied he took Lai Mee by the hand and led her back into the homestead. Some time later, while curled in a foetal position with her buttocks pressed against him, Lai Mee murmured,

"This is probably a good time to tell you that no matter what now happens there will be no further need for us to seek IVF treatment." For a moment it seemed Luc had either not heard or understood and his silence prompted Lai Mee to continue.

"I am fairly sure. At least three months, I think. There has been no sign of bleeding and I think it safe to assume that if we take care, I might present you with a son or daughter."

"But, Lai Mee, you should have stopped me. I had no idea. I entered you from behind and rutted with you like an animal. Our baby is far more important than my lust." Lai Mee chuckled softly as she turned to face him.

"I would have stopped you had I believed it would harm our baby. It might have been difficult though, as my need was the equal of yours. Are you happy?" Her question was altogether unnecessary as the expression of sheer joy on Luc's face was clear to see.

# Chapter Eight

There was time for reflection as Kate sat in the small twin-engined Fokker aircraft on a scheduled service from Ho Chi Min City to Hanoi. The flight had been in the air for less than twenty minutes when she was just able to see the picturesque city of Da Lat spread out beneath them through a gap in the clouds. Seeing this, prompted her to remember a recent time that she had spent there while visiting her friend Lily Tanaka.

Lily was now lecturing at Da Lat University and the pair had become firm friends while studying at Cambridge. In the first instance Kate had helped the young Vietnamese woman with her poor understanding of English. Later, when Lily became pregnant following a casual relationship which had little or no chance of going anywhere, it was Kate who gave welcome support and Lily's father had arrived unexpectedly. It had then fallen to Kate to find a clinic and make arrangements for the termination which both daughter and father insisted should happen.

Admiral Tanaka's family had changed its citizenship from Japanese to Vietnamese several generations before and the Admiral had also foreseen the change from French Colonialism to Ho Chi Minh's form of communism.

Displaying a wisdom which was later to stand him in good stead, the younger Tanaka had adapted accordingly. Thanks to this and his then later war career, Lily's father was given various ministerial positions within the civil administration until acquiring his current post as Minister for Marine Affairs.

The Admiral was an honourable man and when Kate approached him with a request, he had not forgotten his pledge to repay the help she had previously given.

"Fingers crossed there will be no last minute hitches," Kate thought, as she speculated on the enormity of what she was hoping to achieve. Quite unexpectedly the telephone in her hotel room then rang and interrupted this concern. On picking up the instrument she recognised the voice of one of the hotel receptionists and realised that the young woman's tone was more deferential than was usual.

"Admiral Tanaka apologizes for his unexpected arrival and asks if you might receive him?"

Taken by surprise and with serious feelings of alarm, Kate dropped the telephone back onto its cradle and frantically sped around her suite, picking up an assortment of clothes which she had earlier discarded and which were now strewn over furniture in some disarray.

Thoughts of relief crossed Kate's mind on realising that she had at least showered, was dressed and had combed her hair. These racing thoughts also covered many imagined reasons for the Admiral's unexpected visit as she stowed untidy used garments away from view. Kate had been scheduled to meet him the following morning and now speculated on what might have gone wrong.

"My dear Kate, I am so sorry for my unintentional rudeness. I gambled that you would be staying here and my secretary was able to confirm that this was so. I have a problem. No, there is no need for you to look alarmed. It has nothing to do with the licensing for your new service."

Admiral Tanaka could not have been aware that Kate in her concern had pierced the palms of her hands with her fingernails, as thankfully her face betrayed none of the true anxiety she felt.

"The fact is I have to attend a conference which the North Koreans have arranged to discuss territorial fishing boundaries. I am not really sure why we are involved, although it is something which I am unable to avoid, despite it being arranged at very short notice."

"But, Admiral Tanaka, there was no need for you to come in person. I fully understand the demands on your time. A telephone call from your secretary would have explained everything."

"Not at all, I realise how important the new project is to you and I also happen to think that my country will benefit from the service which you propose operating. On that score you need have no worries. Papers have been drawn up and tomorrow one of my aides will go through everything with you. Once he has witnessed your signature and taken copies for the lawyers, formalities will be complete and you will then be licensed to commence at a date and time which suits. I am only sorry that I will be unable to conclude the matter myself. To make amends would you consider dining with me this evening? I think you will remember how partial I am to the fine Japanese cuisine which is served here at Hotel Nikko."

Several cups of sake had been consumed by both of them when the Admiral asked for his chauffeur to be summoned. Out of deference to some dated custom, the Admiral then took Kate's hand and kissed it.

"I think that what you are setting out to do in my country is very brave. I wish you every success and please remember, if you need help in any small way, you only have to ask. Goodnight, Kate."

Kate bowed and then on impulse bent forward and gently brushed the Admiral's cheek with a kiss. This unexpected and unusual gesture brought a rueful smile to the weather-beaten face.

The strong warm rice wine which they had earlier consumed had not the effect that Kate hoped for. Sleep was slow in coming and her thoughts were in turmoil. Music from the bedside radio also failed to soothe either her doubts or growing anxiety. Previously there had been little time to consider the risk of her undertaking; now in the stillness of night she realised the enormity of it all and hoped that she would not fail the many other people involved.

# Chapter Nine

Lai Mee sighed with contentment and shielded her eyes from the bright sunlight which reflected off the still waters of the paddy field in which she was working.

Since announcing her first pregnancy, life with Luc Tun had been both quiet and peaceful, their happiness marred only by the unexpected death of the deaf mute who had provided a home for them when they had escaped from the medical centre. The old man came to rely on Luc's skill in marketing the produce that they helped him to harvest and in turn he more than repaid them with the expertise he demonstrated when their first child was born. He was unexpectedly gentle throughout Lai Mee's labour and when the baby boy was safely delivered, the old man's pleasure equalled that of her husband and from then on he doted on the child and never lost an opportunity to spoil or watch over him.

It was also the deaf mute who first indicated that he believed that Lai Mee was once more pregnant. Pointing to her stomach he had made expanding motions with his hands while grinning in happy anticipation. His prediction proved correct and seven months later she gave birth to their second son with the old man's further help and assistance.

Miraculously no harm came to either child the day the old man died. Both children had been left in his care while Lai Mee accompanied Luc on one of his regular visits to market. Their return was greeted by the dog meeting them and barking furiously while they were still some way from the homestead. Luc had quickly uncoupled the handcart from his bicycle and raced on ahead with the dog in close pursuit.

Tears were streaming from her husband's eyes when he emerged from the house and Lai Mee feared the worst. When she found both sons safe, she then realised it was the old man's death which was causing Luc's distress.

With some consideration and forethought they buried him on a grassy bank beneath some overhanging willow where there would always be shade during the hotter part of the day. It had been a favourite spot of his, a place where he often retired from the rigours of work.

On returning to the house, Luc insisted that they should honour the old man's memory and wish him an easy journey to the next world with a glass or two of his mature rice wine.

"What will we do now?" Lai Mee had then asked. "We are homeless again. The only difference this time is that we now have two young sons and a dog to care for."

Lai had paused to gauge Luc's reaction to this, when he offered none she continued.

"You will be able to sell all the livestock now that the local people have grown accustomed to you. Although I hope you will agree that the dog comes with us. I have grown very fond of him and he has become a good friend."

"We will do nothing. There is no reason for us to leave this place. So far as we are aware there are no relatives who might claim this property. The people in town have as you suggest accepted us and assume that we are the old man's family. In fact I might never mention his death. It has been some while since he last came to market and the traders seem almost to have forgotten him. Certainly few ask after him these days."

Luc poured two further cups of wine before concluding,

"There is a comfortable living for us here and it is close enough for me to keep an eye on that medical centre. I have not forgotten my pledge and I will do everything possible to bring about its downfall."

Lai Mee's frown should have conveyed something to her husband. That it did not was because Luc's passion for justice was one of the few things which still marred her happiness. She sympathised with his feelings and understood that the crimes of the medical institute should not go unpunished. She feared, however, for her husband's safety and wished it was not him who had to attempt the centre's downfall.

Lai Mee's life in every other respect was as perfect as she could wish for. The air was clean and there was an abundance of wholesome food for the four of them. Compared to the years when she had lived in Cambodia under the Pol Pot regime, their current situation was idyllic.

By attending market on a regular basis, Luc and Lai Mee regularly came across sash-wearing employees from the medical centre intermingling with the townspeople. Because of this, they concluded that their initial reluctance in approaching either police or other authority had been wise.

Luc had quickly learned to converse with the market traders and he was also able to pay for some tuition in reading and writing.

Although fairly fluent in English, French, Thai and Laotian, Lai Mee at first struggled with the local dialect. This problem was partially resolved when Luc insisted that she take produce to the market alone and eventually she became reasonably proficient with conversational Cantonese.

While he was still alive the old man had absorbed much of the child minding duties. With his death this responsibility was forced on either one of them until an idea occurred to Lai Mee.

"Sit there and watch over my sons, dog," she ordered. From that moment on and whenever they were absent through work, the intelligent animal would readily hunker down beside the playpen with his lower jaw on his paws and watch over both their sons.

On one occasion while they were diverting water channels some way from the homestead, they were alerted to a problem by the dog's frenzied barking. Scurrying back, they found both children squabbling, with the older boy attempting to cram a wooden toy down his brother's throat.

On days when she was left alone, Lai often took her sons and the dog to where the old man was buried beneath the willows. The children were allowed to crawl and roll on grassy banks while the dog was free to hunt for rabbits and other game to supplement their food stocks. Lai Mee came to enjoy this peaceful corner and revered the spirit of the old man which she was sure still lingered. Lai's feelings for the memory of him had also developed to a level where she regularly placed gifts on his grave and said prayers for him.

On stumbling across Lai Mee's gifts one day, Luc good-naturedly chided her for indulging in such practices.

"Those small things are of no great significance, Luc! There is usually a little rice wine which he liked to drink and cigarettes or tobacco which he also enjoyed smoking. I am very happy here and I wish that the old man had not been taken from us. He became a substitute for my own dear father who we lost so long ago. While the old man was still with us I often felt papa's presence through him and it was comforting."

Luc's response was no more than a resigned shrug. He had grown accustomed to Lai Mee's beliefs and although he thought of them as foolish superstition, he supposed it did no harm to humour her. Occasionally he would find her spirituality unsettling as she often woke him in the night to recount some discussion which she'd had with his first wife in a dream. When attempting to persuade her that reality had no substance in dreams, Lai would become agitated and tell him of conversations regarding the children from his first marriage and the sons which were now hers.

Luc slowly realised that these supposed links with his dead wife were so real that ridiculing them would serve no purpose other than to create distress for Lai Mee.

Lai Mee's happiest time was when work for the day was complete and she was free to watch wildlife. She admired the iridescent colours of kingfishers and the soaring majesty of the vultures and buzzards overhead.

Lai and Luc rarely quarrelled, although whenever Luc removed the revolver from its hiding place for cleaning, her fears would return and she would plead with him to stay away from the medical centre. In all probability Luc was now as familiar with the place as the staff who worked there as he had returned on numerous occasions. Mostly the compound was deserted, with the only exception being the odd watchman making his rounds.

Regular visits to the town's market also helped Luc to integrate with local people and their acceptance of him was encouraged by the small gifts he regularly gave. Sometimes the gifts were nothing more than a few eggs; at times though, when trade was good, Luc might part with a duck or a chicken.

Lai Mee now remembered an occasion when Luc had failed to return from his marketing responsibilities at the usual time. With the arrival of nightfall she had feared the worst, convinced that his true identity had been discovered and that he had been taken back to the medical centre. The dog's whimpering was a first indication that her fears were groundless and Luc then appeared, if somewhat shakily, in the doorway.

In other circumstances she might have found Luc's intoxication amusing. Lai Mee's very obvious distress quickly sobered Luc, however, and eventually he managed to console her.

With some of Lai Mee's composure regained, Luc described how he had been invited to play mah-jong with a small group of market traders at one of their regular social evenings. Two employees from the medical centre had joined them mid-way through this session and Luc confessed to feeling very uneasy in their presence. The pair were eventually summoned away by a sash-bearing female who came to inform them that all medical centre staff was required to report back for a briefing.

A few sniggering remarks by Luc's other companions followed this hasty departure and while Luc had previously held a still tongue, he now felt reasonably secure in prompting further discussion on the two men.

"Oh, they're not from around here. Although you can be certain that when their bosses call, they sure as hell have to jump." This remark was accompanied by a very obvious sarcastic sneer.

"I thought their manner of speaking and their accent was rather strange," Luc prompted.

"Dr Chang's people almost all come down from the north. I have heard them talk of someplace called Tianjin which I believe is in Beijing province," the talkative man next volunteered.

"This Dr Chang, is he an industrialist? He must have a very large organisation to employ so many people," Luc then continued, before his companions were able to offer an explanation,

"It seems strange that it is necessary to transport employees from the north when there appears to be an abundance of local people who could do the doctor's work?"

"Ah, but the people he employs are skilled in medicine. People from around here are mainly farmers and fishermen. The work they do at the centre would be too complex for the likes of us."

"And what work would that be?" Luc asked. There was a moment when he thought he had gone too far and was not going to receive an answer. Casting a furtive look in the direction of the door the previous speaker then continued,

"It is not wise to discuss the activities of the centre. Dr Chang's henchmen have cruel ways of discouraging gossip. You and your wife are isolated out on that farm and so you have probably not heard of the punishments which are exacted against any of the staff who give free rein to their tongue."

Further hesitation indicated that the man was uneasy and this was confirmed by his continued glances toward the door.

"This is for your ears only. So far as we know, people from other countries are donating parts of their bodies for transplant. Once they are through this process they are paid a lot of money and then returned to their homes where they enjoy the wealth which their sacrifice has secured. Things sometimes go wrong, of course, and some poor souls forfeit their lives. Desperate people are, however, always prepared to resort to desperate ways." The man paused to refill his cup.

"There was a full-scale and very extensive search some years back when a young woman escaped from the compound. It was suggested at the time that she had contracted some serious disease before coming to the island. They never found her, or at least that was the story we were told. After weeks of searching without success, the institute people concluded that she had strayed into a bog on the marshes and drowned."

Luc had attempted to show sympathy and suggested it was a terrible thing to have happened.

"Certainly she never left the island, as they had every possible route covered and this included all types of shipping, together with the fishing boats."

There then seemed an unwillingness to discuss the matter in further detail and Luc thought it might help if he purchased two further flasks of wine. Instead of helping to ease their tongues this seemed to have an opposite effect; the players lost interest in the game and he described how he had left all but one of them sleeping off the effects of alcohol.

"This woman the staff was searching for. Do you suppose it was one of the group that was with me? It seems tragic if she managed to escape only to then perish out on the marshes," Lai suggested.

"No, I think it was the same occasion when they were searching for you, little one. In fact I feel certain that it was you."

"Me?" Lai Mee questioned. "How come you're suggesting that it was me and not the two of us? Your friends at the market told you that the staff were looking for a woman with some disease. I can understand that they would invent disease as a reason for her running away, although surely they would have alerted local people to the fact that they were looking for two patients if it was really us that they were searching for?"

"You have overlooked the fact that I killed the thief in the showers and left him in my place. If they ever noticed that he had rid himself of the ankle bracelet, they probably assumed the adhesive had failed and that it had been flushed down the sluices."

"Surely his family would have inquired after him when they lost contact?" Lai Mee questioned in an unconvinced tone.

"Maybe he didn't have a family. Perhaps the sort of man who is capable of co-operating in such evil and then cheats on his accomplices would not be the type to have family ties. When he failed to report for work, his colleagues may have assumed that he had deserted the medical centre for something more lucrative."

The after-effect of Luc's evening of excess was then beginning to tell and Lai Mee realised that she was unlikely to extract little more of interest from him. She was about to suggest that they retire for the night when one further thought occurred.

"You seem to have forgotten the woman we took the yellow band from. The same woman that we left trussed up before we stole the bicycles. Would she not have alerted the others that it was two people who had tied her up and then left her beneath that hut?"

The question was barely out before Lai Mee realised that she knew the answer. It seemed obvious that on one of the occasions when Luc had been back to the centre, he would have checked beneath the building.

"Unfortunately she didn't manage to free herself. I think she probably suffocated on the gag we used." Lai's look of horror prompted him to continue,

"I am not sorry and certainly do not regret being responsible for her death. The mere fact that she was in the compound and wearing one of those yellow sashes indicates that she was certainly involved with the mass executions."

A sceptical look from Lai Mee prompted Luc to add to this.

"In my opinion she deserved to die the way she did. Suffocation is the method used by those people and it would seem a fitting way for the world to be rid of them."

"Then is her body still beneath the hut where we left her? Lai Mee asked.

"No. I managed to dispose of her remains in a cess pit during darkness on the first occasion that I stole back into the centre. It had already decomposed quite considerably and despite my reluctance to move it, I feared it might eventually be discovered."

Lai Mee was saddened by her husband's seeming callousness, although she realised that throughout the entire time that she had known him his gentleness was a quality which had always been very apparent. Despite her love for him there had been numerous occasions when Luc had demonstrated a ruthless streak which always shocked her, none more so than when he believed that the weak and defenceless were being disadvantaged by the strong and powerful.

The alcohol that he had consumed at the social gathering was beginning to take its toll and Luc's speech was becoming increasingly slurred. Lai Mee took his arm and gently steered him to their sleeping platform.

The information which Luc had gleaned from his night at the traders' social gathering served only to strengthen his desire to learn more and, as the days passed, Lai Mee realised it was becoming something of an obsession for him, an obsession which did nothing to allay her fears.

If the purpose of the medical centre was to obtain organs for transplant, Luc felt that it was essential for him to acquire an in-depth understanding of the doctor's overall operation. That was always supposing that he would eventually find some weakness in the organisation that he could exploit.

Thus far Luc had been frustrated by his inability to damage Chang Jin-Ming's murderous regime. Now at last he felt he was slowly gathering intelligence with which to work and in the following weeks he went about acquiring additional information in a manner which he hoped would not raise suspicions.

Learning the name of the principal had been important and on two occasions he had actually seen Dr. Chang Jin-Ming. The first of these was when a large black Russian-built Zil limousine slowed for some ducks which were crossing the road close to where Luc's trading stand was positioned in the market. In that fleeting moment, Luc was allowed no more than a glimpse of the face of a passenger reclining on the deeply-upholstered rear seat of the automobile.

The owner of the ducks, after muttering some profanities, then confirmed that this was indeed the infamous head of the nearby medical institute.

On the second occasion Luc had been observing the centre from a secure place outside the perimeter fence when he witnessed Dr. Chang have one of the staff half beaten to death for some minor infringement of duty.

Luc had seen and personally experienced the brutality of Khmer officials; he had always considered them to be thugs of low intelligence. Dr Chang, he assumed, was of above average intelligence and yet he seemed to derive similar enjoyment from inflicting pain on defenceless people.

When the medical centre was not in use, Luc was able to explore the place at will and while doing so he gradually came to understand the low mentality which prevailed amongst a majority of the staff. He also learned that they were both lax and lazy.

Luc Tun's basic knowledge of air compressors was learned through his earlier years of practising dentistry and this experience allowed him to quickly understand how the shower blocks were made airless.

Through frequent visits to town, Luc was also given ample warning of when further shipments of refugees were due and he regularly observed disembarkation and transport arrangements from places close to the port.

Following the arrival of yet another group of unfortunates, Luc had stolen across to the same cell where Lai Mee and others had been awaiting their fate. As on that occasion, a number of confused and somewhat stressed people were patiently waiting.

Discovering that the door was now secured by a heavy padlock quickly removed all thoughts of releasing the detainees. Luc was in any case aware that foot patrols now guarded the perimeter fence and the possibility of people in a confused state successfully escaping was improbable. With feelings of helplessness and despair Luc had returned to his former hiding place and then waited to see what might happen.

Trucks eventually arrived and when ramps had been erected against the rear of these vehicles, stretcher bearers began carrying corpses from the shower blocks and depositing their gruesome bundles into the empty vehicles.

A silence descended over the complex when the last of the bundles was carried out and the convoy had driven away. Following this departure, Luc had decided to stay on in an attempt to learn what might happen to the small group who were left behind in Lai Mee's old cell.

The morning passed slowly and the sun had sunk low before signs of further activity occurred. A cloud of dust from off the dirt road preceded the arrival of a small bus which in turn was followed by a smart limousine. When the two vehicles came to a standstill inside the compound, Luc watched as one of the waiting staff opened a rear door of the following expensive looking vehicle. A man of unusual appearance then emerged, this character was unusually tall and his long hair was kept in place by a fastening at the rear. His clothes were of western design and yet his facial appearance suggested origins of an oriental background.

Although Luc was unable to hear the conversation which then took place, he thought the newcomer appeared to have some distaste for his surroundings and the people who greeted him. It also became obvious that the tall man was inpatient and his conversation appeared both clipped and abrupt. The consequence of this was that one of the staff promptly escorted the internees from Lai Mee's former cell and noisily urged them onto the waiting bus.

There was a moment of hesitation when one of the refugees appeared to question what was happening. A slashing whip-like blow from the tall man's riding crop was the only reaction he received and this appeared to deter further attempts at protest.

With little more gesture than a curt nod, the tall man then stepped back into the limousine, which sped off in pursuit of the bus and its obviously reluctant passengers.

Lai Mee later insisted that they should offer prayers for the unfortunate victims and the good fortune which had allowed both of them to escape a similar fate. This was when Luc had arrived back at the farm and given her an account of all that had happened. She pleaded with Luc not to become complacent while also accepting that his clandestine surveillance had as yet gone unnoticed. Lai Mee's plea and her concern for Luc's safety registered with him despite the appearance of not having done so. His determination, however, was growing ever stronger with each new piece of evidence that he was able to gather.

On the occasion that the doctor's car had slowed for the ducks at the marketplace Luc had been quick to observe a small sign on the rear fender which declared it to be the property of the Fan Chee Medical Institute.

Eventually, and after some prolonged haggling, Luc had managed to persuade a book stall trader to exchange a second hand medical directory for one of his ducks. From the medical directory Luc read with some difficulty that the Fan Chee Institute was situated in the city of Guangzhou on the mainland and that Dr. Chang Jin-Ming was listed as the Institute's principal.

With the location of the doctor's base established, Luc next investigated the possibility of crossing to the mainland and these inquiries revealed that security checks on the ferry had not been in place for some while.

"I am going to risk visiting the mainland, little one," Luc announced later that evening when Lai Mee had settled both sons on their sleeping mats.

"It is possible that I will be away for some time. Will you be able to manage without me?" Realising that this could only mean further pursuit of his plans to expose the medical centre, Lai responded with no more than a shrug of resignation.

"Of course I will. Our eldest son already helps with feeding the poultry and both children can travel to town with me on market days. On those occasions I will leave the dog loose and he can guard our property." Having expected stronger resistance, Luc's relief was very obvious.

"I will go to the ferry terminal tomorrow and obtain the cost of a return ticket together with sailing schedules. Please trust me. Lai Mee. I will do nothing in haste and promise that I will take great care in Guangzhou."

# Chapter Ten

While waiting at the airport departure gate for the first leg of his journey back to London Charlie's attention was drawn to an attractive young woman who had hurriedly joined the economy class queue. This young woman was without doubt the most stunning he had seen in a very long time and it brought back memories of an experience many years before. Charlie had been at university and had also been similarly smitten by one particular young student and his subsequent involvement was in all probability the reason for his still being a bachelor.

An announcement that business class passengers should commence boarding distracted him from further thoughts of what had then been a thrilling although brief and sad encounter.

Charlie stowed his bag, accepted a glass of champagne and was about to settle down with the previous day's edition of the Daily Telegraph when he became aware of the same young woman that he had noticed earlier. She appeared to be studying seat numbers until, looking confused, she asked,

"Is this 14A, do you think? Luckily I've been upgraded, although I don't seem able to find my seat."

"I guess it is," Charlie faltered. "At least, I thought mine was 14B. Although if it's not, I reckon someone will soon claim it. Would you like a hand to put that bag in the overhead locker?"

"It's all right, thanks, I can manage. I suppose it is on the large size, although I always travel with just the one bag. It saves having to wait for luggage at the other end."

"Good idea, so do I." Charlie replied. This remark was lost on the young woman as a steward came forward with a tray of drinks and apologised that cabin staff had not shown her to her seat. The fact that the steward seemed in awe of her amused Charlie and he thought she was oblivious of the effect that she was having on the man.

"No champagne for me, although might I have some fruit juice, please?" When she had taken the glass, she then offered her free hand across.

"My name's Kate." Charlie had barely time to introduce himself before they were being urged to buckle their seat belts.

The heavily-laden plane seemed to struggle for height after leaving the runway and for a while Charlie peered out of the window at skyscrapers and the interlacing road system which cluttered the outskirts of the city.

Prior to boarding Charlie had assumed that he would sleep for most of the fourteen or fifteen hour journey home; his companion, however, seemed to have other ideas. She fidgeted briefly before opening a conversation.

Initially Charlie thought Kate's urge to talk was because of a fear of flying, although when the giant Airbus dropped violently into an air pocket she showed little sign of concern or even that she was aware of what had happened.

"I'm sorry, Charlie. I expect you would like to read or maybe watch an in-flight movie. Please forgive this intrusion. I am on such a high and I'm desperate to share my excitement with someone. You also seem a nice person who might be patient enough to listen." It then seemed as an afterthought when she asked, "Do you mind if we talk for a while?"

Charlie realised that his face had reddened with mild embarrassment. It had been some years since he had been paid a compliment by an attractive female and because of her forthright and confident approach he felt distinctly awkward when he muttered a reply.

"Um yes, sure, that will be okay. I have nothing other than the newspaper to read and I am not much into movies."

Encouraged by this the young woman then launched into telling him how she and an aunt had recently purchased a ferry company in Vietnam.

Fascinated by both the location and the fact that someone as young as her would embark on such a venture, Charlie realised that he was rapidly gaining interest.

"When you say a ferry company, would this be with seagoing vessels like roll-on roll-off ships?"

"Oh no, not at all. In fact we are operating hydrofoils, mostly for carrying foot passengers. Our routes currently begin and end at Ho Chi Min City on the Mekong Delta. Hydrofoils, you see, are ideal for negotiating the shallows and continually shifting sand banks which abound there."

Charlie's many years of involvement with marine contracts had brought him into contact with a variety of sea going vessels, jack-up platforms and other ancillary support craft.

"When you say hydrofoils, I presume you mean those weird craft that ride up on skis?"

"Yes, that's right. I always assume that people are familiar with them. They are used an awful lot by Greeks, Italians, Albanians and a whole host of other countries."

"Are they anything like those strange bug-eyed craft which I've seen in the Aegean? I think the Greek operators call them Flying Dolphins."

"Yes, that's right. Ours are exactly like those, although there are of course other types. The fleet that we have acquired are the Meteor Class, which were built by Zavod Gorkogo at some place in Russia. When we have successfully developed a recently acquired new route, we hope to be introducing larger vessels that are capable of carrying up to four hundred passengers."

"Really! I am surprised. That's huge, and my guess is that this aircraft would have a similar capacity," Charlie retorted.

"How many people can you take on the smaller craft which you are currently operating?"

"Around a hundred, although on the new route which we have just been awarded the capacity will be slightly reduced, as we intend installing larger cafeterias on the craft that are assigned to the longer routes."

Kate's knowledge and enthusiasm was infectious and Charlie was captivated by both her enthusiasm and confidence. Because of this he managed to prolong the discussion by asking what he hoped were intelligent questions. Charlie had not been looking forward to the long and tedious flight home; now he was happy that the seat next to him had been vacant. Kate was certainly proving to be a very agreeable travelling companion.

"This is the third time that I have been upgraded by this particular airline. Normally I travel economy class as it would be unfair to inflict the extra cost on our company at this early stage." Charlie thought Kate's stunning appearance might be a contributing factor with regard to the upgrades and certainly so if her boarding was processed by a male attendant. He omitted, however, to suggest that this might be the explanation.

"Am I talking too much? My friends all suggest that I have a tendency to babble. I am sorry; I hope I am not boring you?"

"Not at all, in fact I will miss your company when you leave the plane at Bangkok."

"Oh, but I'm not. I'm travelling on to London and then down to Bournemouth. There are some papers with my aunt's lawyers which require our joint signatures."

While food was being served by in-flight attendants, there was an opportunity for Charlie to discreetly observe his travelling companion and he once more remembered his early fascination with a young woman of equal beauty.

Kate demonstrated an appreciation of both good food and fine wine during this interlude. Coffee and liqueurs had been served when the overhead address system announced that passengers travelling on to London should remain seated while Bangkok passengers disembarked. Charlie understood this to mean that he and Kate would remain together throughout the rest of the journey and that Kate would not now be displaced by someone with a business class ticket.

"In my usual way when I am excited or enthusiastic about something I tend to talk too much and pay little attention to my companions. It has been rude of me and now I would like to learn something about you, Charlie. What were you doing in Hong Kong? Was it a business trip, or a holiday? Or maybe I shouldn't ask personal questions?"

"No, that's okay, although compared to your involvements my routines are going to seem rather dull and boring." Charlie then briefly described the purpose of his trip to Hong Kong and explained that he was heading back to head office to report on the outcome. He also surprisingly realised that he had then described his recent dissatisfaction with work.

"Is there nothing which might take you away from what you are so obviously not enjoying?" Kate asked.

"Well yes, as a matter of fact there is. My company has asked me to take charge of an overseas harbour contract which will certainly give me some respite from the tedium of head office."

Charlie was then about to change the subject and tell her something of his interest in horses, when Kate asked,

"Where is this harbour contract? Is it some place nice where you will be able to relax and, more importantly, unwind?"

"It's certainly not going to be a picnic. The programme is very tight and as for being nice, I know very little about Sri Lanka."

"Pardon, did you say Sri Lanka?" Kate asked with obvious renewed interest.

"Sri Lanka is where I'm from, I was born there. In fact apart from leaving for education it's where I have spent my entire life until now." Kate paused and it was difficult for Charlie to imagine what was going through her mind; the germ of an idea was also beginning to creep into his own thoughts.

"Is your contract in Galle? I have heard that there are plans to extend the harbour to cater for an increased flow of quarry materials." Charlie told her it wasn't Galle and that his contract was in the port of Colombo. Some sixth sense and a nagging suspicion then prompted him to say,

"I knew someone once who came from Sri Lanka. She lived at a place called Koggala. It's close to Galle, I believe. Do you know it?" A moment of startled disbelief followed until Kate managed to say,

"Gosh Charlie, this gets more and more intriguing. Koggala is my home and I can tell you that there are not many people living there. There is every chance that I will know your friend if she is still around. What's her name?"

"Lorna, she was Lorna Savage, although I guess she married and so she would be called something else now."

Kate had shown surprise when Charlie mentioned Sri Lanka, although it was nothing by comparison to her present reaction of disbelief. Her mouth opened and a look of incredulity came over her until eventually she spluttered,

"But that's my mum. You have to be kidding. You must be setting me up. The coincidence of meeting a complete stranger on a plane and being told that they know my mum is just unbelievable." Charlie then explained that only moments before he had thought there might be a connection.

"There was something about you which reminded me of Lorna. Possibly a facial expression and, although I didn't realise it at the time, there was also something which caught my attention when I noticed you at the departure gate back at the airport." Disbelief was very evident in the expression on Kate's face until eventually she murmured,

"You must have known her well for it to have left such a lasting impression?" The fact that Kate was still coming to terms with what she had just learned was now very obvious.

"I was at Birmingham University when we met. Your mother was attending some lectures by someone famous in the aeronautical world. I can't remember why, but I was in a hurry and ran slap bang into Lorna and sent her flying. When she picked herself up she brushed aside my apologies and this left me feeling more of a dolt than ever."

A steward reaching over to take away the trays that their food had been served on interrupted him and Charlie had a moment to wait before continuing.

"Later that evening a group of students came into the pub where I worked and Lorna was with them. I plucked up courage and asked if I might buy her a meal to make amends. Surprisingly she accepted and we arranged to meet the following evening. Over dinner Lorna talked a lot about Sri Lanka and Koggala in particular. She also told me about someone called Rory and I realised that it was her way of letting me know that having dinner was the only thing which was on offer. The following day she travelled back south to Cranfield, where she was learning to fly, and I never saw her again."

A long drawn out silence followed until Kate did something which momentarily startled him. Gently reaching across she took his hand in hers and then spent further seconds studying him. With an expression bordering on awe she eventually murmured, "I believe you actually fell for her. No, please don't be embarrassed, it's written all over your face." A moment of further scrutiny followed until she gasped, "How romantic, nothing like that has ever happened to me and I think it might be such a sad story. In fact it seems that it could be like something from an opera or a ballet." Kate then paused in obvious thought before suggesting,

"There is a saying that time heals all wounds. I suppose you eventually married and then pushed all thoughts of my mum to the back of your mind?"

Shocked by her perception, Charlie realised that he would now have to tread warily. He then told her that the unsociable way he had lived through work had prevented his marrying and that his commitment to horse racing had also not been the ideal basis for a committed relationship. In an attempt to remove himself from further embarrassment, he then suggested,

"Our chance meeting seems incredible. In a short while we will be touching down at Heathrow. We will then both go our separate ways and I realise even now that there will be lots of questions which I shall regret not having asked."

Kate then admitted that after the initial shock of meeting by chance someone who had once known her mother, she was also intrigued and happy to talk.

"I can still hardly believe that I am actually on a plane sitting next to Lorna's daughter. Are you sure you won't mind my asking personal questions?" She told him she couldn't think of anything that she would not want him to know.

"Do you have brothers and sisters?" Kate shook her head.

"No, sadly my father died the day he and my mother married." It was now Charlie's turn to look shocked.

"Rory, the man who you said Mum mentioned to prevent you from having wrong ideas, was in fact my dad. Mum and Rory were brought up together at Koggala; they played together as children and eventually became childhood sweethearts. When Mum went off to England to train to be a pilot, Dad joined the island's security service and much later, during a covert operation against the Tamil Tigers, he was badly wounded and taken prisoner. Incredibly this coincided with my mother's plane being hijacked by the Tigers. Both she and the crew were then forcibly taken to the same rebel stronghold where my father was being held. Some weeks later the rebel settlement was attacked by a strong force of government troops. In the midst of the melee that was raging all around, my father escaped and managed to free Mum together with the other people in her crew. Unfortunately in an attempt to shield my mother Rory then sustained further wounds from small arms fire. With help from government troops that they had managed to link up with, they were able to retake the Catalina and fly it out. A Catalina by the way is an amphibian aircraft and Mum had been forced to land it on one of the large tanks in the north when the plane was hijacked."

Charlie's puzzled frown prompted Kate to explain that in Sri Lanka large tracts of man-made inland water are referred to as tanks. Charlie nodded to indicate that although he knew what a Catalina was, he had no idea that a lake was a tank. There wasn't an opportunity for him to tell her this as a stewardess arrived with yet more refreshments. As the woman then moved further down the aisle, Kate continued,

"I have always found difficulty in talking with my family about the circumstances surrounding my father's death. All I know is what I have pieced together from that which Kuli has told me. Kuli, by the way, is my grandfather's longest-serving employee and he acted as a nursemaid to both Mum and my uncle Richard when my grandmother died after giving birth to Richard. Kuli loves to gossip and I can wheedle almost anything out of him."

Pausing to savour some of the white wine that she had been given by the stewardess, Kate then asked if he really wasn't bored by her monologue of family history. Charlie assured her that he was finding it more than interesting and encouraged her to continue.

"I understand my father realised that he had not long to live and he persuaded my mother to land further down the tank where there is a tiny island on which a Roman Catholic priest was living. Father Schyns had in the past helped the security forces with information and through this he and Dad had become firm friends. Although realising that his officiating was no more than an act to honour the wishes of a dying friend, Father Schyns married my mother and father in the fuselage of the old Catalina. With the conclusion of the ceremony my father appeared to sink rapidly into something that he was unlikely to recover from and Mum flew him off to a military hospital. It was sadly too late for Dad and he died in the air. It has always seemed to me that the last thing Rory fought for was to do the honourable thing by Mum. It was obvious that she was pregnant with me at the time."

Charlie's attempt at expressing sympathy felt ponderous and awkward; despite this he murmured that it was an altogether remarkable chapter of events. Sensing his feelings of awkwardness, Kate hurriedly reassured,

"It's okay, I never knew Dad and so I guess it has been much easier for me. Mum has had a strange life though. Mostly she has buried herself in work and that hasn't always been easy. The world of flying is male dominated and she's had to contend with a lot of prejudice over the years."

Charlie then found himself in a position of uncertainty and the question he so desperately wanted to ask felt like cotton wool in his mouth. Unsure of how to put the question, he nervously spluttered,

"Did Lorna remarry?" It was the first time for some minutes that the expression on Kate's face had changed and he wasn't sure if it was a smile or a grin.

"No, she never married again and so there may be hope for you yet, Charlie." This was said with a mischievous grin and if Kate was aware of the further discomfort that this remark created she pretended not to notice.

"How about you? You have so far used work and horses as an excuse for not marrying, although there must have been the odd relationship somewhere along the way?" Charlie's mumbled retort was interrupted by an announcement that they were on Heathrow approach and that all passengers should return to their seats.

Both Kate and Charlie sped through the usual airport formalities and then quickly boarded the Heathrow express. At Paddington, she kissed him lightly on the cheek and told him she was truly sorry that their journey had come to an end.

"I have a feeling, though, that our paths may cross again. Will you look Mum up when you are established in Colombo?"

"I'm not sure; a lot of water has passed under the bridge since Birmingham and it would probably be quite embarrassing for Lorna if I pitched up at Koggala out of the blue."

"No, it certainly would not. Please take my word for it. She will take it in her stride and if you promise to go, I will not tell her that we have met. She doesn't have too many surprises and I think your turning up might just be the nice surprise she really deserves."

# Chapter Eleven

At certain times, when the medical centre was not in use, Luc was happy with his role of being a peasant farmer and Lai Mee desperately hoped he would become so involved that his vendetta against Doctor Chang Jin-Ming's evil regime might be forgotten.

The morning after Luc had left to check out ferry sailings, Lai Mee spent a day miserably anticipating disaster. On his return, albeit a little later than expected, her feelings of relief quickly changed to anxiety when she sensed a noticeable change to his mood. It was some while before she was able to discover the reason for this as both boys clambered over their father in an attempt to find what treats he might have brought home for them.

Eventually the boys found some candy which Luc had hidden in his cycle panniers and Lai Mee was then able to question him.

"Please tell me that you have not taken risks. I realise I'm being foolish but I am so afraid. The fact that you are thinking of crossing to the mainland frightens me and I don't know how I would cope if anything happened to you."

Luc was rarely demonstrative, although on this occasion he put his arms around her and told her that he had a confession to make. There was a moment of thoughtful silence while Lai Mee tried to imagine what her husband might have done to warrant a confession.

"You will think me foolish as I have spent money from our hard-earned savings on something which you may consider a poor investment. In fact, in its present condition most people would think it fit only for the salvage yard. The price I've agreed to pay, is, however, marginally above scrap value."

This unexpected statement brought a confusion of thoughts to Lai Mee's already troubled mind, until finally she asked,

"What is it, Luc? Please don't keep me in suspense. I have had a horrible day worrying about you and I'm really not in the mood for further torment."

Sensing his wife's ever-increasing agitation, Luc told her that while cycling through the port area in search of the ferry reservations office he had come across a large four-wheel drive tractor, which seemed to have been abandoned.

"I had gathered all the information I needed on fares and sailing schedules and was cycling back past the machine when I spotted a man who appeared to be surveying an area adjacent to the tractor. As this person was carrying both a clipboard and a portable radio I thought he might be someone of authority. I was right and it transpired that he is a storage supervisor."

"Please get to the point Luc, the suspense is almost more than I can bear."

"Well, I asked the supervisor about the tractor and he told me that a farming co-operative had been about to ship it back to one of its holdings on the mainland when the engine failed. The port authority later discovered that because of past poor performance, the co-operative had been disbanded by the state agricultural secretariat. The man also told me that the port management was thinking of towing the machine off to a salvage yard." Luc hesitated and Lai Mee sensed this was because of some embarrassment.

"On impulse I asked the supervisor if the authority might consider an offer and from that point things developed rather rapidly. The man left what he was doing and took me off to the accounts department." A further pause followed. "Subject to my returning with some cash tomorrow, we are now the new owners of a tractor."

Had there been anything to add, it is unlikely that Luc could have continued as Lai Mee demonstrated her relief and told him she didn't mind in the least that he had spent money on a piece of machinery. What she did not say was that she didn't care if the thing never worked. Lai was simply relieved that Luc might have stumbled across a project which would distract his thoughts from Dr Chang.

Luc returned to the port the following morning and paid over the agreed price for the defunct tractor. On his return to the farm Lai Mee was amused by her normally restrained husband's further excitement.

"Guess what, little one?" She was given no opportunity to respond as he continued breathlessly,

"I met one of the port mechanics and he had heard of our purchase. The mechanic says that there is little wrong with the tractor other than the fuel pump. I asked him if it could be fixed and he says he has a similar pump which has been discarded from another machine. If it is recalibrated and then fitted, he considers the machine will be in good working order." Luc paused for a reaction. Lai Mee, however, was attempting to absorb this latest development and to assess if the conclusion was good or bad.

"I hope you will not think that I have indulged in further foolishness as I agreed to pay a further three hundred and fifty yuan for the mechanic to supply and fit the replacement pump."

"Dear Luc, I know better than anyone that you would not squander our savings and whatever you do has my blessing."

Supper that evening was a special dish of crayfish, which Lai Mee knew Luc particularly enjoyed. Her relief at his enthusiasm for something which she hoped might distract him from thoughts of damaging the medical centre, was sufficient for her to go to untold lengths in an attempt to please him.

In due course the large lime green-coloured American John Deere tractor made its homecoming, although this feat was only accomplished with some difficulty. The tractor's four giant-size tyres had previously been fitted with even wider flotation cages to enable it to operate over water-saturated paddy. When the cages were removed, the machine was the same width as the track which led to the homestead and Luc had flattened a number of small trees and shrubs on the journey home.

"With this machine I will now be able to cultivate land that was never manageable with the buffalo. I believe there are lots of old tree roots buried, although the disc plough should make easy work of breaking up the soil. I can also use the bulldozer blade for levelling." Luc proudly showed Lai Mee the additional equipment which had also been included with his purchase.

"The extra produce that we will harvest from the new land will hopefully generate sufficient income to enable us to send our sons to school."

Faith in the tractor's potential was more than justified. Luc not only cleared and cultivated large tracts of land which had hitherto lain unused; he was also offered work for his tractor by neighbouring farmers.

Somewhat surprisingly, one of the first calls for this service was from the port authority. Following two further meetings and some formality, the authority then contracted him to level land adjacent to the port which was destined for new development.

Luc used his bicycle to travel to and from site each day as the cumbersome machine was unsuitable for frequent journeys through the town.

A residential area lying between the port area and town contained several large and impressive houses; one mansion in particular attracted Luc's attention as he cycled past. Access to this mansion was through a pair of massive iron gates which were supported by stone pillars, on top of which sat an equally impressive pair of ornately carved dragons. Finelymanicured lawns bordered a gravel driveway leading up to the house, which was shrouded by a rich green pan tiled roof. Whenever passing this property Luc marvelled at its opulence and realised that he had never seen anything as magnificent in Phnom Penh.

One evening while peddling home, Luc, as was now his custom, glanced through the railings and his attention was drawn to a familiar figure stepping from a car. Realising that it was the same tall man with the pony-tail who had escorted living refugees from the medical centre, Luc quickly dismounted and leant his bicycle against a wall.

Concealed behind one of the pillars, from where he had clear view of what was happening, Luc witnessed an exquisitely-dressed woman greeting the tall man. When the tall man failed to re-emerge from the building after a considerable wait, Luc decided further time spent watching the house might attract unwanted attention.

The port mechanic had fallen into the habit of eating his food with Luc when they stopped for breaks each day and the two men had become good friends.

Following on from the morning when Luc had seen the tall man at the large imposing house, he described the building to the mechanic in detail.

"Ah, my friend. Looking in from the outside will cost you nothing, although stepping in through those gates would be an entirely different matter!" The port mechanic chuckled. When realising Luc's further curiosity, he continued.

"It is a house of pleasure! Unfortunately it is not for the likes of you and me. It is rumoured that the women are highly skilled in their profession and that most of them come from far away. My second cousin is a gardener there and he has told me that women are not the only pleasures the house has to offer."

An inquiring look from Luc encouraged the man to elaborate.

"Opium pipes have been outlawed in our country for many years although there is little risk for those with influence. I understand that other substances are also available," the man exclaimed with a knowing wink.

"A very tall man with long hair tied behind his neck entered the house as I passed yesterday and I felt sure that I had seen both him and his car somewhere before."

"It's more than likely. He comes through the port regularly. From your description I imagine it was Bax, General Zin Bax. I have heard it said that his great-grandfather was a Dutchman who served as a military adviser to one of the warlords when our country was still ruled by the emperor." The mechanic then paused to retrieve some small grains of rice from his mess tin.

"These days Bax is employed as secretary to the Fan Chee Medical Institute and he regularly crosses between here and the mainland."

Had the mechanic not been engrossed with the remainder of his lunch packet it is possible that he would have seen Luc's change of expression.

"His position would seem to carry a large remuneration for him to afford the pleasures of that house," Luc knowingly chuckled.

"Yes and my cousin says he takes full advantage of everything the house has to offer. He is a mean bastard though, and gives nothing but grief to the servants. If he thinks one of them has been neglectful in their duties, he is quick to have them disciplined. In fact there was a time when some foreigners came to the house looking for one of the ladies of pleasure. It was rumoured that she had fallen foul of the general, although nothing more was ever seen of her."

A knowing look passed between the two men and the mechanic paused for Luc to form his own conclusion.

"My cousin suggests that the ladies of the house are terrified of Zin Bax. He expects much more than simple relief from them!" Here the mechanic picked up some flex and whipped it viciously on the ground; this left Luc unsure as to what his friend was insinuating.

"Apparently he not only enjoys taking it, he also enjoys dishing it out." The conversation then momentarily faltered and Luc was none the wiser.

"There is a large family who live in the shanty area to the north of town. Like most people there, the mother is extremely poor. She learned to her cost that General Bax has a liking for young boys. As she had a son who was unusually pretty, she offered the boy to the general through an intermediary. For a while the woman benefited from this liaison and then quite suddenly the gifts and payments petered out."

One of the port's noisy container handling machines trundling past interrupted the mechanic's flow.

"The ladyboy's mother eventually sent her eldest son across on the ferry to investigate. This boy showed some initiative. He quickly located the general's home and then kept watch until Bax was driven away. Assuming that it would be safe to do so, the older son then went into the grounds of the house to see what he might discover. He found his younger brother chained to a post in an animal pen. The boy was in a filthy state with a broken arm and a badly mangled foot. On managing to free his sibling, the older boy then learned that the boy was unable to walk. The wretched lad had been exposed to some despicable practices and had incurred serious internal injuries. Remarkably the elder son managed to carry his brother back to the ferry and eventually they made it home. Tragically the ladyboy died two days later. When his mother attempted to claim compensation from the general, she was badly beaten and lost an eye."

Luc's grunt of horror caused his friend to falter until he finally concluded,

"I suppose she was lucky not to lose her life. Bax is a real bastard, he seems to be above the law and you will do well to give him a wide berth, my friend."

Sickened by yet another example of the inhuman excesses of the people he hoped to bring to justice, Luc assumed some consolation from the fact that he had discovered the name of yet one more person who was involved with the Fan Chee Institute.

Involvement with the farm and other work now kept Luc and Lai Mee busy, and yet more time slipped by with Luc not finding ways of harming the institute. They were now harvesting a great deal more produce from the land which had been cleared and Lai Mee suggested that they should consider alternative transport for carrying goods to market.

"If you continue to do tractor work for other people we should find a way of using your time more efficiently. We could afford a small truck and that would save considerable time on your journeys to and from town."

This proposal was considered rash by her husband and the expenditure unjustified. Despite his stubbornness Luc eventually saw merit in Lai Mee's proposal and they purchased a sturdy motorcycle, together with a small trailer which was designed to be towed behind. Luc had been using this combination for some time when word ran round the market that a fresh intake of refugees was about to dock. Quickly uncoupling the trailer, Luc left Lai Mee and their sons to deal with the remaining market business while he went off to investigate.

Luc's knowledge of the port had improved considerably during the time that he had worked there and he took up a position behind a warehouse from where he had a clear view of the quayside which was normally used by Dr. Chang's organisation.

Three buses were already in place and Luc assumed the vehicles were waiting for passengers to disembark from the incoming freighter.

"There must be more to come?" Luc silently questioned. He knew from past experience that three buses would have insufficient capacity for the groups that had previously been landed. While he was considering this unexpected development, a very noisy and throaty exhaust note distracted his thoughts.

Curiosity compelled him to search out the source of this and he had not long to wait before an unusual-looking craft hove into view.

The vessel appeared to be riding on fins and was travelling at speed as it came through the harbour entrance. Luc watched with interest as it negotiated the narrower confines of the cluttered fish wharf; it then lost some way when speed on the strange craft was reduced. With a reduction in forward motion it seemed to settle in the water and then travelled slowly toward the quayside.

Luc wondered next if the rumour of incoming refugees was correct, as the newly arrived craft manoeuvred alongside the same wharf where refugee ships normally docked.

Explanation for this quickly followed when a hatch opened and three crew members secured the craft with mooring lines before placing a gangway onto the quayside.

A group of somewhat bewildered-looking people then followed the crew ashore and Luc watched as they were ushered onto the waiting buses. His first inclination was to follow the departing refugees until deciding it might be useful to learn something of the different craft which had been used to transport the new arrivals.

There was not long to wait before the arrival of a smart limousine which Luc instantly recognised. General Bax stepped from this vehicle and removed a cigarette holder from an inside pocket. When the tall man had fitted a cigarette to the holder, he struck a match and then casually blew smoke out through his nostrils.

Feelings of animosity by Luc were almost instantly forgotten as he watched a lone figure coming ashore from the newly arrived craft. General Bax spoke briefly to the man, who was wearing a merchant seaman's pea jacket and cap at a jaunty angle. There was then a moment of hesitation as the pair shook hands. Something about this greeting caused Luc to think it was probably the first time that the two men had met.

A brief discussion followed and a large manila envelope was taken from the general's briefcase and handed to the seaman. The man then opened the envelope before nonchalantly peering inside and with less than a moment's hesitation a smile creased the man's face. Luc guessed then that the seaman was satisfied with the envelope's contents.

Following up on the initial greeting and exchange of what Luc assumed to be payment, Bax said something which Luc was unable to hear before pointing in the direction of his car. When both men climbed into the vehicle, Luc decided to follow although fortunately there was no great distance to travel.

The highly-polished limousine slowed before turning into now familiar gates with the dragons on pillars at either side. When it came to a standstill adjacent to the very imposing entrance, Luc watched the same woman he had previously seen approach the limousine and bow deeply.

Based on previous experience, Luc decided that the general and his guest might be preoccupied for some while and he then returned to help Lai Mee tidy up at the end of market trading.

"There were not as many in the group as on previous occasions and the vessel they arrived in was nothing like the freighter that was previously used."

A quizzical expression fell over Luc's features until his silence was broken when he announced excitedly,

"I remember now. I have seen pictures of similar craft and think it's probably a hydrofoil." Luc was describing earlier events to Lai Mee when the family had eaten and their sons had been put down for the night.

"I was not able to accurately count the number of people who came ashore, although I would estimate that there was less than a hundred. In fact they all managed to squeeze onto three moderately-sized buses."

The sound of a muffled snore alerted Luc to the fact that his narrative had lost interest for Lai Mee and not for the first time he wished he could forsake his sworn oath of exacting vengeance against Dr Chang's organisation.

Since acquiring a portable radio, Luc regularly tuned into world news channels and learned that Pol Pot and many of the Khmer officials were still at large and enjoying a freedom which they had previously denied an entire nation. Knowledge of this served only to increase the Cambodian's resolve.

One more softly-sounding snore brought Luc's brooding thoughts back to the present and he paused only to set aside a cup of rice wine before carrying Lai Mee to their sleeping mat.

"Go to sleep, little one. Tomorrow will be another day and I will do all I can to take care of you and the boys." The mother of his children stirred sleepily and she appeared comforted by Luc's murmurings.

The following weeks passed quickly and as there were no further signs of people arriving at the centre, Lai Mee's happiness continued unabated. In the early hours of one morning, however, she woke her husband in a state of rare excitement.

"I have had another of my dreams," she told him.

"Who was it this time?" Luc asked irritably. "Was it your sister? Perhaps it was one of our parents? Or maybe it was all of them together with the children?" Annoyed at being disturbed, Luc's retort demonstrated his considerable grumpiness. Oblivious of this irritation, Lai Mee continued,

"No, oh no. It was the old man." A blank stare from her husband suggested that he had not understood.

"The old man, the deaf mute who gave us shelter when we were in need. It was him and he visited me in my dream. You will remember that we never knew his name? Well, it's Lin Yen. And the incredible thing is that in my dream he was able to speak and his hearing was perfect."

Despite not wishing to hurt his wife Luc was unable to suppress a snort of derision, although this fortunately passed unnoticed.

"Lin Yen told me he thought that you were wise to buy the tractor and he is pleased that you have cultivated the land which he was unable to plough. He says to tell you that because you now have a machine to do the work, you are not to sell the buffalo. Lin Yen was emphatic that they will provide us with milk and curds and their breeding is very fine. He says that if we put them back to good bulls, their heifer calves will always fetch high prices."

Tired and still aching from the previous day's work, Luc's retort was more from a need for further sleep than a wish to be cruel.

"What other words of wisdom did the old man wish to have passed on?"

"He's called Lin Yen. Now that we know his name we shall have to be more respectful when we talk of him. Lin Yen suggests that you work hard to finish clearing the last of the untilled land as the monsoon will come early." Another derisory grunt interrupted Lai Mee's flow.

"Many fish and eels will be washed out onto the paddy and Lin Yen says when the rains have stopped we will be able to trap them by controlling the sluices. He says we should smoke the catch, keep what we need and then sell the rest."

"Perhaps he would like to come back and lend a hand with the extra work." Luc's patience was now beginning to show signs of strain.

"Hush, Luc. We should not offend him. He will watch out for us. He says our sons will become strong wise men and that we shall be proud of them. I think he also said that the boys will take care of us in our twilight years."

"What other words of wisdom did he pass on?" Lai Mee once more allowed this sarcasm to pass.

"Well, he was quite excited and I am not sure that I understood everything. I have, however, kept the best news until last. We are to have an addition to the family, although I'm not sure that you will be pleased. Lin Yen says we will have a daughter and she will be very beautiful. I am so happy, Luc, as he says that she will always be close to me."

Luc smiled and thought the retelling of Lai Mee's dream might amuse some of the market traders at one of their social evenings, although in his heart he knew that loyalty to Lai Mee would prevent him from ever mentioning the dream.

"If Lin Yen's prophesy is correct, it's ironic that we ever thought we would need IVF treatment. Had we known that we would eventually have children, we may have stayed in Cambodia and been blissfully ignorant of what happens here at the medical centre."

Mention of the centre dampened Lai Mee's mood; despite this she felt further explanation was called for.

"In time my pregnancy may well have happened in Phnom Penh, although I think it less likely. My contentment and the good life we have here has contributed to our having children and if we were rid of that cursed place, I would probably have many more!"

Luc realised that the medical centre was the cursed place referred to and when she added nothing more, he realised that she had gone back to sleep.

Luc's scepticism was shaken six days later when the monsoon returned early and, as the old man had predicted in Lai Mee's dream, their land took on the appearance of an inland sea. They also used the sluices to trap an abundance of fish and eels which were then smoked and the considerable surplus was sold at market.

Chinese New Year saw Luc, Lai Mee and their two boys going into town each day to join in the festivities. While their sons were engrossed with one of the many spectacular fireworks displays, Lai Mee whispered,

"Lin Yen was right when he predicted that there would be a flood and his other prediction was also correct. Let me have your hand."

Lai Mee then moved Luc's fingers through the loose fold of her wrap and as he explored the smoothness of her belly, he was surprised to feel movement.

"That is your daughter taking her exercise," Lai Mee whispered happily.

# Chapter Twelve

Kate was beginning to feel the effects of the long journey as she settled onto the seat of a train which was slowly moving away from Waterloo Station. There had been a moment of panic when she looked up at the destination board and discovered that departure was imminent. Had she not managed to scramble in through the barrier and then the guard's open door, she would have waited another hour for the next train to Bournemouth. The guard was obviously about to reprimand her for the reckless way in which she had gained access to the train, although his manner faltered and changed when she smiled at him and he then helped her to find one of the few vacant seats.

Kate was surprised that she had been so forthcoming on the journey from Hong Kong; she supposed that she had felt comfortable with Charlie Greenwood and realised this was often the case with older men.

As the train gathered momentum and the backs of terraced houses became a blur, she stared vacantly out through the window. Taking the business card from her pocketbook, she read that Charlie Greenwood was a director of engineering and this did not altogether surprise her.

"If it wasn't for the fact that I believe Charlie is okay, I would find it rather strange how things have turned out. It is weird that he knew Mum and it was all too obvious that she had once created quite an impression on him."

"Can I see your ticket, miss?" Kate resented this intrusion into her speculative mood, although she quickly forgot her annoyance when it was necessary to explain to the conductor that she did not have a ticket. When the railway official produced a machine and she had given him a credit card, she was then left to return to her thoughts.

"I wonder if Charlie and Mum were lovers. Surely not, he said they only spent one evening together, although it is possible that he didn't tell me everything."

Kate was also having doubts about the promise she had made and wondered how her mother would really react if Charlie reappeared in her life. She thought it probable that he would in fact show up at Koggala and hoped it might bring a change for the better to her mother's life.

As her aunt's seafront hotel was some way from the main railway station in Bournemouth, Kate was relieved to find a vacant taxi waiting on the cab rank. The first person she encountered on entering the hotel reception area was the familiar large and imposing figure of Uncle Lenny. Lenny Rouse had been her grandfather's business partner for most of his working life and the two men had served together as pilots in the RAF during the Second World War. With the cessation of hostilities, Bob Savage had purchased a war surplus Catalina aircraft and invited Lenny to join him in what became a successful freight hauling business.

"Uncle Lenny, it's good to see you, and it's wonderful to be back!" Kate rushed forward to embrace him.

"God, you're a sight for sore eyes, young Kate! How did you get here?" When she told him that she had taken a taxi from the station, he scolded her for not calling him to meet her with the car.

"Your aunt's up in town with her accountant. Seems the company that have purchased the other hotels now want to get their hands on this place. They have made her a good offer and I'm urging her to sell. I'm not sure she will, though. She feels some attachment to the place; although if I thought it had anything to do with my being here I would pack my bags and find somewhere else to live." Lenny paused, probably to reflect on what such an undertaking might involve.

"Your aunt has been good to me, almost like the daughter I never had, although I wouldn't want to stand in the way of a good business deal."

Uncle Lenny had been living with Ruby at the small hotel since his retirement and it was here that Kate had spent a great deal of time during holidays from both school and university.

"I'm sorry, child. If you've travelled down by train from London you must be famished. I can hear chef moving around in the kitchen. Shall I go through and ask if he can knock you up an omelette or something?"

"No thanks. Apart from a nap on the train I've not slept in the last thirty hours. What I would really like is some tea and then I'll crash out in my room, if that's okay with you?" Kate then went through to the kitchen and was given a cup of tea by the chef before making her way up to a comfortable and very familiar room where she immediately fell into a deep sleep.

Daylight was streaming in through the windows when Kate next came too. Glancing across at the bedside clock she saw that it was eight thirty and with a gasp of annoyance she leapt out of bed.

"Ruby, it was rude of me to crash out like that. I am sorry. I should have waited for you to get back." After quickly washing and dressing, Kate had made her way down to her aunt's private quarters. She kissed the older woman and Ruby instantly brushed aside her apologies.

"Uncle Lenny and I hoped you might be down soon. Neither of us has had breakfast and we thought it would be nice for the three of us to eat together. Hopefully we can then catch up on all of the things that have happened since I left you in Saigon. What would you like for breakfast? Will it be grilled bacon and eggs or would you like a nice Finnan haddock?"

"Oh yes please, and with a poached egg if I may?" The peculiarities of English cuisine had been introduced to Kate by her aunt many years before.

While Lenny was replenishing their coffee cups from the pot, Ruby suggested,

"Now then, perhaps you'll satisfy an old woman's curiosity by telling her how things are progressing with your business?"

"It's not mine, it's ours, and you're not old. Is she, Uncle Lenny?" Lenny's response to this was simply to hold his hands up, indicating that he had no wish to become embroiled with that particular exchange.

"Well, after you left, I spent some time in the offices on Bang Dang jetty getting to know the staff and that sort of thing. On the whole I would say they're a pretty good bunch, although I'm still not too sure about the Chinese captain who tried to be smart at our initial staff meeting." Ruby's thoughtful nod indicated that she also recalled the incident.

"I was impressed with Captain Wang, the senior skipper; he struck me as a very dependable sort and I asked him to make arrangements for the first trial run on the new route. To his credit, he never once asked for detail regarding the destination and the fact that I told him to ensure that we had charts covering the whole Vietnamese coastal region should have aroused his curiosity."

A tap on the door was followed by one of the hotel staff telling Ruby there was an urgent telephone call for her. When she returned to the breakfast table she told both Kate and Lenny that the call was from yet another prospective buyer for the hotel.

"I have told them to put their offer in writing, although unless it's outstanding we are staying put, Lenny. This old place is what got me started. It was my aunt's and now it's my home. Anyway, you were telling us about Captain Wang?"

"Yes, well after leaving him and Molly to make the arrangements I flew up to Hanoi to meet Admiral Tanaka. The Admiral actually caught me on the hop as instead of a meeting in his office as had been arranged, he came to my hotel. Seems something had cropped up with the Koreans over fishing rights and there was an urgent meeting which he was required to attend. He really is a lovely man. It would have been so easy for him to have passed me on to one of his subordinates, although that's not him. His manners are impeccable and he has a good eye for detail. He arranged things so that our route licence was issued the next day and it only required signatures to complete the formality."

"It sounds to me as though you two have cracked it. Although I guess it means that I'm going to be seeing much less of you in the coming months." This remark was directed at Ruby, although it was obvious Lenny was pleased that their new business venture was making good progress.

"So what did you do after you'd dealt with the formalities at the Admiral's office?" Ruby asked.

"As I had allowed a whole day for the meeting and assumed I would be dining with the Admiral that evening, I found there was time to spare and I was able to change my travel arrangements and take an earlier flight to Sri Lanka. My arrival at Koggala was then a day earlier than anticipated. The following day Grandpa Bob came with me to the bank in Colombo. He's dealt with the manager there for years and I rather think his presence helped smooth the transfer of monies from my trust to the new business account. On the way home we stopped off at Galle and found Gongy going over the Dolphin before it's to be shipped across to Ho Chi Min."

Kate stifled a yawn and Ruby sympathetically said that they should wait to hear the rest of the story.

"I'm okay, I slept like a log last night and certainly shouldn't be feeling tired. Anyway, Gongy surprised me by offering to come over to Vietnam for six months to run his eye over our maintenance set up. I hope you won't mind but I've taken him up on his offer and told him that we will cover his expenses. He was adamant that he wouldn't take a salary, as since his wife died he has been at a loose end and looking after the Dolphin in Galle harbour is the only thing which has kept him sane. Grandpa was pleased that I said yes and he's sure that if our maintenance crews are taking short cuts, Gongy will root them out."

With something that sounded like a snort, Ruby interrupted.

"I've told you on countless occasions that the everyday running of the business is down to you. I have simply bought in because, like Gongy, I am at a loose end. I also happen to think that it will be good for you to have the occasional bit of company as it might prove a little lonely, particularly so if we move from the Continental and find somewhere to set up home."

This remark caused Kate to drift from her narrative and, with a small start of excitement, she then proudly announced,

"Molly just so happens to have an uncle who owns a sort of hardware store which has a very nice apartment above it. The furnishings are mostly Vietnamese and not altogether designed for Western comfort, although it has a nice upper terrace which is facing the waterfront and it's only a stone's throw from the office. The old chap is asking a reasonable rent and I thought that if we decide to go ahead, we can put furniture in which will be more comfortable. There are two very large bedrooms, an adequate kitchen-dining area and a nice size lounge."

"It sounds ideal. I'm sure we will manage and if we find it a bit cramped, there will be time for us to look for something larger. Now tell me about the trial run, how did that go?" Kate drank some coffee and helped herself to more toast before continuing,

"Well, despite getting back to Saigon earlier than expected, I found that Captain Wang and Molly had completed all the arrangements for the trial. Molly was delighted when I told her that I wanted her to come along. In fact the crew Captain Wang had chosen were quite excited when I revealed our destination. Molly seems to me to be wasted in her present role; I think we should bear her in mind for something more demanding." Ruby's nod indicated that she agreed.

"On the morning of our departure I surprised everyone by telling Captain Wang that I wanted to take the Dolphin down to Vung Tau. He in turn surprised me by voicing some strong opposition. His reasoning seemed to be that I didn't have a master's ticket. I argued that this was only a requirement when carrying fare-paying passengers and as we were not doing so, I had an entitlement as one of the owners. I wasn't at all sure that this was correct and neither I suspect was he. When I suggested that I would like him on the bridge, it seemed to settle his concerns."

"I know very little about maritime law although I would suggest that was a load of bunkum, young lady," Lenny retorted.

"I don't think I would have persisted had Tommy Jung not been part of the crew. I still remembered with some irritation his arrogance on that first morning meeting with the staff." Kate's frown reflected the distaste that she still felt when recalling the incident.

"Gongy regularly allowed me take the helm on Savage Air's Dolphin and I have berthed the vessel in Galle harbour more times than I can remember. I was also confident that I would be able to show smart-assed Tommy Jung that I know a little more than he gives me credit for." A disapproving tut from Lenny was more or less ignored by Kate.

"Anyway we slipped the moorings at the Bang Dang jetty and I put the ship astern against a flood tide. Once clear of the river moorings, I put her about and increased power. We were running light and so she quickly came up onto the foils. With Captain Wang acting as lookout we made it down to Vung Tau without mishap and, although I say it myself, I berthed her very smoothly. On leaving the bridge I attempted to act as though I'd been performing manoeuvres like that for most of my life. Tommy Jung's face was a picture, although I pretended not to notice and talked instead to Molly about the food we would be preparing for the evening meal."

"Good for you, darling!" Ruby approved. Kate then had a moment of respite while one of the hotel staff cleared away the breakfast dishes.

"Over the next few days we seemed to fall into a routine with either Captain Wang or Tommy Jung in charge of piloting the ship. We slept and ate on board with Molly and me sharing galley duties. You'd be surprised at the quality of meals we served, given the small space in which we had to work. It was a good insight into what can be achieved for passengers when our regular service starts. Berthing at Nha Trang was a little tricky and we have asked the harbour authorities there to make some alterations to the landing stage. In fact we called again on our return leg to check things through. While we were there we entertained the harbour master and his senior staff in the yacht club. I think it was a good PR exercise although I'm still dubious about that particular facility. On both occasions we met strong winds and I think future crews will need to take particular care."

Lenny once more interrupted by suggesting that the exercise had surely encountered other problems.

"No, apart from that everything ran rather smoothly. At both Qui Nho'n and Dha Nang the authorities regularly handle all kinds of shipping. I think when they've got used to us, everything will run like clockwork." Kate then cast a glance in her aunt's direction before continuing,

"Aside from the fact-finding mission, I found the scenery as we entered Ha Long Bay some of the most stunning I have ever seen. You really should take time out to go up there once we're established, Ruby. It is breathtakingly beautiful."

"Well yes, I should like to. It will be another excuse for me to get out from under your feet."

"Oh, don't go fretting about that. I expect to begin with we will both be so darned tired that crowding each other's space will not be a problem." A frown from Ruby indicated that she was not so sure.

"After leaving Hai Phong, we then went round Cat Ba Island to take a look at Cam Pha. I'm now having second thoughts about using it as a staging post. For one thing the facilities would need a large injection of capital and for another there is a perfectly good highway linking it to Hong Gai and Hai Phong. My guess is that local trade wishing to use our service can easily board at Hai Phong." Kate paused for a second before then saying,

"That's about it. I can't think that there is anything left to tell."

"It seems to me, girl, that you have inherited a great deal of your mother's energy. I'm feeling quite breathless just listening to you," Uncle Lenny chided.

"I agree, dear. It seems obvious that you must be exhausted. Would you like to crash out here for a couple of days before we complete paperwork at the lawyers and my bank?"

"No, Ruby. I'm desperate to get back. What I would like to do is to set up the meetings with both your bank and the lawyers and when that's settled I can then arrange my return flight. Will that be okay with you?"

"Of course, dear. Although I think we should make that two tickets. I have about wrapped things up here and we might as well travel together."

When Kate parked her aunt's battered Mini at the rear of the hotel three days later, she felt satisfied that she'd completed everything she had set out to do.

"So you're home, my lovely." Her aunt's voice greeted her as Kate made her way across to where a cosy fire was burning in the hearth of the guest lounge.

Ruby was then about to pour tea from a large china pot when she hesitated.

"I am so sorry, I almost forgot. I received a letter from your mother at least two weeks ago. Lorna is asking if I will be able to make it to Koggala in three months' time. It's your Uncle Richard's fiftieth birthday and she is planning a surprise celebration for him. I guess there will also be an invitation waiting for you when we get back to Saigon."

Kate's response to this was to show that not only had she forgotten the important occasion, she was also aggrieved that she would be spending yet further precious time away from their business.

"I think you should go. There really isn't a need for me to be there. I can stay on at the office while you're away, to keep an eye on things. Perhaps by then we will have one of those telex machines installed and it will be easy to stay in touch. Richard is not much of a one for parties, least of all surprise ones. Although I know that he will be really disappointed if you're not there," Ruby added.

# Chapter Thirteen

The woman on the stretcher felt the air ambulance accelerate and then race across the tarmacadam. Nancy Schmitt had flown regularly until her health had deteriorated and dictated otherwise; for her this was a very familiar sensation. The safety harness tightened against her chest as the plane rose from the runway and she listened to the satisfying sound of the undercarriage thudding back into its fuselage.

Glancing across at the two in-flight nursing attendants, Nancy smiled sympathetically. The nearest, a pretty young woman strapped to her jump seat, looked terrified and her knuckles showed white as she gripped the armrests.

"The poor young thing has probably not flown much before," Nancy decided. She then tried to focus on the face of the other attendant, although the frame of the dialysis machine partially obscured her view.

Nancy's transfer from a Zurich clinic to the airport had gone smoothly and little time had been wasted in loading her aboard.

"I would probably be nursing a glass of champagne and trying not to spill any if I was still working and flying first class," she mused.

Nancy's thoughts had been a source of comfort and her only refuge for some considerable time. When first diagnosed with kidney failure her family was unusually attentive and Rolf, her husband, surprisingly showed some out of character concern. Nancy quickly discovered, however, that long-term illness was stressful for family and friends and hospital visits quickly petered out. Only Helmut, her eldest child, continued to persist with his concern and devotion. Realisation that the bond was often close between mothers and their sons did nothing to lessen the pain she felt through any lack of concern that her daughter Chantille demonstrated.

Nancy had been born in Thailand and had grown up in the southern city of Phetchaburi. Her grandparents were Chinese immigrants who had fled the mainland prior to Mao Tse-tung and the people's revolution. Nancy's father eventually inherited a considerable fortune from his father who had traded in precious gemstones. Like most rich men, her father's main preoccupation was adding to his wealth. Thailand was kind to him and business had flourished in his family's adopted country.

Nancy's birth in an expensive Bangkok nursing home was exactly one hour and twenty minutes later than that of her twin sister. There were a number of half-sisters and brothers although there was never a possibility of the twins being displaced by offspring from their father's many associations with other women. The twins' mother was independently wealthy and also in a position to impose influence over their father through powerful family connections.

To his credit, the girls' father was instrumental in ensuring that the twin girls received the best education that English public schools were able to offer. Both had excelled and from England they had elected to go on to University College, Dublin. If this had seemed an unusual choice of university, their parents had done nothing to interfere.

Sin-lee, Nancy's sister, showed some aptitude for the arts while Nancy studied economics and politics; she also excelled with a passionate interest in the French language.

Despite demonstrating an unusually high work ethic, Nancy had managed to integrate within the Dublin social scene and a gap slowly widened between the two sisters.

Sin-lee's interests became focused on making money and the family business in particular. Nancy, on the other hand, came to despise the jewellery trade, believing that it simply indulged narcissistic tendencies.

Despite early good intentions, Nancy was lured into investment banking after serving an impressive spell in the chemical industry. Sin-lee had by then returned to Thailand and the family business.

To his credit, their father continued to support the younger twin, probably because he had the foresight to see Nancy's future potential. If this was so, he was surely gratified to observe her successful progress in a highly competitive commercial world. Less than three years after joining an international banking group Nancy was headhunted by an even larger and more influential investment group. From this career move Nancy went on to become one of the youngest heads of investment securities in the City of London. Her ever-growing expertise, however, was not always directed to the sole benefit of clients. An independent broker bought and sold stock on her behalf and almost always in front of market fluctuations. Unlike many of her race, Nancy was not an habitual gambler, and she became a very wealthy woman before reaching the age of thirty.

The twin girls had borne a striking resemblance to one another until reaching maturity, when Sin-lee's fine looks began to fade and her face became hardened through greed. Nancy, on the other hand, retained her fine features and was also unusually tall for someone of her race.

There were brief relationships during Nancy's student years although, once embarked on a career, she decided that involvements with men interfered with an ambition to succeed. Her close friends were therefore surprised when she eventually married a much older businessman of Swiss nationality. Nancy had then very quickly discovered that there was an ulterior motive behind Rolf's pursuit of her. If Rolf had, however, thought that Nancy would immediately invest in his ailing automotive parts business simply to support him, he was mistaken.

Despite early misgivings Nancy quickly recognised the true potential of Rolf's business and she understood that with skilled management it could be returned to profitability. Nancy's eventual investment was made with imposing conditions and was not at all what Rolf had initially hoped it might mean. She became the non-executive chairman and immediately recruited a chief executive whose loyalty was solely to her. Rolf was generously allowed to retain a seat on the board although this was without any authority to influence or interfere.

Once he overcame feelings of hurt pride Rolf then found additional time for philandering. Had he hoped to wound Nancy by this behaviour he had certainly not reckoned with her very strong Chinese upbringing.

Despite a strange and somewhat strained marriage Nancy eventually became pregnant and Helmut's arrival allowed her to love and give as she had never previously loved. From the outset Helmut was engulfed in an affection which was so strong that reciprocating those feelings was a natural path for the young boy to follow.

Initially Nancy believed that Chantille's birth was the result of a brief affair which she'd had with a married colleague. Despite these doubts she intended that she would also shower the same feelings of love and affection on her daughter that her son Helmut enjoyed. As the little girl developed it soon became clear that she possessed an entirely independent attitude and her mother's feelings were regularly rebuffed; these acts of coolness led Nancy into thinking that Rolf might after all be the girl's father. Certainly any act of affection that Chantille might display was generally reserved for Rolf.

Nancy's kidney failure was compounded by the fact that her blood group was extremely rare. When the medical team treating her, advised that finding a suitable donor would be difficult, Helmut immediately offered to forfeit one of his in the hope that his mother might resume a normal life. The risk of her son forfeiting a vital organ was one which Nancy was not prepared to take and his very generous offer was initially rejected. As the months passed and dialysis treatment became more essential Nancy realised that her constant need of care was becoming a burden to both her colleagues at work and also her son.

Neither Rolf nor Chantille appeared overly concerned although Helmut persisted with his offer to act as a donor. The medical team treating Nancy also continued to pressure her into accepting her son's offer.

Helmut's full recovery from the operation was some consolation for the total disappointment which both mother and son experienced when Nancy's body quickly rejected the transplanted organ.

"Things will work out, you will see, Mama. We will find another donor and in no time you will be living a normal life," Helmut had hastened to reassure.

Some time later it seemed all too obvious that it was Helmut who had persuaded Chantille to come forward with the offer of one of her kidneys. Nancy had decided from the outset that she would not allow her daughter to risk the same sacrifice that her brother had made. Nevertheless, she was pleasantly surprised by her daughter's approach; that is until Chantille explained the reason behind her rare act of generosity.

"I would expect you to pay, of course." Then sensing her mother's distress the girl had paused in an effort to understand the reason.

"Oh, come off it! There's no need for you to show surprise or to look shocked! You can afford the money and it's me who will really be taking the risk. Why wouldn't you expect to pay for regaining a normal life? Surely being rid of all this clutter on a daily basis must be worth something?" Chantille indicated the dialysis machine with its incumbent array of tubes. There was then a further pause while she attempted to gauge her mother's reaction.

"I should like the money in cash. American dollars, if that's okay? I thought one and a half million would be fair." Nancy had blown her nose and taken time to compose herself before replying,

"Thank you, Chantille. I am overwhelmed by your offer. The fact that Helmut's health has been compromised by what proved to be a fruitless exercise compels me to decline." Aware of her daughter's disappointment and growing anger Nancy then asked, "What on earth were you planning to do with one and a half million dollars?" Chantille knew that her mother rarely changed her mind once she had reached an important decision and the reply she offered demonstrated some of her somewhat childish petulance.

"I'm surprised you bother to ask, since you have only ever been interested in your own high-flying lifestyle. What I do with any money that I generate is my business and should not interest you."

Surprisingly hope for a cure arrived from an entirely unexpected source. Nancy's contact with her twin sister had at best been irregular. When Sin-lee needed surgery to fit an artificial heart valve, Nancy had in fact visited her sister at the hospital in Bangkok and also on another occasion when bypass surgery was required. Other than that, the two women maintained the distance which had developed when they graduated from university. Sin-lee's telephone call therefore was both brief and unexpected.

"Nancy, I can arrange for you to have another kidney transplant. A donor will soon be available and you needn't concern yourself over the blood group. It is, I am assured, the same as ours."

Nancy's immediate reaction was one of both gratitude and surprise, since she believed her sister to be simply possessed with self-interest. When she marvelled at the rarity of finding a donor, Sin-lee's true motive was revealed. It transpired that she had been told by a coronary specialist that if she wished to extend her own life, a heart transplant was the only option left open to her. Following the specialist's pronouncement and after many months of searching, Sin-lee had located a clinic in China where both the donor and treatment was available.

"It's going to cost a great deal of money, although I've thought about it and naturally don't want to die. Neither, I imagine, do you." In her usual brusque manner, Sin-lee then mentioned a figure which made Chantille's proposal appear generous. She also informed her sister that the surgeon would only perform the operation at his clinic in Guangzhou.

"Who is this man and what is the name of his clinic?" Nancy asked.

"The surgeon's name is Dr Chang Jin-Ming and his clinic is the Fan Chee Medical Institute. It's all right; I have had both him and his clinic checked out by an independent source. I understand that the institute only offers a service to very rich people who are able to afford the fees and who have rare blood groups or other abnormalities."

Nancy was less concerned about money than the necessity of having to visit a country from where her grandparents had fled nearly a century before.

"Could this Dr Chang be persuaded to perform the operation somewhere else? That hospital which treated you in Bangkok offered a highly professional service and most of the medical staff were trained in the West. Surely he would be able to find the necessary backup in a place like that?"

"No. He flatly refuses to operate anywhere other than in his own clinic." Sin Lee paused then before suggesting,

"I am also afraid of having to visit China and wish there was an alternative."

"If we do decide to go ahead, how can this surgeon be so sure that donor organs will be available? It seems strange that he can provide such a service when Western institutions have failed."

"I have made my mind up and if is not a factor so far as I am concerned. I thought you would also be interested, although if you are happy with the situation of having to be plumbed into that dialysis machine for whatever time you have left, so be it."

Sin-lee's brutally matter of fact summary of the situation was typical and with barely a pause she continued,

"As for the availability of organs, Dr Chang guarantees that he can supply them. You have to remember that China is a very large country with a vast population. His secretary tells me that there is a man who shares our blood group and who is not expected to live. Obviously that situation will not wait while we are dithering. There is also a risk factor for both of us, although yours is the simpler of the two operations. Please think about it and then call me back as quickly as possible. Arrangements will take time and I want to start things moving."

Nancy had quickly decided to go ahead. Helmut was the only person she consulted and her son had not needed convincing.

The air ambulance put down at Don Muang airport in Thailand long enough for the nursing staff to be changed. The aircraft was also refuelled and Sin-lee was helped aboard.

If her twin was nervous she didn't show it and Nancy was not about to be upstaged by her elder sibling. They chatted amiably throughout the remainder of the flight and Nancy realised that the apparent normality of the situation was helping to restore her courage.

Both twins expressed surprise at the size and facilities which the airport had to offer and realised that they had been put down on a private landing strip. If either of them found this disconcerting, they were quickly reassured by the clinic staff and general air of efficiency in the ultra-modern but surprisingly small hospital.

Dr Chang visited them that evening and Nancy immediately experienced conflicting feelings with regard to the man. His face was cruel and from her long involvement with people she thought him capable of being totally ruthless. Yet when he spoke in cultured English he demonstrated the usual concerned and solicitous tone of a skilled surgeon. His words were reassuring and he talked to each of them in turn, explaining the complexities of both operations. Dr Chang described the preparations they would be expected to endure prior to surgery, the aftercare they would receive and explained that the danger areas were infection and rejection. When both women appeared satisfied that they understood everything, he gave them the gratifying news that donor organs were immediately available.

"Your arrival has been perfectly timed and with your permission I shall operate on Madam Sin-lee early tomorrow morning?"

While he was addressing himself solely to Sin-lee, Nancy thought the surgeon's suit was Saville Row; the cut was perfect and clung to the man's muscular frame with not a crease showing. In addition to his clothes, she also detected the aroma of a cologne which might only be acquired from an expensive perfumery. The surgeon also wore gold rimmed pince-nez perched on the end of his nose. This in itself was not a cause for mistrust although over the years Nancy had developed a dislike for things which were designed to draw attention.

Dr Chang turned to Nancy next and explained that her kidney would be replaced the day after her sister's operation and asked if she had any further questions.

"I do, doctor. May we be given the donor's name and some details of his family? I feel sure my sister will agree that we should offer some recompense for the valuable gift of his organs." Sin-lee's expression in fact suggested that she had considered no such thing.

"Alas, I am afraid not. We have strict rules with regard to donor anonymity and you need not concern yourself with thoughts of further compensation. That has already been taken care of. We have a reputation to maintain and we are entirely dependent on the goodwill that we enjoy as benefactors."

It was all too obvious that Dr Chang Jin-Ming had found Nancy's request irritating as, without further ado, he bowed curtly and left the room. As the door was closing Nancy saw a break in the seam of his well-cut trousers and a speck of pink was peeping through.

"Perhaps he's human after all," she thought, with some amusement. To Sin-Lee, she suggested,

"I'm glad transplant surgeons don't have to win popularity contests. He really gives me the creeps. Are you sure you can trust this investigator that you hired to check him out?"

"Yes of course! I have already told you that he met with three people who were given a new lease of life by Dr Chang. Now, if you don't mind, I think I would like to sleep. I have suddenly become very tired. Perhaps there was something in those injections which has made me feel drowsy. I will speak to you again in the morning before they take me down to the theatre."

Considering the situation they were in, it was surprising that Nancy also slept soundly that night.

# Chapter Fourteen

"There's something that I would seriously like to talk about," Ruby announced, as she and Kate were having early evening drinks on the terrace of their rented apartment.

"I hope it isn't work, it's nice and relaxing out here. I've had a full day and I imagine yours has not been any easier?"

"No, quite the contrary. In fact what I was about to say is that you shouldn't allow work to interfere with your social life. You're young and I think you should go out and meet people of your own age. Perhaps a man, or is there already someone special in your life?" Kate's shrug and raised eyebrows suggested that this was a topic which had been raised by others many times before and one which she would rather avoid.

"Sorry to disappoint, but there's not." The wry smile on Ruby's face told Kate that she would not be allowed to fob this off and with a sigh of resignation she responded.

"I had an affair with a science professor at university during my first year. I suppose I thought I was in love although when he insisted on keeping me hidden from his friends I realised his instinct for self-preservation was stronger than his feelings for me. It was wrong of me to become involved with someone who was already married and my only excuse is that it began at a party where drinks were flowing and my power of reasoning was poor. When the professor eventually thought there was a strong possibility of his wife finding out, he showed a cowardly streak which I had never seen before. I had a couple of brief affairs after that, neither of which gave me any feelings of security. Since then I have given men a wide berth. My problem seems to be that I'm mostly attracted to older men." Kate paused and Ruby thought something more interesting was about to follow.

"There was a man that I met recently. It was in fact on the recent flight to London via Hong Kong when your lawyers required me to return to swear that affidavit." Ruby's rueful expression reflected the irritation that this had caused for both of them.

"I judged the man on the plane to be in his early forties, although through an unbelievable coincidence I learned that he was several years older. I will describe him first and then explain the coincidence. He is attractive in a rugged sort of way, not very big although I would guess he's strong both mentally and physically." Kate fished around in her folder and then produced Charlie's business card.

"Here, this is him," she handed the card across to her aunt. "Before I explain the coincidence, I have to admit that I found him rather attractive and finished up telling him things about our business which I would never normally divulge."

"Charlie Greenwood! I've heard of his company. He's a director of engineering, so there must be something going for him."

"Perhaps, although remarkably it transpired during our flight that he had known Mum." This unexpected revelation brought a revised and serious expression of interest to Ruby's face.

"Yes, apparently it was while Mum was studying in England and he was a student at Birmingham University. It seems Mum had gone to Birmingham with a group from the Cranfield aeronautical college to listen to some lectures."

"Gosh! That is a coincidence. It must be a million to one chance getting onto a plane and meeting someone who claims to have known your mother some thirty years before. Do you think he's genuine?"

"Oh yes, there was no doubting that. He even trotted out Dad's name and said Mum had used her relationship with Rory to keep him at arm's length. Despite that I rather think she created quite an impression on him. In fact I would go so far as to suggest that he was fairly smitten by her and it rapidly put paid to any romantic thoughts that I was harbouring. In fact, it was quite a slap in the face."

Ruby offered some words of comfort and suggested that Kate shouldn't waste time on older men; she also said it was unlikely that her niece would run into Charlie Greenwood again.

"I wouldn't be so sure. The other uncanny thing is that he is about to start a contract in Colombo. I persuaded him that Mum would be pleased to catch up with someone from her past and I think he will eventually be making his way down to Koggala." Kate paused before continuing.

"While we were discussing his brief involvement with Mum, I sort of promised not to tell her that Charlie and I had met. At the time I was carried away with romantic notions and thought she deserved a nice surprise. Do you think I should tell her, or should I honour that half promise?"

"I wouldn't worry, Kate, Lorna has been around for long enough and I'm sure she will cope. If and when this man Charlie turns up, she will either make him welcome or politely find a way of getting rid of him."

"I hope it isn't the latter. He is such a nice man," Kate added thoughtfully.

Some weeks later all thoughts of Charlie Greenwood were forgotten. The new ferry service from Ho Chi Min City to Hanoi was now running and every third day one of their hydrofoils headed north while a second made the return journey south. That the service was operating smoothly was in no small part due to the efficient systems that Captain Wang had introduced.

The smooth trouble-free sailings had also been assisted by the arrival of Gongy from his hitherto base in Sri Lanka. Savage Air's retired chief engineer had initially caused some disruption among the maintenance staff when he introduced new and strict maintenance schedules. Thorough monthly inspections were implemented and arrangements made for the company craft to undergo dry dock surveys on a bi-annual basis.

Initially Kate had found Gongy's presence reassuring, although as time passed his insistence for perfection created problems which, if left to her own devices, she might have let slide. Within weeks of his arrival Gongy decided to take one of their more experienced marine engineers from the workshops at Vung Tau and relocate him to the new facility at Hai Phong. Kate had been in Vietnam for enough time to know that despite the war finishing some years before, people from the north still found integration with people from the south difficult. Kate's quick intervention, despite strong protests from Gongy, prevented the loss of a valuable employee and also avoided an embarrassing situation.

The latest problem that Gongy had unearthed was the fact that they were using more fuel oil from the Hai Phong source than at Vung Tau. Kate suggested prevailing winds or tides might be a contributing factor although the old engineer was unconvinced by this explanation. Gongy was certain that with two Dolphins running in each direction week in and week out that the consumption of fuel oil from both bunkering facilities should be comparable. With usual persistence the elderly engineer had pointed to his graphs and shown Kate that the surge had in fact so far only happened on two occasions.

"I realise you will think me a bloody nuisance, girl, but if there's one thing I can't stand it's thieving, and I'm convinced that's what it is." Encouraged by her failure to respond, Gongy had continued,

"There was a time when your grandfather was operating from a small base at Mangalore and something similar happened. I eventually discovered that the transport fitter was shoving cans of gasoline under the security fence for his brother-in-law to collect."

"Well, I would guess from the quantities involved it's not being pilfered in jerry cans!" Undeterred by this sarcasm, Gongy was obviously hell-bent on following his theory through.

"I think the fuel was transferred to another vessel, possibly a trawler, or maybe a privately owned coaster. It needs sorting, Kate. Perhaps I should plant someone reliable up there to see if the mystery can be unravelled."

With memories of the Vung Tau-based engineer incident still fresh in her mind, the last thing Kate wanted was for Gongy to blunder in and cause further disruption.

"Okay, you've convinced me that we have a problem and it is something that I will deal with."

By assuring Gongy that she realised the seriousness of the situation, Kate had then managed to wrest some respite from her grandfather's elderly engineer. Had either of them known the eventual outcome of her investigation, they may have decided to leave well alone.

# Chapter Fifteen

Weak sunlight was attempting to penetrate through early morning cloud as Charlie parked his car in its usual slot. He had arrived home from Hong Kong late the previous evening and was not finding the change in temperature to his liking. As he was buttoning his coat and pulling up the collar, a voice startled him.

"What ho, Charlie! I'd say from the way you are trying to disappear into that coat, you're finding it a bit chilly this morning. It's all right for you bloody globe-trotters. There's some of us that have to stay back here and suffer the cold to keep things ticking over."

Turning, Charlie saw the bearded face of the chief executive grinning over at him.

"I'm glad I ran into you. If you have a minute, I'd like you to come up."

The smell of freshly-brewed coffee greeted them as Charlie and the CEO passed through his PA's outer office.

"Morning, Mrs Finch. Bit cold this morning. How were the roads when you came in? Bloody council hadn't put a bit of salt down and I all but lost the car coming out of the Great Staughton turn. Coffee's smelling good. Reckon Mr Greenwood would appreciate a cup when you're ready."

The door closed as Jean Finch left the inner sanctum and Charlie's boss motioned him to take a chair.

"I'm flying out to Jamaica this afternoon. Our Caribbean set-up is in a mess and I will need to kick some arse when I get there. Like as not Con Cassidy will be on the next plane home, although that's in strict confidence, mind."

Charlie knew that Con Cassidy was the regional operations director for the whole of the Caribbean.

"Alistair McKown was pleased with your efforts in Hong Kong. He wrote me a long report which in a nutshell implies that you had the client's chief engineer eating out of your hand. Says you suggested ideas which had previously been rejected and the bugger finished up believing they had been his from the start." The big Geordie grinned.

"Ay, a lot of folk make the mistake of believing that you East Anglians are half-baked, although that will always be to their disadvantage. Thanks, Charlie." Jean Finch's gentle tap on the door interrupted this discourse.

"There is a call on line from Macclesfield. Jake Vander-Oust said not to interrupt your meeting although he thought you would like to know that they have discovered how fuel oil is seeping into the tunnel. I asked him to hold as I thought you might like more detail."

"Ay, I would. Put him on, would you?" As Mrs Finch left the room her boss motioned for Charlie to remain seated.

"Another bloody job that's gone tits up," he mouthed across as the telephone rang. Charlie spent the next few minutes trying to take in an item which appeared in a recent edition of The New Civil Engineer. It was not easy to concentrate and despite not wanting to eavesdrop, he was aware of the CEO's changing mood for the better.

When he finally replaced the telephone the chief executive's attention returned to Charlie, although it seemed obvious that his thoughts were elsewhere.

"Now then, where were we, Charlie?"

"Talking about our contract in Hong Kong." Charlie thought this more tactful than reminding the man that he had been discussing the possible dismissal of a fellow director.

"Ay, that's right, so we were. By God, Charlie. That old adage of one's misfortune being another's good fortune seems very apt this morning. You will have heard that we are having difficulties at Macclesfield and that's putting it mildly. Bloody method we've been applying was wrong from the start. Anyway, we had further problems a few days ago when fuel oil began seeping into the tunnel. That was Jake Vander-Oust telling me that they've discovered the source. There are some old storage tanks situated above ground on the line of the tunnel run and they are leaking like sieves. The health and safety people have been called in and declared the site unsafe. Now my guess is that this latest problem will give us some respite and we can come at the work from a different angle. That is, of course, while everyone else is figuring out how to deal with the leeching fuel oil." There was a gleam in his eye as he continued,

"Shouldn't be surprised if this doesn't result in a nice little claims situation." Charlie knew that the chief executive had built his reputation on a thorough understanding of contract law and had made use of it while still at contracts management level.

"Sri Lanka; I don't want there to be any balls-ups on that job, Charlie. That's why I have asked you personally to take it on. It starts in eight weeks so I would suggest you organise someone to take over the running of your division as quickly as possible."

"That's not a problem. Gerry has always looked after things when I've been away. He's a bright young man and the other engineers all respect his ability."

"Great. Then if that's all sorted I would advise you take the holiday that Bill Arthurs suggested. There are not going to be too many opportunities for you to have time off once the job is up and running and the contract period is thirty months."

As he drove home that evening Charlie began to feel that the Sri Lanka contract was at last a reality and that there would be some respite from his tedious spell at head office. He had been in the business long enough, however, to realise that things could still go wrong. There had been too many false starts in the past for him to be lulled into complacency, although from what he had thus far discovered it seemed preparations were well under way. Materials and new equipment had been sourced and shipping arrangements completed.

Charlie felt warmth from the central heating as he opened the front door of his house and was glad he had remembered to set the thermostat timer that morning before leaving for work.

Feeling a need to tell someone of his changing fortune he next decided to call his cousin. Yvonne had also been raised with him by his grandmother Lizzie and was one of the few remaining family members with whom he was close.

"Charlie! How good to hear from you. In fact I was just about to call to see if you can help."

"Why? What's the problem?"

"It's not me, it's a friend. She is taking up a post at the hospital in Bedford and it's all happened rather quickly. She needs to rent an apartment or small house for a while so as to give her time to look round for something to buy. I wondered if you or any of your drinking pals might know of anything suitable."

"What's this friend of yours like?" Charlie asked. "Is she trustworthy?"

"Trustworthy! I should hope so! She's a senior registrar at Guy's and one of my best friends. Will that do for a reference, or would you like a copy of her bloodline?" Charlie laughed and an idea which had begun to germinate led to his suggesting that his own house might be suitable. It was uncharacteristic of him to act impulsively although he quickly decided that any friend of Yvonne's would surely make a good tenant.

"This place might not suit, although it would certainly be convenient for me. I was calling to tell you that I am going back overseas to work for a while. If your friend is interested, I can negotiate a better than fair rent with her."

"Charlie, what a brilliant idea! I'll phone Eve straight away to see what she thinks, although I'm sure I know what the answer will be. Give me a few minutes and I will ring you straight back. I want to know all about this trip of yours anyway."

Within minutes Yvonne called back to say Eve was delighted to learn that there were some positive prospects and that she would be in touch to arrange a viewing and to discuss terms.

"So Charlie, now that's sorted, tell me all. Where are you off to next?"

"To a new harbour project in Sri Lanka. It's just the usual stuff, although I have some free time before the job actually starts. The schedule is so darned tight it's been suggested that I take some leave from Friday week to compensate for not having time off while I'm out there."

"Quite right too! It will do you good to go off and enjoy yourself. What will you do?"

"Well, I have had an idea on that score. Do you remember Lizzie's stories about Ali Baba? He was the porter she employed in Bombay when Grandpa was posted to India with his regiment. Ali was the man whose real name she could never at first remember or pronounce. Anyway Lizzie and this Sikh bearer developed a close relationship over the years and he left her a legacy which she eventually bequeathed to me. She had no idea what it was although she made me promise that I would one day go out to collect. I think her motive was for me to make a pilgrimage to some of the places that she had loved and always remembered. There is never going to be a better opportunity than this, so I'm off to India first and then on to the job in Sri Lanka."

"You lucky so and so! I wish I could come with you. I imagine the places she described will have changed a lot, although it should still be quite an experience!"

Yvonne next asked Charlie questions about his contract and was unable to disguise the fact that she was worried for his safety. He reassured her that the port area of Colombo was considered reasonably secure and free from the terrorist activities which she had read of in newspapers.

"Well, if that's true I may come out for a holiday. I presume you will be able to tear yourself away for a few days and then perhaps we can explore some of the safer parts of island?"

Eve, an unattached lady from a Caribbean background, proved to be as honest-looking as Yvonne had described and Charlie had no qualms about leaving his house in her hands. The morning after she had settled in, Eve drove him to the station and that afternoon he was looking down over the snow-crested peaks of the Alps. As the huge airliner passed above this majestic spectacle Charlie wondered if he would get close enough to the Himalayas to witness some of the things that his grandmother had described.

The Foreign Office had been off-putting when Charlie applied for visas, especially advising British travellers not to visit the region around Srinagar. The reason for this was that in recent years Western hostages had been taken by Kashmir separatists to extract ransom monies. There had been little or no time to consider the full implication of this as Charlie had miraculously arranged airline tickets and now felt more relaxed than he had for some time. Charlie's reason for travelling to the Northern frontier was to fulfil the promise he had made to his grandmother and official warnings were not going to rob him of this ideal opportunity. Apart from Yvonne, Charlie had no immediate family and reasoned that there was little to hold him back.

Stepping from the aircraft into a link span Charlie was uncomfortably aware of the scorching heat which bore down on the artificial tunnel. Inside the airport terminal the air-conditioning plant had cooled the temperature to a comfortable level, which was fortunate as his passage through immigration was at best tedious. Temperature outside the airport terminal was still stiflingly hot when he eventually joined a long queue of people waiting for taxis. As the queue gradually thinned there was just one family group and a solitary turbaned Sikh waiting in front of him. Two cabs arrived at the same time. The Sikh turned and then asked in perfect English,

"Would you care to share, sir? My destination is the city. This car has air-conditioning and it may save a tiresome wait in the appalling heat."

Gratefully, Charlie accepted the offer and followed the man into the rear of an Ambassador taxi which reminded him of the Morris Oxford that he had once owned.

"Please allow me to introduce myself. My name is Sarwan Kumar. I am returning from a visit to the UK and travelling back to my home in the Punjab." Charlie then found himself telling the amiable man that he was partially fulfilling a duty and described the promise to his grandmother and her involvement with India.

"My dear chap, how very interesting! What, may I now ask, is your immediate destination?"

"I would like to find a comfortable hotel and then spend at least two days in Bombay."

"Then I am pleased our paths have crossed. Bombay, or to be correct Mumbai, is one of the more expensive places to stay in India. Our beautiful city is frequented by visitors from the oil-rich states of the Middle East and hotel rooms are at a premium. These taxi driver fellows are all looking for baksheesh and they will take you to any establishment where the doorman pays an attractive commission."

The Sikh glanced through the dividing screen, presumably to discern whether or not their driver understood English.

"Before retirement I was commissioner of police for the Colaba district and I still maintain contact with the Garden Hotel. A very good friend of mine has also managed the Ascot for a number of years and I am sure a room can be found for you at one of those establishments."

"Thank you; I really do appreciate your suggestions. Would it be possible for me to be dropped at the Ascot, do you think?"

"Certainly. As a matter of fact I am staying there myself, just for the one night, you understand. I will introduce you to my friend and he will ensure that you are made comfortable."

The hotel was moderate in size and Charlie formed the opinion that it was well-managed. His new acquaintance Sarwan Kumar was greeted by both the doorman and reception clerks with a familiarity which suggested that he was well known to them and within minutes of their arrival the manager appeared and was introduced. A quick exchange between this man and a smiling young woman behind the reservations desk followed and this immediately secured Charlie a pleasant room overlooking a well-tended city park. When he discovered from reading the hotel tariff that he had been given a fifteen per cent discount, he realised his Sikh travelling companion was responsible and was pleased that he had accepted an invitation to meet for drinks before dinner.

Exhausted from the journey, Charlie showered quickly and then lay on the bed. The quiet swishing sound from an overhead fan was soothing and the room was in darkness when he next came to. Switching on the bedside lamp he was relieved to see that it was only a few minutes after six and that there was still time to shave and get scrubbed up before going down to keep his drinks appointment.

Charlie insisted that the first round was his and was slightly amused when his companion requested a large Johnny Walker Black Label.

"May I ask; is the room to your liking? Recommendations to friends are not always wise." Charlie assured his new-found companion that the room was perfect and thanked him for the discount which had been secured.

"I do hope you will forgive my curiosity and perhaps excuse it as being part of my police training. In the taxi there was no hesitancy on your part with the choice of hotel?" Charlie smiled before replying.

"I don't mind you asking at all. There was nothing unusual in my decision other than that Ascot is the location for a famous horse racing venue in England."

"Ah, the sport of kings, or so I'm told. Do you enjoy the races?" Charlie replied that he did, although modesty prevented him from explaining that Ascot was where he had enjoyed winning on three occasions. They talked on amiably for a while until on impulse Charlie asked if his companion would join him for dinner. The man accepted and suggested there was an excellent restaurant he knew of where the curried goat was considered the best in Bombay.

Over their meal, Sarwan asked what plans Charlie had for the rest of his stay in India. When he explained that his final destination was Srinagar, the elderly Sikh showed concern and asked if his journey there was really necessary. Charlie then told him that his grandmother had enjoyed a very close relationship with a Sikh man and explained that there was a legacy left her which she in turn had passed to him.

"How strange! This Sikh man, did he have no family who might inherit his estate?"

"No, from reading my grandmother's diaries I have been able to establish that her friend was something of an outcast. At some time in his past he had fallen foul of the law and after serving his punishment, he relinquished both his faith and all family connections."

"Then you should go. If you do not take this risk, you will have failed to meet an obligation. Tonight I will write a letter of introduction to the police commissioner in Srinagar. He is the son of my father's youngest brother and a very good friend to both me and my family. I shall ask him to provide some security for you while you are there and I am unable to emphasize strongly enough that you really should look him up and deliver my letter." Charlie assured him that he would and they arranged to meet the following morning before the elderly Sikh continued his journey home.

"Here is the letter of introduction that I promised to write and you will also find my address inside this other envelope. If you have time to visit me in Amritsar before leaving India, you will be most welcome. Now my friend, if I am to catch the Rawalpindi Express, which stops at Amritsar, I should leave now." Sarwan held out his hand, Charlie took it and then embraced the man strongly with his free arm.

# Chapter Sixteen

The port area of Mumbai had almost certainly changed out of all recognition from a time when Charlie's Grandmother Lizzie spent two days camped there in a disused salt warehouse. Charlie tried to imagine the scene of that bygone era in which confused soldiers and their families had disembarked from a steamship anchored out in the roads.

With the aid of an English-speaking tuk-tuk driver, he also attempted to retrace the battalion's route out through the city and away from the port. There were several large pieces of waste ground on which the regiment might have camped on that first night of their march to Pune and from where his grandmother had first engaged Ali Baba.

Spending a further day wandering around Mumbai, Charlie then tired of the city, checked out from the Ascot and managed to secure a seat on an overcrowded bus bound for Pune.

Overwhelmed by the noise of passengers and the sultry heat inside the vehicle, Charlie thought of the toughness of the soldiers' wives who had trekked through India with his grandmother a hundred years or so before and also of how Ali Baba had wheeled a handcart along behind them.

The plains scenery they passed through was scorched and oppressive and when the bus overtook a camel train, Charlie thought the scene was probably unchanged from when Lizzie had travelled this same route.

Both his head and back ached from sitting too long in a cramped position and he was relieved when the bus driver called out something which he hoped was "Pune terminus".

Alighting at the northern bus station, Charlie was immediately accosted by a number of tuk-tuk drivers. He selected one with a pleasant grin and asked to be taken to a hotel. After rejecting the first dilapidated building which they stopped at, he rattled some coins in the palm of his hand and insisted that he be taken to a good one. This seemed to do the trick and in no time his bag was being carried into Hotel Amir. The next day he was taken by an elderly porter and shown where the British garrison had once been. A few buildings occupied by an Indian cavalry regiment were all that now remained. There was little or no sign of the powerful presence which had once occupied the same site and Charlie found no one who remembered the Suffolk Regiment ever being garrisoned there.

There was a feeling of anticlimax as Charlie boarded the train to Bombay en route for Ajmer and Delhi. From Delhi Charlie took another train to Gujrat where he disembarked and spent one final night in a hotel before catching an express bus to Srinagar. As his journey had progressed by train and bus he began to gain some understanding of why his grandmother had wished him to visit this vast country. He enjoyed the diversity of passengers and the countryside through which they travelled. At every fresh stop vendors boarded the trains, selling goods ranging from cigarettes and cheap jewellery to cooked foods with appetising aromas. When Charlie was not walking the trains or visiting the dining cars, he spent time watching the world outside slide past from the seclusion of his shared sleeping compartments. There were scrubby plains, temples and palaces in various stages of disrepair. When they entered the Punjab, Charlie was surprised by the variety and lushness of the crops which abounded in well cultivated fields. The final part of his journey from Gujrat by bus took him through mountainous foothills with distant snow-capped peaks clearly visible.

Relieved to be stretching his legs after many days of travel, Charlie felt some confusion when catching sight of water. At first he thought he was mistaken until remembering that his grandparents had spent time on a houseboat in Srinagar during one of their infrequent leave breaks.

"How stupid of me to forget the lakes, but they're huge. I really thought I was looking at the sea," Charlie mumbled to himself as he stared out over a wide expanse of water. Then all too quickly he became the focal point for touts as he walked to where he hoped the centre of town might be. Most of these very different-looking high country men were offering cheap rates for houseboat accommodation, or so they claimed. Shouldering his way through the revolving doors of the Grand Hotel in an attempt to rid himself of the touts, Charlie found a clean friendly atmosphere and decided it would be as good a place as any to stay.

Despite some travel weariness he decided against taking a siesta and opted to explore Srinagar instead. Charlie had not consciously attempted to locate the central police station although when he looked at its impressive front entrance, he decided to go in and attempt delivering Sarwan Kumar's letter. On asking the duty desk sergeant if he might make an appointment to see the commissioner, the policeman reacted in a manner in which he might not have shown more astonishment had Charlie asked to see the very Lord Krishna!

"The commissioner is an extremely busy man, sir," he spluttered. "He normally does not grant interviews. Are you by any chance a journalist?"

"No, I am not a journalist. In fact what I have is a letter to deliver. Will that be possible?"

"You can leave the letter with me. I will make sure that it is delivered."

"I would rather not. The correspondence is something which I pledged to deliver in person."

"May I know from whom this correspondence comes?" Charlie was rapidly tiring of this irritating exchange and the sergeant's dated use of English.

"Yes, I can tell you that. The writer's name is Mr Sarwan Kumar and he lives in Amritsar." Charlie saw an immediate change to the man's attitude, although he was unsure if it was mention of his former acquaintance's name, or Amritsar which had caused this.

"I will send someone to tell the commissioner that you are waiting to see him, sir."

Charlie thought the high-ranking officer sitting behind a desk was a younger and less friendly carbon copy of his cousin. There was no attempt at formal greeting and Charlie immediately felt that his presence was an unwelcome intrusion.

"I am told that you have a letter which you insist on delivering in person? May I see the letter please?" The man's features then relaxed a little as he read from the handwritten paper.

"So, you are a friend of Sarwan Kumar?"

"Yes, we get on very well." Initially Charlie had not intended soliciting help from this man, although now that he had, he thought there was no harm in exaggerating his relationship with the policeman's cousin. He also thought it likely that he was not the first person to have been steered along a similar path.

"I presume you will be staying on one of the houseboats?" Charlie explained this was not so and told the commissioner that he was staying at the Grand Hotel.

"That is a pity. It is much easier to keep an eye on the houseboats. You realise, Mr Greenwood, that in these times Kashmir is a dangerous place for Western travellers?" Charlie said he was aware of the risk and explained that he had important business with the law firm of Alexander Haggart.

The senior policeman's tone softened at mention of the law practice and he next described it as being highly respectable.

Charlie's meeting with the commissioner had lasted barely fifteen minutes and as he re-emerged from the police station he believed it to have been a waste of time. His meeting the following morning with James Galbraith, a senior partner at the law firm Alexander Haggart, was an entirely different matter. When Charlie introduced himself and produced his birth certificate, passport and copies of papers from Alexander Haggart to his grandmother's solicitors, he was received with great courtesy.

"Western visitors have not been coming to Srinagar for many years, although we thought it likely that we would one day receive some communication regarding your instructions, Mr Greenwood. Instead, we are now delighted to receive you in person."

It was obvious that there was mixed blood in James Galbraith's lineage although what Charlie found intriguing and surprising was the man's strong Scottish accent.

"Unfortunately my father retired some years ago. It was he who was originally commissioned to manage the estate of the late Sikh man known as Ali Baba. Following Ali Baba's death my father attempted to trace the man's real identity. Although the will had been legally drawn up and attested, father felt that some blood relative might one day come forward to contest it. That has never happened and so over the years we concluded that our client had made a thoroughly good job of burying his past. His instructions to my father were that the residue of his estate should be managed in such a way as to achieve safe but steady growth and until such time as Mrs Lizzie Greenwood or her nominated beneficiary should decide to take that responsibility from us."

The lawyer hesitated then before suggesting.

"I sincerely hope that when you have had an opportunity to peruse and evaluate the estate accounts, you will be satisfied that they have been managed in an efficient manner."

As he was considering James Galbraith's words, Charlie's thoughts centred on the legal charges and management fees which would have accrued over some forty years.

Having always struggled when it came to analysing balance sheets, Charlie knew enough, however, to be shocked by the figures shown on the last half-yearly statement. Doubting the evidence of his own eyes, he swallowed hard and then scanned the columns of figures for previous year endings.

Charlie next began to wonder if some enormous practical joke was being played out at his expense. Eventually he managed to croak,

"These figures are shown in Indian rupees, Mr Galbraith?" The lawyer appeared to misinterpret the question. Looking a little abashed, he replied,

"They are incomplete in respect of investments which have been made with banks in the Channel Islands and the Isle of Man. We chose those

135

places as we felt that one day the estate beneficiaries would require easy access to funds. I presume, Mr Greenwood, you are aware that to take currency from our country is no easy matter and that was why those decisions were made."

Charlie, though still unable to grasp the implication of what he thought he was looking at, decided that a request for water might allow him some respite.

"Mr Galbraith, mental arithmetic has never been a strong point of mine. Would you be so kind as to convert that figure into pounds sterling, please?" The lawyer then looked at what appeared to be a recently received telex message before reaching for a calculator.

"Based on today's exchange rate of 18.5331 rupees to the pound, I calculate the value of the estate to be two million, two hundred thousand and thirty-three pounds, although as I mentioned a moment ago, this takes no account of offshore investments."

Charlie swallowed hard once more and then pinched his thigh to make sure he was not dreaming. He had been prudent throughout his life and with some personal investments and a small ownership of company stock, he considered himself to be comfortably well off. Never, however, in his wildest imagination had he any reason to believe that a windfall such as this would fall into his lap.

"I suppose you wouldn't have something stronger?" Charlie motioned to the empty water glass. With a smile of understanding the lawyer produced a bottle of Chivas Regal from a desk drawer.

Anxiety for some calming effect caused the malt whiskey to almost choke him and Charlie, with tears in his eyes, next asked,

"Have you any idea as to the value of those offshore investments, Mr. Galbraith?"

"Based on our last appraisal they will be comparable to that of your Indian holding."

Attempting to buy time to regain further composure, Charlie reached for the whiskey tumbler and turned pages of the accounts in front of him. When he felt able to speak normally again, he next asked,

"There are some supplementary accounts listed. Can you explain those, please?"

"Ah, yes, of course. That is the livery stable covenant. It is a sum of money which was set aside by Mr Ali Baba to be used as a subsidy to his former business. This will remain in place until such time as the stables cease to function and demolition of the buildings has been paid for from a separate fund. There are a number of other clauses and conditions applying and if you wish, I will attempt to explain them."

"Thank you, but not now. The fees for managing both the covenant and the estate, have they still to be taken?"

"Should you wish to terminate instructions with Alexander Haggart, we will need to calculate a final settlement fee. On the other hand if it is your wish that we continue to manage the fund, the fees are to be collected in the normal way on an annual rolling basis." Charlie deduced from this that the only outstanding fees were those for the current year.

"Ali Baba's livery stables are still operating, Mr Galbraith?" The lawyer nodded and when Charlie expressed a wish to see them, James Galbraith gave him directions. Before leaving the advocate's office they shook hands and Charlie had stepped out through the door before realising that he had not been entirely gracious in his manner of leaving.

"Mr Galbraith, please forgive my poor manners. There has been a great deal for me to absorb this morning and I have been remiss. Would you consider having dinner with me? I shall be around for the next few days and if there is an evening that suits, I would welcome your company." Charlie detected pleasure on the man's otherwise impassive features and realised his gesture had been correct.

A haze of conflicting thoughts next swirled around in Charlie's mind as he desperately tried to come to terms with the fact that he had just learned that he was now a relatively rich man. He realised, however, that in terms of true wealth his new-found fortune was at the lower end of the scale. It also occurred to him that Lizzie could not have known the extent of her old friend's wealth.

Yvonne, being the older, had inherited the family home, together with the bulk of any monies in Lizzie's bank account when the two cousins were sadly deprived of any future relationship with an old lady whom they had both loved dearly.

It had been typical of Yvonne's generosity that she attempted to persuade Charlie to accept half of her inheritance. With a reasonable salary and bachelor only expenses he in turn had persuaded Yvonne that her generosity was unnecessary. Now though, Charlie realised that circumstances had changed and he would need to find a way of sharing this windfall with his cousin.

Standing across the road from a large wooden barn-like building, Charlie's thoughts were still in turmoil. Less than an hour before he had learned that he had inherited a considerable fortune and he was now staring up at a sign which read Ali Baba's Livery Stables, the very place from which his new-found wealth was created.

With some hesitation, Charlie realised that he had skated through his grandmother's diaries and had not truly appreciated the unique relationship which had existed between her and the Sikh porter whom she had engaged during her first days in India.

"I always realised that Lizzie was a very special person, although she must have created quite an impression on the man who started this," Charlie thought.

One thing which Charlie did remember was that before leaving India, his grandmother had gifted her old retainer a sum of money for past loyalty and with which to offset his loss of employment.

"There doesn't appear to be anyone around. I think I'll chance taking a look," Charlie murmured as he strode in through the doors.

The inside was cool and carried an all too familiar smell of horses. Making his way into the cavernous building, Charlie's progress was arrested by a voice which initially startled him. When he peered into the gloom he saw the silhouette of a man seated on a filled corn sack with a bridle across his knees.

"Can I be of assistance, sir?" Charlie imagined the man to be around his own age and as he stood, there was evidence that he was someone who possessed the bandy gait of a true horseman.

"Yes please. I was wondering if I might rent a hack." The man cast an appraising eye over Charlie before responding.

"Is it your intention to ride in those clothes and shoes, sir?" It seemed a fair question; Charlie smiled and explained that he had not set out with the intention of going for a ride. Then, remembering that he was now wealthy, he asked if there was an outfitters close by which might kit him out with jodhpurs and Jodhpur boots.

"There is, although if you have no objection to wearing boots and clothes which have been worn before, we can hire them to you."

The short brown Jodhpur boots were highly polished and Charlie imagined them to have been little worn since their arrival from a boot maker. Thick cavalry twill jodhpurs were also spotlessly clean and carried a strong smell of mothballs.

Dressed now in familiar rider's garb, Charlie followed the man, who he believed to be the proprietor, down past rows of loose boxes. Some were empty and had obviously been so for some time, while others contained horses whose heads were mostly looking out over stable doors.

Each loose box door bore a plate on which was printed the name of its occupier. As they approached the very last box, one which commanded a view out through the open doors of the main building, Charlie saw a well-remembered name on the door plate. It was the name of a horse which his grandmother had owned in India. Tadger had been her father's nickname and the name Lizzie had used when buying her first horse.

Charlie remembered his great-grandfather as a lovable old scoundrel and was about to ask when the box had last been occupied, when a handsome head with intelligent eyes peered out.

"I would like to rent him for the afternoon." Charlie had been around horses for a great deal of his life and there was no doubt in his mind that he was looking at neither a mare nor a gelding.

"I'm sorry, sir. He is not available for hire. No one other than my son or me ever rides him. He is an important part of the establishment and carries the name of five former occupiers of that box. So long as our livery business continues to operate, it has been decreed that only a horse of special character shall carry the name and occupy that space." Charlie was not about to be fobbed off and when he described his grandmother's past relationship with the original owner, the man's attitude changed completely.

"Memsahib Greenwood is still spoken of by the older people of Srinagar. I obviously cannot remember her, although I do know that she is still very much revered by those few who do. Have you ridden a mettlesome horse before? Tadger can be quite lively and he has not been out today."

Charlie asked if there was a schooling paddock and on learning that there was, he suggested the owner tack Tadger up and judge for himself.

Ignoring the offer of being legged up, Charlie went first to the horse's head and then breathed into the animal's nostrils before talking softly to him.

"Okay, I don't know if he's ready but I am." Charlie vaulted up to a point where he could lie face down over Tadger's neck. It was obvious that the horse had never previously been mounted in this manner and to the alarm of the proprietor he shied violently sideways.

Tadger had listened to Charlie's softly spoken words and probably enjoyed the introduction; he was proud, however, and not prepared to allow a stranger onto his back until that person had been put to the test. Twice he reared, the second time almost to the point of vertical. When this failed to unseat his rider, the horse put in a series of bucks which would have done credit to a rodeo horse. Charlie had been through this performance many times before on horses equally as spirited. He chuckled quietly to himself and Tadger eventually sensed that he was not after all in complete control. Charlie next walked and then hack cantered quietly around the paddock.

"Has he been schooled over fences?" The proprietor nodded and after taking up another hole on the girth, Charlie turned and put Tadger at a set of coloured jump poles.

Tadger's timing was a split second slower than his rider's reflexes. Charlie had felt hesitancy and knew instinctively that the animal was going to make a fool of him by running out. He took a firm hold on the bit and dug his heels into Tadger's flank. Taken by surprise, the horse took off three strides before the kicking board and described a perfect arc over the obstacle.

"Okay, Mr Greenwood. I think you and Tadger are going to get along fine. How long would you like him for?" James Galbraith had earlier made an appointment for him to meet the branch manager at the Bank of Delhi and so Charlie suggested he would like to ride out to the edge of the foothills which he estimated was an hour's ride away.

As the noise of traffic was replaced by the song of larks and the scent of countless sundried herbs wafted on the pleasantly warm air, Charlie began to relax. He felt closer to Lizzie than he had for a very long time and imagined her riding over this very same ground on a horse quite like the one on which he was now mounted. On returning to the stables he asked the proprietor his name. The man grinned up at him.

"Everyone around here calls me Ali Baba. I have grown accustomed to it and it is certainly easier for Westerners. My grandfather worked for the original Ali Baba, and when the old man died my grandfather took over the business and people began calling him Ali. It was a joke at first, although it stuck and so my father also became known by the same name." Charlie was intrigued and wished he could stay longer.

"My grandmother wrote in her journal of a place in the hills which was occasionally populated by migrating Tibetan peoples. Do you know if the village still exists?" Ali Baba told him that he had never heard of such a place, although he seemed delighted when Charlie asked if they might go in search of it the following day.

"We shall need to take bedding rolls and provisions with us. I am sure my grandmother always spent at least two nights out when she travelled to the settlement. Can you provide the things we will need and a third mount which can be used as a pack horse?"

"I can do better than that. We have a few mules out grazing. I will fetch one of those up." Charlie then arranged for an early start before hurrying off to keep his appointment at the bank. Later, when having what he thought might be a quiet drink in one of the hotel bars, he was surprised to receive a visitor.

"Please forgive the intrusion. It seemed easier than leaving a message for you at reception." Charlie was delighted to learn that James Galbraith was able to accept his invitation and was even more pleased when the lawyer recommended an exceptionally good restaurant overlooking Dal

Lake. The two men then arranged to meet on the evening when Charlie hoped to return from his short expedition.

Throughout the next day Charlie felt a great peace within himself. He was mounted on an interesting and lively horse, trekking through foothills and majestic ravines and along paths where he felt sure his grandmother had once trod. They camped out that night and when the horses had been fed then hobbled and made comfortable, Charlie regaled Ali with some of the stories that he had read from his grandmother's diaries while the two men ate supper.

Everything was so perfect it seemed inevitable that there would be at least one disappointment. The two men searched valleys and the habitable mountain slopes without coming across signs of the settlement where Lizzie had befriended a Tibetan woman. When they came across two goatherds who had never heard of such a place, Charlie decided that they should start back.

On the return journey Ali Baba was drawn into talking about his life and Charlie was pleased to discover a contented man. Only one thing appeared to mar Ali's security and this was that business in Srinagar and the livery stable in particular had suffered from many years without tourists.

The following day was mostly spent attending to the paperwork which had been prepared by both bank and lawyers. Charlie welcomed this respite as he was feeling the effects of three hard days in the saddle.

When James Galbraith arrived at the hotel to collect him, Charlie was looking forward to a convivial evening. They rode the short distance to the restaurant in a beautifully preserved SS Jaguar saloon and James explained that it had been purchased in England by his father in the late nineteen-forties.

Surprisingly, their table discussion did not centre on Charlie's inheritance. Instead, the two men talked about the complicated issue of Indian politics, outside interests and in particular James's love of golf and hockey.

With the culmination of an enjoyable evening, Charlie elected to walk the short distance back to his hotel and the two men arranged a final meeting before his onward trip to Sri Lanka.

As the sound of the Jaguar's engine faded in the distance, Charlie looked out over the lake. A full moon illuminated the waters to such good effect that he could clearly see myriads of tiny fish gathering in shoals around the tethered houseboats, which gently rose and fell to short pitched waves.

With thoughts of a nightcap before turning in, Charlie decided to take what he thought might be the shortest route back to his hotel. This entailed walking through a narrow passageway which ran adjacent to what appeared to be a series of industrial buildings. He had travelled half the length of this poorly-lit walkway when he became aware of the sound of footsteps from behind. Glancing over his shoulder, Charlie saw that three men were rapidly overhauling him and he lengthened his stride. Feelings of alarm did not really occur until he next spotted the silhouettes of two further figures approaching from the other end of the passageway.

While attempting to stay calm Charlie tried a number of the warehouse doors and realised that panic would only worsen the situation. It seemed all too obvious that five men could easily overpower him; his one slight consolation came with the realisation that the narrow walkway would make it difficult for them to launch a concerted attack.

Backing into the recess of a single doorway, Charlie reached down and pressed back against the woodwork to give him additional leverage. In doing this his right hand made contact with a heavy chain hanging from the door lintel. In desperation he pulled hard and the rotting door frame yielded to pressure.

As a weapon the length of chain was cumbersome, although much better than anything he'd had a moment before. Running his free hand down its length, Charlie grunted with satisfaction on finding that the heavy fixing staple was still attached.

The width of the alleyway dictated that his now all too obvious assailants had to approach him in pairs, one from either side. If the men were expecting him to defend himself, they certainly had not anticipated his having a weapon and Charlie used the length of chain to good effect. It missed the man on his right by inches although was sufficiently close to halt him in his tracks. The figure on his left was less fortunate. There was a scream of pain as the end of the chain made contact and Charlie felt the shock of its impact ringing down his arm. Both attackers fell back until urged on by a voice from their rear.

"Go and get him you imbeciles. He is only one man. Are you all cowards?" Despite the desperation of this situation, Charlie was surprised that these words were spoken in poor, barely understandable English.

Using the length of chain continuously proved successful in keeping his attackers at bay, although the element of surprise had disappeared and the assailants were now much more cautious. One of the men leapt forward as the twirling chain passed him, although Charlie had anticipated this and managed a swinging full force kick to the man's knee. Despite this and the

142

grunt of agony which followed, the same voice of command was continuously urging the attackers on and demanding greater effort.

Assuming that he had immobilised and accounted for two of the five men, Charlie then made a fateful mistake as he decided to go on the offensive. His arms were tiring and he knew that unless he could drive his way out of the alleyway, it would only be a question of time before he was overwhelmed.

Swinging at the lone assailant coming from his right, Charlie managed to force the man to link up with the two on his left and the ferocity of his renewed attack began to tell.

The chain which had thus far been so effective then unfortunately became entangled with an overhead protrusion. Charlie should have abandoned it and ran; instead he attempted to free the chain and in that brief moment two of the remaining assailants leapt on him. Going down under a hail of kicks and blows he was trying to protect himself when he clearly heard a voice say,

"Secure and gag him. There will be plenty of time to take our revenge when we have him back at the safe house."

Charlie's hands were next roughly secured behind his back with plastic ties which cut into his flesh. When he attempted to kick, he also discovered that his ankles had been lashed together and he fought desperately against attempts to insert some cloth into his mouth. The end result of this was that he received a further sustained and violent clubbing.

Whenever faced with a crisis in the past, Charlie had always managed to think positively. Now as he was rolled into some coarse cloth and then bodily picked up, he felt both bruised and completely beaten.

From this situation of helplessness there seemed only one explanation and that was that he had been successfully overcome and was now about to be taken off to some remote place and held there until payment of a ransom might secure his release.

These despairing thoughts were then dramatically interrupted by fresh sounds and it seemed obvious that they were not being made by his erstwhile attackers, who were struggling with the awkwardness and weight of his body.

A series of shrill whistles and yelled commands could now clearly be heard. This was despite muffling from the shroud which his attackers had wrapped him in.

What followed next became a blur of unsighted confusion. First he was dropped or dumped and the jarring sensation from hard packed earth caused Charlie to bite his own tongue. Blinded by the cloth and with the cloying taste of blood in his mouth, he tried to envisage what was actually happening although it seemed fairly obvious that he was in the midst of some struggling melee.

He heard curses, screams and the sound of blows. Eventually, and after the frenzy of noise and confusion had slowly died away, Charlie was unceremoniously rolled from his cloth cocoon.

As he began to struggle in an attempt to break free, fresh hands restrained him and a vaguely familiar voice gave renewed hope to his previous thoughts of despair.

"Mr Greenwood. I had hoped that we would next meet in more convivial circumstances. Here, let me remove that filthy rag from your mouth and then we can set you free."

Charlie's blood circulation had been restricted, his arms and legs were not functioning as they should and his concern for maintaining balance momentarily outweighed an urge to respond. Eventually he gasped,

"I am unable to remember an occasion when I was more pleased to see a policeman."

An urgent flow of adrenalin had carried him through his own earlier struggles; with this now drained from him he was left with overwhelming feelings of relief as he stumbled into the police commissioner's steadying arms.

"I confess to being relieved that my team remained vigilant. Had they not, I dread to think how Sarwan Kumar might have reacted."

Intense feelings of gratitude was magnified by the relief Charlie felt and, when he asked that his appreciation should be expressed to those involved with his rescue, a thoughtful look came to the senior policeman's face.

"You have also rendered us a service, Mr Greenwood. When news of your inheritance spread through the city, I felt sure that the separatists would attempt to kidnap you. It was too good an opportunity for them to miss and so I'm afraid that we allowed you to become the sacrificial goat."

Momentarily distracted by some commotion coming from the now handcuffed gang of would-be kidnappers, it was some seconds before, with thoughtful consideration, the policeman continued,

"In fact you were a large enough carrot to tempt one of the Iranian ringleaders to make the rash mistake of becoming personally involved. He is one of their top men and it is rare for him to participate in the rough end of the separatist's filthy trade. Fortunately for us we have him now and I can assure you that it will be many long years before he is free to ferment further troubles in my territory or for that matter return to his own country."

Charlie's confusion was what prompted his next response.

"I have talked to no one about my legacy and I feel sure James Galbraith's professionalism would never have allowed him to reveal such things."

"James wouldn't need to. It has been common knowledge for many years that your grandmother or her heir would one day collect the proceeds from Ali Baba's will. When you showed up at the livery stable and introduced yourself, word of your arrival spread quickly and the purpose of your visit would not have been difficult to imagine."

"I suppose that might explain things, although what in hell's name would have happened to me if your men had not been alert and things had gone wrong?"

His previous mood of gratitude was rapidly changing and Charlie was now experiencing anger through realising that he had been used as the bait for a police trap.

"If your men were so much on the ball, why didn't they intervene when I was fighting off those thugs?"

"I understand that you might feel aggrieved, although please understand, we did not invite you to come here and neither unfortunately did we have it within our powers to forbid your entry." It seemed obvious that the police commissioner was now rankled by Charlie's aggrieved mood and was responding in like manner.

"My cousin, Sarwan Kumar, reminded me that we had a duty to protect you and that is precisely what we have done, Mr Greenwood. I also understand that he warned you of the dangers of coming to Srinagar."

It seemed that the senior police officer was about to add to this when there was further commotion from one of Charlie's would-be kidnappers.

"Get those men down to the station, sergeant, and make sure there are armed guards in place for the rest of the night. We will move them to the military prison tomorrow and the army can then take responsibility for them."

When the police commissioner next refocused on Charlie, it seemed the rest of his retort had been forgotten.

"Now, Mr Greenwood, there will be a report which has to be completed and, unless you are prepared to stay over for the trial, I shall require a very detailed statement from you."

Feeling completely bushed after a long and tedious spell at the police station and a more or less sleepless night, Charlie made his way back to the livery stables the following morning and found Ali Baba in a subdued mood.

"Mr Greenwood, the police were here earlier and they told me that there was an attempt by the separatists to kidnap you. They also implied that it was my fault. My only excuse for telling people that one of Memsahib Greenwood's relatives had paid me a visit was that I knew many would be interested and also pleased that her family has not forgotten this region."

"It's all right, Ali. I realise that you wished me no harm and also understand why you would tell others of my visit. I have come to say goodbye. I am leaving tomorrow, as there is work that I have to go to in Sri Lanka. When my task there is complete, hopefully I will return to Kashmir. Next time though, I shall certainly steer clear of poorly-lit passageways."

Relief was evident on the other man's face as he stepped forward, although Charlie ignored the outstretched hand.

"During our ride together the other day you told me how difficult things have been since travellers stopped coming to this region, Ali. I hope one day there will be a peaceful settlement to the troubles and that outsiders will return to admire the things that Kashmir has to offer. In the meantime it may help you to know that I have arranged with James Galbraith for an equal sum to be added to the money which you receive from the original Ali Baba stable subsidy. My grandmother would certainly have approved such an arrangement and I hope it will help to tide things over for you."

"You are indeed Memsahib Greenwood's grandson." Ali grasped Charlie's hand and his almost imperceptible gasp of pain from previously bruised knuckles went unnoticed.

"You will always be welcome here, Mr Greenwood. May you travel in mercies, have a safe journey and please God return to Srinagar soon."

"Rest assured, Ali, I shall certainly try."

# Chapter Seventeen

Lorna Savage was lonely; she was also missing her daughter who was mostly away in Vietnam. Apart from Kate and immediate family, Lorna had been alone for more years than she cared to remember. Rory, her childhood sweetheart, had died from gunshot wounds the day after they had been married in the fuselage of an old Catalina aircraft.

Radio traffic interrupted these thoughts and she clearly heard the voice of a Chennai air traffic controller directing a China Air 737 onto final approach. Lorna smiled at being reminded of her age; she still thought of Chennai as being Madras.

A call to deliver some medical supplies which were urgently required on the Andaman and Nicobar islands had necessitated Lorna abandoning preparations for her brother's surprise birthday party and taking the job herself. Under normal circumstances there would have been other pilots available and this particular task would not have presented a problem. Now she was desperately hoping that there would be no unforeseen delays.

Although there was a good landing strip at Port Blair the supplies were required by a clinic at Jagannath Dera on North Andaman. Lorna had made a similar delivery some years before and knew that the bay there offered a relatively well-protected area to put down in and from where the light cargo could easily be taken ashore by boat.

Visibility was good and as Lorna set the Cessna Caravan amphibian aircraft on a course out over the Bay of Bengal she could clearly see white capped waves some fourteen thousand feet below.

India's land mass gradually faded from view over the port wing and it occurred to Lorna that her love of flying was on the wane. During the early years of her career she had regularly flown twin engined Catalina amphibians. The Cessna Caravans which Savage Air now operated practically flew themselves and today's put down on water was a rare event.

Lorna was at a loss to understand her mood of melancholy although she realised that because of her brother's birthday she would soon need to snap out of it.

Through the shimmering heat haze ahead she eventually spotted a series of islands which indicated that she had sighted her destination on cue.

"At least I can still set an autopilot," she told herself with some irony, before disengaging the device prior to losing height. Twenty minutes later Lorna was concentrating all her powers of observation as she circled Jagannath bay.

A major hazard when amphibian aircraft put down on water is unseen floating objects which can so easily rip float struts from the fuselage.

Satisfied that the bay held no such hazards, Lorna made her final approach over the small hamlet of Madhyamgram and after a smooth touch down she taxied to a point within safe distance of the tender which had come out to meet her.

Lorna next instructed two men in the boat on how to lay out a forward anchor before unloading their stores; when this was complete she went ashore with them to get a signature on her copy of the bills of lading.

An offer of refreshment and the opportunity of stretching her legs before the flight back home was too good to miss and darkness had fallen before half the distance of the return crossing was achieved. The twinkling lights from vessels far below was in fact the only sign that there was other life on the planet earth.

Feeling more than a little tired, Lorna eventually spotted the street lights of Matara off the starboard wing and breathed a sigh of relief. The control tower at Koggala quickly responded to her call and almost immediately after she had flown over Ahangama the runway lights came on.

Touch down on the asphalt runway was not as smooth as it should have been and Lorna hoped there were no critical eyes watching this poor if somewhat fatigued performance. As she walked across the apron she became aware of one of the wireless room operators rushing out to meet her.

"What's wrong? Have we a problem?" A negative shake of the young man's head was sufficient to ease Lorna's immediate concern.

"I am sorry to bother you the moment you've touched down, Lo. Your timing is, however, convenient as we do have a minor problem. Kate telephoned some while back. She was about to board a train at the Fort Station when she discovered that due to maintenance work on the line all southbound trains are terminating at Alutgama. Apparently there are buses laid on, although she's still scared of using those after her accident." Some years before Kate had been in one of the many coastal route express coaches when it had been involved in a major incident and five people had been killed.

"There's no one else around to go and pick her up or to relieve me in the wireless room. I was about to call one of the taxi firms when we learned you were on approach."

"It's all right, I'll go," Lorna sighed. "What time is she due at the station?"

"Providing the train's not late, in about forty-five minutes." Lorna thanked the young wireless operator and made her way across to the transport pound in search of a spare vehicle. She knew that if the train was on time, Kate would almost certainly arrive before her.

"There she is," Lorna murmured. "She really is a sight for sore eyes. No wonder I'm feeling old." She watched with admiration as her daughter descended the high steps leading from the railway station.

"Sorry, darling. Have you been waiting long?" Lorna had all but fallen from the pick-up truck in her rush to greet Kate.

"I've just arrived back from The Andamans and it's as well that I got back when I did! There was no one else around to meet you." Kate brushed aside both the apology and explanation while smothering her mother in a long, lingering embrace.

It seemed family matters were high on Kate's agenda and once she had been assured that her grandfather was well and preparations were on stream for her uncle Richard's birthday celebrations, her mother was then able to ask what progress was being made with the new ferry routes and how things were developing in Vietnam.

The drive back to Koggala was uneventful and they ate a late supper in the canteen soon after their arrival. As most of the staff had already eaten, the dining room was quiet and this allowed the two women to continue their discussion regarding developments at the Mekong Express Company.

"I managed to get some live time on television. The interviewer obligingly asked the right questions and I was able to obtain maximum publicity for our new routes. I rather think Lily's dad, Admiral Tanaka, had a hand in that small coup. He has been wonderful, although as you probably realise it is nigh on impossible to achieve anything of importance in Vietnam without help from a party member. I did, however, manage to get interviews on two of the radio stations without his help and Molly, our reservations manager, came with me to translate. We have taken advertising space with both state-controlled newspapers and a number of the independents which are springing up. This seems to be paying off as bookings are on the increase."

"I am so pleased that you have been able to tear yourself away. Your Uncle Richard will also be happy that you are here. He hasn't been told anything about the party and certainly won't be expecting to see you. Oh and I almost forgot, he is not due back until tomorrow. Our forwarding agents in Dhaka are in on the secret, so I'm keeping my fingers crossed that there will be no hold-ups at their end."

Kate smiled. It was good to feel her mother's excitement. On previous visits she had worried that Lorna had lost her usual zest for life and but for her own preoccupations she might have made greater effort to discover the reason.

A long drawn out yawn from her daughter prompted Lorna to suggest it might be a good idea to turn in, although Kate surprised her by asking if they might have a nightcap first. A clatter of snooker balls indicated that there were still people in the games room, otherwise the two women once more had the lounge area to themselves and they were able to continue their reunion catch up.

"How has Gongy settled? He has been out there with you for some time and I thought we might have seen him back here before now."

"I rather think not. He has found himself an apartment and seems to be in his element. Which reminds me, I promised him some while back that I would look into why we are using more fuel oil from the bunkering facility at Hai Phong than is the case at Vung Tau. He is convinced that someone is stealing the oil and selling it to local fishermen. Gongy actually wanted to plant someone reliable up there to spy and see on what's going on. He had previously taken steps to move one of our very best marine engineers to the north and, had I not got wind of it and intervened, all sorts of staff problems might have been created." Kate then explained the integration problems which still exist between northern and southern people in Vietnam.

"I have been so darned busy that I haven't been able to do anything about the fuel deficiency." Kate sighed and Lorna placed a sympathetic hand on her daughter's arm before suggesting it was a mistake to attempt to do everything and that she should try to delegate.

"I realise that, although when I get back I will need to follow it up, if for no other reason than to get Gongy off my back. He really is a treasure, Mum, although sometimes he's like a dog with a bone. Once he gets his teeth into something he will not let go." Lorna's reaction to this was that she didn't need reminding of Gongy's persistence.

Sitting in her office the following morning Lorna breathed a sigh of relief when the operations room told her that the Hercules was on final approach. Lorna watched with pleasure as the large bulbous aircraft put down and then decelerated on a surprisingly short stretch of runway before turning onto the perimeter track and making its way round to the bonded store. Using one of the base bicycles, Lorna pedalled across and was just in time to catch the crew as they exited down the rear cargo ramp.

"What brings you out to meet us, Lo? Couldn't you sleep?" Lorna smiled; it was typical of her brother to tease.

"Do you know what day it is?" Richard appeared puzzled by the question and was thoughtful for some seconds before responding,

"It's Thursday unless I'm mistaken, or maybe I've lost a day somewhere." Lorna was almost the equal of her brother in height and when she pulled him to her before planting a resounding kiss on his cheek, his face reddened with embarrassment.

"Happy fiftieth birthday, little brother. I was sure you wouldn't remember." Richard's embarrassment was then further compounded when his crew cheered before breaking into an exaggerated version of Happy Birthday. His discomfort quickly disappeared and was replaced by genuine pleasure when Kate appeared.

Richard, the archetypal bachelor, was not given to expressing feelings and Lorna was once more touched by seeing his obvious affection for her daughter. He was then given just sufficient time to change from his work clothes and take a shower before being whisked off to the mess and his surprise birthday party.

The party was a huge success and Lorna managed to persuade her brother onto the dance floor. Not to be left out, Kate also danced with her uncle. Everyone consumed lots of alcohol and it was as well that none of the pilots were required to fly the following day.

Attending to some paperwork Lorna was surprised when Kate, looking bleary-eyed and somewhat out of sorts, put in an appearance the next morning.

"There is a flight back to Ho Chi Min city late tomorrow that I would like to take, Mum." She paused for a reaction before continuing,

"Well, actually it's in the early hours of the morning and the agency is holding a ticket for me. I hope you won't think that I can't wait to get away, as that's certainly not the case. I have really enjoyed being back. This is my home and it always will be although I really shouldn't leave Ruby to shoulder the responsibility for everything at this crucial time."

"Yes of course, darling! I do understand. It was good of you to take time out to be here. Richard was certainly pleased and we all appreciate your concern. If I were in your shoes, I expect I should be feeling exactly the same. Can we have dinner together tonight?" Kate agreed and Lorna found the quiet family evening with her father, brother and daughter as enjoyable as the previous day's party.

The sound of a vehicle pulling into the visitor's parking slot passed almost unnoticed the following morning, it was an occurrence which happened so frequently that it barely registered.

Lorna had thought her daughter still in bed and so was surprised to hear both Kate and the confusion in her voice as words drifted in through the open window.

"Gosh! You didn't waste time getting down here. I am surprised." A short silence followed and then a man's voice replied,

"I am also surprised to find you here, Kate; I rather thought you would be busy in Vietnam." There was something about the man's voice which was vaguely familiar, although Lorna was confused by the accent and thought it might be Australian.

"I've been home for a couple of days. It was my uncle's fiftieth birthday the day before yesterday and we all got together to celebrate."

"Sounds nice, although I hope that my visit will not now prove to be an intrusion into a family gathering. Should I go away and come back another day, do you think?"

A tremor in the man's voice suggested that he was nervous and Lorna tried to remember if Kate had known any of the commercial travellers who frequently called.

"No, Charlie, I think you should strike while the iron is hot." Determination had replaced amusement in Kate's tone and while Lorna had initially been conscious of the man's nervousness, she was now equally aware of the assertiveness in her daughter's voice.

"Charlie? I can't think of any of the travellers who are called Charlie," Lorna silently questioned.

With her curiosity aroused, it took a deal of self-restraint to resist going to the window to witness Kate's amusement. When her daughter next suggested that her mother was in the office and that it might help if she went in first to break the ice, Lorna could no longer contain herself and she had a fleeting vision of some suitor who had come to plight his troth.

Two faces swung in unison as the window opened wider. There was something about the man who stood facing Kate that was almost certainly familiar and Lorna thought she had previously seen the same awkwardness in the way he was standing. Assuming Kate was the reason for the stranger's discomfort, she ran an appraising eye over him. While Kate was still living at home it was an infrequent occasion for her to invite men friends to visit, although when she did Lorna always scrutinised them for suitability and noticed with parental concern that they were almost always much older than her daughter.

This particular man, standing with a hand resting on the door of an ugly Land Cruiser, was certainly older than she might have expected and he was also small in stature. His face was weathered and yet the smile when he looked up was both warm and sincere. Lorna also thought that despite his lack of size, there was an air of strength about him.

"I was not eavesdropping, although when I heard it was me that you were hoping to see, curiosity compelled me to establish who you might be. I'm Lorna Savage, although you have the advantage as I cannot recall our previously meeting."

There was no immediate response; instead the man's staring appraisal seemed literally to absorb her appearance in every detail.

Embarrassment was a sensation which Lorna rarely experienced. Now, however, with this stranger looking like a stray dog who had just found a new owner and Kate's ridiculous grin, she felt colour rising to her cheeks.

Lorna's embarrassment further increased when she realised that the man's scrutiny was one of admiration. It seemed that a very long time had passed since any man had looked at her in that way and it was the more puzzling because of Kate's obvious relationship with him. His accent was what she again noticed when, with some slight hesitancy, he began to explain.

"It was at Birmingham University. You had travelled up with some other students to attend a Barnes Wallis lecture and I knocked you flying when I burst out from a lecture room. We met by chance in a bar afterwards and you were gracious enough to allow me to buy you a drink. In the conversation which followed, you talked a lot about Sri Lanka, and Koggala Lake in particular. You also suggested that if I ever visited your island I should look you up and so on impulse here I am."

"Charlie Greenwood! Now I remember. But my God, you've changed! I'm sorry, that was not tactful. Please forgive my rudeness. It's just that it was such a long time ago and I'm now feeling rather confused."

Lorna's embarrassment further increased as she remembered the two nights of abandonment which she and this man had shared. Glancing across at her daughter, Lorna was grateful for Charlie Greenwood's tact, as it seemed from Kate's inquisitive expression that she knew no more than that which Charlie had just related.

"Are you two going to carry on with this conversation out here or should I fetch Charlie round to your office, Mum?" An affirmative nod was the best Lorna was able to manage.

Desperate for some respite, Lorna was thankfully aware that Charlie was now asking Kate if there was somewhere in the village where his driver might find refreshment.

"He can use the staff canteen. There is almost always something hot available and if that's not to his liking there will be a selection of cold snacks and drinks which he can choose from."

As her daughter and the long-forgotten man disappeared from view, Lorna attempted to compose herself. She was thoroughly confused, and pondered over the reason for Charlie's visit. Lorna also questioned what had prompted him to turn up now after a gap of more than thirty years. There was insufficient time to dwell on this, as Kate strode into her office with Charlie in close attendance.

"I'm sorry, Mum, Charlie and I met on a plane while travelling between Hong Kong and London. That journey as you well know is a long one and there was a great deal of time in which to talk. I'm afraid that I did most of the talking during the early part of the flight, although you can imagine my surprise when it transpired that Charlie had once known you."

Lorna's nod indicated that she was trying to understand, although her confusion was very obvious.

"Charlie, when he had an opportunity to speak, explained that he was going to be working in Colombo and I sort of encouraged him to look you up. He thought I should tell you that he might call down but I decided that it would be a nice surprise if you were not forewarned."

Lorna was all too familiar with her daughter's attempts at matchmaking and wished Kate would direct some of that energy toward her own unattached status.

"I will go and fetch Charlie's driver and show him where the canteen is, Mum. You two can then get reacquainted." Lorna's discomfort was not helped by the still silly grin on her daughter's face.

Surprisingly, it was Charlie after his faltering start that now broke the unease created by Kate's departure.

"I am sorry. It would be easy for me to suggest that my being here was a spur of the moment decision, although that would not be true. I have harboured thoughts of paying you a visit for as many years as it is since we parted in Birmingham." Lorna's frowning concern was all too obvious and Charlie hastily added,

"Please understand that I have no wish to cause embarrassment. Kate told me when we met on the plane that she never knew her father and explained the tragic circumstances of his death. I do, however, fully understand that you have family and many other things to consider. I also understand that my discretion should be paramount." Lorna studied her unexpected visitor before responding

"It seems obvious that I have been unable to disguise the fact that your visit has thrown me. Were it not for the fact that I am used to Kate springing surprises, I would also be quite cross with her. Kate is Kate, however, and as my only child, I suppose I have been guilty of spoiling her." Charlie mumbled that although this was understandable, he thought Lorna's daughter was one of the more balanced young women he had encountered in a very long time.

"As you probably now realise we live in a rather isolated community here and our socialising is mainly limited to family and staff. If my manner has appeared unwelcoming, please accept my apologies." Kate's reappearance prevented further explanation and Lorna was at last regaining some composure.

"Now then, Mum. Has Charlie shaken a few of those skeletons from your cupboard?" Lorna parried this by picking up a telephone and asking someone if tea and coffee might be brought over for a visitor.

"Oh and bring an extra cup for Kate would you, please, she is also with me." Lorna felt a need for her daughter's presence until she could at least get to grips with the situation.

"If I'm going to catch that late afternoon train from Alutgama, I am going to ask to be excused very shortly," Kate reminded her mother.

"There are things I need to do and I still have to throw a few clothes into my overnight bag." Charlie's inquiring look prompted her to explain that she was catching a train back to Colombo and returning to Vietnam on a scheduled flight in the early hours of the following morning.

"You can ride back with me if that will help?" Kate without preamble accepted Charlie's offer and then eased the situation with her light-hearted conversation. It seemed to Lorna that her daughter was intrigued by what might have taken place in the past and she was pleased that Kate had accepted the offer of a lift. Lorna realised that had her daughter not been leaving, she might have been subjected to some serious questioning.

When Kate finally announced that she would abandon them to finish packing, Lorna asked if Charlie would like to be shown the base.

"If we finish down by the lake there is a good chance that you might see some fish eagles. The weather has been quite humid and the thermals should give them good platforms to work from." Charlie, who was also in need of stretching his legs, readily agreed to Lorna's proposal.

The pleasure he gained from being alone with Lorna was good and the fact that Charlie found his tour of the base interesting was an added bonus. Lorna explained that both the lake and airfield were used during the Second World War by the RAF and that Sunderland flying boats had then operated from the lake.

"Sunderland's were not the only aircraft to use Koggala. Big planes, such as Liberators, Halifax's and DC3s often used the metal runway, together with an assortment of light aircraft. There are lots of old photographs on the walls over in the mess if you are really interested. Quite a few are of amphibians, as we operated a pair of Catalina's until a few years ago." Charlie's genuine interest and enthusiasm encouraged Lorna to continue. She explained that her father had started their business with Catalina's and was unable to prevent herself from smiling when Charlie asked, in a voice which betrayed some awe, if she enjoyed flying amphibians.

Lorna was not at all surprised when Kuli put in an appearance. His natural curiosity and over-protective nature dictated that the old Sri Lankan should give this stranger the once-over. She then observed how easily Charlie made conversation with the older man and realised that the normally discerning Sri Lankan had quickly taken to her companion.

When Charlie showed more interest in the lake cormorants than the Pallas's fish eagles which were circling overhead, Kuli seized the opportunity of telling him that there had once been a flock of trained fishing cormorants on the lake. Kuli's approval of the Englishman seemed to further increase when in turn Charlie told him that he had more than once watched trained cormorants fishing on the Yangtze.

They ran into Richard as they were making their way up from the lake and once more Lorna was surprised by her brother's reaction to their visitor. In response to Charlie suggesting it must be quite an experience to fly an aircraft such as the C130, Richard offered to take him up whenever it was convenient.

"If you keep in touch with Lo she will let you know when there is a short hop scheduled. Just make sure you bring along your passport."

Before Charlie's return journey to Colombo, both he and Lorna took afternoon tea with Sidi, the company's commercial director, and also Lorna's father Bob Savage. Lorna was also by now growing used to the stir that Charlie's visit was causing. She felt sad when the time came for her to kiss Kate goodbye and was honest enough to admit that separation from her daughter was not her only regret.

It was then difficult not to giggle when Charlie offered her his hand to say goodbye and Lorna wondered if it was normal to shake hands with someone that you had once slept with.

# Chapter Eighteen

The large four-engined 747 jumbo was rumbling its way out to the holding apron, despite distraction from the noise it was making there was a great deal to occupy Kate's mind. Her mother's embarrassment had been strangely touching and it was obvious that Lorna had not the faintest idea who Charlie was when he had first appeared. When Lorna was in fact reminded of their previous meeting, it then seemed that there had been more to the relationship than a casual drink prompted by an accident.

Kate had also seen Charlie's expression when her mother appeared at the window; his initial curiosity was quickly replaced by first approval and then something approaching a long and forgotten adoration.

There was adequate time for them to talk on the journey up from Koggala as Charlie had insisted on taking her all the way out to the airport. From the moment Kate stepped into his car, however, Charlie had shown a strong resistance towards discussing her mother. They had reached Kalutara when Kate's patience finally ran out.

"Look, Charlie. It's very obvious that you are doing everything to avoid talking about Mum. I respect a need for discretion and wouldn't expect you to recall anything which might compromise or embarrass her."

A noticeable relaxing of Charlie's hitherto taut shoulders encouraged Kate to continue,

"The pair of you obviously met before mum married and so in my book she was a free agent. I do, however, find difficulty in visualising someone as keen as you appear to be wanting to renew a fleeting acquaintance which actually happened before I was born." Kate then paused briefly with a thoughtful expression.

"I wonder! There is the possibility of course that it is as I suggested during our flight from Hong Kong, that you developed some really strong feelings for Mum during that first brief encounter." Kate's theorising was then interrupted when Charlie turned and appeared to be studying her in light from passing traffic with what appeared to be a changing expression.

"I was certainly attracted to you when we were waiting to board that plane in Hong Kong. I thought then that I had only ever seen one other person equally as attractive. It was complete chance or maybe an act of fate which decreed that person just so happened to be your mother. Had we not sat together, I would never have made the connection and the empty void in my life would have continued. Your complexion is darker than hers and you are also smaller than she is. The one striking similarity is your hair colouring and yet there was obviously something which drew me to you."

The wailing blast from the horn of one of the express coaches charging its way through heavy traffic caused Kate to catch her breath and interrupt Charlie's flow. With her heart rate returning to normal Kate had then quickly realised that Charlie was very aware of their not being alone and she was quick to reassure him that their driver only understood a very basic form of pidgin English. Encouraged by this, Charlie continued,

"I'm sorry if I give the impression of being a sentimental old fool, but there you have it. I have travelled continuously throughout most of my adult life and I have never ever found another person that I was more attracted to than Lorna. Obviously she has had a great deal to contend with, the loss of your father must have been a terrible blow, and yet the years have been kind to her. In fact she is more beautiful now than how I have always remembered her."

A small tear was apparent while glistening on Kate's cheek and Charlie thought his sentiment had gone too far when she groped for a tissue to blow her nose. Words had then seemed to lodge in his throat while attempting to offer further explanation; fortunately Kate's resumption, when it came, offered him some respite.

"Thank you for being so candid, Charlie. I suppose offspring rarely think of their parents in terms of relationships, although now you've mentioned it I can understand that Mum might be considered attractive by a great many people of all age groups." Kate appeared to ponder this for some seconds before asking,

"Do you think you will be seeing her again?" Charlie, looking thoughtfully ahead, had hesitated before replying.

"I shall certainly try, although there is a very tight schedule on my contract and I am not expecting to have too much free time. When I can, I shall make every effort to see Lorna. She may have other ideas, of course. There has been an awful lot of water under the bridge since our first brief meeting and she may find my reappearance irritating."

It occurred to Kate even as he was speaking that she badly wanted Charlie to go on seeing her mother and so she had encouraged him.

"My guess is that she will want to see you again. When she was over the shock of you appearing out of the blue, her spirits lifted to an extent which has not been apparent for a very long time."

Explanation of how she had neglected to follow through on fears for Lorna's low spirits had then been related by Kate.

"Your turning up might just be the fillip she needs. If you do get together, please be kind to her, Charlie. Mum has had a tough life, mostly because she has had to compete with arrogant people in a man's world."

Following this, Kate remembered wondering why Charlie had never married and felt touched when realising the answer.

"If you are going to be seeing more of Mum, perhaps I should briefly describe our family. My dark colouring comes from my paternal grandmother. She is a Tamil from Kandy and almost a native of our island. Her grandparents, like so many other Tamils, arrived in Ceylon, as the island was then known, from Tamil Nadu in southern India to pick tea. It seems they prospered and their son, my great-grandfather, eventually became a successful trader in general merchandise. My paternal grandfather is Caucasian, a true Scot in fact, from Lewis in the Outer Hebrides. I think he and my grandmother met when my grandfather was stationed with the RAF at Trincomalee during the Second World War and you couldn't possibly begin to understand the love they have bestowed on me over the years. It sometimes feels a little awkward, as I often think that I am something of a substitute for the loss of their son, my dad."

Kate had gone on to say that she knew little of her maternal grandmother although her maternal grandfather had played a very big and influential part in her life. She also told Charlie what little she knew of her father and how her parents' marriage had lasted just the one day.

"Mum hasn't actually told me that she was pregnant at their wedding although it's unlikely she conceived afterwards as Dad was very weak and probably dying during the ceremony." Kate had then followed this by relating stories of her upbringing at Koggala and how she finally went to school in England.

When Charlie described Kuli as a delightful old chap, Kate grinned and warned him not to be taken in by the old Sri Lankan.

"He would give his life to protect my mother. He acted as nursemaid to her after Granny Savage died while giving birth to Uncle Richard, and as you might imagine, Mum and Kuli are terribly close. They were involved in an incident at the lake some years ago. I was told by Grandpa Bob that they, alone, actually saw off a bunch of Tamil Tigers who were attempting to steal or sabotage one of the old Catalina's. It was serious at the time, a real gunfight in fact, and only weeks before the Tigers successfully hijacked Mum's aircraft and took both her and the crew hostage. I think that I've previously described what happened then."

Kate had been surprised by the warmth of Charlie's affectionate kiss when they finally parted at the Katunayka air terminal, particularly so as she'd noticed the formal handshake her mother received when they left Koggala.

Kate's next recollection was of someone waking her to make sure that her seat belt was fastened.

"Hello, Molly! How are things?" Molly was the first person Kate ran into as she walked back into the offices on Bang Dang jetty.

"Hi, Miss Kate, it sure will be nice having you back. Things are okay, ticket sales are up, the operational crews are happy and I have not heard anything untoward regarding the normal grouses we get from shore-based staff. Although I reckon that situation won't last," she added philosophically.

Ruby, looking very relaxed, was ensconced behind her desk when Kate next walked into one of the small portakabin's which they both shared.

"I needn't have worried about racing back. You lot seem to have everything under control." Her aunt grinned.

"That's the trouble with you high-fliers. You always seem to think that you're indispensable." Ruby smirked again before rising to embrace her niece.

"There are no problems for you to fret over and I can see that you are tired, so let's call it a day and go home."

On the walk back to their apartment Kate described Richard's birthday party and also the surprise of Charlie turning up two days later. Ruby suggested that it would be nice for Lorna if something developed from this and Kate teasingly expressed a view that she hoped it would be Ruby's turn next.

The following morning, after countless cups of coffee and two freshly-baked croissants, Kate was beginning to feel that her short break had never happened. Admiral Tanaka's telephone call, when it was put through, certainly did little toward easing her back into the commercial routine which she had previously created.

"Kate, how are you?" It was then typical of the high-ranking government official to come straight to the point and his follow-up question caused shock waves to reverberate through her system.

"Would you consider running a regular service up to Chau Doc on the Cambodian border?" He paused briefly, presumably to give her sufficient time to absorb the question.

"You will be aware that there is a government-backed schedule currently operating, although I'm afraid that service leaves a lot to be desired. In fact the current recently appointed operator has continued in much the same way as it has always been. Late departures and late arrivals are the norm and customer satisfaction seems not to enter into the equation." Kate then clearly heard an interruption as someone asked the Admiral a question.

"Now, where was I? Ah yes. You see, Kate, the most important development for our country in the next two decades will be tourism. We are determined that our standards shall equal those of other tourist-led economies and Thailand in particular." This time Kate discerned annoyance in his voice as she heard a further unseen question.

"Government ministers are most impressed with your new service and I have been instructed to ask if you will consider taking other routes. Chau Doc would be the first of many which you will be offered."

Kate quickly realised that opportunities such as had been briefly outlined did not readily occur and her every instinct was to treat this seriously.

"Admiral, I just don't know what to say. In fact, I'm dumbfounded. Can I have a little time to think things through and also to discuss the matter with my aunt? Although before I do, I know that a first stumbling block will be finance. We have stretched ourselves getting the current operations off the ground and I rather think Ruby will err on the side of caution." The Admiral said this was understandable and then created a further shock to Kate's already frayed nervous system.

"I have been authorised to offer financial help from our state bank. My government will back you to the extent of some sixty-eight million US dollars and our finance minister has agreed interest rates shall be fixed at one and one half per cent over seven years." Some throat clearing followed until the Admiral continued,

"By initially supporting you we will save a great deal in both capital outlay and the training of personnel for government operated services. Our ministers are also rapidly concluding that civil servants are not the ideal people for running commercial enterprise. This approach of ours has the added benefit that if successful the project will give my government a return for its backing, plus a small percentage profit increase. So you see, Kate, our motive is definitely not coming from a sense of thoughtless generosity. The Mekong Express Company has already demonstrated its professionalism and a professional portrayal is what we in this country are now going to achieve in the shortest possible time." Kate was still attempting to absorb all that had just been said when the admiral continued,

"I appreciate that you will require time to think our proposals through and there will also be numerous questions which you will need to ask. Take your time and please feel free to call me as often as you wish."

Realising both the enormity and importance of the proposal, Kate promised to drop everything and said she would get back to the admiral as quickly as possible. Placing the telephone back on its rest, she then noticed that her hand was trembling, and she thought it sensible to remain seated until some composure was regained.

Frustrated at not being able to immediately locate Ruby and realising it was unlikely that she would be able to concentrate on other work, Kate decided to go out onto the jetty to think things through.

"The offer of that money on those terms is a once in a lifetime opportunity. Can we really afford to walk away from it?" she asked herself.

"Obviously we will need to employ more people, preferably people with experience and local knowledge." Kate was now convinced that they should think positively and was considering how they might attract staff from other ferry operators when a voice beside her exclaimed,

"There you are, Kate! I was on my way to see you. Can you spare a few minutes?" Without waiting for an answer Gongy plonked his backside down on an adjacent Samson post and proceeded to roll a cigarette.

With her thoughts in turmoil the last thing Kate wanted was some lengthy discussion on maintenance. Unable to think of a good reason for fobbing off the old engineer, she smiled and said,

"Okay, Gongy. Yes, I realise I have done nothing to sort out your concern with regard to the excessive fuel consumption at Hai Phong. I'm sorry, although with having to go back to Koggala and other commitments I have simply not gotten round to it. I promise I will. In fact, I will make it a priority."

An unconvincing nod from Gongy indicated that he doubted Kate's commitment and she felt further reassurance was necessary.

"One thought has occurred. Do you think the tanker driver is somehow short-changing us when he makes deliveries? I realise that you receive printouts of the quantities which are fed into our storage tanks and I'm sure you check those against invoices, but could the meter reading be rigged?"

Gongy pushed a greasy and very soiled cap to the back of his head, spat a gobbet of phlegm far out into the muddy water and then agreed that of course meters could be rigged. "I hadn't thought of that," he murmured, in a tone which suggested he should have.

"Well, I think something like that is far more likely than one of our shore-based staff selling fuel to local fishermen. There is always so much activity around the wharf that someone would surely spot something and blow the whistle? Anyway, leave things with me."

Kate had known the old engineer for the whole of her life and so it felt quite natural for her to place a reassuring hand on the older man's arm.

"Please trust me. I have promised that I will look into your concerns and I really will."

As though on cue, she then spotted Ruby making her way down the quay. Seizing on this opportunity to disengage, Kate suggested,

"I have been waiting to catch Ruby all morning. Something urgent has cropped up and I need to grab her while I have the chance."

Kate cursed under her breath. She had almost reached Ruby when Lung Chen, the elderly Chinese accountant, came from his office and intercepted her aunt.

"I'm sorry, Uncle Lung Chen. I really do need some of Ruby's time as there is something terribly important to be talked through. In fact it might be a good idea for you to sit in and participate."

"Sounds rather mysterious. If it's that important maybe we should use Lung Chen's office. It's much quieter and we are less likely to be disturbed by incoming calls."

Water lapping at the piles beneath them was soothing and against this background Kate gave both Ruby and Lung Chen a resume of the Admiral's proposal. She was half expecting immediate rejection on the basis of their overstretched financial position. Instead, Kate was surprised by her aunt's reaction.

"Well, we will have to consider it. This is Vietnam and the Vietnamese government holds all the cards. We have licences for the routes that we currently operate simply because the government allows us to be here. What has previously been granted, however, can also be easily removed." Ruby paused to allow time for this to be considered.

"We would certainly be foolish to turn this down without careful consideration." Lung Chen then also surprised Kate by his nodding agreement.

"Did the Admiral suggest a timetable for the start of this new service?"

"No, his proposition took me by surprise and in my state of shock I forgot to ask. I realise now that it was stupid of me, although it just seemed so unreal and in fact I had to pinch myself to make sure that I wasn't dreaming."

Ruby and Lung Chen both nodded their understanding before settling down to debate the proposal in detail.

One early and important point then made by the elderly Chinese accountant was that despite the large sum of money which would be at their disposal, they would still require additional funding if they were to set up more than one new operation. Lung Chen also further surprised Kate by suggesting,

"We wouldn't need to use the backing money, of course! In fact with large amounts deposited in our accounts and evidence of other secure bond investments, banks and the financial institutions would be falling over themselves to lend us even greater sums at very competitive rates."

The elderly accountant paused to allow both Ruby and Kate to ponder this announcement.

"If and when we finally decide to go ahead, I feel confident that I will be able to produce some interesting and attractive financial proposals."

Time sped by quickly until the sound of staff leaving to go home for the night seemed an indication that further discussion would serve no good purpose until a more detailed study was available. It was then finally agreed that Kate should telephone the Admiral to arrange a meeting.

"Perhaps we can have further discussion on the matter tomorrow morning before you put your call through to the Admiral," Lung Chen suggested.

"It may be that we will have thought of other considerations when we have slept on the matter."

A cultured voice with a Western accent informed Kate that Admiral Tanaka was not expected back until after lunch. Disappointed, Kate thought she really should now concentrate on the many other things which were waiting to be dealt with.

Catching sight of Gongy as he was about to board one of the recently docked hydrofoils reminded Kate of one important commitment and she dialled the number of the company that provided a bunkering service for their Hai Phong operation. A voice responding in Vietnamese prompted Kate to ask if there was someone available who was able to speak English. As no discernible reply was forthcoming, she left her office to go in search of someone who might translate.

"Molly, will you telephone our fuel supplier at Hai Phong and ask if it will be okay for me to call on them in the next week or so, please?" This request was quickly arranged and with more ease than Kate had anticipated.

"The commercial director says he will be pleased to make himself available at any time convenient to you, Miss Kate. He suggests a telephone call the day before will ensure that he's around." Molly also confirmed that the man spoke no English.

"I am hoping to arrange a meeting in Hanoi. When that's fixed I would like to combine the two things. It will obviously be necessary to have an interpreter with me and it might help us to get even better acquainted if you came along."

Kate was not sure if it was surprise or pleasure which registered in the other woman's smile.

Molly's telephone ringing then prevented further explanation and Kate, who was about to leave, was surprised when told that the call was for her.

"I am sorry, Admiral. I was not expecting to hear from you until after lunch. Your office indicated that you would not be available until then."

"Ah, but you have overlooked the fact that we take early lunch here, my dear Kate. Was your call to clarify something from yesterday's brief discussion?"

"Well, in a way, yes. In fact it was to ask if I might come up to discuss your proposal in detail." Kate was vaguely aware of Molly closing the door as she left her office and, despite preoccupation, she was grateful for the young woman's sensitive discretion.

"As you might imagine, considerable time was spent yesterday talking over your proposal and we think it will be better to discuss the matter with you in person. Is it possible that you might spare me some of your valuable time?"

"Of course and I must say I am now feeling optimistic. Your request suggests you are interested in taking the matter further. If that is the case I agree we should get together as quickly as possible, although when is the problem. My diary appears to be full for some weeks ahead." Kate's heart sank until the admiral then suggested that his secretary would attempt to rearrange things.

"How flexible can you be if we throw a few dates at you?" Kate told him she could be very flexible and that she would attend the meeting alone as her aunt was of the opinion that too many voices round a table tended to complicate matters.

"Your aunt is a very wise woman. Quite often people interject at meetings simply because they think their presence calls for it."

The admiral's aide, who had guided Kate through the initial documentation for their coastal route, telephoned the next morning.

"Miss Savage, the admiral asks if a ten thirty appointment on the twenty-fourth will be convenient."

"Would that be the twenty-fourth of this month, Captain?" Kate drew a sharp breath as she replaced the telephone. She now realised that this was yet another monumental milestone which she had not envisaged when setting out to create a business in Saigon.

# Chapter Nineteen

Charlie watched with mixed emotions as Kate disappeared down a long tunnel leading to the airport concourse. He still felt the warmth from her kiss and realised that his strong feelings sprang from both an admiration for her and reawakened feelings for her mother. Making his way out through parked vehicles he slowly returned to where the company driver was waiting for him and they then began the tedious journey back to the port.

"I hope it won't be long before I see them again," he murmured.

"What's that, boss? Traffic noise big problem!" As the driver wound his side window up, Charlie realised his thoughts had been uttered aloud.

"It's okay, I was talking to myself. Speculating on whether the crane barge will have arrived when we get back." The Singhalese man grunted an acknowledgment, although Charlie thought it unlikely that he had understood.

When the window was opened again and the sound of chaotic traffic flooded back in, Charlie's thoughts returned to Lorna and the strong emotion she had aroused in him when she first came to the office window. The only other occasion that he could recall such feelings was when they had first met and although he considered himself to be both rational and sensible, he was uncertain as to what his future strategy should be.

On driving into the site compound these thoughts were distracted by the sight of one of the company's crane barges being manoeuvred alongside. Climbing from the Land Cruiser he was just in time to see a large Dutch ocean-going tug slip its tow and a smaller harbour tug begin the process of shepherding Neyland onto a temporary berth. Charlie watched this arrival through an almost carnival array of bright lights with feelings of pride; he was aware that more impressive crane barges existed although he had used this particular vessel on numerous contracts and knew it to be a very stable work platform.

Another aspect which pleased him was that Bill Arthurs had ensured that the additional ancillary equipment was secure before the barge began its long journey from Wrabness on the Stour in Essex. Charlie also made a mental note that the two hundred ton Manitowoc crane should be hosed down with fresh water as sea spray had left it encrusted in a sheen of salt. He also thought that a wooden crate which was lashed to an area of forward decking might contain the Delmag diesel piling hammer he had requested.

"I will check the Mani over in the morning, Charlie." A sandy-haired man with a Northern Irish accent had joined him on the quayside.

"When I'm satisfied she's okay, I will pick the boom off its supports and swing the rest of the equipment ashore." Jack Henderson had operated practically every crawler crane owned by the company and when Charlie had failed to secure the services of Martin Mansfield, the Ulster man had been his next choice.

"When you have dealt with that, would you couple a fire hose to that hydrant and give the crane a good sluice down, please? Doubtless we will have visits from the European Grant Fund people and also bods from the World Bank. They will arrive unannounced and when they do, I would like them to find a good shipshape operation in progress." Jack's nod indicated that he understood: Charlie Greenwood was renowned for running both tidy and well-organised contracts.

"I am going to turn in now. How's your cabin? Not too stuffy I hope! Has the sparky fixed you up with one of those portable air-con units?" Jack Henderson told him yes and that everything was fine.

Having spent the next two days dealing with the many mundane problems which occur when a construction site is being set up, Charlie's mood was to say the least agitated. A light tap on his office door caused him to groan inwardly, convinced that yet another minor irritation was to be passed his way.

"Yes, come in if you must," he barked and then refocused on a drawing which he was studying.

"My, Charlie! This is a side of you that I certainly don't remember. The young man who directed me to your office suggested I should tread carefully. He said you were a bit liverish this morning." Unable to believe his ears, Charlie hesitated before looking up.

"Lorna, what a lovely surprise! In fact I would go so far as to say that you just might be the perfect antidote for my ill humour." Charlie rose from his chair, hugged Lorna and briefly brushed her cheek with a welcoming kiss. Her very presence was intoxicating and the subtlety of her perfume was an additional distraction. He had certainly thought of her a lot since leaving Koggala, although was now completely flustered by her unexpected visit.

In an attempt to find somewhere for Lorna to sit he dislodged a pile of papers from his desk and then heard himself asking if she would like coffee.

"I'm sorry; your appearing out of the blue has completely thrown me," Charlie explained with a frown of embarrassment.

"I suppose it should be me apologising. My visit was on impulse. Would you like me to go away and drop by another day?" Lorna's reaction caused yet further embarrassment and confusion to Charlie's racing thoughts. Eventually he managed to stammer,

"I wasn't expecting to see you again so soon. What brings you up to Colombo and how on earth did you get in through port security?" Lorna smiled before once more apologising for her unannounced visit. She then explained that she had business in the port and as a regular visitor to the restricted area, possessed a security pass. They chatted over coffee and she showed interest by asking questions about the contract. Responding to this, Charlie took her through to the engineer's office and showed her an overlying site plan. With Lorna showing more than just polite interest, Charlie was encouraged to ask, "Would you like to take a look round? There isn't much to see yet as the only progress we've made thus far is to set up the compound. If, however, you just happened to be passing in a few weeks' time, I think you might see a difference."

Charlie was conscious that his attempt at a further invitation had not disguised the fact that he wanted to see her again. Then deciding he didn't care and that he didn't want her to leave, he asked if she would have lunch with him.

The reunited couple were shown to a table in the yacht club restaurant with a view out over the inner harbour and Charlie rediscovered that making conversation with Lorna was much easier than anticipated. He also found himself telling her how dissatisfaction with life at head office had led to his taking the contract in Colombo.

Lorna in turn explained that she was also becoming dissatisfied with work and how Kuli had suggested that she should take a holiday to rekindle some enthusiasm.

"Holidays are okay, although they always seem to end just as you are beginning to relax!" she added.

Prompted by this Charlie told her of his recent visit to India and how his grandmother had requested that he should visit some of the places she had known as a young woman. Lorna was a good listener and with this as encouragement Charlie went on to describe Srinagar, the lakes and the mountainous border region through which he had briefly trekked.

"It would seem Kashmir made quite an impression on you," Lorna eventually observed.

"My dad and Uncle Lenny hauled freight up there in the early days and I heard them describe its beauty and how they felt they were intruding when putting down on the lakes. Perhaps I should take Kuli's holiday advice and go there myself."

With genuine concern Charlie told her that if she was serious she should be very careful and certainly not walk around without some extremely good protection. He then also described his own brief encounter with hostage-takers. Expressing sympathy for Charlie's harassing experience, Lorna shrugged and explained that living on a war-torn island had taught her that it was pointless to spend one's life worrying about such things.

When it became all too obvious that the waiters were anxious to clear their table, Charlie was prompted to pay the bill. This was not without regret as he was unable to remember an occasion when he had enjoyed lunch more.

"Can we do this again soon?" Charlie asked as he opened the door of an ancient Standard Vanguard with RAF roundels still showing through the paintwork on its front wings.

"I haven't enjoyed myself so much in years." Lorna ignored his outstretched hand and then placed her lips to his mouth.

"I have also enjoyed our being back together," she breathed. "We shouldn't rush things though. It would be nice to develop a firm and lasting friendship this time round. It's something which is very much missing in my life; the location of Koggala and my job is unhelpful with forming strong relationships." Charlie desperately wanted to hold onto her; instead he simply opened the car door.

"Thank you for lunch, Charlie. I enjoyed the site tour and will keep you to your promise of letting me see how things develop." He thought she was about to start the engine, but instead she looked up and asked,

"How about trying to get down to Koggala for Sunday lunch once in a while? I realise that when things get under way here it might be difficult for you to find time, although hopefully there will be the odd Sunday afternoon when you might be free?"

Attempting to disguise his delight for the proposal, Charlie told her that the invitation was too good to miss and that he would make every attempt to take her up on it sooner rather than later. Both agreed to keep in touch by telephone and Lorna had started the engine when on impulse Charlie leaned in and kissed her again.

Chattering telex messages were a novelty when the machine was first installed but the noise now barely registered, and Charlie continued writing yet another letter to the client. When the junior site engineer burst into his office without preamble, it occurred to him that the young man should learn some manners.

"Sorry, boss. I couldn't help reading this and I knew you would want to see it straight off." Charlie murmured a somewhat grudging thanks before glancing down at the flimsy piece of paper. Unable to then believe the completely unexpected content, it was necessary for him to read the message through a second time.

Charlie,

We are experiencing contractual difficulties. Do not continue with further work on current project. Repeat, cease operations forthwith at present location. Legal staff estimate a minimum of three weeks to resolve. Advise, secure site, lay off local employees and send expat staff home on short-term leave. Please telephone Head Office. I shall be in from seven thirty a.m. UK time.

Duncan Hardcastle

Contracts Director International Division

"Oh, bollocks! And just as we were getting under way! Why in the hell can't those useless buggers in the legal department get things sorted before we arrive at this stage?"

"I dunno," the site engineer responded. Charlie had overlooked the fact that the young man was still in his office. Looking up, he felt his earlier irritation returning.

"Right, take yourself off and find the works manager, tell him that there is to be a briefing here in fifteen minutes and that all personnel should attend." The young man was turning for the door when Charlie added,

"If you mention one word of what you've read in this telex to anyone out there, I'll have your guts for garters. The crew will need to hear this from me." He then added, "Are you clear on that?"

Charlie felt drained when he finally sat back at his desk. Darkness had fallen at least an hour before and it had not taken long for the site to have an appearance of neglect and dereliction.

All but one of the expat staff had elected to take up the offer of unexpected home leave and Charlie thought the junior site engineer's reason for staying had a lot to do with a relationship which was forming with one of Colombo's fairer sex.

While laying off local employees and ensuring that airline tickets were in place for those wishing to return to the UK, Charlie had not given thought to his own position. With everything finally taken care of he now had an opportunity of considering what he would most like to do with the unexpected free time that stalling on the contract had created.

In waiting for Lorna to come to the telephone he worried that he was acting rashly and that she would dismiss his idea as being totally unacceptable.

"Hello Charlie. It's now my turn for a surprise. I hadn't expected to hear from you until at least the weekend. Are you calling to say that you can make it for lunch on Sunday?"

"Not exactly." He briefly hesitated. "In fact, I was wondering if you would consider taking a short holiday with me." Then casting caution to the wind he explained what had happened and apologised for making such an outrageous proposal at short notice.

"Not at all! It's a lovely idea," Lorna responded, and as Charlie breathed slowly out, she continued, "I realise I will need to make my mind up quickly! Your contract is unlikely to be suspended for ever. Can you give me fifteen minutes to see if I can organise things at this end?" Still unable to believe her willingness, Charlie said that he would sit tight for as long as was needed. Her return call in fact came in under ten minutes.

"Yes, Charlie. I am okay for up to two weeks. Where shall we go?" He then heard a throaty chuckle echoing down the telephone line when he told her that he had not given too much thought to a destination.

"It seems you are more interested in getting me away than where you will actually be taking me." Charlie's denial produced another sound of merriment and then Lorna said that an idea was forming.

"Your description of Kashmir made it sound wonderful. How about taking me there?" She gave no opportunity for a reply and it was obvious from what she said next that her mind was already fixed on visiting Srinagar.

"There is a small freight parcel in our warehouse waiting to be transported to a pharmaceutical company's laboratory adjacent to the airfield in Delhi. We could drop that off on the way."

"What? You mean you would fly us up?" Charlie asked, feeling now rather overwhelmed with the speed that things were being suggested. Lorna said unless he had some firm objection it would shorten travel time and create more holiday time.

"It is possible of course that you will find our being alone together for two whole weeks difficult to cope with," Lorna again giggled, and he realised that she enjoyed teasing him.

Charlie retorted that he felt confident of being able to manage two weeks although longer might prove difficult.

"Well, if that problem occurs, I shall have to think of ways of keeping you amused!" Charlie had not remembered Lorna having a sense of fun during their earlier short time together and on realising it now, he was rapidly gaining enthusiasm for the trip.

Lorna's tone then became more serious when she suggested that she would try to obtain permission for them to land on the same lake that her father had used when flying to Srinagar.

Charlie was finding difficulty in keeping up, although it was now clear that Lorna had set her heart on going and he reminded her again of the dangers which they might be exposed to. Her reaction was dismissive and she reiterated the same feelings she had expressed when they had lunched together. Their conversation then ended with her asking him to get down to Koggala as early as possible on Wednesday morning.

"We will need to make an early start so that our landing at Delhi does not coincide with the custom people's lunch break."

Replacing the telephone back on its rest Charlie paused to take stock of what arrangements had been agreed. One thing which immediately occurred was thoughts for Lorna's safety. She had clearly expressed feelings on the issue although he realised that she couldn't possibly understand the danger which existed in Kashmir.

With memories of his own foiled kidnap experience still fresh, Charlie first considered contacting Sarwan Kumar to ask if his cousin the police commissioner might be enlisted to help once more. This idea was quickly dismissed when realising that his previous encounter had probably used up most of the good will initially created.

As he was considering the danger that a return to Kashmir might create, a vague memory came flooding back. On closing his eyes to concentrate, the image of a newspaper article was slowly remembered, as was the photograph of a man he had once known.

"Bloody hell! Why not? I am wealthier now than I ever thought I would be and can surely afford to pay for some protection."

Glancing down at his watch, Charlie was relieved to see that with the time difference he would still gain a response from head office. Reaching for the telephone he once more dialled the all too familiar number and was quickly put through to his secretary's extension.

"Tina, I apologise in advance for calling to ask favours. Do you think you might be able to trace the telephone number of a security agency which is fronted by a man named Mustapha Al Hameed? I think their offices might be in Chelsea or Fulham." To explain his reason for making this request, Charlie told Tina,

"It's not easy locating international telephone numbers from this end as you might imagine, and if you are able to help, I will certainly be grateful."

"Sure thing, Mr Greenwood! It's no trouble. Are you still at the office? What's the time in Colombo?" Tina promised to get back to him as quickly as possible and was as good as her word.

"It was easy! The company is called Al Hameed Securities and they are based just off the Hammersmith Broadway. I called them and the receptionist eventually told me that Mr Al Hameed was in. She was a bit cagey at first, although I said I was calling on behalf of a prospective client." Charlie wrote down the number and then asked Tina if she would write a note to Duncan Hardcastle saying that he had decided against coming back to the UK for leave and would instead take two weeks' local holiday. He finished dictating the note by suggesting that he would be in touch when he had settled in at a local resort.

"Greenwood? Would that be Sergeant Greenwood? Yes of course I remember you! I always hoped that you would re-enlist. How is your Greek these days?" Charlie told Mustapha Al Hameed he had not used that language in years and would now find difficulty in conversing with anyone who spoke only Greek.

"Um, bit like riding a bike after a long layoff. It would soon come back. Don't suppose you would be interested in a job? We pay well and also award exceptional tax free bonuses to skilled operatives. From what I remember you would quickly come up to scratch. In fact, there is a Greek shipping magnate who is looking for someone reliable to manage his personal security. Nice little number based on a private island in the Aegean."

Charlie thanked him for the offer and then explained the reason for his call.

"Kashmir, you say. Not our usual operational area, but do you know, I believe you may be in luck. It's going to be expensive though. The people I'm thinking of work as a team. There are three of them and they are back home in Nepal waiting for an assignment right now."

Tentatively Charlie asked the cost and breathed more easily when the fee quoted by his former boss seemed reasonable. The two men talked for a while longer, making arrangements for dates, times and meeting places. Finally Charlie asked the names of the three retired Gurkha soldiers. Mustapha Al Hameed hesitated before suggesting,

"It's probably better that I let them introduce themselves. One of their first clients called them Bing, Bang, and Boom. He had difficulty with their names, as do I. It appealed to their sense of humour and is now how they usually introduce themselves. Jolly little fellows on the surface, although if anyone took their good humour as a sign of weakness they would certainly be misguided. Between them they boast a Military Medal and a

Distinguished Conduct Medal; two of them have also been mentioned in despatches."

Momentarily Charlie mused over the coincidence of his and Lorna's future security being in the hands of men that worked under aliases, while at the same time the stable management in Srinagar was also burdened with a similar handicap.

Two one-way road systems in Colombo proved Charlie's temporary undoing very early on Wednesday morning while travelling to his rendezvous with Lorna. The site driver had been paid off along with other locally recruited staff and Charlie decided that driving to Koggala would not be difficult. He reasoned that if he kept the ocean to his right, he could not go wrong. Confident when starting out, he eventually resorted to hiring a somewhat bemused early breakfasting tuk tuk driver to lead him out through the suburbs. Consequently his arrival at Koggala was much later than hoped for.

"We will need to get our skates on if we stand any chance of making it to Srinagar before dark." Charlie decided this wasn't chastisement as he had been reassured by the warmth of Lorna's greeting and realised she was simply anxious to be off.

"Sit up front next to me. We will be able to talk more easily that way. Normally the rear seats would be removed to make space for cargo although this machine was used to ferry part of a replacement oil rig crew across to Myanmar a few days ago." Lorna indicated four seats immediately behind the ones which they would be occupying.

While the engine warmed and Lorna was going through pre-flight checks she told him that she had been unable to obtain permission to land on the lakes at Srinagar.

"Normally there wouldn't be a problem, now though there is a large religious festival taking place at a mosque which is situated right on the shoreline. You needn't worry though, I have filed a flight plan to the airport and from there we can take a taxi into town."

Charlie's concern was not one to which Lorna was alluding. His thoughts were that by using taxis it exposed them to hostage taking more than public transport might, although he kept those concerns to himself and instead expressed disappointment at not being able to land on one of the lakes. He also told her that he had never flown in an amphibian before.

"It's a shame, although if you would really like to we can put down on the lake here when we return."

From the outset it was obvious that she was a competent pilot. Their take-off was smooth and each adjustment to trim and change of course was calmly dealt with. Conversation was distorted by noise from the engine although Lorna kept up a running commentary throughout. She explained the controls and the purpose of the numerous dials on the instrument panel. Charlie thought starting a holiday together this way was a good omen and the long haul up to New Delhi passed all too quickly.

Contrary to expectation there was no delay in acquiring customs clearance and disposal of the small cargo went smoothly. Communication with flight control was then dealt with in a jargon which was difficult for Charlie to follow.

"That's good," Lorna told him. "Traffic's light at the moment and there shouldn't be a long delay." There had barely been time to take this in when Lorna next announced that they had been cleared for take-off.

Throughout the second leg of their long and laborious journey Lorna's attention was mostly concentrated on continuous radio traffic and Charlie contented himself with watching the ground and then early evening lights pass by beneath them. Eventually, and after a further long flight, he spotted much brighter runway lights on the airfield at Srinagar. It still seemed a long time, however, before their landing wheels make contact with the runway.

Exiting the airport coincided with a throng of passengers who had just arrived on a domestic flight from Amritsar and they joined a rush of people scurrying for taxis.

Charlie felt a sense of relief when their cab then joined a queue of other vehicles, all heading into the city. He assumed that there was safety in numbers. Lorna appeared not to notice his preoccupation and the frequent glances he made through the rear view window. Instead she cleared her throat and asked, in the amused tone which he was now becoming used to,

"I presume we are checking in at a hotel? How are you going to register? Do we take adjoining rooms, or would you like me to be your wife for our stay?" Studying his face in the poor light before continuing, Charlie was treated once more to a husky peal of Lorna's laughter.

"I'm not sure but I do believe you are blushing, Charlie Greenwood. I realise that my suggestion is somewhat forward although it isn't as though we haven't done something similar once before. If my memory serves me well, I seem to recall that you were most anxious to get me up to that room of yours at the pub in Birmingham." Yet another bubbling peel of amusement prevented her from continuing until she finally gasped,

"I am sorry, Charlie. I can't help behaving badly. It's been so long since I suggested anything as outrageous or that anything as exciting as this has happened and I'm feeling rather like the young woman you met all those years ago. In fact I thought it might never happen again." Charlie grinned and asked their driver to take them to the Grand Hotel.

"My, that sounds impressive!" Lorna exclaimed.

"I stayed there when I was here last. It's comfortable enough and I have arranged to meet some people there in the morning."

"Ah, so you've taken advantage of the situation and arranged a business meeting!" Lorna again teased.

"Not exactly, although you will just have to wait and see," Charlie countered, and a few minutes later they were pulling up in front of what was, to Charlie, a now familiar building.

"Of course we have your reservation, Mr Greenwood. I am so pleased you risked coming back to us following that last frightful experience. We also hope that Mrs Greenwood will be comfortable throughout her stay." Charlie flinched as Lorna kicked his ankle, unnecessarily so as he had no intention of dissuading the receptionist of her misunderstanding.

As details were being taken from Charlie's passport, Lorna browsed through brochures which were neatly stacked on the reception desk.

"Oh, how lovely! Look at this, Charlie. The hotel rents out houseboats. Could we stay on one, do you think?" Responding, the receptionist told her that there were just the two available and Charlie asked if she had a more detailed description of the facilities on board. Lorna's enthusiasm gathered momentum when they then spent further time studying a very descriptive brochure.

Another pleasant surprise awaited them when a porter had carried their bags up; a comforting fire was waiting for them in their suite of rooms.

"Gosh Charlie, this looks cosy!" Instead of immediately responding to Lorna's obvious delight, Charlie rang room service and asked if it might be possible for them to have dinner brought to their room. Before replacing the telephone back on its cradle, he also requested a magnum of champagne.

Lorna came to him then and placed her arms around his neck. When they kissed, she opened her lips and murmured something unintelligible into his mouth. Charlie's immediate arousal came as more than something of a relief; it had been some time and he was concerned that masculine capability might have deserted him. Before disengaging from their embrace, Lorna whispered seductively in his ear,

"Mmm, same old Charlie Greenwood. I do remember you now, although we shouldn't. The menus and our drinks may arrive. There is a whole night ahead and there isn't a need for us to rush things."

There was some hesitancy as she untangled herself from his grasp and it seemed something of a diversionary ploy when she suggested,

"If it's okay with you, I think I would like to freshen up? We've had a long journey and it will be nice to get out of these travel clothes."

Charlie was in the throes of placing more peat turfs on the fire when both the champagne and menus arrived.

"I will send one of the backhouse boys up to attend to that for you, sir," the wine waiter offered.

"Thank you, but there will be no need. I grew up with open fires and although they were not peat, I feel sure I shall manage." Lorna, emerging from the bathroom as the waiter was leaving remarked,

"I hope that waiter's not able to read your motives as well as I do." Her tone had lost some of its former teasing and was now quite alluring. Charlie also noted with approval that she had changed into a close fitting gown of some sheer quality.

"I think a magnum was rather extravagant, although I am pleased that you ordered it. I feel like being pampered and I really want to savour our first evening together. Can we sit here and enjoy some wine while we choose from those menu cards?" Lorna patted the sofa in front of the fire.

"Three days ago I wouldn't have dreamed anything like this might happen," she murmured, as Charlie kissed her again.

With the arrival of their food they were surprised to find that a bottle of Remy Martin cognac had also been included, with compliments from the management.

"I am not going to get tipsy and spoil things," Lorna told him, with a hand shielding her glass as Charlie was about to pour more brandy.

"My food was delicious and I want the next two weeks to be equally special. At my age there will be few other opportunities and I am determined this is going to be something that I will treasure for a long time." Charlie responded by saying that she shouldn't put herself down by being sensitive over maturity and hoped that their holiday together might be the start of many other good experiences.

"If we put the trays outside we shouldn't be disturbed and I want you now," Lorna murmured unexpectedly. She then moved behind his chair and placed a hand through the open buttons of his shirt. What followed was then a blur of unimagined pleasure and Charlie realised that age and experience was an apt alternative to youth and inexperience.

The ruddy glow from their peat fire bathed Lorna's beautiful body in an aura of enticement, which in turn injected feelings of uncontrollable vigour into Charlie's almost adolescent enthusiasm.

A crescent moon was illuminating their bedroom in pale surreal light when Lorna eventually moved Charlie's slumbering body to a more comfortable position.

Somewhere a song bird of unknown species woke him to a melody of delight and this almost equalled the sheer magic that he had experienced the night before. Peering sleepily out through the open window, Charlie was momentarily disappointed at not being able to catch sight of the tiny creature which had provided such a perfect setting for his awakening. Closing his eyes to concentrate on some of nature's more pleasant music, he briefly wondered if the previous twenty-four hours had been real and not something which he had simply dreamed. Touching warm flesh as he stretched out an arm was a relief and his happiness from the previous evening came flooding back.

"I wish I could wake like this every morning," Lorna murmured, as she turned to face him.

"I hope at the end of this holiday you will still be feeling the same way. I missed you like hell when we parted in Birmingham, and while you were still at Cranfield I toyed with the idea of travelling down a number of times. Perhaps it was weakness on my part, although you had described strong feelings for Rory and your plans for marrying him." Charlie would have continued had Lorna not placed fingers to his lips and then wriggled beneath him.

Breakfast was served in their room and while Lorna appeared to be enjoying a very large helping of kedgeree, Charlie returned to the subject of their relationship. Lorna was about to fork more savoury rice to her mouth when he noticed something which resembled frowning disapproval. Realising that he was now pushing boundaries too far, Charlie quickly decided to be more circumspect.

"I'm sorry. There's no need for you to look alarmed. I am not about to embarrass you by proposing something which you are not ready for. When and if you ever are, I hope I will know."

Lorna responded to this with a kiss which suggested that she was still not in the mood for getting up. Much later while she was pouring coffee, the bedside telephone rang. Struggling to extricate himself from beneath her, Charlie managed to wrest the instrument from its cradle and then heard the now somewhat familiar voice of the hotel receptionist.

"There are three men in reception asking for Sergeant Greenwood. Would that be you, sir?"

"Yes, and I am expecting them. Would you ask if they have had breakfast?" A background of murmuring then indicated that his request was being dealt with. When the receptionist next told him that his visitors had not eaten, Charlie asked if they could be shown to the dining room and to say that he and Mrs Greenwood would join them shortly.

"Come on! We've no time for more coffee. There are three individuals in the dining room that we have to meet." Surprisingly, Lorna did not ask who the visitors were and Charlie approved of the speed with which she dressed and made ready to go down.

Had the three very noticeable individuals seated around a breakfast table been attired in the Gurkha Regiment's number one dress uniform, they could not have looked more impressive.

"Sergeant Greenwood?" with his hand outstretched, the broadest of the three enquired, and Charlie immediately felt strength from the formal greeting that followed.

"It has been a long time since I was addressed by that or any other rank. Please, call me Charlie. And this is Lorna."

"Memsahib, it is a pleasure to meet you." There was no doubting the sincerity of his greeting and as Charlie glanced sideways he noticed that Lorna was also returning a very warm smile.

"Our employer, Mustapha Al Hameed, painted a rather intriguing picture of you, sir. He suggested that although it may have been some years since you served with the colours, we would do well to remember that you are to be relied upon in a crisis. In fact it is the very first time that he has presented a client to us in such a way."

Charlie was aware that his own complexion had changed and Lorna's look was one of renewed interest. There was no time to dwell on this, however, as their visitor continued,

"If I may, I would like to introduce both myself and my colleagues. This is Subedar Major Gane Limbu and Jamadar Kulbir Khapa. My name is Gaje Lama and I was once privileged to hold the rank of Senani. I believe you have been told that most of our clients refer to us as Bing, Bang and Boom. If it's okay with you we are happy for you to do the same? Should you, however, still find some confusion with our identity, we won't mind in the least."

The eyes set in a mahogany face gleamed with amusement and yet, as had been suggested by Charlie's former police chief, there was something about the trio which displayed both strength and personality.

"Please, will you continue with your breakfast, and would you mind if we pull chairs up to join you for coffee? Lorna and I breakfasted earlier, although we would both welcome a further cup."

From the outset it was obvious that all three men enjoyed food; despite this they managed to ask questions about their assignment. When everything was explained Charlie then also asked about their military experience.

"We served with the same unit throughout the Malay campaign and after some easy postings in Europe we were returned to Borneo and Sarawak. For a great deal of our time in service we were fighting communism. It seemed then that the Western governments' greatest preoccupation was concentrated with what they saw as a threat from extreme socialism, although I must confess to sometimes feeling that the dangers were exaggerated. Given time I felt sure, as has been proved, that the harshness of those regimes would moderate. Alas though, we were merely soldiers, mercenaries if you wish, and certainly not in a position to influence things other than by fighting."

The man's rugged appearance was misleading, Charlie decided. It seemed Boom was well-educated and independently minded and his expression glowed with interest when Lorna told him that she often visited Kuching in Sarawak, modestly explaining that she worked for an air freight company. Charlie was impressed by her omission to explain that she was a joint owner of the company and that she regularly piloted one of its planes.

The discussion then returned to the task of ensuring that neither Lorna nor Charlie should fall victim to hostage-taking. Charlie's previous experience in Srinagar was also described.

A concerned look on Lorna's face may have prompted Boom to explain that he and his colleagues had developed the art of being unobtrusive.

"We will want you to enjoy your holiday, although it will be helpful if you are able to provide us with some advance indication of your movements. Other than that, you should relax now and leave security arrangements with us."

Charlie warmed to the three men and judged them to be competent. When he next explained that they would be transferring to a houseboat following breakfast, Boom nodded approvingly.

"It will make our task much easier. We served with a special boat section in Indonesia and discovered that it is extremely difficult to approach a moored craft in open water unnoticed. Our practice is to follow the standard British Army procedure of each man completing two hours on watch and four hours off. That is of course when we are not moving."

Some while later, when their belongings had been transferred, Charlie and Lorna were delighted to find that there was ample space on the houseboat to accommodate the three bodyguards. They were also surprised to learn that catering and cleaning was to be taken care of by a local couple who lived on a smaller houseboat which was tethered alongside.

While having pre-lunch drinks, Lorna chided Charlie for his secrecy and his failure to tell her about the Ghurkhas. She also suggested with some amusement that he had surely done some considerable creeping to have ingratiated himself into their employer's high opinion.

"What shall we do this afternoon?" Lorna asked sleepily, when they had lunched on curried lake fish and the fluffiest pilau rice either had ever tasted. Charlie told her that at some point during their visit he would like to call and see his lawyer James Galbraith. Then, having never discussed his involvement with horses in detail, he was unsure if his next suggestion would meet with Lorna's approval.

"I had also rather hoped to fit in a visit to Ali Baba's livery stable, or would you find that too boring?"

"Not at all! In fact you told me that when you were last here you went trekking and camped out overnight. If one or more of the Gurkha's rides, can we do something similar?"

Thoughts of his grandmother Lizzie crossed Charlie's mind yet again and he knew instantly that there was nothing he would like more. It then occurred to him that he should ask if Lorna rode.

"Not well, and never since school, although I'm sure that I will manage if your friend Ali has a nice quiet horse for me." She then explained that she had no suitable clothes for riding and Charlie told her it wouldn't be a problem if she hadn't any objection to wearing men's jodhpurs. They next consulted Boom and were delighted when told that he and his two companions had ridden mules while serving in the Malay jungles.

Ali Baba was delighted to see Charlie once more and when introduced he greeted Lorna warmly. The three of them then discussed another trekking expedition and Ali suggested he would tack some horses up to establish the competence of Lorna and the three Gurkhas.

It was obvious from the outset that Boom was far from comfortable and Charlie suggested someone should stay behind to mind their belongings and the houseboat.

The sun had still not risen when they arrived at the stables the following morning and Lorna enjoyed the strong smell of hay and horses. She then watched carefully as one of Ali Baba's sons showed her how to put tack on. Under harsh artificial light the process looked complicated, although she was determined to cope and not rely on Charlie.

In addition to supplies, the mules carried feed for the horses, although Ali suggested that they should allow the animals to graze out whenever possible.

Lights in many of the houses were being lit as the small group made its way out through the suburbs of Srinagar, and a new dawn was slowly lighting their path. On reaching the lower edge of the foothills there was sufficient light for Charlie to identify landmarks which he had seen on his earlier excursion with Ali Baba.

Ali had provided them with two hunting rifles, an axe for chopping wood and a compass, in addition to their provisions.

Bing and Bang politely declined the offer of the rifles and then sheepishly produced two Israeli machine pistols which were hidden in the folds of their bulky clothing. Charlie presumed that these weapons had somehow been carried in through border checks when they travelled down from Nepal and wondered how this feat had been accomplished.

There was a plentiful supply of brushwood to light a fire when they stopped mid-morning for a brew up and the coarse grasses appeared suitable fodder for the mules and horses. Much later Lorna and Charlie were both feeling the effects of their long ride and realised that they had spent more than four hours in the saddle following on from their mid-morning break.

Anticipating saddle fatigue, Ali Baba had provided them with some cream, which he assured would relieve soreness. Lorna was surprised, however, when her companion also confessed to feeling some tenderness around his nether regions.

"I am surprised. You look good on that horse, almost a part of him in fact."

"I don't ride as often as I should any more, and when you are out of the saddle for a while it tells. I will certainly be grateful for Ali's salve when we've pitched camp, and I guess the two Gurkhas will also be feeling some stiffness. It's obvious that they are two very fit individuals. Today, however, will have exercised muscles which they never knew they had."

Looking back, Lorna was just able to see Bang bringing up the rear as he passed round a bend in the track which they had earlier decided to follow. Bing, to his credit, was already unloading the two mules prior to turning them out to graze.

The late afternoon sun was disappearing behind a ridge when they finished making camp, and while Lorna busied herself gathering wood for building a fire, Charlie discussed the night's guard roster with the two Gurkhas.

"I wouldn't expect us to be troubled up here, as the country is too rugged and there are probably richer pickings down in the city. All the same, we will do the usual two hours on and four hours off and I will be included in the rota."

Responding to Bang's protest on the question of guard rosters, Charlie pointed out that, with Boom missing, the balance was wrong and he wanted both of them to stay fresh, alert and fit for the next day's trekking.

"Ah, Sergeant, it seems that you have done this before," Bing whispered with a grin. Charlie had a hunting rifle at the ready seconds before the flap of his bivouac was pulled back.

"What time is it?" Charlie asked quietly as he slithered out into the open.

"A few minutes after ten, are you sure you want to stand watch? I can easily do another before waking Bang." To avoid disturbing Lorna, Charlie motioned for the Gurkha to move further away from their tent.

"You go and get your head down; just because I have a few grey hairs it doesn't mean that I am not up for this." Bing nodded with a look of amusement before then moving off in the direction of his bivouac.

With the hunting rifle across his knees and his back resting against a stunted tree, Charlie reflected on times, many years before, when standing guard on some bleak hillside in the middle of the night was a part of his everyday life. He next thought it likely that Bing was unable to sleep as rekindled flames from their fire showed that someone was awake in the camp below.

Dismissing this as understandable given the rocky ground on which they had pitched their tents, his thoughts then turned to his unbelievable good fortune in finding Lorna free and the fact that their relationship might now develop. When a softly-spoken voice startled him, Charlie's immediate reaction was one of annoyance at his lack of vigilance and also for allowing another person to creep up on him.

"I thought this might drive away the chill night air," Lorna quietly suggested, as she squatted beside him with two steaming hot mugs of cocoa and a sleeping bag draped over her shoulders.

"Bloody hell, it's as well you're not one of the Kashmir separatists. Had you been, it's probable that I would now be trussed up like a chicken on a butcher's block and endangered the freedom of both you and our two Gurkhas."

"Oh, come off it, Charlie, you have to be exaggerating. We're surely secure up here away from their normal city patch? Now take this mug, it will help to warm you."

"Um, I don't remember it ever being like this," Charlie told her. Moments before Lorna had suggested that if he moved slightly she could use part of the tree as a back rest and Charlie had put an arm around her as she draped the open sleeping bag over them.

"When were you involved with this sort of thing?" Lorna asked, after cursing because she had burnt her lip on the scalding hot rim of a mug. Charlie told her it had been before they met and that he had been in Cyprus completing national service.

"Is that where you met this man, Mustapha Al Hameed?" Charlie explained by sheer chance that the senior police officer had discovered he spoke passable Greek and that he had then been seconded from an army infantry unit to a special branch of the Cypriot police force.

"A separatist movement, rather like the one here, called itself Eoka and had as its aim enosis, or if you wish, complete union with mainland Greece. It also wanted to rid the island of its Turkish community, which incidentally had been living alongside the Greeks for many hundreds of years."

Charlie next suggested that further historical detail would be boring and that by living in Sri Lanka, Lorna was unlikely to have read anything of the Cyprus troubles.

"No, it's not boring, and if we are going to be close it will be nice to learn something of your past. How come you speak Greek? Has your family some Greek connections?" Encouraged by Lorna's intimation of future closeness, Charlie explained that his Greek was learned by going to a Greek Cypriot café in the small Suffolk town where he had attended school.

"At the end of a normal school day I would regularly take my homework into the café, before stopping off at stables to do further work and then cycling on home. The grandparents who brought me up had travelled a great deal as my grandfather was a soldier, and they often used foreign phrases which they had picked up in both India and other countries. Because of that, I developed an interest in languages and was studying classical Greek for A level examinations at school. My friend the café owner and his wife were usually quiet in the afternoons and took a strong helping hand with my studies. My spoken Greek was certainly not classical and in fact may also have been difficult for mainland Greeks to understand."

"So how did Mustapha Al Hameed discover that you spoke Greek?"

"I was present at the interrogation of two terrorist captives, standing guard in fact. The interrogating officer was British, with a Greek interpreter. From listening in, I quickly realised that the interpreter was not only distorting answers given by the captives, he was also prompting the two men and was an obvious sympathiser. Unfortunately for him, he believed he was able to converse secure in the fact that the interrogating officer had no understanding of his language. I decided to bide my time and not enlighten the officer until the interrogation was over. Some hours later I was driven into Nicosia and found myself also being interrogated. This time it was by a high-ranking police officer who turned out to be Mustapha. Although of Turkish origin Mustapha also spoke Greek fluently and my interrogation was conducted in that language. I was told at the conclusion of the meeting that I was to be transferred from the army to a special branch of the Cypriot police force and given the immediate rank of sergeant. I was given no choice in the matter and even my demobilisation from military service was later deferred by Al Hameed who pulled strings at senior level. The man threatened me with all kinds of retribution in an attempt to persuade me that I should remain as part of his team. My only let out came through threatening to involve our local Member of Parliament back home, and eventually I was released."

"And this was all before we met in Birmingham?"

"Yes. I had decided to put conscription behind me before going on to university. I suppose because I'd no wish to eventually complete military service with men who would be so much younger than I was."

"What a coincidence. Rory spent his entire adult life combating terrorism and now I learn that you have also had a hand in something similar."

Lorna would have liked to ask more, although Charlie was finding the warm closeness of her a major distraction.

"No Charlie, not now. You are supposed to be keeping watch. There will be plenty of time when you have completed your guard duty and we are back at the tent. Now tell me some more about Cyprus. It might help to distract you."

Charlie was about to recall some lighter moments from those earlier days when movement close to the camp below held his attention. Swiftly brushing aside the sleeping bag and working the bolt action of the hunting rifle he threw himself forward onto his stomach in an offensive stance. Taken by surprise, Lorna suggested that he should stop fooling around and mind not to spill his cocoa.

"There is someone approaching the camp from our left flank. Keep your voice down," he quietly told her. Something in Charlie's tone indicated that he was very serious and Lorna craned her neck to see what it was that had so alarmed him.

"Where? I can't see a thing." Charlie pointed to an area which certainly appeared darker than its surroundings.

"My God, he is getting awfully close to the tents, should we call down to warn the two Gurkhas, do you think?"

"No, let's give him a little longer. If it is a separatist he won't be alone and I would like to know where the others are. Kidnapping for ransom is their main aim and so I don't think Bing and Bang's safety is immediately threatened. The kidnappers are probably assuming that we are all snug in our bedrolls and that their task is going to be made easy. At some point other separatists in the party will show and from this position we will have the perfect drop on them. This small bore rifle is not the ideal weapon, although it should be capable of winging one or two and causing confusion amongst them. Hopefully then our two Gurkha friends will have been alerted and they can use their machine pistols to good effect."

Lorna's reaction to this was to say that she wished she had the other rifle and then without warning the camp fire imploded in on itself. With reinvigorated flames to illuminate the area, Charlie grunted with an expression of amusement.

"It's okay, Lorna, there will be no fighting for you tonight and there's no need for alarm. It's one of the hobbled mules moving closer in search of sweeter grass." Despite the casualness of his explanation, it was obvious Charlie was relieved that the incident had not been anything more serious.

"I am pleased that the fire flared up when it did, but for that we would probably now be faced with the expense of providing Ali Baba with a replacement mule. On reflection, it would also have caused some high amusement amongst the three Gurkhas."

There was now no doubt in Lorna's mind that had the mule moved closer, Charlie would have shot it.

"So, still the soldier boy? I am surprised. Your life since those days has surely changed a great deal?"

In an attempt to divert attention from himself, Charlie then told her he was aware that she had also been involved with a life-threatening experience while she and Kuli had been protecting an aircraft at Koggala from interference by Tamil Tigers.

Surprised that he would know of the incident, there was then no opportunity for Lorna to respond, as Bang's arrival to relieve Charlie coincided.

Had their provisions lasted, they may have stayed longer in the foothills. For Charlie it was once more a wonderful experience as he had been allowed further insight into the life that his grandmother had probably experienced while travelling the region.

Both he and Lorna had marvelled at the sight of majestic peaks which often seemed about to engulf them and together they had discovered a mutual interest in wildlife. Apart from watching numerous kites and other birds of prey, the couple were delighted when catching sight of a rare breed of wild sheep which were grazing precariously on a cliff overhang at least two hundred feet above them.

"I have had a truly marvellous holiday, Charlie. The last few days have been wonderful and I am ashamed to confess that going back to Koggala and work leaves me feeling sad. I realise that I will have to snap out of it though, as all good things eventually end." Moments earlier they had caught a glimpse of Srinagar in the distance.

When Charlie responded by saying that he hoped their all too brief time together would be the start of something which could be built upon, Lorna's expression suggested that he might not be disappointed.

Night was closing in fast as they made their way from the stables and Charlie hoped that the two Gurkhas were somewhere close by.

"I should make a telephone call. Would you mind if we stopped off at the hotel, darling? I promised Sidi that I would check in to make sure everything is okay back at base."

"Sure thing. I will wait for the Gurkhas to catch up and explain what's happening. I will also order drinks and see you in the bar when you have finished your call. Maybe I should also check in with head office, although like you, I have no enthusiasm for a return to normal life at present."

Charlie's concern that making telephone calls might intrude and spoil their last few days together had quickly dissolved with the realisation that Lorna had called him darling. He thought it unlikely that she would ever use that term of endearment lightly.

# Chapter Twenty

While immersed in work, the days of waiting for her appointment had passed quickly. Now, feeling a little like a tour guide while showing Molly the sights of Hanoi, Kate was pleasantly surprised by her companion's apparent awe when visiting Ho Chi Min's mausoleum and the many other monuments erected to commemorate the northern people's victory over America and the south. Arriving early in the capital had offered them the opportunity of seeing and doing things which Molly had previously never experienced.

On the evening prior to Kate's crucial meeting with the admiral, the two young women ate in a nearby restaurant and, when sightseeing fatigue dictated, they retired early.

Surprised the following morning by not being shown to the admiral's now familiar office, Kate instead discovered that she was to attend a meeting in a large conference room, where a number of other unknown people were already waiting. This unexpected occurrence had the effect of adding additional concern to her already nervous state.

As though anticipating Kate's disquiet, a small man in a light grey uniform suit rose to greet her.

"Miss Savage. Please will you take a seat and make yourself comfortable." The small man indicated a solitary chair on one side of a long confrence table behind which two women and three other men sat. With the late arrival of Admiral Tanaka Kate was, however, instantly reassured by the warmth from that man's smile.

"Miss Savage, my name is Le Long and I am privileged to hold the post of minister for tourism."

After first introducing himself, Kate's welcoming official next proceeded to introduce the government's deputy finance minister and an official from the Hanoi Bank. He also indicated those people who were seated to his right before continuing,

"Madam Zuc Zen and Comrade Ding are government advisors in the field of international banking and maritime law respectively. Admiral Tanaka is, of course, well known to you."

Assuming that the formalities of introduction had been dealt with, Kate rose and stood nervously, before bowing first to her left and then to her right.

"Honourable ministers, ladies and gentlemen, thank you for receiving me this morning. I would first like to ask for your tolerance in my having a very poor understanding of your language. This is despite the considerable time that I have now spent in Vietnam. I also confess to finding many Vietnamese words and place names difficult to remember. If my responses to your questions are therefore not as immediate or as clear as they should be, I would also ask for your further patience and understanding."

There was barely time for Kate to regain her seat when questions were directed at her in a constant flow. From the outset it seemed obvious that the group confronting her were already assuming that the Mekong Express Company would be unable to reject an offer of operating a ferry service from Ho Chi Min City to Chau Doc.

With some very obvious attention to detail, timetables were discussed and fare structures queried. The craft which would be used also appeared to be of importance to Kate's inquisitors.

Improvising despite considerable nervousness, Kate suggested that they would run a twice daily service in both directions and that this would be extended as and when passenger numbers increased. She told them that fares for the complete journey would initially be priced at 269,000 dong with reduced increments applying to the variable shorter stages. Kate added that the fare structure would be similar to that which was used on their current service between Vung Tau and Da Nang.

The assembled group also appeared to show some real enthusiasm when Kate suggested that, if awarded the contract, her company would create new pick-up points at Tra Vinh, Vinh Long and Long Xuyen. Fortunately there was insufficient time for her to consider the implications that these improvised undertakings might create.

As the dialogue continued Kate came to realise that the delay in setting up this meeting had been invaluable. It had in fact given an opportunity to familiarise herself with the proposed new route.

When at some juncture in the proceedings she received a nod of approval from Minister Le Long, Kate realised that the time and cost of travelling the route on both the existing service and completing an independent survey in a company craft with Captain Wang had been invaluable.

"We will almost certainly be using the Meteor Class hydrofoil as it is a well-proven vessel and our aim will be to standardise where possible."

This piece of information was offered in an attempt to stall for time and to also gather her thoughts for the more difficult questions which she thought were still to be asked. Glossy brochures depicting the type of hydrofoil referred to were also passed around, although from the brief scrutiny that these received it seemed probable that the recipients were familiar with the vessel in question.

Kate might also have added that if they were awarded the contract, the company would in all probability replace the older Meteors with larger craft on their existing coastal service and reschedule the number of daily sailings on that route. She was not given an opportunity to elaborate, however, as Admiral Tanaka caught her eye, and his barely discernible negative head shake suggested that further elaboration was unnecessary. Kate also hoped this indicated that her many unasked queries were still to be dealt with.

When the meeting eventually wound up she was complimented on her performance by both the admiral and the minister for tourism, who had remained seated as the other assembled members gathered up their paperwork before leaving the conference room.

"Please accept my apologies, Miss Savage. I rather fear that you were put on the spot this morning and I confess to being the source for your discomfort. When I learned of your meeting with my good friend, Admiral Tanaka, I realised that the opportunity of bringing other people on board was too good to miss. The admiral assured me that we could rely on you to respond in a manner which would satisfy our colleagues and without doubt you have this morning given a very good and polished account of your company's capabilities. Personally I am impressed and I do assure that you will have the full backing of my department."

As the minister next rose from his chair, Kate assumed their meeting to have been concluded and was further surprised by the small man's parting remark.

"I shall leave you now in the admiral's capable hands. There will be many questions which you still have for him and I will stand by whatever is eventually agreed. Good day to you, Miss Savage. We will, I hope, meet again soon."

On regaining access to Admiral Tanaka's office, Kate's many questions were in fact quickly and efficiently dealt with. The admiral stressed his government's flexibility with regard to start-up dates and said that he and his colleagues would ensure a smooth running takeover from the existing operator. He also suggested that he understood the complexities and problems of both equipping and staffing such a project.

Eventually, it seemed to be by way of a conclusion when the admiral finally handed Kate a pre-prepared list of the people who had attended the earlier meeting, together with their contact telephone numbers and a list of banking officials with whom she should liaise in Ho Chi Min City.

When satisfied that she had covered everything of importance, Kate then asked if the admiral would join her for lunch. She was not unduly disappointed when he declined as she thought it offered further opportunity to reflect on the outcome of that morning's meeting.

Chimes from a clock somewhere high up on one of the many impressive buildings indicated that it was two fifteen in the afternoon when Kate was delivered back to their hotel. Finding that Molly was already waiting in the lounge was also gratifying and Kate quickly explained that while passing through reception she had arranged for a taxi to take them out to the fuel supplier's storage depot.

Before setting out on the next stage of their scheduled journey Kate attempted telephoning Ruby at the Ho Chi Min office and was slightly irritated to be told that Miss Ruby appeared to be involved with a lengthy incoming international call. Realising that this might take time, time which they could ill afford, she left a message for her aunt saying that the meeting had gone very well and that she would be telephoning later with more detail.

The fuel storage depot was surprisingly large, particularly so as Kate had expected to find no more than two large holding tanks; instead there were numerous rows of containers holding unimaginable quantities of fuel oil and other substances.

Molly asked their taxi driver to wait and the two women then set off through a maze of pipe work and metal containers in search of the offices. When the entrance was eventually found a receptionist showed them through to the commercial director's somewhat unimpressively small office.

On hearing her name mentioned Kate assumed that Molly was going through the formality of making an introduction and once those pleasantries had been exchanged, Kate asked questions while Molly interpreted.

There was a moment of silence when the commercial director appeared at first thoughtful and it was some seconds before he responded.

"The honourable director is surprised by your question. He agrees that the metering systems on their tankers could be rigged although he thinks this is unlikely as they are the largest supplier of fuel oil into the port of Hai Phong. The director is also emphatic that their long-standing reputation would be destroyed if such an occurrence ever came to light."

Following this, a staccato-sounding discourse was next added for Molly to translate.

"The honourable gentleman would also like me to explain that the company's delivery drivers have, without exception, been employed for a very long time and are unlikely to attempt any kind of theft. If, however, there just so happened to be one amongst them who was so inclined, the likelihood of his making deliveries to our company on a regular basis would be most unlikely." Something was added by the commercial director and when Molly had absorbed this, she continued,

"They also have a simple system in place for random checks on the tankers' metering systems. The director suggests that when we have taken tea, he will demonstrate how this works."

When satisfied that the check system was adequate and that it was used regularly there seemed little point in prolonging their investigation and a return to the offices for more refreshment was suggested. In responding, Kate asked Molly to decline and to express her gratitude for the commercial director's valuable time and also to apologise for any inconvenience which their visit may have caused. The quietly-spoken man assured them that it had been no trouble and hoped that his company would be able to continue serving them for the foreseeable future.

"Although it's late I would now like to carry on out to our jetty, please, Molly. Will you ask the driver if he is happy to extend the journey?"

Kate realised, however, that there was still considerable distance to travel and that it would be dark before they reached the port of Hai Phong.

"Do you think the driver might stop for some refreshment when we next spot a roadside food vendor?" Kate eventually asked. "I'm ravenously hungry. It's probably because I missed lunch," she added.

Their driver, in fact, appeared as much in need of sustenance as at least one of his passengers. Stir-fried shrimp and noodles in cardboard containers were mouth-wateringly delicious and while the three ate in the car at the side of the road, Kate enlightened Molly with something of the reason for her meeting that morning. She did not over-elaborate other than to say that she hoped their workload would increase and if that was the case it would entail employing additional staff.

It seemed very obvious that the prospect of more work and further responsibility was greeted with enthusiasm by her companion and Kate was once more reminded of Ruby's early observation that Molly was an obvious candidate for further promotion. With this in mind, on resuming their journey Kate made a concerted effort to learn all she could about the young Vietnamese woman and they chatted amiably until reaching their destination.

"Will you ask our driver if he can switch his lights off, please, Molly?" They had driven in through the dock entrance gates moments before.

"I would rather that we did not announce our arrival to any company employees who may still be working on the jetty," Kate added.

As the two women alighted from the cab and moved off along the wharf, Kate felt secure in the knowledge that their driver would content himself by reading a local newspaper and wait for them.

Seeing little or no sign of activity, Molly glanced at her watch before suggesting that she thought they were unlikely to achieve anything by being there.

"The southbound sailing should have left at five thirty this morning and there is not another service due in until nine thirty tomorrow. My guess is that everyone will have gone home and that is why the place seems deserted."

This observation was, however, almost instantly disproved when they saw lights in the office complex and the silhouette of a person moving around.

"Would you expect someone to still be working when the staff all appear to have left for the day?" Kate asked.

"Maybe it's one of the cashiers attempting to balance ticket receipts against takings. There isn't a ticket office at Nha Trang and one of the stewards has to issue tickets and take fares from passengers boarding there. Sometimes the fare money gets mixed in with takings from the buffet bar." Kate was considering this possible explanation when Molly unexpectedly grasped her arm.

"I thought there was something missing, although I couldn't immediately place what it was. The standby craft is not on its moorings and if you listen carefully you will hear a sound which I feel sure is the exhaust note from one of our hydrofoils."

Kate prided herself on having good hearing, although she could now hear nothing other than wavelets lapping against the jetty wall. She was on the point of telling Molly she was imagining things and that the spare Dolphin was probably round at the ship repairers having some minor defect rectified, when she also heard the now very familiar sound.

"It must be a long way out. It's a clear evening with little other noise to distract, although I heard it for no more than a second. What do you think? Is it coming or going?" Molly shrugged and said she was unsure.

"I think we should now hang around and wait to see what happens."

An area of stacked containers provided what seemed like a good place to conceal the two young women and when satisfied that it would be difficult for them to be seen from the quayside, Kate asked.

"Will you go back to our driver and ask if he will wait on a little longer. Give him this money on account and tell him that there will be a worthwhile gratuity when we get back to the hotel. Try keeping to the shadows if you can. I would rather we were not seen by whoever it is in the office as I don't want them having an opportunity of warning the Dolphin out there of our presence."

It occurred to Kate as Molly moved away that she was acting in a somewhat reckless manner. If there was something happening which she was not supposed to know of, they were simply two defenceless women who had no right to be groping around in a dark and deserted port. Kate also thought that perhaps she was making too much of the incident and that she should simply walk across to the office and find out what was actually happening. Standing alone in shadow behind rows of cargo containers, she now felt very vulnerable and was relieved when Molly finally reappeared.

"Unless I'm mistaken that exhaust note is getting louder and probably indicates that it's heading this way. I also now feel sure that it is our reserve hydrofoil."

Concealed behind a stacked row of towering containers the two women waited for what seemed like an eternity and as the minutes ticked by the sound of the approaching craft became increasingly louder.

It seemed that the deserted port, together with darkness and the suspense from waiting, was also causing both their imaginations to run riot and when Molly noticeably shivered, Kate instinctively put an arm around her.

White curling waves pushing away from a semi-submerged hull was the first indication that a Flying Dolphin was entering the harbour. Both women watched with some trepidation as the craft then manoeuvred alongside. When the outrigger platform was less than a metre from the quayside, two figures leapt from it and scurried to secure bow and stern lines.

Both engines were still idling as two more figures followed ashore and then the four men rode off on two motorcycles which they had collected from the cycle shed. When the engines were finally cut and the cabin lights extinguished, a further figure stepped down onto the quay. As this individual strode off in the direction of the offices, Molly quietly exclaimed,

"Captain Jung! What on earth is he doing here? The woman he lives with telephoned in three days ago to say that he was reporting sick and was going to be off work once more." Kate said she was not aware that Tommy Jung had been ill and Molly quickly outlined what little she knew.

"The doctor's original sick note described a suspected duodenal ulcer. I spoke to his girlfriend when it was delivered and she hinted that it might be something more serious. Because of that, I have not pestered her on the few other occasions that Tommy has been off. Perhaps one of the other skippers has also reported sick and he has struggled in to fill the gap."

"I don't think so," Kate whispered. "It's unlikely that he would be brought in simply to move the standby craft for whatever reason. Something is going on, Molly. I don't yet know what, although when we have the answer, I rather think Gongy's concern over fuel imbalances may be explained."

Watching as the youthful looking captain strode off across the dockyard, Kate thought there seemed little wrong with him. When his stride suddenly faltered she then wondered if she was judging him too harshly. Those doubts disappeared when he turned and quickly retraced his footsteps at an increased tempo. Both women watched with renewed interest as Tommy Jung climbed back onto the outrigger platform and then disappeared inside the hydrofoil.

When Tommy reappeared the cabin lights were once more extinguished and the two hidden women could clearly see that he was clutching a small, barely-concealed white parcel.

With a great deal of uncertainty they then waited for some time until the sound of a vehicle eventually faded in the distance and Kate moved slowly out from behind the containers.

"Come on, Molly. I would think it's all clear now. We'll go up to the office and see if we can find out what is going on."

The office manager's startled expression turned to one of alarm when recognition slowly dawned on him.

"Mr Nygen! Working at this late hour is very commendable. May I ask what it is that keeps you from your family?" Although Molly rapidly translated, Kate was aware from previous discussions that the man had a very good grasp of English. His eventual reply in a mixture of Vietnamese, however, resulted in incoherent babbling.

"I hope you will quickly realise, Mr Nygen, that I am not about to give you the opportunity of insulting my intelligence. And neither am I going to wait around while you concoct some fanciful story. I would like to know what on earth Captain Jung and his crew have been up to with the standby craft which came alongside barely twenty minutes ago."

An expression of either fear or guilt came over the man's face and, but for Molly's quick response, it is possible that the erstwhile trusted manager would then have made it out through the still open office door.

"That was rather foolish, Mr Nygen. Now unless I'm satisfied with your next response and believe you are telling the truth, I intend picking up that telephone and calling Admiral Tanaka. Unfortunately I do not know anyone in the local police, although I feel sure that the admiral's influence will quickly bring someone down to extract the truth from you."

It seemed obvious that Nygen had heard of the admiral and also that he believed Kate's threat to be real, although he then appeared to lose control and some form of trembling fear caused his hands to shake violently. This unexpected reaction reminded Kate of stories which she had been told of local police methods for extracting information.

"They will kill me if I tell you what has been happening, Miss Kate." There was now no doubting fear in the man's voice and although shocked by it, Kate was not about to weaken.

"It is painfully obvious that something underhand has been happening, Mr Nygen, and you can choose between the police taking you away to the station and forcefully extracting the information from you, or you can now tell me everything here in the quiet seclusion of your own office."

Seeing first hesitation and then something resembling renewed resistance in the manager's face, Kate picked up the telephone and began dialling. She had quickly concluded that if she was going to extract the truth from her northern office manager, she would have to play on the man's fear of police methods.

Had Nygen been less fearful and more observant he would have realised that Kate had no knowledge of area codes and it should have seemed unlikely that she would have memorised the admiral's telephone numbers.

"All right, all right, I'll tell you," the office manager gasped. "First though I want your assurance that you will protect me from Captain Jung and his people."

Despite believing that she should make no such concession, Kate nodded agreement while crossing her fingers behind her back to excuse the false commitment.

"Captain Jung has been using the standby craft to transport people over to the island of Hainan."

For some seconds Kate speculated as to the location of Hainan until remembering from an earlier study of regional charts that it is a large island in the Gulf of Tongking and also that it belongs to the People's Republic of China. Somewhat taken aback by both the revelation and the location, Kate asked,

"What people are you talking about and who on earth would want to go to Hainan on unauthorised transport?" Despite asking these questions, suspicions were already forming in Kate's mind.

"Refugees, people who hope they are travelling to a better world."

When Kate asked where the refugees were from, the badly-shaken man shrugged, before telling her he thought that most would be from Myanmar, although Laos and Cambodia were also strong possibilities.

A glance in Molly's direction indicated that the young Vietnamese woman was equally puzzled by this revelation.

With a brief break to his interrogation it appeared that the slightly-built manager was regaining some composure and without prompting he now offered further explanation.

"You will probably remember that there were many of my fellow countrymen, particularly those from the south, who attempted to escape by boat in the years following repatriation. That was, of course, when our army's magnificent effort had succeeded and the Americans fled in disarray. Mostly those people were unsuccessful and either drowned or ended up in Hong Kong where the British authorities eventually returned them to this country."

A noise from outside caused him to hesitate and after pausing to peer through the window he shrugged and then continued.

"Happily things here are now much improved and our people generally no longer wish to leave. It is, however, not so in many of our neighbouring countries. Those people who are able to raise money for an illegal passage will still risk everything by taking that route."

Trying to envisage the complexity of such an operation prompted Kate to ask how refugees from the countries that Nygen had suggested might be transported the considerable distance from border crossings to Hai Phong.

"They arrive by road in covered trucks. I imagine remote land crossings where there are no checks will be used. Our glorious Vietcong knew of many such trails leading into neighbouring countries and will probably have passed this information on, or there is a possibility that some ex-Vietcong are directly involved with the people smuggling operation."

The office manager's speculation was then abruptly interrupted when his office door crashed open and a bewildered-looking taxi driver was thrust violently into the room by Tommy Jung.

"So, boss! You had to come up here snooping and this fool has spilled the beans." The youthful sea captain gestured toward Nygen with a handgun which had hitherto been pressed into their taxi drivers' neck.

Realising that the situation was now rapidly deteriorating and becoming something which might endanger their lives, Kate's concern increased when she clearly saw that there were also three crew members in the corridor behind their captain. Each of these men was brandishing a firearm together with grim expressions on their normally impassive features.

With her troubled thoughts quickly changing to a sensation of creeping fear, Kate wondered how she might extricate them from what she now realised was a very dangerous situation. Desperately trying to figure out what might happen next, Kate was also aware that they could expect no help from outside as the dock was deserted.

Glancing across it seemed obvious that both Molly and the office manager were equally alarmed, none more so than Nygen. Kate was given no further time to speculate, however, as Tommy Jung continued,

"It was lucky that I spotted your taxi when driving out from the port. Alas, though, I had to disturb your driver's precious sleep. When with some persuasion he described his passengers, I quickly decided that you were unlikely to be paying a routine visit out of hours and thought you might be on to me. Realising that I would need help if that was the case, I locked your driver in the trunk of his vehicle and went off to find my crew. Fortunately their habits are predictable and the bar that they regularly use is no great distance from here."

It was impossible to discern next whether Tommy's long pause was to allow either his crew or him time to consider their predicament.

"I suppose I should shoot all of you," he eventually announced, with no greater emotion than would have been the case had he suggested that he was thinking of taking them on a picnic.

"Fortunately for you I have so far not resorted to murder. I also think that if I took that option and your bodies were discovered the crime might be traced back to me. My life here in Vietnam has been more pleasant than anything that has gone before and at the moment I have no wish to leave this country prematurely."

Nonchalantly pushing a captain's cap to the back of his head with the point of the revolver, Tommy then appeared troubled by the problem and deep frowns creased his oriental features. Some further seconds ticked by until the hydrofoil skipper appeared to reach a decision.

"Despite this dilemma we will certainly have to do something with you. There are plans to ship one more group across before the current transport method is changed and my contacts on the other side will be most displeased if they are told that these arrangements cannot go ahead. In fact even as I speak there will be small groups assembling before heading to the various rendezvous points and in all probability arrangements for the next shipment are now past the point of either change or recall."

There was something totally matter of fact in Tommy Jung's manner which Kate found altogether unacceptable, and his callous attitude aroused one of her rare moments of anger.

"Do you not realise the seriousness of what you are mixed up in, Captain Jung? You talk glibly of shooting us and yet you suggest that you would like to remain here in Vietnam. Surely you can see that the truth of what has been happening will eventually come out and when it does, you and your crew are likely to go to prison for a very long time."

Kate's attempt at reasoning, albeit in an agitated manner, was not at all how she really felt. Realisation that Tommy Jung and his men were likely to do whatever was necessary to keep their criminal activities from the attention of the authorities was an altogether alarming thought.

The young Chinese ferry captain appeared to ignore Kate's angry outburst, until eventually responding after a further spell of silent thought,

"My crew are not going to be happy as they had settled for the night. Despite inconveniencing them, I have decided that we will make another trip across and hope that the absence of the standby craft will go unnoticed when the routine service docks tomorrow morning."

Tommy's next words, spoken in some Chinese dialect, sounded like a command and in response to this a newly arrived crew member stepped into the room and fastened both Kate's and Molly's wrists behind their backs with lengths of electrical wiring, which had obviously come from the engine room of the docked hydrofoil for just that purpose.

"There is no need to take me, Captain Jung," the office manager pleaded, as his wrists were also roughly pinioned behind him.

"You, my friend, have already demonstrated a willingness to talk. Your version of the operation was most enlightening. Listening to you from outside that door one might be forgiven for believing that you had previously travelled the entire route with the refugees. If left behind you will sing like a canary when our friends here are reported missing. I also think that you might find the next leg of the refugees' journey rather enlightening."

Chuckling at his own mean-minded attempt at injecting further terror into the office manager's mind, Tommy then issued an order which neither Molly nor the office manager appeared to understand.

Having been roughly manhandled along the quay the four captives were next bundled into the saloon compartment of the standby hydrofoil and then left to ponder their dilemma.

The hydrofoil had exited the harbour and they were beginning to experience movement from open sea when Kate realised that she was suffering from the effects of a raging thirst. Initially she attributed this to the shrimps and noodles which she had eaten earlier, although she also understood that fear and her current concern might be a contributing factor. Whatever the cause, she realised that she was now desperately in need of fluids.

Molly watched on hopelessly as first access to the pantry was gained with some difficulty and then the near impossible task of Kate attempting to remove the top from a bottle.

"Here let me hold it for you, it will be much easier with two pairs of hands." Standing back to back, Kate then decided that breaking free from their wrist restraints was more important than her thirst.

"Let me see if I can untie the flex from around your wrists. Drinking with my hands free will also then be made that much easier."

Freeing Molly was not as difficult as Kate had supposed; the flex was simply twisted into a plat and unravelling it was easily dealt with.

Freed from their bonds they were then also able to steady themselves against the constant movement of the vessel and immediately set about freeing both their driver and the office manager.

On discovering that the waist door exits had been secured from outside, Molly next tried the stout aft door and was frustrated to find that it was also securely locked. Kate sympathetically remarked that it would not have helped had they gained access to the small stern deck, as while the craft was travelling under full power any attempt at going overboard would have been suicidal.

With a shrug of resignation, Molly next decided to light the galley stove so that she might make some hot drinks.

Finding a half bottle of cognac in the gimballed spirits rack, Kate laced her coffee with a good measure of the warming spirit and some of her natural courage gradually returned. She then thought it might help if they knew what to expect when they arrived at Hainan. Nygen, the office manager, was unable to throw any light on this, although it seemed obvious that they would remain captive until at least the last shipment of refugees had been transported across.

The office manager, who appeared almost paralysed by fear, said very little when the subject of escape was discussed and as the elderly taxi driver understood no English, it was left to the two young women to talk things through.

An early dawn light revealed a choppy sea and they were soon able to make out white waves crashing against the rocks of a rugged shoreline.

Armed with a heavy champagne type bottle which she had found in the galley waste bin, Kate hoped that she might disarm at least one of their captors when they were sent for. Molly had agreed that if they were able to overcome a crew member and take his weapon, they might then be able to remain in the saloon and create a situation of standoff stalemate.

As the hydrofoil slowed and came off its foils there was the clear view of a well-developed port area and next the sound of scrabbling feet on the coach roof indicated that they were about to dock.

Unfortunately for the two young women and their male companions, their earlier resistance plan was thwarted when the waist door opened and Captain Jung's voice simply ordered them out. Kate briefly considered ignoring this instruction until realising that, without a weapon, there was nothing to prevent their captors from entering the saloon en masse and forcibly ejecting them.

# Chapter Twenty One

A small minibus was waiting for them as they stepped ashore and on entering the vehicle it quickly became apparent that two of the armed crew would be travelling with them.

Kate followed their vehicle's progress with interest as they travelled through avenues of stacked timber and many other items of dry goods. Also evident was a series of aggregate processing plants which gave the impression that large quantities of sea-dredged materials were also processed in what appeared to be a very busy port.

If an opportunity to escape occurred, Kate thought some knowledge of their surroundings might be useful and she was intent on absorbing as much of the area as their dusty journey permitted.

When their driver braked sharply and his vehicle veered across the road before coming to a standstill, Kate was unprepared and was thrown headfirst onto the forward bulkhead. On collecting her thoughts in a somewhat dazed manner she next realised that a voice was being raised in anger and when her head cleared she saw that they had all but collided with a very large green bulldozer.

It seemed obvious that the raised and agitated voice belonged to their mini coach driver and that he was verbally haranguing the machine operator. This appeared to have little or no effect as the man on the machine simply gazed down from his lofty perch with what appeared to be unconcerned contempt. Momentarily Kate thought that this standoff might create an opportunity for them to escape, as their escorting crew members were following the verbal exchange with obvious amusement. Then all too quickly Kate's hopes were dashed when the large machine moved into reverse and out of their path.

On exiting the port Kate noticed that there was a security office with the usual weighted barrier pointing skyward; she also observed the fact that the security post appeared to be unmanned.

The town that they then passed through was unremarkable in appearance with just two temples standing on either side of the road; both were adorned with ornately scrolled serpents which appeared to be guarding almost identical entrances. Kate thought it strange that the two places of worship should be in such close proximity although she realised that oriental religions had not previously been of great interest.

Their vehicle next passed through an area of market stalls which were in the process of being provisioned by traders and there was also evidence of a few early morning shoppers examining the produce. This scene was all too familiar and was in fact one which was replicated throughout the numerous other South East Asian towns and cities which she had previously travelled through.

It then seemed to take only a short time before the suburban surroundings gave way to a rural landscape, and in other circumstances Kate might have enjoyed the scene which unfolded as they sped along a well-paved road.

Rice appeared to be the main crop in the fields and groups of women wearing coolie hats were wading ankle deep through muddy waters while clutching bundles of fresh green rice plants.

They passed a team of water buffalo pulling a wooden plough and the countryside then changed to tidal marshland. Some time of driving through this changed terrain had lapsed before they turned onto a gravel track; their vehicle then lurched over potholes with clouds of dust billowing in its wake.

While still intent on absorbing as much as possible of the surrounding countryside, Kate eventually focused on a cluster of incongruous looking buildings which appeared ahead through the shimmering heat haze. These buildings and their location seemed out of place in what appeared to be at best water saturated marshland and certainly unsuitable for agriculture. Kate at first thought that the complex might be a facility for collecting sea salt. Seconds later, however, some intuition told her that the compound was in fact their destination and she was not surprised when they swung into it through high wide open gates.

A woman wearing a yellow sash, who was unfortunate to have very coarse Chinese features, came to meet them as they climbed from the transport and this individual beckoned that Kate and the others should follow.

Their short walk took them past two out of character buildings from which the distinct sounds of dripping water came. Still intent on learning whatever she could from the locality, Kate speculated on the possibility of the buildings containing some form of refrigeration or freezer installation.

On being ushered into a large modern complex, which was very obviously a medical centre, they were confronted by two people, one male, and the other female. Both these individuals were wearing white housecoats and each had stethoscope's dangling from their necks. Behind this pair stood a man whose very presence suggested that he was someone of authority; he was also unusually tall for a person bearing obvious Asian features.

"My name is General Zin Bax," he announced without preamble.

"Captain Jung has explained his reason for bringing you here and I have told him in no uncertain terms that in his place I would have shot you and spared myself the unnecessary journey. His failure to deal with the situation, however, has placed me in the position of having to decide what is to be done with you."

Kate immediately decided that the man's verbal demonstration of arrogance and cruelty portrayed a dangerous and ruthless character; there was also no doubt in her mind that he was more than capable of killing another human being.

"Please don't think that you are going to intimidate us with your brutal talk, General whatever your name is. You might now be holding all the cards, although I do assure that when we are repatriated I will bring a whole heap of trouble down on you and this establishment."

With a glower of contempt, General Bax briefly studied her.

"Miss Savage, your presence here is an inconvenience and I think you do not fully appreciate the situation that you have placed yourself and your friends in. If you all cooperate you will be processed through our standard procedures. If you or any of your companions fails to cooperate, I will have you personally shot through the palm of your hand."

Kate realised the pause which followed was to allow time for all of them to understand the sincerity of this threat and she sensed from the others that it was having the desired effect.

"It will make little difference to me if your time here is spent in pain," the general continued.

"I am told that a bullet passing through one's hand is excruciatingly painful."

Although now less composed, Kate's anger surged. She had never before been threatened in such a cruel manner, although she decided that further provocation would serve no good purpose.

"Each of you will now be subjected to a thorough medical check by our staff." General Bax indicated the two white-coated individuals.

"When that has been dealt with you will be taken across to one of the shower blocks, where you will have an opportunity to freshen up before continuing on the next stage of your journey."

Although surprised by what appeared to be an attempt to add to their immediate comfort, Bax's statement suggested that they were to be sent on from their current location and Kate speculated that they might then join up with the illegal immigrants who had been shipped across the previous day. She drew some comfort from this and hoped that an opportunity to escape might yet occur.

"I'm afraid that it will be necessary for you to take communal showers, as lighting a second boiler for your small group would seem unnecessary. If your modesty is offended then so be it. Clean underclothes will be provided when you have bathed and I suggest for the next stage of your journey that you wear those under the clothes which you arrived in. Are there any questions before we continue?"

"I gather from what you have told us that this is not to be our final destination. Would you mind now telling us where we are going to from here, please?"

"You should not concern yourself with destinations, Miss Savage; all will be revealed in due course. Now will you please cooperate with our medical team?"

A brief interruption then occurred while Molly explained everything to their taxi driver. Following on from this, each of them was in turn examined by the white-coated medical staff.

Surprised by the extent and thoroughness of these examinations, Kate decided that being x-rayed and having blood samples taken for testing might indicate that they were to be moved on to another country where an absolutely clean bill of health was essential.

Kate's thoughts were then distracted when the general appeared to be having a whispered conversation with an individual who had appeared from an adjacent room which reminded her of a school science room or laboratory. Both Bax and the newcomer then cast frequent glances in Kate's direction until the General finally appeared to nod agreement.

When yet a further blood sample was taken from Kate and then passed to what she thought might be a laboratory assistant for a second appraisal, her earlier concern increased.

"It would be ironic if they have now discovered that something is seriously wrong with me," Kate speculated. She was given no opportunity to ponder this as she was motioned back to a desk to have her blood pressure checked once more. One of the medical team then took her pulse and again listened to both her heart and lungs. Kate found this disturbing and more so as none of her companions had been subjected to the additional examination. These fears were further compounded when the General instructed that the other members of her small group should follow yet another individual through to the showers.

"Not you, young lady, there are further tests which we wish to make and you will need to be patient for a while longer."

This, coming from Bax in if anything a more deferential tone, did little to allay Kate's fears, as she had previously thought that the group should try to avoid separation from one another at all cost. Despite this concern she was given no time to protest as someone wearing a yellow sash forcibly escorted her from the room.

When Kate decided to resist and dug her heels in, the escort was quickly joined by another rough-looking individual who simply twisted her arm painfully up behind her back and frogmarched her before him.

Stumbling along through an avenue of barrack-like buildings, Kate's discomfort was replaced by yet further concern when they arrived at a smaller hut with bars let into the upper part of what appeared to be a stable style door.

Once inside Kate quickly concluded that she was in a room which was designed to be a detention centre or prison cell. Apart from a plain wooden table and a pair of uncomfortable looking straight-backed chairs, the cell was unfurnished. As the heavy double doors closed behind her, Kate distinctly heard the sound of what she assumed were metal bolts being thrust into place.

She thought briefly of creating a commotion, but quickly realised that it would be wasted effort when watching both escorts quickly turn a corner and disappear from view.

While remaining glued to the heavily barred upper part of the door, Kate was now unable to see any further sign of life or movement. Testing the door's security only served to prove that it was heavily constructed and that the bars in the upper section were deeply embedded into hard timber.

Collecting her thoughts Kate decided that inactivity was unlikely to help her situation and she next explored the cell, while hoping to find some weakness which she might exploit. When this proved fruitless she sat at the table and once more worried over her separation from the others.

Left to consider this predicament her imagination quickly concluded that the General's suggestion of wanting to carry out further medical tests was nothing more than a ploy to mislead her, one with which to secure her cooperation and reduce any resistance that she might be tempted to make.

"The General and his minions will almost certainly now be thinking of ways to dispose of me," she decided.

"It's obvious that Molly and the two men will pass along the refugee chain unnoticed, whereas my Western and dark features will stand out like a sore thumb."

It was at this point in her deliberations that Kate reinforced her previous view of the necessity to escape. She was aware that from the outset her plans for doing so had failed and although as yet there had been little or no opportunity of acquiring one, she decided a weapon of some kind would be essential if she was to succeed.

Both high-backed chairs appeared cumbersome and she thought they would prove unwieldy in the confined space of her cell. By next using all her strength Kate eventually managed to worry one of the heavy chair legs free from its mortise joint. When satisfied that it would make a useful club, she thrust the dismembered chair into a darkened corner and then settled down to feign sleep.

Lying with the chair leg concealed beside her, Kate hoped that when one or more of her captors arrived she would find an opportunity of surprising them and using the improvised weapon.

The monotony of pretending to sleep was only broken by the sound of a heavy diesel engine's continuous throbbing and Kate assumed it to be a standby generator; despite this assumption, her somewhat airless cell remained devoid of little else which might hold her attention. When the irritating noise from the diesel generator was eventually closed down the silence that followed was equally spooky.

Daylight was rapidly failing when Kate risked leaving her position on the cell floor to drink water from a container which she had earlier discovered. Fear that the water might be contaminated was eventually overridden by thirst and a certain regret that she had found the shrimp and noodles so appetising the previous day.

Before returning to her former position, Kate succumbed to an overriding urge to peer out through the bars of the upper door once more and was then utterly dismayed to find a pair of eyes looking in at her.

Silently cursing her weakness and need for fluids, she was further angered by feelings of hopelessness when realising that she had once more lost the advantage of surprise.

"What do you want? Have you brought food? I hope so. I have been locked in here for hours and unless you intend starving me to death, I must eat."

Kate had no wish to appear weak and thought a tone of aggressive authority ought to be what she should now use.

"Do you understand?" The eyes boring in were disconcerting as the light was poor and she could barely see the outline of a darkened face. Silence followed until a man's voice offered her the smallest glimmer of hope.

"You are in grave danger, miss. I cannot be caught here and we must talk quietly. Guards will, I think, eventually bring food to you. Until they do, there is little that I can do to help. This door is locked and the padlocks are far too strong to be forced."

Panic momentarily invaded Kate's thoughts as the blurred shape moved from sight and she thought that she had once more been abandoned. When the voice spoke again, Kate felt an unusual surge of relief.

"When the orderlies come, one of them will unlock the door and they will enter the cell. You must then do something which will hold their attention. Scream faint, point to something in the corner or pretend to have a fit. Do anything which will help to distract them."

"Who are you and how do I know that I can trust you?"

"You don't. Although I'm afraid the alternative for you is death." This brutally frank statement, although shocking, rang true and Kate suffered further spasms of fear as palpitations coursed through her body.

"My identity is of no importance and for the moment it is better that you do not know. I will explain everything if and when I get you out of there. It may help you to trust me, however, if I tell you that my wife was also once held in this very same cell."

On hearing this Kate's hopes were raised once more and she thought that if his wife had truly been in a similar predicament it might be reason enough for his helping her.

"Before I disappear, there is one more thing. Getting you out of this place will not be easy, although getting you away to safety is going to be far more difficult. If I am to help, I have to have your assurance that you will do as I say and not offer resistance to any of my proposals. Will you accept those terms if I attempt to free you?"

Kate had barely time to nod and murmur yes before the man's silhouette disappeared once more. Fear and a sense of loneliness returned, although she now believed that there was little choice other than to go along with what her surreptitious visitor had suggested.

Waiting in the failing light next gave Kate the added opportunity of considering ways in which she might distract the food orderlies when they arrived, and she thought of many options before deciding on one course of action.

Light from a torch finally warned Kate that people were approaching and she then steeled herself for the part which she now knew was crucial for her to play.

As the bolt slid back a guttural command in barely understandable English was issued and Kate realised with some relief that not two but only one orderly had arrived.

"Stay away. I have gun and shoot if you move. Food go on floor. You only move when door close."

Although surprised by its gruffness Kate immediately realised that the voice belonged to a woman, probably the same coarse-featured individual who had escorted them into the medical centre following their arrival. There was no time to dwell on this as Kate first groaned pitifully then immediately followed this up with an agonised and very loud moan, before then opening her eyes wide and clutching at her chest in an attempt to feign severe pain. As the beam of the torch swung full on her, Kate felt a sense of satisfaction that her ploy was working. Next collapsing face down on the floor, she managed one final strangled gurgling gasp before sensing the orderly move.

In the next instant a heavy crushing weight fell across her and Kate at first thought that the woman had thrown something over her. As she struggled to replace the breath which had been driven from her, she was surprised by feeling a warm sticky wetness trickling onto her neck and running into her hair. She had insufficient time to consider the implication of this as the weight was next lifted from her and the previous man's voice was urging her to her feet.

"Oh my God, is she dead?" Kate gasped, as she looked down on a still form with the hilt of a knife protruding from it.

"Come, there is no time to waste. If we are to get you away from this cell we must leave now."

"But she might still be alive. We should see if we can help." Kate pulled at the woman's shoulder in an attempt to discover a pulse and as she did so pink frothy foam erupted from the mouth and nostrils and then the man was once more urging,

"We are wasting time and there is nothing that we can do for her. My knife probably pierced a lung before entering her heart. Please remember your promise and do as I say. We are both in grave danger and I have no intention of allowing the people here to recapture me."

It is possible that further explanation may have followed had Kate not chosen that moment to vomit. Tears coursed down her cheeks and mucus from her nostrils threatened to turn her stomach a second time. Despite this, there was something about the man's tone which made her understand that she must do as he ordered. Fighting to overcome nausea and take control of her trembling limbs she took a handkerchief from her pocket with which to wipe her eyes.

Valuable time was undoubtedly lost while Kate struggled to compose herself. Eventually she rose to her feet and was about to put the handkerchief away when she noticed from the light of the fallen torch that the cloth had changed to a dirty rust red colour.

"Oh hell! I must have hit my head and cut it open when I collapsed on the floor," Kate announced, to no one in particular.

"Here, give me the cloth. It will be sensible to clean the blood from you before we go outside as it would certainly attract unwanted attention."

Finding a part of the handkerchief which was still dry the man scrubbed at her face and neck before explaining,

"It's okay, you haven't injured yourself. The blood is from her." The man gestured down at the still form of the woman at their feet. This unemotional reaction did little to help Kate's queasiness or to reinforce the trust which she was now prepared to place in him.

"I am unable to clean you with this rag as it's completely saturated with blood." Kate then watched open-mouthed as the man bent and stripped a large section of cloth from the dead woman's overall.

"Is there some water in the cell?" Kate nodded and motioned to the container from which she had earlier taken a drink.

While peering out through the bars of her cell she had been unable to distinguish any of the man's features. Now in weak light from the fallen torch she was able to study a completely calm facial exterior which in their current situation was, she thought, completely out of place. In those fleeting seconds Kate's rescuer's appearance also reminded her of someone she had previously seen and she thought his features registered more pain and grief than most people were normally exposed to.

"Here, put this over your shoulder." The man had taken one of the uniform yellow sashes from the corpse when he was tearing strips from her overall and Kate then noticed that he was also wearing one.

"We are going to walk out through a side gate. If we come across anyone, just act as well as you did when you feigned that heart attack. Try to give the appearance of belonging and keep this hat pulled well down over your face."

The man had passed her a rather soiled and ragged-looking straw hat, which she obediently placed on her head.

"In the poor light outside it should help to hide your appearance. Come, we must leave now."

On exiting the cell Kate followed her rescuer past darkened buildings while he quietly explained their objective.

"On the other side of a perimeter fence there is a cycle shed. We will take two bicycles from it and ride to where I have a motorcycle hidden." He motioned ahead to where she supposed the bicycle shed to be.

"I presume that you can ride a bicycle?" Kate's affirmative nod allowed the man to continue,

"I walked when I came to find you, although travelling on foot will now be far too slow. When that woman's body is found, there will be panic amongst the staff and they will scour the countryside looking for you. The punishment that their masters will exact for allowing you to escape will be extreme. General Bax is certainly ruthless enough although their top man is the most sadistic human being I have ever seen. I once watched him have someone punished and it is something that I hope not to witness again."

It seemed to Kate strange for someone who had recently killed another person to express distaste for cruelty. Despite these uncertain and racing thoughts she now pondered on her rescuer's remark of setting out to find her and she then remembered where she had previously seen him.

Realising now that he was the same man who had been operating the green bulldozer which their transport had all but collided with in the port, caused her to remember that she had not been alone and that Molly and the two men should also be rescued. Tugging at the man's sleeve she quietly explained,

"There are others who were brought here with me. We have to find them and take them out to safety. It would be unthinkable for me to leave without them."

Kate had become accustomed to the gloom and could now clearly see a pair of deep brown eyes studying her.

"They will be dead. I heard the compressor running as I was making my way here."

Kate was unable to grasp the significance of this remark although neither was she about to accept that she would leave without the people that she had been abducted with. Molly and the taxi driver had to be freed from wherever they were. The office manager was partially responsible for his own predicament, although Kate realised that had she not bullied him into revealing what little he knew, Tommy Jung would have allowed him to remain behind.

"I realise I gave you an assurance that I would follow your instructions and do whatever was required of me to escape; now, though, I will have to go back on my word. I cannot leave without first attempting to free my friends. If this puts your life in danger I will understand if you decide to leave without me."

Kate's rescuer sighed deeply, shrugged his shoulders and then motioned for her to follow.

They had not far to go before reaching the first of the large buildings that had caught her attention while being escorted into the medical centre.

While Kate remained concealed in shadow from an adjacent building her rescuer then made sure that there was no one around before first removing a retaining bolt and then rolling one of the doors aside and motioning that she should come to take a look for herself.

The inside of the building was silent, save for the sound from a leaking shower head as it dripped water into a small pool. It was then that Kate once more remembered that they had been told there would be an opportunity to shower and freshen up before going on to the next stage of their enforced journey.

"My guess is that they showered together in the other facility," her rescuer murmured as he closed the rolling door.

With finding the first shower block unoccupied, Kate also expected to find the next unit empty. Instead, what she saw caused her to gasp with horror.

Molly's naked body was lying just inside the double rolling doors with her arms and fingers outstretched in an attitude of final desperation.

Unable to move or turn from this new mind-boggling tragedy, Kate was vaguely aware of her rescuer kneeling to feel for a pulse. When he next looked up and shook his head, she saw that there was a deep sadness etched in his very expressive eyes and she instantly understood there was nothing she could do that would help Molly.

"Your companion realised she was being asphyxiated." The man's shudder when he told Kate this was very noticeable.

"I wish that I didn't, although I know exactly how she felt. The memory of my own experience still haunts me." It quickly registered with Kate that her rescuer had in fact at some previous time experienced the same horror which her friends had now been subjected to.

"Had they been in the other shower block, it is possible that this young woman may have saved herself." Motioning to Molly's still form the man explained,

"There is a flaw in the other door seal which she might have found. Hopefully we will one day find a way of avenging her death, together with that of the many others who have gone before," he added sympathetically. "Now though, we should concentrate on saving ourselves and getting you away from this evil place alive."

Every instinct suggested that Kate would be failing if she left without trying to do something for the dignity of the people that she felt responsible for, if nothing other than to arrange their bodies in a less distressful way. She took a pace to where Nygen's body was lying and this time there was no mistaking the determination in her rescuer's voice.

"Both of them will have died before the woman. She was obviously fighting for her life. We must leave them as they are. If Bax suspects that you have witnessed this crime it will serve only to fuel his determination in recapturing you." Realising that there might be some wisdom in this logic, Kate reluctantly turned away.

"Come, their fate will be ours if we are caught." When the door was once more closed on the horrors which the shower block contained, Kate followed passively. Absorbed in thoughts of the horror which she had just witnessed she was now relieved that for once the responsibility of what lay ahead was not hers.

Only one other person was seen by them while making their way to the gate. Fortunately the man was some way off and dressed in what Kate thought might be a chef's hat and chequered trousers.

On reaching the cycle shelter, Kate's companion took a machine from one of the racks and handed it to her. Despite still feeling deep shock from what she had moments before witnessed, she realised that she still did not know who her rescuer was. As the man was selecting a second machine, she quietly suggested,

"I still have no idea who you are and I guess the same goes for you. Do you think it might be a good idea for us now to introduce ourselves before going on?"

"My name is Luc Tun. There will be time for us to talk as we cycle to where I left the motorcycle. Now please, we must put distance between ourselves and those people. If we see lights coming from either direction, we will have to hope that there is somewhere for us to hide."

Luc Tun's fears of encountering other people did not materialise and they reached the place where his motorcycle was hidden without mishap. When he had wheeled the machine out from a dilapidated building, Luc Tun then took both bicycles and threw them out into a large pool of water. As they sank from view, Kate looked around and deliberated on where they might be. A tall structure which she thought might once have supported an irrigation pump stood beside the building. She was then given no opportunity for further deliberation as the motorcycle sprang to life and Luc Tun was urging her to climb on behind and hold tight.

"Although the path is badly rutted it will be too risky for me to use the motorcycle's light; the surrounding countryside is very flat and illumination from the machine would be seen for miles around."

Riding at a steady pace the track snaked along through what Kate assumed was some kind of salt marsh. Surprisingly the unlit ride seemed less dangerous than she was expecting it to be.

Eventually, riding off the track and into the deeper gloom of some scattered buildings, they were greeted by furious barking from a very large dog. It seemed obvious that the animal had come out to greet Luc Tun and Kate assumed from this that they had arrived at their destination.

Light flooding out from a doorway was followed by a feminine voice which seemed to be asking questions. A brief but what seemed a somewhat heated exchange followed and then Kate was being helped from the motorcycle by a slightly-built young woman.

"I am sorry if my tone sounded less than welcoming. I should explain that each time Luc ventures near that awful medical centre I am overcome with fear and as it is now way past the time that he normally returns from his work at the port, my imagination was running riot."

Sighing with what appeared to be troubled concern the woman then paused for breath.

"I also feel sure that after what I imagine you have experienced, your thoughts will be in turmoil and there will also be many unanswered questions which you wish to ask. You will also be suffering from deep concern for the other people who were with you and my earlier agitation will be of little importance in your present state of mind. Now though, please come inside. My husband will join us once he has put his machine away."

Surprised by the young woman's fluency, Kate next felt a sense of unreality as she was ushered into a warmly-lit dwelling and then told to take a seat at a very low table.

A steaming bowl of soup was next handed to her and they were then quickly joined by Luc Tun.

# Chapter Twenty Two

While eating a very satisfying meal with Luc Tun and Lai Mee, Kate realised that it had been more than twenty-four hours since she had stopped for food on the side of the road with Molly and the taxi driver. Thoughts of her former friend and colleague brought convulsive tremors to her throat and she had also experienced extreme feelings of both guilt and grief.

Earlier Kate was shown to a small room in which there was a simple sleeping platform with an assortment of bed coverings placed to one side, although the tiny alcove was bare of furniture.

"This was where Lin Yen slept and the covers have been freshly laundered," Lai Mee had explained, after showing Kate the room where she was to spend the night. It had also previously been explained that Lin Yen was the deaf mute who had given shelter to the Cambodian couple when they too had escaped from the medical centre.

"I feel sure your experiences of the past days will have left you exhausted and I hope that you will be able to sleep. It may help if you try to erase all recent horrible memories from your mind and think of more pleasant things," The young woman also quietly suggested, as she held a lighted candle high for Kate to familiarise with her new surroundings.

Although not the most comfortable bed in which she had ever slept Kate was weary and sleep came surprisingly quickly. She was woken shortly afterwards, however, by a noise which she did not immediately recognise and, from the light of a torch which Lai Mee had left in the room, Kate learned it was less than two hours since she had lain down.

"Croak, croak, croak," the noise rose and fell. At its peak the crescendo of sound was an echoing reverberation of throaty melody which echoed throughout Kate's cell-like room. As the waking seconds ticked by, with no sign or sound of anyone else stirring in their small dwelling, she decided it was not a frightening noise and eventually realised it to be a species of giant bullfrog uttering mating calls. Similar sounds could sometimes be heard coming from the lake back home, although at much lower volume.

In thinking of Koggala, Kate next experienced feelings of homesickness and speculated on whether she would ever again see the lake from where her family regularly flew amphibian aircraft.

With recognition of the marshland sounds a partial peace returned to Kate's turbulent thoughts. Despite this she realised that further sleep might prove difficult and the recent distressing turn of events was proving a problem to dismiss.

Molly's cruel murder had created a vacuum of deep grief for Kate, who strongly abhorred its sheer waste of life and a talent which would have gone far. It was also proving difficult to rid herself of the guilt which she felt for the demise of Nygen and the taxi driver.

Images of three prone bodies lying in a cold and lifeless shower block haunted her, and as she tossed and turned she tried in vain to obliterate thoughts of spending the remaining seconds of one's life gasping for air.

Kate also realised with feelings of shame that she had not so much as even known the taxi driver's name. This neglectful act helped her to decide that, should she be fortunate in escaping from Hainan, she would never again take anyone for granted.

In trying to override unpleasant feelings of guilt, Kate's thoughts turned to her present dilemma and she remembered the extraordinary story which had earlier been told by Luc Tun and Lai Mee over supper.

On realising that the food had been prepared in expectation of Luc Tun's return from work, initially Kate had felt that eating in her emotional and troubled state might prove difficult. Despite these thoughts she realised that she should attempt to show some appreciation for her new hosts' generosity and hospitality.

Before settling down to eat, Luc Tun had introduced his wife Lai Mee and explained that they were Cambodians and how they came to be living on the island. He also told her that he had been surprised by the arrival of her small party at the port, an arrival which was both unscheduled and unannounced.

"I was fortunate to be working close to the jetty where the refugees are normally landed and even more than a little surprised by the small number in your particular group. In fact it was one of the reasons why I travelled out to the medical centre to investigate."

"It was fortunate for me that you did, as despite thoughts of attempting to escape it now seems unlikely that I would have succeeded. The woman who came to that cell with food was armed and it was very obvious that her caution would have prevented me from surprising her."

Kate had concluded by sincerely thanking Luc Tun once more for his intervention which she now realised with an absolute certainty had saved her life.

Her host's explanation for her present predicament seemed incredible and had Kate not witnessed the dead bodies of her former companions, she would have found difficulty in believing it.

When her rescuers described how she would almost certainly need to be hidden in a very secure place the following morning, she slowly began to understand the seriousness of her situation. Both Luc and Lai Mee emphasised they were sure that the countryside would be combed in an attempt to recapture her and her place of concealment should be very secure and carefully chosen.

"We both submerged ourselves in an irrigation ditch on the occasions when they came searching for Lai Mee." Kate's surprise and raised eyebrows prompted Luc to explain that they were able to breathe under water by using hollow reeds and that this had been suggested by Lin Yen, their former host.

"Unfortunately the water is at present too low for such a purpose. Despite these concerns we should have ample warning of an approach as the surrounding countryside is very flat and we also have the old dog whose hearing is still good, despite his age."

Between them the young couple had then told Kate all that they knew of the group that had made her a prisoner and the reason for the medical centre's existence. She had responded by asking why the matter had not been reported to the authorities and Luc explained the influence that the principal of the Fan Chee Medical Institute held over the island community and its ruling council.

"What the infamous doctor is unable to buy, he enforces through brutality and extreme fear," Kate was told.

"People on the island are terrified of falling foul of him and it is rumoured that a number have disappeared over the years. He has a henchman; a man who calls himself General Zin Bax and who practically lives here. Bax also has paid spies everywhere on the island. Had we not been regarded as being relatives of Lin Yen when we escaped, we would doubtless have quickly been recaptured. It also helped that we were a couple and that they were actually only searching for a single woman." Kate had been about to ask for further explanation when Luc continued,

"As Lin Yen was a deaf mute throughout his entire life the local people were not particularly surprised by discovering that he was Vietnamese. Or so they believed when we appeared with him on market days. Because of our very noticeable foreign accents, Vietnam is where they all thought we were from."

"It was General Zin Bax who received us when we arrived this morning." Kate remembered telling them and also that she had immediately judged him to be an extremely unpleasant and dangerous character. Confirmation that her initial intuition was correct did little to stave off her present fears of insecurity. Luc Tun's continuing enlightenment of the dangers to her was also disconcerting.

"Your escape will generate a great deal of fear amongst the staff and Zin Bax will also be concerned for the consequences, as he will not be immune from the retribution which will follow."

Luc Tun had then explained the security measures which had been put in place when Lai Mee escaped and eventually Kate asked the question which was still troubling her.

"I am finding it difficult to understand my separation from the others in our small group. If Lai Mee was also singled out for similar treatment, why was that, do you think?" This prompted Luc to ask,

"Do you know what blood group you are?" When Kate told him it was O rhesus negative his nod indicated some understanding.

"I am not surprised that you know this. Most people would not carry that sort of information around in their heads. The fact that you do is because you have been made aware that you have a rare blood group and that in an emergency medical staff should, if possible, be notified." Kate had also then explained that both her father and paternal grandfather were of the same blood group.

"Should your human leucocyte antigen be class one or two it would make you a very valuable commodity and Dr. Chang's organisation will have been treating you as such. In fact, I imagine that he will leave no stone unturned to secure your return, as you will certainly have been regarded as a rare asset."

Kate was vaguely aware of what Luc Tun was telling her as she had been taught from an early age about varying blood groups and hers in particular.

"How is it that you understand these things?" she asked. Her rescuer then explained that he had practiced dentistry before the genocide which had placed his country in turmoil.

"It was a genocide which wrecked our country and in fact resulted in Lai Mee and I becoming refugees."

Luc had also suggested that his dentistry training had given him a limited knowledge of medicine.

"Doctor Chang Jin-Ming's principal interest is transplant surgery. His organisation, although efficiently run, simply exists through first taking money from people such as us. Gullible refugees, if you wish." A gesture towards Lai Mee and himself indicated that regret for his earlier ill-advised act still rankled.

"Refugees like us, who wished for nothing more than to escape a life of hardship and repression. We, of course, all had our reasons, although most simply hoped to find peaceful sanctuary in a welcoming country." Luc Tun had then paused for Lai Mee to reach across and refill both his and Kate's cups with rice wine.

"You will by now, I hope, understand that none of the doctor's illegal refugees ever reaches the paradise that they had hoped for. Instead they are brought here to this island and to the medical centre. People such as yourself and Lai Mee are treated as special cases of value because of the rarity of your blood groups." Kate's inquiring look was then immediately explained.

"Yes indeed, Lai Mee also has a rare blood group which is why she was placed in that same small cell with others who shared both yours and her rarity." Luc had then paused to savour the wine in his cup.

"The shipment of people who came across with the two of us was much larger than the numbers who have been arriving recently. I imagine that fact accounts for the higher percentage of rare blood group people who initially shared the cell with Lai Mee. Her group, by the way, is AB negative. My understanding is that blood group O negative is capable of mixing with other groups, although I believe a greater number of failures in transplant surgery occurs because of rejection. I also understand that if donor organs from the same blood group are used the risk of rejection is greatly reduced."

"So what happens to the people who are not selected because they do not have rare blood groups?" A moment of hesitation was followed by Luc Tun telling Kate it might be better if she didn't know.

"A colleague, someone whose friendship I was beginning to value, has been murdered, along with two other people that I felt responsible for. I think I should be told, irrespective of how insensitive the truth may be. In fact, I would like to know."

A moment of further silence followed, until Luc then told her that a small percentage of refugees with common blood groups were also chosen as donors and he added that some physical features almost certainly contributed to their selection.

"Problems obviously arise from holding a large number of prisoners for long periods, not least the cost of food and somewhere to house them.

When refugees with common blood groups are chosen they are shipped off to a place called Guangzhou, along with the people who have rare blood groups." Luc Tun paused briefly, with an expression which suggested he was concentrating on what more it was necessary to tell.

"Once I had established what the purpose of the medical centre was, I also managed, through some minor research, to establish that body parts can be stored for up to five days in a patented organ preservation system. I also learned that a group of Western medical researchers has been able to extend this to seven days when they were experimenting with animal organs. In my opinion Dr Chang Jin-Ming's organisation will, in all probability, have achieved unreported improvements to those official research figures, although it obviously would not be in his best interests to have any such personal success published."

Luc Tun had peered at Kate over the rim of his glass until he sighed, a sigh which may have indicated that he sympathised with her ignorance on the subject.

"I realise that my lengthy explanation will appear to be something of a digression and of no possible use in solving our present dilemma," the Cambodian continued.

With little or no knowledge of medicine or the human anatomy, Kate had in fact been struggling to understand what was being explained. She was pondering this when Luc Tun appeared to add to his explanations.

"I imagine that Dr Chang's fees for transplant services will be greatly enhanced when the recipient has either a rare blood group or some physical abnormality which is similar to that of the intended donor."

At this point in his explanation a child's whimpering cry from somewhere at the rear of the dwelling had caused Lai Mee to go scurrying off to investigate.

"It's okay, nothing more than a bad dream," the young mother had told them when she returned.

Luc Tun had then motioned for his wife to help herself to more of the rice wine, although it was noticeable that Lai Mee did not share her husband's enthusiasm for the stomach-warming alcohol. With something which vaguely represented a frown, Luc had then continued to theorise.

"I have read that people throughout many countries who are in need of transplant surgery generally expect to wait for long periods until a donor is found, and also that the patient often dies before a suitable match is made. What Dr Chang Jin-Ming and the Fan Chee Institute offer is unique. When a client first approaches the doctor they are almost certain to receive instant attention and avoid the crucial risk of delay. Following a thorough medical examination, Dr. Chang then simply selects a suitable matching donor from his very large cache and ends that donor's life on the day of the operation."

"The man deserves to rot in hell," Kate had gasped. Previously she had remained silent, until a strong sense of loathing for someone she had never met prompted her to ask,

"What happens to the bodies of the people who are not selected as donors?"

"I earlier asked if you were sure that you really wanted to know. Now I will ask again if you really do need to know." Kate's exasperated expression had then appeared to convey the answer.

"Some time ago I discovered that the centre for Dr Chang's operation is at Guangzhou, the place I mentioned earlier. After agreeing with Lai Mee that she would take care of things here, I crossed to the mainland and journeyed there by train. It was quite an experience for me as I had never travelled on a train before. On reaching the city of Guangzhou, I set out to discover where the Fan Chee Institute was located and after finding it I secured a room in a cheap lodging house close by. Some rather boring days of inactivity followed and I simply watched the comings and goings from a derelict house which stands close to the institute. On a number of occasions I witnessed ambulances arriving at the centre and saw patients being stretchered in."

Lai Mee had at that point interrupted her husband by describing the deep fear she had felt during the entire time of his absence. This had unexpectedly prompted Luc to put an arm around her shoulder in a rare show of affection.

"The people of Guangzhou appeared to be even more in fear of the doctor than they are here on Hainan. Whenever I asked a question about the institute I met a complete wall of silence and in fact felt quite vulnerable. My foreign accent is very noticeable and I had no wish to be reported to any of the institute spies. My eventual break came when I noticed one particular individual leaving the centre on a regular basis. On following him I discovered that his destination was no farther than a food vendor's stall some two blocks away. It seemed obvious from the outset that this individual was interested in company and I deliberately took my food bowl to his table. In the days that followed I made a habit of joining him and it transpired that he is an anaesthetist who had travelled down from the Anhui Province to work at the institute. I learned that he has assisted Dr Chang on numerous occasions and certainly appeared in awe of the man. From our conversations I also learned that, in addition to admiration for the doctor's skill, this new acquaintance of mine has a great fear of him."

Once more Luc's description of events was interrupted by a child's cry and when Lai Mee eventually returned he had continued.

"I formed the opinion that the anaesthetist is inclined toward homosexuality. If my suspicion is correct, it may account for his fear of the doctor and the hold that the man has over him. People of that persuasion live dangerously here in this part of China and any threat of exposure would be very worrying for him."

Kate expressing sympathy for the repression of people with homosexual tendencies once more interrupted Luc Tun's flow and with brief signs of slight irritation he ignored her remarks.

"My new acquaintance, the anaesthetist, described heart and kidney transplants as commonplace and in fact gave the impression that he considered operations such as those to be little or no more difficult than the removal of an appendix. What the man seemed to have enthusiasm for was the transplanting of other body parts and in particular a face, which was recently grafted onto a man who had been badly disfigured in an industrial accident. This, I concluded, explained the use of donors with common blood groups who may have certain bone structure and other body features which can be recycled."

Briefly Luc reached for the earthenware jar and Kate thought the strong spirit suitable sustenance while listening to Luc Tun's imagined account of the doctor's gory practices.

"Pretending to be in need of money I asked the anaesthetist if it might be possible for me to donate a kidney. The man immediately went on the defensive and suggested that there was a more than adequate supply chain of donors in place. He also became quite agitated when I pressed for more detail; I think he was afraid that I might request an introduction to the institute and he actually offered me the loan of some money." Lai Mee interrupted her husband then by asking if Kate would like more soup.

"When I was not taking food with the anaesthetist I followed other leads and learned of Dr Chang's many other interests. There is one business in particular which he owns and which I believe explains how he is able to deal with one of his more problem areas. This organisation runs a slaughterhouse where carcases considered unfit for human consumption are processed into canned animal foods. Chinese society is gradually becoming more affluent and people now own pets in a way which did not happen during the years of austerity."

With the realisation of what was about to be explained, Kate had gasped in further horror before asking,

"Have recent experiences so warped my mind that I am now capable of imagining even greater atrocities?" Luc Tun's sad nod indicated that she had indeed arrived at the correct assumption.

"I recognised many of the vehicles which reversed into the food canning factory, as I had previously watched the very same trucks being loaded with corpses at the medical centre."

Following this incredible observation her rescuer's face remained impassive and during the silence which followed Kate was unable to contain her anger and revulsion.

"That monster has to be stopped. Will you be able to take me to a telephone in the morning?" Kate's question had prompted a look of incongruity from the Cambodian man.

"I'm sorry, Kate, but you have still not grasped the situation that we are in." Luc then went on to explain that it would be unsafe for her to be seen. He told her that with her Eurasian features she would be very noticeable and everyone on the island would have been warned to be on the lookout for someone of her appearance, a patient who had in fact escaped from the medical centre by killing one of its staff.

"Zin Bax's cronies will have told the people that your mind is unbalanced and the islanders without exception would immediately turn you in. If that was to happen, it is more than likely that Lai Mee and I would also be picked up as being your accomplices."

Luc Tun then next told her that it was almost impossible and also quite dangerous for anyone to attempt making surreptitious telephone calls as there was a strict monitoring system on the island for all outgoing and incoming calls.

With a sinking heart and feelings of despair Kate then frantically raked her brain as to how she might overcome the problem of communicating with the outside world. These thoughts were eventually interrupted by a less than reassuring suggestion.

"It may be possible for me to make a telephone call on your behalf, a call which should not attract unwanted attention." Kate's inquiring look had encouraged Luc to explain.

"For some months I have been working in the port with my tractor and the office staff have become used to me. Occasionally when I need fuel oil or other consumables they allow me to use one of the office telephones. More recently they have insisted that I should feel free to make these calls as and when the need arises and also without asking for permission."

In response to Kate's next question his work in the port was briefly explained.

"The port authority, as you might imagine, has regular contact with the outside world and their telephone calls do not attract the same attention as those from other sources. If the call I make could be to a shipping agent or some other maritime organisation, I imagine it will go through untapped."

"Would the telephone number of our ferry company be acceptable, do you think?"

Until then Kate had not mentioned that she was part-owner of the vessel which had transported her and others to the island. When this and her abduction were briefly explained, Luc suggested that he had thought it strange for someone of her appearance to be brought to the clinic.

"There are many people throughout this part of the world who are not accounted for and when someone goes missing, it is generally thought to be no big deal, on the other hand, if someone of European lineage fails to turn up, I imagine it starts alarm bells ringing which in turn creates a great deal of fuss. A fuss that I feel sure Doctor Chang Jin-Ming would normally avoid at all cost."

Following further discussion on the topic of getting news of the island's atrocities to the outside world, Luc suggested that Kate write a message containing something which would categorically identify it as coming from her. He also emphasised that the message should indicate that it had not been written under duress.

In the brief respite which followed, and despite her rescuer's steady intake of rice wine, Kate was forming a high regard for Luc Tun's intelligence.

"It is possible your friends will assume that you have been taken hostage for ransom purposes and you will need to convince them that is not so."

While her husband was stressing the importance of how the content of the message should be convincing, Lai Mee busied herself by finding paper and pencil with which to write.

When Kate was finally satisfied that she would be able to compile a message that would have the desired impact, Luc again told her that they should expect staff from the medical centre to come searching the following day.

"In all probability it will be necessary for you to hide in a safe place for long periods during the time that you are with us. If and when we are successful in concealing you they will eventually give up searching, although until that happens we cannot be too careful," he had added.

"They searched extensively for Lai Mee during the days following our escape, although since then they have never bothered us."

In answer to Kate's next question Luc explained how it was that the medical centre staff had only been searching for Lai Mee. When the substitution he had made for himself in the men's shower block was explained, Kate was neither shocked nor surprised. She was very aware of how Luc had dealt with one of her gaolers and was slowly accepting that on occasion the end justified the means.

The story of how a deaf mute, the former occupier of her small room had befriended and taken them in was another part of the couple's recent history which Kate found quite incredible. She also marvelled at how they had used this new-found friendship to develop alternative identities and she realised that they were two quite remarkable and resourceful people.

The fact that the medical centre has never knowingly had one of their people killed by an escapee was another topic for concern.

"I am not suggesting that the doctor will be shedding tears for a dead employee, although the woman's colleagues may adopt a more positive attitude, not that they will need added incentive. Chang Jin-Ming's punishment for allowing you to escape will be extremely severe." Luc then described a punishment which he had secretly witnessed under the doctor's supervision.

"Those yellow bands on the receiving end of the doctor's fury will leave no stone unturned and we must ensure that your hiding place is absolutely secure. I shall go to the port at my usual time tomorrow and at some point during the day hope for an opportunity to make that telephone call to your contacts."

Hesitating, Luc then seemed to take time before following up on an earlier point which he had stressed.

"I cannot emphasise strongly enough that the person I manage to speak to is capable of grasping that it is essential that official intervention is not requested. Any approach by the Vietnamese authorities will simply be rejected as unfound nonsense and access to the island will certainly be refused. That is the sort of influence which Dr. Chang has over the island's ruling council."

"It all seems quite hopeless," Kate dejectedly exclaimed. "If official intervention won't work, how shall I ever be able to convince the outside world of what is happening here?"

Luc Tun's response was not immediate, as he had been encouraged by Kate's concern for alerting others ahead of her own precarious position. While pondering what he considered to be the young woman's brave and selfless attitude, he reached across to refill Kate's cup. On this occasion and in an attempt to retain a clear head, she had politely declined.

"The surest way for us to make the outside world aware of what is happening here on the island is by you doing so in person. It is so important for all of us that you make it back to Vietnam or some other country which is not influenced by Doctor Chang Jin-Ming." Luc had then lapsed into further silent contemplation until asking if Kate knew anyone who might be able to organise a rescue attempt through unofficial channels.

Admiral Tanaka was immediately rejected as Luc Tun felt certain that a Vietnamese government official would assume an official approach to be the only way of handling things.

"If your rescue is to succeed it should be carried out by a small party, preferably men or women with military experience who have been battle hardened by conflict. Do you know anyone capable of organising such an operation?"

In realising that Luc Tun had survived in his present situation simply by the implementation of guile and cunning, Kate decided his experience qualified him to propose a plan to deal with her dilemma and she thought it foolish to ignore any suggestion by him.

"My uncle Richard is an airline pilot and although he has no military experience his training will enable him to deal with crisis situations. I feel sure that, given time, he will also be able to recruit a team capable of getting me off the island. Had my father been alive he would certainly have known what to do, as his adult life was dedicated to freeing Sri Lanka from terrorism. In fact he managed many dangerous missions against the Tamil Tigers and was eventually killed by them."

Thinking her uncle's involvement to be a safer option than dealing with officialdom, Luc nodded his somewhat sceptical approval.

Emerging the next morning from the small cubby hole where she had spent a rather restless night, Kate was confronted by three pairs of inquisitive eyes staring up at her from the low table around which two young boys and a baby girl were seated. Their mother's timely arrival prompted an introduction and both boys immediately stood and bowed deeply; the very young girl child had, however, remained seated with a look of bewilderment on her pretty face.

On complimenting Lai Mee on her beautiful and well-mannered children, the young woman responded with delight and then thanked her for the compliment before explaining that her husband had already left to go to the port.

"Luc thinks we should behave as we always do while you are here and the port authorities have become accustomed to his regular routine. He also asked me to say that he will attempt to make your telephone call later today."

Instinctively Kate understood that Lai Mee was very concerned for her husband's safety and she realised that they were both risking a great deal.

Before eventually falling asleep in the early hours of the morning, Kate had thought of the enormity of what was being done for her and she knew that had Luc Tun not intervened, she would certainly have suffered the fate of previous refugees with rare blood groups.

Thinking of ways in which she might try to repay a little of her debt to the Cambodian couple, Kate decided one way might be to help with farm chores and amusing the children. Now realising that her stay would probably be for much longer than hoped for, Kate was determined to add to her host's lives rather than becoming a tiresome burden.

With the breakfast things removed and while Lai Mee was engrossed with needlework, Kate washed the dishes and then organised a game of hide-and-seek for the boys in which she pretended to have difficulty in finding them. Their near hysterical laughter and joy was finally interrupted when the old dog began barking furiously. A response from Lai Mee was instant; rushing out she urged,

"Please, there is not a moment to lose." Lai Mee then took Kate's hand and led her to a hole which had been dug in ground adjacent to a rotting heap of refuse and animal dung.

"Lie down on those rugs," the young woman instructed. "There is a battery-powered torch, a bottle of water and some rice cakes in case our visitors prolong their stay. Whatever you do, don't make a noise. My sons and I will cover you with these boards and then spread a canvas cover and some manure over them. There is one other thing which may deter the searchers from digging. We have a badly decomposed animal carcase which my husband retrieved while you were still sleeping this morning. My sons and I will partially rebury it in the manure heap on top of you, although I'm afraid the smell will be horrible. You should try to console yourself with remembering that the stench may provide some additional and essential protection."

Kate allowed the two boys to help her down into the hiding place and daylight was quickly blotted out as the coverings were placed over her. She was now very afraid and a terrible sense of claustrophobia threatened to overwhelm her as the dog's barking became muffled.

In addition to her fear, Kate was aware that the sickly sweet smell of rotting flesh appeared stronger in the small cramped area of her hiding place and it required mental strength to refrain from gagging aloud. Once she had overcome this urge, her grave-like confinement gave further opportunity to reflect on the horrors which she had been subjected to in the previous forty-eight hours.

Her own immediate predicament and a huge sense of responsibility for the deaths of Molly and the two men was an overriding factor. Although outraged by Doctor Chang Jin-Ming's total disregard for life, Kate now believed that anger alone would not assist with the downfall of him or his clinic and she resolved to remain calm.

Despite an intense fear of being buried alive and the awful stench from a rotting carcase, her determination was rapidly gaining momentum and she vowed that destroying the doctor's organisation would become a priority if and when she managed to escape from his sphere of influence.

Desperately trying to overcome an urge to panic, it then occurred to Kate that if Lai Mee and the children were taken away she might never escape from her hiding place and would eventually die of thirst. These fears were reinforced when she heard the sound of muffled voices immediately above her. When she felt the soil vibrate under the trample of feet, Kate prayed that she would not be discovered.

A whimpering yelp of pain suggested that the old dog had received a kick or a blow from one of the searchers. Further sounds of numerous snarls and more yelps carried down to her and Kate realised that search dogs were also being used in the quest to find her. Once more she marvelled at the wisdom of Luc Tun and his wife in burying a stench-ridden carcase alongside her.

Helplessly entombed inches beneath the feet of people searching for her, Kate prayed not only for her own safety. She now knew for a certainty that both Luc Tun and Lai Mee would forfeit their lives if she was discovered and desperately hoped the unbelievable help that they'd given would not endanger either them or their children.

# Chapter Twenty Three

Ruby had been waiting in the office for over an hour when most of the staff had left for the day. Kate's second telephone call had failed to materialise and she assumed her niece to be lunching with Admiral Tanaka. When the junior clerk had placed Kate's message on her desk some time earlier, intuition suggested something out of the ordinary and Ruby experienced emotions bordering on both exhilaration and excitement.

"My guess is that whatever Kate has agreed is beyond our expectations." Ruby sensed that the simple message, although giving little detail, contained something which would be beneficial to their company.

In the short time since they began working together, Ruby had more than ever come to respect both her niece's judgement and sound business sense. The young woman's attention to detail and her clear thinking would, she felt, have done credit to many older and more experienced people.

The years had seemed to pass quickly since Ruby's first meeting with the very pretty, although somewhat precocious, little girl. Since that early introduction, had Kate been Ruby's own daughter she could not have experienced more pleasure or taken greater pride from her young protégée's progress.

"There is little point in waiting on here now. She will have assumed that I am long gone and it's not fair to keep Wey Ling waiting." Realising that she would be dining alone, Ruby had asked the young Vietnamese woman whom they had recently engaged, to prepare supper for her. She also reminded herself to chivvy the state telephone company along with regard to the home installation which had been requested when taking out the lease on their apartment.

The noise from countless motorcycles and other traffic assaulted Ruby's ears as she made her way home through semi-deserted streets. It had taken a little time, but she was now becoming fond of the little she had so far seen of Vietnam and Saigon in particular.

Ruby firmly believed that the foundation for compassion and integrity were qualities forged in the aftermath of extreme hardship, much of which the South Vietnamese people had been subjected to in the wake of defeat.

She also understood that Saigon had been transformed from a city of decadence to a place where survival itself was an enormous struggle.

Ruby attributed the industry and dependability of the people with whom she now worked to the fact that they had somehow survived in the aftermath of adversity. This judgement was based on a lifetime of travel and a latter experience of working in a profession where honesty and integrity was not always in evidence.

An opportunity to invest in Kate's ambitious undertaking had been Ruby's way of encouraging her niece's entrepreneurial aspirations and the achievements of the company thus far had not caused her to regret that decision. From the outset she had hoped they might gain some small profit in the first five years of trading; now it was rapidly becoming necessary to revise that target. In fact, as the weeks progressed it was clear that a breakeven situation would be achieved much sooner than expected. Kate's dynamism was both infectious and a driving force to which everyone in the company was responding.

Ruby was in the office making coffee before settling to unfinished business when she remembered the expected telephone call which had not materialised the day before. She now felt certain that Kate would telephone before boarding her flight back to Ho Chi Min City and speculated that calling from Noi Bai airport might be easier than from her hotel.

Since moving from the old suite of offices to the facility on Bang Dang jetty, Ruby had fallen into the habit of eating lunch at her desk. The containers of food which one of the office staff collected from street vendors had been eaten and afternoon tea brought to her when finally closing the ledger on a set of accounts which she had been studying. Glancing up at the office clock, she was surprised to see that it was after four thirty in the afternoon and she realised that Kate's call had still not materialised.

Moving across to her niece's desk, Ruby managed to find the directory of useful telephone numbers which she hoped might be lying around. Sitting back down, she then dialled the number listed for Admiral Tanaka's office and was immediately put through to a man with a cultured English accent.

"Mrs Pardoe, how may I help?" Ruby was pleased that there was someone with whom she was able to communicate at her first attempt and ignored the man's mistake with regard to her marital status. It then almost immediately transpired that she was talking to the same aide who had liaised with Kate throughout earlier negotiations.

"Miss Savage was indeed here yesterday morning and there was a meeting with Admiral Tanaka. Our minister for tourism and some other senior government officials were also present. Their session was rather lengthy and not concluded until well after midday; the admiral appeared pleased with the outcome and asked if I would place myself at Miss Savage's disposal. I managed to catch her as she was leaving the building; she thanked me for my offer of assistance and explained that she wished to return to her hotel as a colleague was waiting for her to go on to a further meeting with one of your fuel suppliers. Fortunately I was able to secure the use of a department car and so arranged for it to take Miss Savage back to her hotel. I think it would not be improper of me to mention that like Admiral Tanaka, Miss Savage also appeared to be in high spirits."

Ruby thanked the aide for his help and then turned to the telephone directory once more.

The number for the company's northern fuel supplier was highlighted, which probably indicated that Kate had used it quite recently.

There was further frustration when Ruby discovered that there was no one at the fuel company's office who was able to converse with her in English. She also realised that in Molly's absence she would have to find someone else to interpret.

Further frustration was felt when she discovered that almost all of their employees had either left or were preparing to go home for the night. With some relief a junior clerk readily agreed to stay on and from past experience Ruby knew that the young woman's English was good.

With a measure of impatience she waited while the junior clerk conducted a lengthy conversation in her own language. Eventually the teenager confirmed that both Kate and Molly had visited the fuel depot the day before. The fuel company's commercial director also explained that it had been late afternoon when they left and said that Miss Savage and her colleague were driven away in a Hanoi registered taxi.

The Mekong Express Company's offices at Hai Phong was next on Ruby's list to be contacted, as she thought it possible that Kate and Molly might have decided to call while in the area. When there was no response to this call, she next telephoned Vietnam Air in Hanoi and learned after some considerable wait that the two seat reservations for both Kate and Molly on the return flight to Ho Chi Min City had not been taken up. On hearing this Ruby's earlier mild concern rapidly increased. With a sinking heart she now feared that things were not as they should be. Kate's silence since one brief message the previous day was completely out of character.

Ruby tried to stay calm by telling herself that Kate was not alone and that there would eventually be some logical explanation. She also thought of telephoning Kate's mother in Sri Lanka and then dismissed the idea as serving no good purpose other than worrying a friend.

Managing crisis situations had been part of everyday life in the hotel business and Ruby now reasoned that had an accident occurred, she would quickly have learned of it, as Kate would almost certainly be carrying documentation which linked her back to the Mekong Express Company.

Feeling that there was nothing more to be gained from remaining in the office, Ruby thanked the young clerk for her assistance and suggested that they both leave for home.

An extreme nervous state determined that supper was not high on the agenda and Ruby hoped sleep might be induced through some generous measures of single malt Irish whiskey. Unfortunately for her, the alcohol had lost its effect long before the time she would normally wake and she was walking to Bang Dang jetty as a dawn light was gradually appearing in the eastern sky.

While patiently waiting and listening to the sound of staff arriving, Ruby eventually decided that the time was now right for her to make a further telephone call to the office at Hai Phong. This call was answered by a voice which immediately changed from Vietnamese to English when she announced herself.

"Good morning, Miss Ruby. I was about to call head office. Is Molly available, please?" In that brief instance it was difficult for Ruby to contain her impatience as she had not made the call merely to answer questions. The mention of Molly's name, however, caused her to hesitate.

"I'm afraid she's not here. Can I help?" There was a brief but noticeable hesitation before the voice responded,

"It's nothing that we should be troubling you with." Her intuitive curiosity was aroused and Ruby decided there was no way that the young man was going to fob her off.

"If your call has something to do with company business there is nothing that I would find either troublesome or too trivial. Now please tell me what it is that you wish to speak to Molly about." Further hesitation preceded a rather noisy throat clearing sound before the young man explained,

"It's Mr Nygen. He has not shown up for work this morning and the requisition pads are all locked in his desk. We wouldn't normally bother you at head office other than in an emergency, although we do urgently need the requisition pads as our stock of galley stores is becoming dangerously depleted."

Briefly it occurred to Ruby that sales through the ferry buffet bars was exceeding expectations until she brought her thoughts back to the present and realised that there were more important things which required answers.

"Was Mr Nygen missing from work yesterday?" The man hesitated again and Ruby realised that he was attempting to cover for the absence of his office manager.

"When did you last see Mr Nygen?" Yet more throat clearing was clearly heard before a response to the question was finally given.

"It was the day before yesterday. He was still working at his desk when I left for home." Deciding that changing the questioning might ease the man's feelings of betrayal, Ruby asked,

"Has Miss Kate paid you a visit recently?" The response to this was less hesitant and when she learned that Kate had not been to the northern office her thoughtful silence seemed an opportunity for the man to continue.

"We have a Hanoi taxi in our compound which appears to have been abandoned. It was here when I arrived for work yesterday morning. I assumed that the driver had taken the southbound hydrofoil and risked leaving his vehicle in our private parking lot. I have telephoned a number of the Hanoi based cab companies although as yet none has admitted responsibility for the vehicle. Do you think I should report the matter to the police?" Ruby's thoughts were racing and she was in no mood to be distracted by the trivia of an illegally parked taxi.

"It's no big deal. If the vehicle is in the way you should contact someone and arrange for it to be removed." With continuing thoughts of all kinds of disaster, Ruby muttered some words of farewell before hanging up and dialling the number for Savage Air Freight Services in Sri Lanka.

"Can I speak to Lorna, please?" To test Ruby's patience even further there was a new switchboard operator who did not recognise her voice and twice she was asked to explain who she was.

"I'm sorry, Lorna is on holiday and she is not expected back for at least another week. If you would like me to, I can leave a note on her desk saying that you called," was the eventual unhelpful response.

Ruby then thought of asking if Captain Bob was around, but instead she decided that the commercial director was more removed from family ties and asked if Sidi was available instead.

"Ruby, how are you? How are things with the Mekong Express Company?" She was given no opportunity to respond as Sidi continued,

"I'm sorry that Lorna is not here. An old acquaintance of hers from way back persuaded her to go on holiday. She took off on the spur of the moment and it took us all by surprise," the Malaysian woman added.

"Is there a telephone number where I might contact her?" Ruby asked. Sidi then explained that Lorna had promised to call with a contact number although as yet had not done so.

"I expect she is having a good time, although it's unlike her to neglect us for very long. My guess is that we will be hearing from her in the next day or so."

Ruby swore beneath her breath; concern for Kate's safety was now further aggravated by her inability to make contact with Lorna.

"Is there a problem that I might help with?" Sidi tentatively asked. Ruby then decided to tell her of the fears which were rapidly growing. Kate's unknown whereabouts was adding to a sense of helplessness and she slowly experienced some relief when unburdening her anxieties.

Sidi instantly agreed that Kate had inherited her mother's sense of responsibility and it was most unlike her to be out of reach during crucial stages of their company's early development.

"I think you should report her absence to the police, and it might be a good idea to ask if that Admiral contact of Kate's can offer some assistance. From the little that I've gleaned, the man seems to carry a great deal of influence at high level and his involvement might inject some urgency into the situation." Ruby agreed that she would and suggested Kate's grandfather should not be stressed by their concerns for Kate's safety at this stage. She also added that when Lorna eventually made contact, she was to be told of the situation and urged to telephone Saigon.

An incoming call was all that next prevented Ruby from telephoning Admiral Tanaka's office as she had intended.

"Miss Ruby, there is a call for you. The man has stressed that it is urgent and insists he will speak to no one other than you." Ruby was about to ask the switchboard to tell the caller she was busy, when the young woman startled her by adding,

"He says his call concerns Rory's daughter and that you must take it." With sinking feelings and flashing thoughts of kidnap racing through her mind, Ruby rapidly responded,

"Put him on and while I'm taking the call try to see if there is any way of tracing where he's calling from. This is very important. Don't get diverted by other calls or interruptions. Is that clear?" She had no time to consider if she was acting over dramatically or rashly as she next heard a heavily accented voice.

"If I tell you that your hotel in Bournemouth is called the Ceylon Rest House and that Uncle Lenny Rouse, a friend of yours, is currently living there, will you please listen to what I have to say?"

Ruby's thoughts raced for an explanation. She thought it likely that the man was holding Kate captive and that he had wheedled information from her to establish some authenticity.

"Please listen carefully. I may be interrupted at any time. It is essential that you grasp the significance of what I am about to tell you. I am speaking to you from the island of Hainan. Your niece was brought here with others against her will. I was able to rescue her from her abductors and for the moment she is safe. Kate has written a message which she has asked me to read to you." The man paused briefly.

"Ruby, I have been caught up in a highly illegal operation and urgently need rescuing. Please try to set something up as quickly as possible. The situation is not only dangerous for me; it may also have severe repercussions for the people who are helping me. Uncle Richard and two or three others with military experience would be ideal to attempt my rescue. It will have to be done surreptitiously and I cannot emphasise in strong enough terms that under no circumstances should either the Vietnamese or Chinese authorities be approached. The organisation that abducted Molly and me has absolute influence over the governing body on this island. Any official approach will simply generate denial and a refusal of outside intervention."

The man stopped reading and Ruby's heart sank as she was convinced that the connection had been broken.

"I'm sorry, I saw someone coming in this direction and thought I might have to break off the call. Kate's message to you continues. Under no circumstance should Admiral Tanaka be consulted as he will conclude that intervention through official channels is the only way to proceed. This would most certainly precipitate an even greater search for me than the one which is currently being conducted. Molly is dead and my life is also in grave danger. A small force operating under cover is the only way of getting me off this island alive. I must escape, if for no better reason than to expose the vile organisation which abducted us. It is imperative that their activities are brought to an end as they are responsible for the deaths of countless numbers. I repeat, please, please, do not go official on this. I implicitly trust the man who is making this call. He will lead you to where I am hiding. I am relying on you, Amanda. I know that as we both share the same name you will do your very best to get me out of here." He broke off briefly and for a moment Ruby thought the contact had definitely been broken; she breathed more easily when his voice continued,

"There is someone coming and now I must go."

"Wait, please. How can we make further contact with you and what is your name?" Ruby desperately pleaded, while hoping that the man would not cut her off.

"My name is not important. Tell whoever comes to look for a bulldozer in the port area; there is only one and they will find me by searching for it during normal daylight hours."

Ruby was about to ask for more detail when she heard a click and the sound of a continuous whirring tone as the line was cut.

Struggling to come to terms with what she had just learned, Ruby found a sheet of blank paper and quickly wrote down a resume of all that she could remember of the brief conversation. When she was finished, she remained motionless at her desk, thinking over all that the man had said. A strong intuition suggested that Kate's message was genuine and that it had not been written under duress. Ruby reasoned that had that been the case, there would have been no point in mentioning that her hotel in Bournemouth was called the Ceylon Rest House or that they shared a name other than to lend credibility to the message. The fact that she and her niece used identical second names was known only to Kate's family and a few very intimate friends.

When the telephone operator called to say that she had traced the incoming international call back to a port authority on the Chinese island of Hainan, Ruby's strong feelings were further reinforced. She thanked the resourceful young telephonist for her persistence and hung up without waiting to learn how this success had been accomplished.

At some point during the deliberations that followed Ruby was aware of someone placing tea on her desk. While still in a state of confusion and some considerable shock she reached across for the cup and her trembling hand failed to grip the hot surface of the handle; scalding liquid spilled onto her lap. Pain from the accident caused Ruby to realise that she should drive confused thoughts from her mind and start to act rationally. She then pondered the current dilemma for further precious seconds until deciding to make a further telephone call to Savage Air in Sri Lanka.

"Sidi, it's me again." On this occasion Ruby was relieved by being immediately put through to the company's commercial director.

"There has been a development in the last few minutes. Can I now speak to Richard, please?"

"I'm sorry, Ruby, that will not be possible. Richard is on his way to Rotterdam to collect marine parts for a salvage company. He took off from here around three hours ago and I am not expecting him back for at least ten days."

"Damn and blast!" Ruby swore. "Why in hell's name is everything going so bloody wrong?"

"What do you want Richard for?" Despite Ruby's feelings of utter frustration Sidi's voice came across as a calming influence.

"Have you learned some more of where Kate might be? Or is it that you wished to speak to Richard before telling her grandfather bad news?"

Ruby hastened to reassure Sidi that as yet Kate had not been harmed and then she quickly outlined details of her recent telephone conversation. There was a brief moment of hesitation until Sidi asked Ruby to repeat the message. When she had listened a second time, she asked,

"And do you think the message is genuine? Or might it be that someone has dictated what Kate should write?"

"The message the man claimed Kate had written concluded with reference to both her and my middle names which few people know we share. There was also reference to Uncle Lenny living at my hotel in Bournemouth and I'm sure that Kate, even under duress, would not reveal unnecessary and intimate detail unless she had reason to convince me of its authenticity. Yes, I am definitely convinced that she dictated the message without interference."

Pausing for further deliberation, Sidi then responded by saying that on taking those points into consideration there seemed no other conclusion which could be reached.

"Kate's insistence that we do not approach authorities is one of the stumbling blocks we are going to be up against and if we accept that the rest of her message is genuine, we will also need to understand that there is danger in not complying with her instructions."

Ruby, with little or no idea what this meant, was pondering how they should next proceed when Sidi interrupted her thoughts.

"Let's think on this, Ruby. If we panic now we are going to make a hash of things. I am actually not sorry that Richard is away. Kate idolises him. He has, as you must realise, been the father figure she never had, although in reality he is not the ideal person for this situation. Lorna is much more likely to cope. She has been in similar predicaments and will have a better idea on what to do. I do know that she and Charlie were heading up to Kashmir for their break. I will put some feelers out and see if I can track them down; it shouldn't be difficult checking out the more likely hotels in Srinagar. In the meantime you think about the Admiral and whether or not he might be persuaded to help in a way which will not alert the people on Hainan or risk exposing Kate to further danger."

Being slightly irritated by Sidi's calm, Ruby realised that she was being unreasonable. She had also wanted to ask about Lorna's travelling companion although in the present situation realised it was of little importance. Sidi's suggestion of involving Admiral Tanaka might be sensible, although for at least the time being, Ruby decided she would take heed of Kate's strongly emphasised request and keep officialdom at arm's length. She felt certain that had Kate thought her friend the Admiral was the person to help, she would not have cautioned against approaching him.

Despite the incredible and frightening things which she had now been alerted to, Ruby realised it would also be necessary for her to stay abreast of matters concerning their business. The Mekong Express Company was something which was extremely important to Kate and something which she would expect to be taken care of in her absence. With this in mind she again called the Hai Phong office and suggested that the ship's supplier of chandlery should telephone her at head office to confirm that supplies could be delivered without a requisition if that slight irritation had not been resolved.

"If, however, there is a further problem we can issue an order number. Surely that will suffice." At any other time Ruby's exasperation might have led to an ill-tempered outburst; now she explained that as a last resort they should break open Mr Nygen's desk.

In her haste to react to Kate's predicament, Ruby also realised that there had been little time to consider the shocking news of Molly's death. Only days before she and the young Vietnamese woman had been working on streamlining a system of accountancy which would make the company audit less cumbersome. Faced now with the prospect of breaking the tragic news to Molly's next of kin, she eventually decided to wait in the hope of being able to obtain more accurate detail as things unfolded. It was as she was considering this that she remembered her earlier telephone conversation with the young man at their Hai Phong office and speculated on the office manager's absence being in some way connected. Silently cursing herself for being a dolt, she also remembered her annoyance with the irritating concern over an illegally parked taxi. Ruby now decided that this might be significant as the oil storage director had informed them that Kate and Molly had been driven off in a taxi.

"I suppose the taxi could have been used by their abductors, maybe the driver was in cahoots or even part of their team." She was speculating this as she mechanically picked up the telephone in response to yet another incoming call.

"Ruby, I have just spoken to Sidi and she has told me what has happened. I wish to God it was not true although I know Sidi well enough to realise she would never exaggerate the seriousness of a family problem or be an alarmist unless she was sure of her facts." Ruby thought it typical of Lorna to come straight to the point in a crisis.

"God, Ruby, I am at my wits' end. The whole thing seems quite incredible, although if you wouldn't mind going over it again, I would like to hear from you exactly what was said in Kate's message."

Through considerable relief that Kate's mother had at last been located and was now involved, Ruby almost lost control and broke down. Somehow, despite the physical effort of having to fight back tears, she managed to recount the telephone conversation which had taken place between her and the unknown man. Lorna next queried a number of points and Ruby was glad she'd had the foresight to make notes.

"I am fast coming to the conclusion that we should heed Kate's instruction on the question of alerting the authorities. She was careful to demonstrate that the message was genuine by referring to your joint names and other insignificant but personal detail."

Ruby murmured that was the conclusion she had also arrived at.

"When you and Rory were involved with terrorism there must surely have been circumstances where you both understood that official intervention might be detrimental to the hoped for outcome. The more and longer I consider this, the stronger my feelings are that there is no alternative other than to go along with Kate's instructions."

A background sound of voices indicated that Lorna was calling from somewhere both open and public, and her next request was muffled. This seemed to imply that she was attempting not to be overheard.

"Will you stay where you are? I am going to ring off now. We will need time to think this thing through. When we have finalised a plan it is almost certain that we will require assistance from your end. Please be patient and sit tight."

The connection was broken and Ruby was left to consider the plural in Lorna's statement as opposed to a singular reference.

Speculating then on the nature of Lorna's travelling companion, Ruby thought it unlikely that Lorna would involve anyone unable to contribute. Time to ponder this seemed all too short as it was less than fifty minutes later that Lorna's second call came through.

"Here is what we would like you to do, Ruby. We need you to have a boat available, the type that can be easily inflated from a high pressure air cylinder, and capable of carrying half a dozen men with weapons and equipment. We will also need a four stroke outboard engine of not less than thirty horse power, preferably a Honda or some other make which is quiet running. Will you also try to obtain local charts for the inshore area around Hainan? And one final thing, will it be possible to obtain permission to land a float plane at Vung Tau to collect those items?"

Ruby, after only a moment's hesitation, suggested Admiral Tanaka's department would be the best body to approach for permission to put a float plane down at Vung Tau and she presumed that a flight plan and air traffic requirements would also need to be registered.

"You can leave those final arrangements with me once you have received permission. I feel sure that in the present circumstances Kate will understand the deception played out on her friend's office staff. I would suggest you tell them that we will be delivering urgently required parts for one of the hydrofoils which has mechanical problems. Hopefully the customs people will not then pay too much attention to what we will be bringing in."

"Okay, leave everything to me at this end. Is there a contact number where I can reach you? Lorna suggested they use Sidi as a control centre as she would have access to Lorna via a radio link.

"I presume from what has been said that you will personally be flying down to Vung Tau? Is there anything more you need?" In response to this, Lorna suggested that someone with knowledge of the coastal region around Hainan might be useful, providing they were trustworthy.

"When do you expect to arrive?" Ruby asked, while hoping she had covered everything that she would need to know.

"Expect me in around three days' time. Sidi will update with the ETA as we progress. I realise the wait is going to seem like an eternity although you should try to stay calm. We will need to make refuelling stops on the way down and I will try to snatch a couple of hours sleep at the stopping-off points. Oh, and there is one other thing which I almost forgot. Will you add fuel and a semi rotary pump for refuelling the Cessna to our list of requirements?"

There was something reassuring about Lorna's involvement and Ruby was beginning to feel a great deal easier than she had since receiving Kate's message. In fact she now realised that it was some time since she had last eaten and, as she was considering a simple bread roll with an indistinguishable filling which had been left over from lunch, she heard the familiar sound of a hydrofoil edging onto the jetty. Glancing out through the open window, Ruby immediately recognised the captain, who was silhouetted through the weatherproof wind shield and a further idea occurred.

"Can you spare a few minutes of your precious time, please, Captain Wang?" Ruby had rushed from her office as the craft was made fast alongside and she then waited for the skipper to come ashore.

"Why, of course, Miss Ruby, and if there is some of your excellent coffee brewing my time will be amply rewarded." The senior fleet captain then smiled and she noticed not for the first time how everyone had relaxed since the early days of their new employment.

Ruby poured each of them coffee from the office percolator before leading him through to the privacy of her own office.

"Captain Wang, I have realised for some time that Kate has come to depend on your integrity a great deal. If this was not so, I would not now be taking you into my confidence. I will come straight to the point and not beat about the bush. Are there any charts available for the coastal region around Hainan Island?"

For the briefest of seconds the distinguished-looking captain peered at her with an expression of astonishment on his normally impassive features.

"I was aware that Miss Kate has gone off to Hanoi, as were many of the staff here. We even speculated on the possibility of her negotiating another route, although I for one certainly underestimated her. I never dreamt that she might be dealing with the Chinese. Our boss is certainly an enterprising young woman."

Ruby was about to tell him that he had jumped to the wrong conclusion when the captain forestalled her.

"The company has no charts for that area, Miss Ruby, but I do. While our country was still under French administration I was second officer on an old tramp steamer which regularly shipped scrap metal across to a steel smelting plant at Lin'gao on the island. Fortunately I never throw anything away and so I still have charts for the whole region."

Ruby had no idea what Lorna was planning, although she remembered her friend suggesting that someone with knowledge of the area might be invaluable. If she was going to solicit the captain's help, she also realised that she would have to trust him.

"Captain Wang, the rumours which circulate around companies never cease to amaze me, although sometimes they do contain an element of truth. Miss Kate did go to Hanoi and she was in negotiation for a new route. I am unable to tell you the outcome of those negotiations as she disappeared shortly after they were concluded." A look of confusion blotted the man's features, until he asked with some incredulity,

"Disappeared? Do you think she's had an accident?" Captain Wang gasped, with genuine concern sounding in his voice. Ignoring the question Ruby continued,

"I have since learned that she was taken to Hainan against her will. The people who took her there have great influence over the authorities on the island and we are going to mount a clandestine rescue."

In the short time she had known him Ruby had certainly never seen Captain Wang ruffled, although this was how he now appeared. With the realisation that from now on every minute was precious, Ruby explained how she had learnt of Kate's abduction and also what initial plans were being put in place to mount a rescue. She told him that Kate's mother was flying down to coordinate things and that she would need a trustworthy person with knowledge of Hainan to become involved.

Ruby also told Captain Wang the horrific news regarding Molly's reported death, and asked for his assurance that this would not be revealed until verification of the facts were obtained.

"It will be my responsibility to break the news to Molly's family and I would not want them to learn of this tragedy from elsewhere."

Captain Wang was silent for a while and Ruby hoped she had not made a mistake by confiding in him. Her fears rapidly evaporated, however, with his eventual response.

"I would be foolish to suggest that what you have just told me has not come as a very big shock, Miss Ruby." The man then studied her with deep liquid brown eyes which seemed to be searching the very depths of her soul.

"You can rest assured I will do everything in my power to assist with Miss Kate's safe return to Saigon. I am no longer in the first flush of youth, although certainly the past has taught me many things. Things I have witnessed which still today makes sleep difficult. Our young boss with, I daresay, guidance from you, has demonstrated that a successful business is about people and I believe her safe return will benefit many of us here." Captain Wang then breathed out in what seemed to be an agonised sigh before adding,

"Had anyone other than you told me this extraordinary story I would have thought them crazy." With feelings of overwhelming relief Ruby, on impulse, clasped the man's hands.

"Thank you, Captain Wang. There is no time to waste, so let's get started. First I would like you to take yourself off the duty roster, although no explanation should be given other than to say that you have a special assignment which I have asked you to perform. When you have done that, would you also please attempt to secure everything which is on this list? I forgot to ask Kate's mother about the type of fuel and the quantity she requires for her aircraft although we can quickly rectify that by putting a call through to Sri Lanka."

With so much to organise and someone to confide in, Ruby now felt much easier in her mind. When she next telephoned through to Koggala, it was Sidi who answered the call. Ruby quickly updated her on what had happened and also what she was doing to ensure that Lorna's requirements were taken care of.

"I know that Lorna will want to be in the thick of things when they attempt Kate's rescue, although you should try to dissuade her from direct involvement. She is a good organiser and I think her contribution will be more productive if we encourage her to concentrate on just that," Sidi suggested.

"If you would like me to locate a small force of men who are suitable for a commando-style operation, I feel sure I will be able to obtain some names from your old boss, Colonel da Silva. He will almost certainly have contacts from his days in state security and I know that he still has high regard for both you and Lorna."

"That's a brilliant idea, Sidi. Yes, please do whatever you can. Although don't tell him that Kate is in China or that she has been abducted. I feel more certain than ever that it is important we heed her warning regarding intervention by official sources. I have spoken to Lorna on this and she also agrees that we can't afford interference from officialdom."

"How like Lorna to have engaged such a competent young woman," Ruby murmured to herself. It came as no surprise that an employee of Savage Air would present an image of being clear-sighted and understand the problems of locating a mercenary force of fighting men.

Silently criticising herself for overlooking this point, Ruby placed her head in her hands and pondered what other important things she might have missed. Had Lorna explained her rescue plan in detail, there may have been much more for Ruby to concern herself with.

# Chapter Twenty Four

There was something reassuring when peering over Captain Wang's shoulder at Lorna's silhouette, which was illuminated by weak light from the instrument panel. Charlie noticed, however, that her otherwise attractive features were now lined with fatigue. His initial reassurance came from the many thousands of miles that he had now flown with someone who he had rekindled strong feelings for. Fatigue, he realised, was not the only strain that his pilot was experiencing. Flying at low-level with the sea only a few hundred feet beneath them was hazardous and the added burden of this, together with her fears for Kate's safety, was taking its toll.

Charlie's thoughts turned to their long hours of uninterrupted flying with only Lorna at the controls and once more he marvelled at both her stamina and determination. She had slept for four hours when they stopped off at Koggala to refuel, and a further five hours at the company's base in Malaysia. The latter stop, although planned, had become something of a necessity as low engine oil pressure had been indicated on the instrument panel while they were on approach still some way out over the Malacca Straits.

It had been explained to Charlie that the somewhat dogleg course they had flown added additional miles, although Lorna reasoned that using Savage Air's home base and the Lumut facility in Malaysia to check the aircraft over was an added security precaution. Fortunately a faulty oil pressure sensor proved to be the only problem, and Lorna was able to grab some badly needed sleep while the fault was rectified.

There had been no time for her to have further rest when they reached Vung Tau, as she had brushed aside his reasoning that fatigue might jeopardise the operation and firmly told him that there would be time for sleep once she had returned to the safety of Vietnam.

At Vung Tau they were met by an attractive middle aged woman and in her haste to get the rescue attempt under way, Lorna almost overlooked an introduction. Ruby had, in turn, introduced the man who was now sitting up front with Lorna, in the same seat which Charlie had occupied for all but the latter part of their marathon journey.

Charlie's first impression of Captain Wang was that the man was dour and probably lacked humour. When, however, they discussed plans for getting ashore on Hainan undetected, he was impressed by the sea captain's practical suggestions.

Lorna was also relieved to learn from the hydrofoil pilot that there was a well-protected deep water harbour at Lin'gao and that it was now unused. Captain Wang explained that it had been constructed to offload iron ore for a smelting plant which had long since ceased to function. He also told them that he had talked with a trusted uncle who regularly fished the area and who assured him that the old smelting works and its harbour were, for the most part, deserted.

It had also been Captain Wang's suggestion that bicycles should be taken along as he estimated it to be a road journey of some thirty miles to the port of Haikou.

Charlie was impressed by the obvious effort which had gone into supplying everything that Lorna requested. He attributed much of this to the sea captain's quiet competence while also understanding that Ruby had also played an important role. He learned that it had been Ruby who had thought of providing him and the three Gurkhas with an assortment of peasant clothes for their mission.

While once more peering over Captain Wang's shoulder, Charlie thought he detected a darkening in the sky ahead and speculated on it being their objective. The occasional white from the crest of a wave was the only other sign that the sea was still beneath them.

Before starting out on this final leg of their long journey, Lorna had again stressed the dangers of what lay ahead. She told both him and the three Gurkhas that she would understand if they wished to reconsider. Apart from obvious danger, there was risk of capture by the Chinese and while relations between the People's Republic and the Western world had thawed in recent years, anyone apprehended by the Chinese authorities for illegal entry should expect to be dealt with both harshly and unsympathetically.

There was only the occasional glint from a star overhead and Charlie thought this was not good. Before starting out on this last leg of their journey the meteorological report from the Hong Kong observatory had forecast a full moon and cloudless sky. The observatory had also indicated a moderate wave height from a north easterly bearing. Putting an aircraft down on water in good light was hazardous; to do so in near darkness was highly questionable.

Somewhere on the island ahead, Kate was being sheltered by some unknown person from life-threatening danger. Charlie had never considered himself particularly brave, and certainly not so by comparison to the old warriors who were accompanying him.

Lorna's resolve as their initial plans unfolded had shown him another unimaginable side of her and Charlie understood that hesitation or weakness on his part would destroy any hopes he had for a lasting relationship. He had also reasoned that without personal motive he would still have volunteered, as Kate, on the two occasions they met, had stirred strong and protective feelings in him.

His recollection of all that had happened since Lorna made her telephone call from the Grand Hotel in Srinagar was now rather blurred, although he still remembered his initial reaction of regret to her making the call. His thoughts, of the disruption to their time together that this might cause, had in fact proved all too accurate.

With only noise from the single engine to disturb his thoughts, he now recalled the rapid reaction which had taken place before reaching their present position. Charlie remembered that after returning the horses to Ali Baba they had stopped off at their hotel and he had ordered cold beers while Lorna made use of the telephone. He had taken the beers to a table and been glad of an opportunity to rest from the rigours of their trek.

It had seemed obvious from her expression that Lorna's call was causing concern and this had been when Charlie speculated on the wisdom of interrupting an enjoyable holiday by making business calls.

When Lorna woke him, he came to with his head on his arms. Charlie then realised almost immediately that the happiness of their holiday had been broken and in reply to his anxious question, Lorna briefly summarised all that she had just learned from Sidi. Notwithstanding the shock from this, he had wryly thought of how his recent concern had centred on safety and the danger of Lorna or him being kidnapped while in Kashmir.

It had taken precious seconds for him to grasp that Kate had been abducted and that at least one of her colleagues had been murdered. When he finally shook sleep from his muddled thoughts, Charlie suggested that Lorna should telephone Ruby in Vietnam and ask her to confirm everything in the message that she had conveyed to Sidi.

Finding further coins for the telephone was the first problem for them to overcome and Charlie quickly resolved this by obtaining permission to use the hotel's private line. He had then listened to a one-sided conversation and marvelled at Lorna's self-control despite a background of noise from chattering hotel office staff.

When Lorna eventually rang off she confirmed with increased trepidation that she had been given an accurate account of the anonymous caller's message. Following this they were each absorbed with their own individual thoughts until Charlie eventually broke the impasse.

"If your brother is on his way to Europe it will require someone other than him to co-ordinate bringing Kate home. Mounting her rescue is not going to be easy and it's obvious that we do not have much time. I have thought things through and the obvious solution would be for me to go. There are other things which I would like you to consider and you will obviously have some thoughts on the matter. It might be an idea for us to pool ideas before making final decisions and maybe now would be as good a time as any to air some views?" Lorna had then studied him carefully, before responding,

"During the time we have spent here in Kashmir it has become obvious that you once had some military training." She paused then, as though reluctant to continue, and Charlie realised later that it was because of her desperation to find a solution for Kate's unusual rescue attempt.

"Have you really considered the danger that you would be placing yourself in if I agree to your proposal?" Charlie took his time before responding to this, until finally displaying an expression which Lorna found difficult to interpret.

"One day I hope ours will be a lasting relationship. That can never happen if you fail to allow me to become involved with whatever it is that enables you to bring your daughter safely home."

"You might be killed," Lorna countered. Then as the thought occurred, she added,

"It's also possible that you might have to kill. Would you be able cope with that?"

"I hope that won't be necessary, although please don't doubt my resolve. A great deal of time has passed since I last played at being a soldier although I firmly believe my relationship with Kate, through you, will equip me as well as anyone for what has to be done."

To reassure her, Charlie might have described the two nights he had lain in ambush on a rocky mule path in Cyprus and that he had killed an accomplice of Mikhail Fakharehde. He could also have explained that Fakharehde and his EOKA group had accounted for the lives of countless civilian and military personnel, although he didn't, as the taking of another person's life had always weighed heavy on his conscience. Charlie also realised that unsubstantiated stories of a young conscript soldier's experience would prove nothing. Instead he suggested that they should get down to some serious planning.

Lorna's second telephone conversation with Ruby indicated that she intended flying down to South Vietnam and then on to the island where

247

Kate was in hiding. When she said that she would want to be with the rescue party which then went ashore, Charlie had persuaded her that as the pilot she represented the only known means of escape and it was more important for her to concentrate on the important task of transporting the team out when and if a successful rescue was made.

Reluctantly accepting the wisdom of this, Lorna then asked if he had any thoughts on how they might recruit a group of men with military experience at short notice.

"That is probably not the insurmountable problem you imagine it to be," Charlie had suggested.

"We already have a group of seasoned fighters that are well equipped, more capable and more experienced than most." Lorna's hesitant look of understanding negated the need for further explanation.

"I will to talk to them and if we are able to secure their services I imagine we will be well on our way to resolving that particular problem."

It had been impossible to detect the presence of the two Gurkhas as they made their way back to the houseboat. Once aboard, however, the three small men had shown strong emotional feelings before then taking the news of Kate's abduction in their stride.

As had become customary, Boom acted as the trio's spokesman and simply declared that through association with Charlie and Lorna, the young woman was family. With a display of genuine sincerity he then explained that it was the group's duty to assist with her rescue.

Boom assured them that, as Mustapha Al Hameed had detailed them to an assignment with Sergeant Greenwood from which they had not so far been released, they would honour their contractual obligation until such time as Charlie was satisfied with the outcome and discharged them from their commitment.

When Lorna outlined plans for the rescue attempt and described the risks she envisaged them taking, the three battle-hardened mercenaries made light of the obvious danger.

"We are soldiers of fortune, memsahib. While we were still full-time serving members with the Brigade of Gurkhas we were simply no more than that. It is what we are born to and also what we are best equipped to do. Sergeant Greenwood has demonstrated that he has remembered his military training and we prefer working with people who understand what we might be up against."

There was then a mischievous grin on Boom's face as he cast a look in Charlie's direction.

"Our fee will, of course, need some adjustment, although we are confident that you will demonstrate your usual generosity."

Glancing back over his shoulder to where the three middle-aged warriors were sleeping in a jumble of cargo netting, bicycles and a deflated rubber dingy, Charlie felt a surge of affection for the three men. He admired their courage and was overly impressed that there had been no hesitation and that they were prepared to go with him into a situation which was totally beyond his comprehension. The fact that they were able to sleep while showing no concern for the present situation seemed further indication of their attitude towards life-threatening danger.

Charlie had grown to like and admire the Gurkhas during their trek into the foothills of the Zanskar mountain range, and if there was a need to face unknown danger, he was relieved that it was to be with these three.

Bang had reminded them that a portable communications radio should be added to the ever-growing list of supplies which they were taking, and Charlie was both pleased and impressed to learn that all three Gurkhas were trained radio operators.

These immediate thoughts were interrupted by Lorna's raised voice above noise from the engine.

"Will you wake those three sleeping beauties and get them strapped into their seats please, Charlie? I estimate that we are less than fifteen minutes from touch down."

The three old soldiers had previously demonstrated how quickly they could gain sleep; now they demonstrated that waking easily was something more for which they had trained.

Boom slid in next to Charlie and then both Bing and Bang followed. They'd barely time to fasten their seat belts before the dark scene ahead lightened and was then illuminated by moonlight as overhead cloud parted.

"Let's hope this light holds for the next few minutes," Boom muttered, just loud enough for Charlie to hear. Despite noise and vibration it also seemed that some discussion was taking place between Lorna and Captain Wang.

Peering ahead Charlie thought he had a glimpse of what might be a concrete groin jutting out to sea. He assumed this to be the breakwater of the inner safe mooring which they were aiming to locate. From earlier discussions he understood that Lorna now had no intention of putting down in the disused harbour as the enclosed water might be strewn with debris. Fortunately an old pennant or some other piece of rag was fluttering from the boom head of a derelict crane which was just visible by light from the pale moon.

"Now we have also confirmed which way the wind is blowing," Charlie heard Lorna mutter with some irony.

249

Charlie next marvelled that the port wing did not touch waves as their aircraft was put into a tight turn. He also realised that Lorna's customary and cautionary approach was to be abandoned in favour of minimising noise. Before turning into the wind she then turned to them and warned,

"This is it! We are going in." Charlie understood this to be the moment of no return and felt his stomach muscles tighten.

At the start of their holiday he had thought an opportunity to put down on water would not be realised until they returned to Koggala; instead he had now put down first at Vung Tau and was about to do so again off the Chinese island of Hainan. Had he been impressed with Lorna's handling of the aircraft on the previous occasion, his admiration was as nothing compared to how he now felt.

Charlie knew absolutely nothing about flying although it was impossible not to be aware of Lorna's skill as she prepared for final approach.

Staring with fixed gaze through the side window, he watched as the starboard float kissed water and then trailed a seemingly endless wake behind it. Slowly the float sank deeper and creaming foam then obliterated it from view as spray washed over the Perspex.

"Okay everyone, it's time to go. I've cut the engine as I don't want the dingy being dragged onto the prop before you've an opportunity to start the outboard. Captain Wang and I will moor up to an anchor out here until we receive the signal that you are ashore. Don't forget, when I have seen three long flashes from your torch and one short one, we will be leaving. Good luck and please do your best to bring my precious daughter out to safety."

It was impossible to clearly see the expression on Lorna's face, although the tremor in her voice determined the anxiety she was feeling.

Charlie next found himself struggling to maintain balance as Bing passed bicycles down to him. The Zodiac had miraculously expanded to a very large inflatable when it was lowered into the water and the gas canister nozzles had been attached.

Watching as the Israeli sub-machine pistols wrapped in protective oilskins were handed across to Boom, Charlie once more questioned their good fortune in being able to bring weaponry into yet another country.

When the outboard engine was fired up without difficulty, Bang was then able to steady the craft against swirling and strong currents.

Noise from their exhaust echoed eerily as they slowly entered the confines of the now disused iron ore handling harbour. Nosing gently along the innermost wall they eventually came to the rusting rungs of some metal steps.

Charlie's foot slipped on slime as he climbed; fortunately he had taken a firm hold with both hands and quickly made his way to the quayside above.

The bicycles and other oddments were handed up to him and these were then followed by the outboard. When his three companions joined him they were with some effort then able to haul the dingy up onto firm ground.

Since leaving the plane Charlie's night vision had improved and he now made his way across to the denser bulk of something which stood out in the gloom. It transpired that this was an old steam locomotive which had obviously been out of service for a very long time as shards of rust peeled from its outer surface when touched.

"Come on," Charlie quietly urged. "I have found a good place to conceal both the inflatable and engine."

The outboard engine and spare inflation canisters fitted snugly into the firebox and because of its bulk they wrapped the deflated dingy in a ragged tarpaulin before lowering it into the locomotive's tender.

"I wouldn't think anyone will bother uncovering that," Bang murmured, as they spread cords of rotting wood over the deflated Zodiac.

Four sets of eyes then stared seaward in the direction of where the Cessna's engine could clearly be heard as it laboured to gain altitude. The shore group had signalled that they were ashore once the dingy and supplies were safely landed on the quayside and the four companions now silently wished Lorna and the hydrofoil skipper bon voyage. Each one of them realised the importance of this as Lorna and her amphibian represented their only known means of escape from the island.

"We have a long cycle ride ahead. If we run into anyone on the road, we will have to hope that these clothes will pass us off as locals." Boom warned.

The coastal road to Haikou was fortunately flat and well surfaced. They made good progress and when the raiding party eventually passed a herdsman together with his herd of milking buffalo in the early dawn light, they simply pulled their hats down and rode on by, offering nothing more than a brief wave.

On entering the outskirts of town they came across the first signs of early morning workers emerging from their homes and much to their relief the people appeared only concerned with shaking off the effects of sleep.

By keeping the sometimes visible waters of the Qiongzhou Strait to their left, Charlie hoped the road would eventually lead them into the port area. Twice their way was blocked when they came to the end of streets which led to nowhere. Eventually, however, they spotted the silhouettes of booms and dockside cranes against an ever lightening sky.

251

The group had taken yet one more wrong turn when the sound of chattering voices from behind alerted them to the fact that they were being pursued by another large group of cyclists.

"Take the next turning off this road so they can pass," Charlie whispered to his companions, and when the following group surged on by, he urged,

"Come on. Let's follow them. They may be on their way for an early shift at the port."

Keeping pace with the group ahead helped considerably as yet two further diversions certainly prevented them from wasting time with incorrect routes.

"This doesn't look good," Boom quietly exclaimed as a security box with a barrier became visible over the shoulders of the group in front.

It may have been the early hour which helped or the surge of cyclists which swept under the raised barrier; fortunately no challenge for security checks came and each of them breathed more easily as they passed into the confines of the port.

As the leading group broke up and peeled away in small numbers, the four expressed quiet relief that they had made it to this point unchallenged.

Rough sawn planks of unseasoned timber piled high on raised plinths in an area with convenient walkways appeared to be as good a place as any from where to begin their search.

"I think we should hide our bicycles under these baulks of timber. If we then also need a place to hide there appears to be room for both us and our gear to be stowed out of sight."

Satisfied that they had removed all signs of the equipment which was not immediately required, Charlie then suggested that they should eat some of the food they had brought with them before setting off to reconnoitre.

"We may have to spend time looking for the contact and it's important that we eat. I think we will need all our strength and wits to keep out of trouble in the days ahead."

Once more Charlie was amazed by the sheer unnerving capacity of his companions as, despite the precarious position which they found themselves in, the three Gurkhas ate their food with obvious relish. Eventually, when they appeared replete, he announced,

"I think we will cover the area more effectively if we search in pairs. Please remember that we are looking for a bulldozer and that should be where we hope to find our contact."

Boom and Bang then went off in one direction while Charlie and Bing made their way cautiously through a maze of stacked shipping containers. Eventually they came across an unused area in which there were signs that it was being prepared for redevelopment. Tubular steel piles had been neatly stacked and a concrete batching plant partially erected. Charlie also decided there was every indication that a bulldozer or some other machine had recently levelled the ground and he hoped it might still be working somewhere close by.

Cautiously skirting round the perimeter of this area, Charlie's intuition was rewarded by sounds from a bellowing exhaust which suggested that a machine was labouring on the other side of further stacked containers.

"Come on, Bing, that noise is worth investigating, although it doesn't sound like any bulldozer that I've ever worked with. Let's stay in amongst the stacked containers and try to get a closer look at whatever it is."

Charlie's first reaction was one of disappointment. The machine they had heard was nothing other than a large agricultural tractor and he was about to suggest this was not what they were looking for when he noticed the small angled bulldozer blade mounted at its front.

Concealed beneath a tangle of brambles the two then watched as the tractor hauled its rear-mounted scarifying tines through the rock-hard soil. Heartened by the sight of this, Charlie's experienced eye told him that the operator was breaking up the solidified pan before making use of his bulldozer blade.

When the machine eventually stopped close to where they were both concealed, it seemed an opportunity might occur for them to confirm that this was where they might find their contact.

When the operator clambered down from his high perch they watched as he then made use of a heavy long-handled hammer to knock out retaining pins on the bulldozer stabilising arms.

"I think he is about to rake the blade round at an angle," Charlie's whispered explanation informed Bing. Then next placing his fingers to his lips, he motioned for the Gurkha to remain concealed. If he had misread the situation and failed to silence the man, he knew he could rely on Bing to complete the task. It also occurred to Charlie that if the tractor operator was their contact, he would be expecting someone of Caucasian appearance and be less surprised by him than by the somewhat battle-hardened features of an old warrior springing out from nowhere.

The unsuspecting man was lending weight to the task of rotating the bulldozer blade through forty-five degrees when Charlie took him from behind. With one hand clamping the man's mouth he prodded the sharp point of an assault knife into the fleshy part of the man's throat.

"Where is Kate?" In that brief second of indecision the operator's expression changed from fear to relief and with some difficulty managed to indicate that he wished to speak.

"Okay. Although I warn you that if you make more noise than a whisper you are a dead man. Do you understand?" A slight affirmative nod was sufficient for Charlie to cautiously release his grip while keeping the point of the knife close to the man's jugular.

"We thought it would take much longer for you to get here," the man gasped, while swallowing hard to breathe normally.

"Are you Kate's uncle?" Thinking that long explanations were unnecessary at this stage, Charlie nodded before repeating his question.

"She is not here. I will take you to her when my work is finished for the day. It will be much safer for us to travel in the dark and it might raise awkward questions if I leave before completing a day's work. Are you alone?"

Charlie explained there were others with him and that they were at present out searching for a bulldozer. A nod of understanding satisfied Charlie that his vagueness suggested a force of some strength. He had no intention of revealing anything of importance until he was absolutely sure that this man could be trusted.

"Please try to stay calm. I understand that you will have fears for Kate's safety and it would be misleading if I played down the danger to your niece. When I left home this morning she was helping my wife. She has also been very good at amusing our children during her stay." The man then went on to explain that Kate's time with them had been interrupted on a number of occasions by search parties which were constantly out looking for her.

"These searches that her abductors carry out have been far more extensive than the one they conducted when my wife and I escaped. Thankfully they did not show up at our home yesterday and we are hoping this is an indication that they have concluded Kate is not in our area."

Although his English was heavily accented, Charlie was surprised by coming to the conclusion that their contact was an educated man. He also felt an indication that the man and his wife were once prisoner's of the same people who had abducted Kate was too obscure to be used as some form of a cover story and his trust slowly gained momentum.

"How far is your home from this place and how shall we get there?" The man replied after only a moment of thought.

"It will take at least an hour and that's assuming there are no problems with port security." This explanation appeared to prompt further consideration.

"I think things will be made safer if you leave your men here in the port area and travel alone with me tonight. A large group will be too conspicuous and will almost certainly attract attention."

While thoughtfully contemplating other problems the man unthinkingly completed the resetting angle of his bulldozer while Charlie wielded the hammer to drive home the retaining pins. It occurred to Charlie that it had been many years since he had done similar things and he had certainly not expected to be repeating the exercise on a Chinese island. These recollections were interrupted by his new companion.

"I travel to and from home on a motorcycle; if you keep that hat pulled down it should be safe for you to ride with me in the twilight. When we return daybreak will not have arrived and we will have to hope that poor light will act as our shield."

Separation from the rest of the group was not what had initially been planned, although Charlie could see the wisdom of accepting advice and guidance from someone with local knowledge.

"I think we should move out of sight behind those crates. The supervisor will certainly be surprised to see that I have assistance with re-setting the machine should he come upon us while making his rounds. The two of us may also attract attention out here in the open when passengers for the ferry start arriving."

A traditional ferry link span structure was clearly visible in the direction that the man then indicated.

"I can understand the obvious concern at being separated from the rest of your group and I also understand that there is a great deal for you to take on trust. Maybe it will help if I introduce myself and describe how I became involved." Charlie's affirmative nod prompted him to continue.

"My name is Luc Tun and I am from Cambodia. My wife and I came to this island as refugees, hoping to reach Europe where we thought there might be improvements to the life that we had lived under Pol Pot and the Khmer Rouge. Our passage was arranged by the same organisation that eventually abducted Kate. My wife and I were fortunate as we both managed to escape; the rest of our group, numbering in excess of three hundred, all died. Some were not treated as humanly as animals in a slaughter house. A few with rare blood groups or physical abnormalities had parts of their bodies taken to be used for transplant operations on patients who are able to afford the extremely high prices that Dr Chang Jin-Ming demands. Dr Chang is a skilled transplant surgeon and he heads an organisation which is both brutal and completely ruthless. What the man cannot command through fear he buys and the governing body on this island is completely under his control. When escaping my wife and I were extremely lucky to stumble across one of the few people that Dr Chang had failed to influence. With help from this generous old man, who by the way happened to be a deaf mute, we were able to integrate into the farming community. There are lots of Vietnamese living on Hainan and the local people generally think that is where we are from."

Luc Tun hesitated before peering out from behind their screen of crates and packing cases.

"I really should be working again. If the machine is standing idle for too long it might attract attention from the works engineer or one of his supervisors. More of the situation here can be explained when I take you home to see Kate. I know she will be surprised, as she is not expecting anyone to attempt her rescue for some while."

When Bing emerged from his place of concealment in response to Charlie's signal, the Cambodian acknowledged his appearance with interest before offering further explanation.

"I thought it unwise to give my name to Kate's aunt when telephoning. There is a bad element operating everything of importance on the island and they have almost all the telephone lines tapped. Fortunately my work here in the port allows me some access to the office telephones and because of its commercial importance international calls do not generally attract the same attention."

Charlie's trust in the man strengthened as his explanations unravelled and he decided that separating from the Gurkhas and travelling home with him at the end of the day's work made sense.

Before remounting his tractor Luc Tun suggested that Charlie and his men should remain in hiding throughout the day and suggested a place where they would be reasonably comfortable.

"It will be all too obvious when my work is finished at the end of this shift as there will be a mass exodus of pedestrians and cyclists. When that happens come back and meet me here."

The noisy machine had resumed grading off an area of previously untouched soil when Charlie and Bing stealthily took off in search of Boom and Bang.

When the rescue party eventually regrouped they then took shelter in the hiding place that Luc Tun had suggested, and although the weighbridge had long since fallen into a state of dilapidation, the scales office was still intact. The windows were roughly boarded over and at some time in the past someone had forced the door lock. High ceilings were designed for ventilation and as the morning wore on all four men appreciated protection from the glaring heat outside.

On gaining the hoped-for security of the weighbridge office they made a brief radio call confirming to Lorna that initial contact had been accomplished. Lorna's acknowledgement was also brief apart from wishing them luck and a further request to take care.

With nothing more to occupy them, three rested while one kept watch. Charlie managed a little sleep, although for the most part worried about what might yet go wrong. He was also troubled that a further search by Kate's abductors might locate her before he was able to bring her under the cover of their protection.

In addition to these concerns Charlie worried over Lorna flying back into Chinese air space, being all too aware that they had been fortunate to get this far undetected. Surprisingly he was grateful for these distractions when it was his turn to stand watch.

Ugly blunt-ended ferries came and went and this activity provided some relief from the monotony of waiting. Charlie watched through gaps in the boarded up windows as passengers embarked and disembarked. Vehicles using the ferries assembled at a central holding point while foot passengers were allowed to board first.

Some distraction was also provided by Luc Tun as he went about his work; the weighbridge office afforded a good vantage point from where Charlie could easily view the new port development with more than passing interest. At around mid-day the Cambodian was joined by another man and Charlie watched as they took food from lunch boxes and settled down to eat. Aside from this and other minor disruptions, Luc was left unattended and unsupervised.

It seemed convenient that the late afternoon watch rota should fall to Charlie as in theory he would then be prepared for meeting Luc Tun at the end of his work commitment. Unfortunately the events of previous days without sleep were beginning to take their toll. Stifling a yawn and shaking off an urge to sleep before glancing at his watch, Charlie was surprised to see that it was almost six p.m. Hurriedly peering out he then watched with some concern as a trickle of cyclists began to pass. Quickly rousing his companions he quietly told the three Gurkhas,

"I have cut things too fine and Luc Tun will now be waiting for me. It might be a good idea for you to move back to where we earlier hid our bicycles. If we have been spotted by anyone, I would like you to be someplace where they might not expect to find you. If the authorities do know of our presence, they will probably wait for nightfall before attempting to surprise us." Boom nodded his approval.

"In a situation like this it is always better to be where you are least expected," the old warrior agreed.

"Now we have to hope I won't encounter problems and that we can get away from here some time tomorrow." In response to this Boom asked what they should do if Charlie failed to return with Kate the following morning.

"Good point. If Luc Tun returns to work without me, one of you should try to make contact and establish what is happening. I would stress, however, that particular care should be taken as the abductors or their island lackeys may be using the Cambodian as bait with which to bring you three out into the open. If neither I nor Luc Tun has shown up by the day after tomorrow, assume that we have been rumbled and get yourselves back to the rendezvous point the best way you can." At this point Charlie had to hold his hands up to forestall protest.

"If I am taken by the authorities and interrogated I will say that I was parachuted in alone. With any luck that should buy sufficient time for you to be picked up. I also suggest that you travel separately. If they are onto us, they will probably be watching out for a group of people as opposed to single individuals."

"I am unable to offer a better alternative, Sergeant. Let's hope everything is going to work out and that your contingency plan will be unnecessary."

Boom's two companions each appeared to be on the verge of adding to this; instead one clapped him on the back while the other simply nodded farewell.

"I was worried that you had been discovered. You are late," Luc Tun admonished, with obvious agitation.

"We should have left with the main group of outgoing workers. Now we will have to hope that there is no security in place at the dock gate as they often search stragglers," he added with a grunt of concern.

Unfortunately Luc's fears were more than justified and the barrier was down when they reached it. Charlie's pulse raced and his heart was in his mouth as he clutched the assault knife beneath baggy work stained overalls. Fortunately the security guard was only interested in what Luc might be carrying in his haversack and gave Charlie barely a glance. With a wave of dismissal the barrier was eventually lifted and the pair were ushered on through.

"Phew, that was a close shave. I thought the security man would hear my heart pounding and think it was a bomb," Charlie joked. There was no immediate response from Luc Tun and Charlie realised that he was in the company of an extremely cool character.

Once they had reached the relative safety of open country Luc slowed, the noise level dropped and he was able to talk over his shoulder.

"One of the port mechanics who has become a friend of mine joins me for lunch most days. Today he mentioned in passing that another shipment of donors for the medical centre is expected tomorrow. I have gleaned good information from him in the past and it has for the most part been accurate. He seems to have a flair for keeping an ear to the ground."

The Cambodian's over the shoulder dialogue was abruptly interrupted when he swerved to miss a large monitor lizard which was lazily crossing the road and only became visible in the last few metres of their approach through the poor lighting on Luc's machine. Continuation of his lunch-time conversation was then further explained after a grunted apology was offered.

"I pretended to be only mildly interested although that was not really the case; there is normally a much wider gap between those shipments. Do you think Kate's escape has caused them to fast track this intake through?"

With only sketchy knowledge of what had been happening Charlie thought his feelings on the matter were irrelevant, and as the wind was in his face, it was necessary for him to shout in order to be heard.

Realising that their conversation was one-sided, Luc suggested they would soon be leaving the road and that Charlie should hold on tight. The machine accelerated and in what then seemed only a short distance they veered off the metalled road and encountered the uneven surface of a dirt track. Billowing clouds of dust engulfed them and they completed the remainder of the journey in silence.

Uncertain as to their whereabouts, Charlie dismounted first and then watched with interest as a large savage-looking dog greeted Luc Tun.

"Come, I feel sure you will not be expected and if we enter the house quietly your arrival will be a welcome surprise for Kate."

The young woman's eyes in fact expressed a mixture of amazement and surprise. This was followed by an expression of sheer disbelief as Charlie stepped into the light from an acetylene lamp that was hanging from an overhead beam.

"Charlie! What on earth are you doing here?" There was no opportunity to explain as without waiting Kate had thrown herself into his arms. Loud sobs of relief echoed against his chest and he held her tightly to him while Luc Tun and a young woman looked on. Eventually and with obvious effort to control her relief, Kate continued,

"Dear God, if you only knew how I have prayed that help would arrive and now that you are here I can scarcely believe it." A series of half-choked sobs stifled the words which became inaudible until, with some effort, the young woman blew her nose and then concentrated on regaining some composure.

"We thought there was little chance of anyone arriving for at least another week. Is Uncle Richard with you?" Charlie explained why he had deputised for her uncle and then gave a quick summary of all that had taken place since learning of her abduction. When Kate grasped what was being done to prepare for her rescue, she then had further difficulty in containing her emotions until eventually suggesting,

"I hope I've not endangered the lives of you and those other men, Charlie. I also pray that your efforts will succeed, as I would like an opportunity to meet and thank all the people who have been involved. Most of all I want to escape so that I can inform the outside world what has been happening here. It can't go on Charlie, it must be stopped!" There was near hysteria as she clung to him once more and the volume of her voice petered to a mere squeak.

Kate's trembling limbs indicated that this was a far less confident young woman than the one he had previously met. Charlie also quickly realised that she had been badly shaken and was now suffering from some form of traumatic shock.

When, with extreme effort, she once more regained control, Kate then introduced him to Lai Mee and three young children, who were obviously in the throes of being prepared for bed.

Charlie was next invited to join the family at their evening meal and Kate, with help from the two Cambodians, described what the motives were behind the people trafficking operation. He learned about Dr Chang Jin-Ming and his accomplice General Zin Bax, about the clinic in Guangzhou and the things which took place there. Charlie listened with incredulity as he heard the story of Kate's rescue from the medical centre and a description of how on five separate occasions she had been forced to hide in a hole in the ground while thugs from the medical centre trampled over her.

"I am so grateful to Luc and Lai Mee; they have risked everything and much more than they should have. I am also lucky to still be alive. Unlike poor unsuspecting Molly, who could not possibly have understood the terrible thing that was happening to her and the two men," Kate added with a sob.

Charlie had no idea who Molly was, although he once more placed a consoling arm around her; on this occasion Kate quickly blew her nose before continuing,

"I was really, really frightened when I heard those people looking for me. They seemed to spend so much time standing right on top of where I was buried. If Luc hadn't had the idea of placing a rotten carcase that stunk to high heaven in the dung heap, I am sure that they would have been more persistent and discovered my hiding place. They threatened Lai Mee; they even questioned the children. Fortunately the children have been well schooled and the two boys pretended not to understand. Lai Mee told those people that the children spoke only Vietnamese and that her daughter had not yet learned to talk. Even the old dog played his part. He gave us ample warning on each of the occasions they came and even withstood attacks from the other vicious animals which the searchers brought with them to act as sniffer dogs. I actually heard him yelp with pain and assumed that he had been kicked. It was only his good training and Lai Mee's control which prevented him from retaliating; had he done so, Lai Mee is convinced that the medical centre people would have shot him."

This was the same animal that Charlie had noticed when earlier climbing from the rear seat of Luc Tun's motorcycle and been glad that he was accompanied by the dog's owner.

There was a gap in the conversation at this point, while Lai Mee persuaded her two reluctant sons that they should go to bed. It seemed doubtful, however, that sleep would come easily, as having yet one more stranger in their home was all too exciting.

When they finally left the eating area, Kate asked,

"May I take these food scraps out to the dog please?" They had finished eating a very palatable meal which Charlie thought was of exceptional quality considering the poor peasant surroundings to which he had been brought. The dishes were being cleared from the table and it was obvious that Kate believed the dog deserved all the rewards she could find for him.

"Perhaps when you have seen to the dog you might like to say goodnight and farewell to the children. With going to bed late they will probably sleep in tomorrow and we will be leaving early. I know for sure that they are going to miss you and it has been good for them having you around," Luc suggested.

As she made her way across the yard to where the dog slept, Kate realised that in the days she had spent with Luc and his family she had not only become attached to the children, she had also grown very fond of their parents and the simple but happy life they shared. Since experiencing a little of their harmonious existence she had asked herself on a number of occasions if her ambitious aim in life was really that important.

Kate had spent many happy hours amusing the two boys and was totally captivated by the baby girl. When placed in context alongside Molly's violent death, she realised that there was much more to life than simply being successful. Kate had also decided that if she was fortunate to return to her former life, she would strive for humility and endeavour to always deal fairly with the people around her.

When Kate rejoined Charlie and her rescuers it seemed obvious to them that she was suffering a further bout of sadness.

"If we come through this unscathed the boys will now be able to go to school." This was an obvious attempt by Lai Mee to distract her new friend from her all too evident melancholia.

"One of the fruit sellers at the market told me that a new place has been opened. She says her granddaughter has enrolled and is making good use of the time she spends there." This statement was also partially for the benefit of her two sons, as she hoped it would bring some consolation for the loss of Kate's company and realised that they were probably still awake and listening through the thin wall partioning.

"Will you have to pay for the children's schooling?" Kate asked anxiously. Reading her thoughts, Luc said that money was not a problem. He described how they had carried the family's entire wealth with them from Cambodia and how he had also looted valuables from the shower block where he had so nearly perished. This in turn was explained to Charlie, who viewed their host with new respect when learning that it had been necessary for Luc Tun to kill in order to make good his escape from the showers.

When Kate also described what had been necessary for her to be released from the cell where rare blood group people would normally be held, Charlie realised that the Cambodian stood comparison with his three Gurkha companions and that any suggestions by him should be respected. These thoughts were interrupted when further consideration of family requirements was offered.

"We have more than enough for our needs and sending the children to school will not cause hardship. Before coming to China we spent many years under the harsh resettlement plans of the Khmer Rouge. Very little was gained from that experience, other than we came to understand the soil and we have become proficient in the ways of good land management. The surpluses we market here generate small profits each month and we want for very little. When the monsoon comes we supplement our diet with eels, some frogs and fish." Charlie's obvious interest in this prompted the Cambodian to continue.

"Eventually I will buy a small boat so that the boys and I can do some sea fishing. Things will be really good then as, despite being constantly aware of Dr. Chang and his vile organisation, our lives have never been happier. If you manage to get away and expose the doctor's activities, Lai Mee and our children will have my undivided attention," he told them, before adding,

"I think Lai Mee has never wanted anything more than for our small family to be close. Before Pol Pot and his cruel regime we were part of a very large family. Sadly we lost them all in the harsh conditions which were imposed. Children from my first marriage to Lai Mee's sister were the first to perish and over a period of time Lai Mee's parents and her sister followed the children into unmarked and desolate graves. My parents, together with a younger brother and two younger sisters, were taken to other forced labour camps and after parting from them in Phnom Penh, we never saw them again. Since our unplanned arrival here we have endeavoured to make up for the loss of their numbers and in that my wife has done her very best." This was added with a proud grin and Charlie thought he detected the very slightest blush to Lai Mee's pretty features. Once more his admiration rose for this very resilient couple.

"If exposure eliminates the doctor's organisation and the constant threat to us, Lai's happiness will, I think, be complete." Lai Mee's quickly changing expression and warm smile in response to this confirmed that her husband understood the present precarious lives they led and yet was still prepared to commit himself to the downfall of an evil regime.

# Chapter Twenty Five

Returning to the port the following morning proved less eventful than the outward journey that Luc and Charlie had experienced the night before. Both Kate and Charlie had squashed onto the rear of Luc Tun's motorcycle and on approaching the port security barrier they found it raised with a stream of workers passing through unchecked. When Luc parked his machine they again wished him a hurried goodbye and then found the three Gurkhas once more ensconced in the disused weighbridge office.

"It's good having you back, Sergeant. We are also pleased to see that phase two appears to have been successful." A very warm smile was directed at Kate and then Boom introduced both himself and his two companions.

Having expressed her obvious and sincere gratitude for what they were risking, Kate then appeared to relax in the old soldiers' company. It was also clear that, despite her preoccupation, the three men were quickly captivated by the young woman's charm and sincerity.

"Phase two, as you suggest, has gone without a hitch, although complacency on our part would be foolish. We still have to hope that lady luck continues to shine. So far it has been all too easy and the fact that it has, bothers me," Charlie told them with some concern.

"Luc Tun believes it would be unwise for us to attempt reaching the pick-up point during daylight and that it will be safer for us to travel when nightfall arrives. Leaving this area with the out rush of workers at the end of the day may also ensure that we exit the port unchecked." It seemed there was to be no objections to this proposal, and so Charlie continued,

"I think we should heed Luc's advice, remain here for the rest of the day and then leave with the main body at the end of their shift. We should also not make the same mistake that I did yesterday. By arriving late at security, Luc and I found the barrier down and Luc's valise was searched. Fortunately the security guard ignored me, although I wouldn't like to risk the same thing happening again. It was in fact a quite unnerving experience and you can imagine the reaction it would cause if a body search was to take place this evening and one of our Uzi machine pistols was discovered!"

Expressions of understanding came from the three Gurkhas and this then prompted Charlie to tell all that he had learned during his brief stay with the Cambodian and his family. Extreme shock was then followed by indignation. Abhorrence of the cruelty which was being practised by the Chinese doctor was also expressed by the three old soldiers. This in turn prompted Charlie into giving them additional information.

"I also learned that there is to be a further shipment of refugees which is expected today. Luc was unable to establish what form of transport will be used, although Kate thinks it's more than likely to be one her hydrofoils. The captain who was responsible for both her and her colleague's abduction suggested during their initial encounter that he was expecting to make one last trip across."

Other than to shrug their shoulders in helpless resignation, his companions accepted this revelation without comment. Further condemnation of the inhuman activity seemed pointless and Charlie suggested that the three Gurkhas get whatever rest was possible. In response to their protesting that a watch rota should be shared, he pointed out that, unlike them, he had enjoyed a comfortable night's sleep.

"If Kate is so inclined we can chat while you three rest up and I will certainly appreciate her company. Otherwise you should all get your heads down as soon as you've eaten. There is, as you will recall, a long cycle ride back to the rendezvous point and we will certainly need to keep our wits about us. Because everything has thus far gone smoothly, we shouldn't relax and we will need to be prepared for all eventualities."

While the three men breakfasted and refreshed themselves on the jasmine tea which Lai Mee had sent in thermos flasks, Charlie then explained his thoughts and plans for their evening departure.

"As previously suggested, I think we should tag along close behind the main workforce when they leave at the end of the day and Kate can ride with me. This shouldn't attract attention, as many of the port workers appear to share bicycles."

Agreement to this was eventually accepted when Charlie conceded that carrying Kate would be shared once their group had passed out from the confines of both the port area and town.

When Kate next carried some tea across, Charlie was positioned behind one of the boarded over windows. Waiting while she made herself comfortable he then once more asked her to tell him all that she had learned of the organisation responsible for her abduction. Although this was very much a repeat of what he had learned the night before, anger and disgust flooded his mind when he thought of all the people who had been murdered for no better reason than greed. The tough world of business had given Charlie some understanding of the power that wealth creates. Despite being aware of this fact, he still despised those whose obsession with its accumulation destroyed their very humanity.

Charlie realised that in all probability the majority of staff engaged at the medical centre were driven to their employment through poverty. He could not, however, accept that poverty was sufficient justification for participating in the killing of innocent people.

As the morning wore on it became all too obvious that Kate was yet again finding difficulty in coming to terms with the fact that she felt a deep sense of responsibility for the deaths of Molly and the two men who had been abducted with her.

"If I hadn't insisted on going out to Hai Phong they would all still be alive, and I know that I will have their deaths on my conscience for the rest of my life," Kate sniffled, through a fresh showing of tears.

"None of this would have happened had I not been so dogmatic and gone looking for answers to an insignificant amount of missing fuel oil."

Charlie then gently reminded her that had she not done so, the cruel exploitation of innocent people would have gone on unchecked for the foreseeable future. He also concluded that even if their rescue attempt failed, Lorna and Ruby would at the very least alert the authorities and make it obvious that there was something happening on Hainan which should be investigated at an international level.

"Yes, thank God," she murmured, in shuddering agreement.

"Finding Molly in that shower block was the most distressing thing I have ever witnessed. From the position she was lying and her closeness to the door, it seemed obvious that she realised what was happening to her and was attempting to escape."

A noisy truck making its way from the port momentarily drowned out Kate's next words.

"Had those awful people used the other shower block, Molly may have found the same flaw in the door seal that Luc discovered and then used to make good his escape."

Realising that it might help if Kate was allowed to talk through the horrors which she had obviously experienced, Charlie decided against attempting further comfort.

"Molly and I only worked together for a short while, but it was long enough for me to realise that she possessed some very special qualities. That bloody awful doctor is going to pay for his crimes if it's the last thing

I do." Further sobs of what appeared to be guilt and frustration then caused added disruption to Kate's flow.

"If we are fortunate and do manage to escape, Charlie, I will spend everything I have to avenge the wanton waste of Molly's life. A trust fund which was arranged for me by my grandfather has been very well managed and Ruby has also been extremely generous over the years. If it costs me every last cent I have, I will see that man goes to hell before his allotted time."

A convoy of vehicles then ground its way past and Charlie realised that a ferry was in the throes of discharging its cargo.

"China may seem a very secure place for the doctor now, although he will learn to his cost that there is no such thing as a safe haven for him. Money has made him what he is and if I make enough available, I will find someone capable of ensuring that he suffers a great deal before his cruel life is finally extinguished."

Kate's bitterness was very obvious and Charlie inwardly hoped it would eventually disappear. He also thought a return to normality might release her from an urge for revenge.

Charlie's preoccupation was next interrupted by the sound of Luc Tun's tractor throttling back and this had him peering out to discover the reason.

A man, presumably someone of authority, was beckoning for Luc to climb down and this seemed cause for concern. When Luc joined the newcomer on the ground, he was then engaged in a lengthy discussion. Some arm gesturing followed and it seemed to Charlie that supervision in China was not far removed from what he had experienced while working on similar if somewhat larger projects. Eventually the new arrival tucked some drawings under his arm and then made off in the direction of where Luc had told them the port offices were located. When the man had disappeared from view, Luc, instead of remounting his machine, began hurriedly walking in their direction. Fearing that this might indicate approaching trouble, Charlie quickly roused the three sleeping Gurkhas.

"I thought you should know that the latest intake of refugees has been sighted and, as tugs have not gone out to meet them, I presume they are again using one of Kate's hydrofoils. That was the port engineer, who came across to check progress, and he happened to mention the expected arrival while also suggesting that I stay clear of the disembarkation wharf for the next few hours. It seems my near collision with Kate's transport when she arrived precipitated a complaint from the driver of her minibus." For one brief instant, Luc then displayed some rare signs of amusement.

"Little did the employee of an evil trade realise that my intervention was intentional. I was determined to have sight of his unexpected and unannounced passengers and in that quest I happily succeeded. Had I not, discovering Kate out at the medical centre would have been far from certain."

Charlie thanked Luc for keeping them posted and then urged him to return to work so as to avoid drawing attention to their area.

"Good luck. I hope everything goes smoothly tonight." Kate embraced Luc Tun once more and took further opportunity of expressing her gratitude for all that he and Lai Mee had done for her. Briefly watching while the Cambodian returned to his machine and the task of levelling a site for future development, Charlie next suggested,

"I would like to witness at first hand what happens to those poor unsuspecting people. It will probably also be useful if we can give a full and accurate account of what we might then witness to the authorities in Vietnam, when hopefully we make it safely off this island. Do you think we can get close enough to the berth where you came ashore and where presumably the next shipment of refugees will be landed?" This question was directed at Kate who, after only a moment's hesitation, said she thought so. Mentally chastising himself for not asking Luc for precise directions while the Cambodian was still with them, Charlie sought further reassurance.

"Are you sure you will be able to guide us back to that same dock?" This time there was no hesitation.

"Yes, it's close to that unusual-looking crane." Peering through gaps in the boarded over widow, Charlie followed the direction which Kate indicated before nodding his understanding.

"That's a Scotch derrick. It will be used for lifting heavy loads. They have greater lifting capacities than the standard dockside cranes." Then yet again he asked,

"Are you certain that is the right location?" Kate, now with small signs of irritation, told him that she had paid particular attention to her surroundings when she and the others came ashore, as she thought it might be useful if she was familiar with the area and a chance to escape occurred.

"And besides there is not another crane like that one," she added tetchily, while seeking reassurance by casting a further glance out over the cluttered skyline. Seemingly satisfied by this reassurance, Charlie suggested,

"Okay, Boom, you go first. Keep to whatever cover there is and try to find somewhere close to that derrick where we can observe things on the wharf without being seen."

All three Gurkhas were stealthily making their way from the weighbridge when Charlie asked,

"I suppose there is nothing we can do for this latest group that has been brought across?" Although having sympathy for his feelings Kate reminded him of the problems Luc had encountered when attempting to warn the people in Lai Mee's cell of impending danger. With the realisation that she was making a valid point and that there was in reality unlikely to be anything they could do, Charlie motioned her out through the weighbridge office door. Despite feelings of helplessness, he was still drawn to witness what was about to take place.

While watching her grandfather's former Flying Dolphin skimming into the harbour at speed and then berthing without preamble, Kate decided there was much to admire with regard to Tommy Jung's seamanship. This was despite the fact that she now knew him for the merciless person that she had previously thought him to be. She and Charlie had rejoined the three Gurkhas behind the skeletal remains of a disused gravel-washing plant. From this point of partial concealment they were able to observe escorts waiting beside vehicles which would eventually transport the unsuspecting refugees out to the medical centre and their ultimate fate.

The location chosen by Boom afforded a very good view of the wharf although the angle iron support on which the washing plant rested barely provided adequate concealment for the group. On considering this, Charlie thought it might be better if they moved to the inside of the washing plant's large elevated cylindrical screen. Their only way of reaching this position without being spotted was by climbing the gently sloping wide conveyor feed belt which very conveniently hid them from view as they made their ascent.

The washing plant's heavy tubular main screen was perforated with holes through which fines and smaller aggregate had been allowed to pass before falling onto a secondary screen for further grading. The purpose-built perforations fortunately provided a reasonably clear view of the dockside beneath them while the heavy metal screen also concealed their party from anyone curious enough to look up.

Of the five watching people the three battle-hardened old soldiers seemed if anything more affected by the helplessness of the situation. They watched with increasing anger as the unsuspecting victims were herded without consideration onto waiting buses.

"I would like nothing more than to go down there and take a few of those stooges apart. I realise, however, that it would jeopardise our mission and serve no good purpose. It's much more important for us to get off this island and alert the outside world to what is happening. By doing so, we will hopefully then prevent others from following in these poor unsuspecting wretches' footsteps," Bing exclaimed, in a tone barely loud enough to be heard.

While her four companions were angrily absorbed with the scene below, Kate's thoughts were elsewhere.

"An easier way of escaping would be on the Dolphin," she murmured.

Anguished cries prevented further explanation as the hidden group's attention was drawn to distressed families who were coping with both separation from one another and also their luggage.

Charlie almost never allowed anger to cloud his judgement but while watching helplessly he felt a rage within himself that he rarely experienced. Sensing this, Kate threaded a restraining hand through his arm and they then watched quietly as the refugees were driven away.

The observing group of five were about to climb down from their eyrie when further disturbance from below caused them to pause. The last bus had disappeared and the wharf was returning to a scene of abandonment as crew from the hydrofoil came ashore. Two of the crew members took cigarettes from a shared packet while a third retrieved a fresh water hose and connected it to the vessel's water spigot. A fourth man also began neatly re-coiling unused mooring line.

"My guess is that they will not be hanging round for too long," Kate quietly murmured.

There was then a short interval during which the group considered if it would be possible for them to descend from their observation post without attracting the attention of the men below.

Tommy Jung's voice next clearly carried up to them and from what was being asked by the Chinese skipper the group realised that the hydrofoil's departure was being delayed by the nonappearance of a courier or some other expected messenger.

"No, skipper, there isn't any sign of him and so far as I can see the wharf is now deserted." This reply came from the man at the water spigot who Kate recognised as one of the company's Portuguese bosun's; a man who generally spoke English with a very poor understanding of Vietnamese and Chinese.

"I'll come ashore and go to see where the hell he's got to. He's probably still in that blasted whorehouse."

There was a noticeably troubled look about the youthful-looking hydrofoil captain's features as he stepped ashore. Pausing briefly to run a critical eye over his craft, Tommy Jung, with further signs of irritation, then instructed the two smoking members of his crew that they should stop loafing around and make themselves useful by helping to prepare the vessel for departure.

"The bloody man is probably spending time with one of the girls, although whatever happens I am not leaving without our regular package. It's certainly the most profitable part of this job and I hope Zin Bax is not trying to pull a fast one simply because he realises that this is to be our last trip."

Tommy Jung could clearly be heard grumbling below and as the sound of his voice died away it was replaced by the distinct sound of an approaching vehicle. Thinking it might be one of the buses returning, Charlie was therefore surprised when an expensive-looking limousine came to a halt beside where the hydrofoil was moored to the quay.

As the dust settled a rear door opened and a very smartly dressed and attractive young woman stepped from it.

"Kapitan Jung?" Seeming to then assume that she had located her intended contact, the young woman continued speaking in English, with what Charlie assumed was a German accent. Without waiting for confirmation, the new arrival then continued in a somewhat breathless manner which probably indicated some haste.

"General Bax has sent me to inform you that the courier, while on his way to you and carrying your last bonus payment, has been detained by some officials who have recently arrived on the island. Although angered and alarmed by this unexpected event, the general is currently attempting to arrange for a replacement package to be delivered to you. He suggests that you remain patient and delay your departure for a short while longer."

With little more than a moment's hesitation this announcement brought what sounded like a string of oaths from Tommy Jung, until next, and with some signs of even greater irritation, he switched to replying in English.

"If your general is playing me for a fool, he may live to wish that he hadn't. Where is he now?"

"He is back at the club and, as I have already explained, he is currently involved with arranging for an alternative package to be delivered." Despite being heavily accented there were now sounds of high irritation in this retort.

"To hell with waiting here for whatever chicanery Bax might be up to, I'm coming back to the club with you." Tommy Jung then gestured toward the car and indicated that he wished to travel with the foreign-sounding woman. In what then appeared to be something of an afterthought, he turned back to his crew.

"Paco, you make sure that the craft has been made ready for departure the moment I return. Once I've got my hands on the smack we won't want to be hanging around here." This final instruction was obviously addressed to the English-speaking bosun.

Tommy Jung's departure from the quayside created a flurry of activity from the crew and in patiently waiting for them to finish their deck chores, Kate sighed with relief when the last of them eventually disappeared into the passenger saloon.

Placing a hand of restraint on Charlie's arm as he was about to follow the three Gurkhas down the conveyer belt, she asked,

"Do you think it might be possible for us to overpower Tommy and his crew?" Charlie's puzzled look prompted her to continue,

"If we can take the Dolphin, it will save us a long cycle ride out to that disused harbour and would also eliminate the risk of mum having to re-enter Chinese airspace."

Having now had some time in which to think her proposal through, Kate realised that highlighting the risk to her mother might lend added weight to her suggestion and she was prepared to use every possible means of persuasion.

"If we can pull it off, we would also stand a good chance of making sure Tommy Jung and his crew face up to their crimes and that they are eventually brought to trial." Kate paused in order to gauge whether her suggestion was gaining any enthusiasm.

"I also feel certain that with the weight of Admiral Tanaka's influence, neither Tommy nor his crew would be allowed to buy immunity from a severe sentence."

It occurred to Charlie that Kate had now spent sufficient time in Vietnam to have some understanding of the complexities which prevailed in the country's legal system and, while making his way cautiously down the conveyor belt, he also had time to consider her proposal.

Although accepting that the Dolphin offered them an altogether easier route home, Charlie next questioned their ability to force Tommy Jung and his crew to sail the vessel back to a life of certain imprisonment.

"Oh, but we won't need to rely on them!" Kate retorted indignantly, when Charlie had voiced this concern.

"In fact, that is an altogether minor consideration. If you and your Gurkhas are able to overpower the crew, you can be sure that I will get us back to Hai Phong. It will obviously be necessary for me to take care while exiting the channel through to the Gulf of Tonkin, although there are bound to be marker buoys as international shipping of considerable tonnage use the port." A momentary pause, while she cast around for further ways in which to convince, followed.

"I also feel sure that Tommy Jung will have suitable navigational charts available on board and there will be radio directional aids to guide us all the way across," Kate added hopefully.

From the unconvinced look on Charlie's face, Kate concluded that yet further persuasion was required.

"Look, Charlie," she suggested, in a tone which registered some desperation. "Before leaving Sri Lanka for Vietnam, I spent many, many hours with my grandfather's old engineer learning all the quirks of that particular vessel. In fact I would go so far as to suggest that I probably know more about it than Tommy Jung does."

Having convinced Charlie, all three Gurkhas were then easily persuaded and Boom thought taking the vessel would not present a problem. His two companions also welcomed the suggestion when realising that a long cycle ride back to Lin'gao might be avoided.

A suggestion by Boom of entering the water and boarding the craft from the seaward side was quickly discarded and eventually the group decided to go with an alternative plan put forward by Bang.

"Two of us can act out the part of Lascar seamen trying to relocate their ship while under the influence of alcohol. Bing is a good actor. He has also had plenty of experience when leaving the regimental mess at Shorncliffe while full of Shepherd Neame ale and in a state of inebriation." This remark, said with a grin, brought a similarly sarcastic retort from his companion.

"When we have gained access to the vessel the rest of you will need to follow in quickly as we may require help in overpowering the crew."

Watching with baited breath, Kate gasped with dismay when Bang appeared to miss his footing on the outer wing and was only prevented from falling into the harbour by Bing and two of the crew who had laughingly reappeared. Prior to this incident, both Gurkhas had stumbled along the quayside in perfect mimicry of two drunks with their arms entwined while raucously conversing in a dialogue which would have been difficult to understand by anyone other than those who had been born or who had lived a long time in Nepal.

"Come on! They may need our help," Charlie urged, as he and Boom ran from behind the gravel plant with Kate in close pursuit. Their haste proved unnecessary as, on gaining access to the hydrofoil's saloon, they found two of the crew spread-eagled on the deck, one obviously unconscious while the other was attempting to stem blood from an ugly head wound. Their two terrified companions were also hemmed in a corner while avoiding the gleaming steel of Bing's kukri as it circled before their eyes.

Some time later it seemed obvious that the expected replacement package had taken longer to arrange than had been anticipated. On eventually regaining access to his craft, Tommy Jung's expression when he saw Kate was one which she would remember with pleasure for a very long time. On discovering that his crew had been overpowered, Tommy swallowed hard before attempting to make a hasty retreat. This move was far too late as Charlie had moved instantly to cut off the captain's retreat. With a look of resignation Tommy then attempted to regain some of his former cockiness.

"They told me that you had escaped." This remark was all too clearly directed at Kate.

"Zin Bax's people thought you had drowned out on the marshes, as there have been others who have perished in that way."

From the expression on his face and the uncertainty in his voice, Tommy Jung appeared to be summoning all his cunning in an attempt to regain some control.

"I wouldn't want to be in your shoes when the general discovers that you are still alive. Because of your escape he has been totally humiliated by the big boss and his staff have suffered a lot more than just humiliation."

A snort of contempt from Boom caused the Chinaman to pause so that he might reconsider his predicament. Realising that there was a machine pistol pointing at his midriff, he quickly came to terms with the vulnerability of his position and changed his tone to one of a conciliatory nature.

"I don't know who these people are." Tommy gestured at Charlie and the Gurkhas.

"What I do know, is that you are operating the Mekong Express Company on a shoestring. There are two kilos of high grade heroin in this bag, that and a similar amount are yours if you set me free in Hai Phong." Kate had seen a similar package to the one Tommy was now clutching when she and Molly watched him come ashore prior to their abduction.

"Four kilos of pure uncut heroin is worth a great deal more than you are likely to earn from ferrying passengers in a very long time." Tommy then suggested if Kate gave him her word that she would set him free in Vietnam, he would arrange for the second quantity of heroin to be handed over on his release.

Had Tommy Jung been half blind he would have had difficulty in not understanding the look of disgust on Kate's face. In response to this, his features changed to a look of desperation before offering to pilot the Dolphin back to Hai Phong.

"What about your crew?" Kate asked. The man's response was unsurprisingly typical of his self-interest.

"Oh, I won't need them. I can sail this thing without their help. You can do whatever you like with them once I have been released and made good my disappearance."

Had it not been for the muzzle of Bing's weapon pressing into his abdomen, the English-speaking Paco would then certainly have caused his captain some severe physical injury.

"You and your offer can go to hell, Captain Jung. I may never avenge the lives of those people that you and your associates have murdered. I will, however, do everything in my power to see that you stand trial for your crimes."

An expression of disbelief shadowed Tommy Jung's features before next turning to Charlie and the three Gurkhas.

"You can easily overrule her. There is still a great deal to be made from a five-way split and it's certainly going to be a hell of a lot more than I imagine you are being paid for this." Then with an air of confidence creeping back into his tone, Tommy Jung continued,

"You shouldn't trouble yourselves with the situation of returning to Hai Phong without her. Once we are at sea, we can wrap her and some ballast in a piece of canvas and put her over the side. Your explanation to Ruby Pardoe, or whoever it was that hired you, need only be that you failed because she had been recaptured and was transferred to the mainland before you arrived. Or if you wish that she had already been processed through the showers." Quite unwittingly this comment proved that the Chinese skipper was perfectly well aware of what happened to the refugees that he had previously transported to Hainan and was further reason for the group's loathing of him.

On this occasion Charlie's reaction was a fraction slow. The Chinese captain had added that no one in Vietnam would be any the wiser when the slashing open-handed chop hit him on the bridge of his already squat nose and flattened it against the rest of his face. A small brown fist then smashed into his rib cage and drove air from his lungs in a loud audible whoop.

It is probable that Tommy Jung would have sustained further serious injury had Charlie not then stepped between him and a very enraged Gurkha.

"There is too much of the gentleman in you, Sergeant. Please stay out of this and I shall then let him taste the bite of my kukri. Better still, I now have an excuse for taking his ears. My youngest nephew in Kathmandu will appreciate owning such a trophy as his brothers have similar souvenirs."

Tommy Jung screamed as the old Senani lunged at him with the scimitar-shaped knife and once more it was Charlie who prevented Boom from permanently maiming him.

"We will have need of him undamaged and in one piece when he faces trial in Vietnam. A clever defence lawyer might make much of the fact that his client had lost a part of his anatomy while being detained."

A murmur of understanding followed and Boom, with an expression of disgust, urged his two companions to take Tommy and lock him out of sight in the aft saloon with the rest of the crew.

"Oh and make sure the others are securely trussed. If one of his men was to get free, it is possible that this piece of human excrement might never stand trial."

It was obvious that Tommy Jung was also aware of that particular possibility, as his muffled pleas could clearly be heard through the closed door of the saloon.

The moment of action had yet again passed in the group's favour and the four men, together with their rescued companion, were savouring this success when Kate suggested that further time should not be wasted.

"If two of you will remove the fresh water hose and then prepare for casting off, I will check the vessel over prior to departure." Charlie then unexpectedly responded to this by announcing,

"While you are going through those checks, I am going to nip back and tell Luc Tun that our plans have changed. I will show him where the bicycles are and, if I describe where the outboard and inflatable can be found, it is possible that he will collect them and put them to good use." Charlie then added that Luc Tun had mentioned owning a boat and that it would add to his family's way of life as it would enable him and his sons to go sea fishing.

This announcement brought an instant reaction from Kate, who told him that she was not happy about his leaving when they were so close to making good their escape.

"It's all right, Miss Kate. I will tag along and keep an eye on the Sergeant. He has not paid us yet and that alone should ensure that he comes to no harm," Boom added, with a broad grin.

"I also think we owe it to that man, Luc Tun. Even if he has no need of the bicycles, they will at least fetch a good price at market and the boat will be one very small way of expressing our appreciation for his bravery and the help that he has given you."

Had any other reason been offered, Kate would certainly have argued against this move more strongly.

# Chapter Twenty Six

By keeping to the protection of shipping containers and other dockside dry goods, Charlie and Boom regained the security of their former hiding place in the weighbridge office undetected.

Peering out through the poorly covered windows, they immediately discovered that Luc Tun was stationary, and his machine was standing only a short distance from them. There was, however, something about the Cambodian's concentration which indicated that site clearance was not uppermost in his mind. In fact, Luc's focus appeared to be concentrating on the last of many vehicles which had so far not been loaded onto a recently docked ferry that was preparing for departure.

"I think we should wait until that thing slips its moorings. There will then be less likelihood of our being spotted," Charlie murmured.

Luc Tun's attention to work had previously never before been distracted during the long hours that the group had watched him; now it seemed strange that he should interest himself in a scene which he had surely witnessed on numerous occasions.

"Come on, come on. Get that blasted ramp up," Boom muttered in exasperation, as a pick-up truck stalled and the ferry deck hands were required to manhandle it aboard. Charlie also felt the need for haste, as he realised that every second was precious if they were to make good their escape. In these final moments of frustration and anxiety something, however, became obvious.

"It's not the ferry that Luc is interested in. If you follow the direction of his gaze I feel sure it's something else!" Boom, after some further observation while shading his eyes from the glare of the early afternoon sun, eventually agreed.

"There, now I have it. The ferry is casting off and there is just one vehicle which has not been loaded. Presumably it arrived on the incoming crossing."

Both men were now able to see that Luc Tun's attention seemed focused on a very large black sedan which was standing in a parking lot adjacent to the ferry loading ramp. Two men in deep, and what appeared to be animated, discussion were very noticeable by the difference in their size as they stood beside this and one other stationary vehicle.

"I wonder why he would be interested in those two," Boom murmured. "Perhaps it's the larger car that has taken his fancy, although I would think it a bit grand for the average man's taste."

Charlie's concentration was now definitely not centred on the vehicle. The animated and angry gestures of the two men beside it suggested that they were in some kind of dispute. It also seemed obvious that the smaller of the two was by far the more aggressive. With yet one further angry gesture, this individual opened the front passenger door of the more impressive vehicle and motioned for the taller man to get in. Slamming the door with some violence, he then made his way round to the driver's side and opened that door.

A vaguely remembered account which Luc Tun had related stirred in Charlie's memory, and for precious seconds he was unable to focus on what it might be, until then remembering the description of a Russian-built limousine.

"Of course! Now I know why Luc is paying so much attention to those two. That has to be Dr Chang Jin-Ming and his crony Zin Bax," Charlie realised, as the man he now believed to be the infamous doctor continued to berate the individual seated on the opposite side of the large automobile.

A throaty roar from the tractor's diesel engine then drowned out further discussion and Charlie almost instantly understood Luc's intention.

Dr Chang Jin-Ming, with his head and shoulders inside the car while still berating his partner, eventually seemed to understand that excessive noise from the tractor might be cause for some alarm. On looking over his shoulder the doctor remained motionless for many precious seconds while seeming to assess the situation. When it eventually became obvious that the green object charging towards him posed a serious threat, his hand went to an inside coat pocket and then reappeared, grasping a weapon.

The John Deere tractor was gathering momentum when the first two shots were fired. Fortunately for Luc Tun these were wide of the mark and the green monster lumbered relentlessly on.

It seemed at first that the doctor and Zin Bax were fortunate, as with the bulldozer's blade raked at an angle, the Zil was swept down the blade's entire length and not into the dock as Luc Tun had obviously intended. In fact, by shunting it sideways the Zil now had its rear fender resting against the dockside barrier. To rectify this mistake and to adjust his angle of attack, the Cambodian moved the power shift to reverse and the machine trundled back towards where Charlie and Boom were hidden.

Somewhat confused, and certainly bewildered by the boldness of this action, Charlie refocused his attention on the obviously damaged car. It immediately became clear that the doctor's leg had somehow become trapped between the driver's door and what appeared to be a distorted door frame. A stain of rust-coloured blood was spreading slowly over the shiny black surface of the large vehicle and it occurred to Charlie with some irony that an abnormal amount of beeswax would be required in future to restore its remarkable body sheen.

Both men watching from their secure hiding place were now expecting Zin Bax to go to the doctor's aid. When an arm snaked out through the passenger window and frantically fumbled with an outer door handle, the reason for the general's failure to offer assistance became clear.

"I think the impact has badly distorted the car's bodywork. Look, the driver is also trying to open his damaged door further." Charlie pointed to where both men appeared intent on their efforts to escape from the damaged Zil while also being aware that the bulldozer was realigning for a second attack. Peering across through the board-covered windows, Boom and Charlie were clearly able to see that there was now a look of very serious intent on the Cambodian's face, and then without warning the windshield of his tractor shattered.

"Those bastards are going to kill him, Sergeant! We have to help!" the Gurkha yelled, as he scrambled from the weighbridge office with his machine pistol at the ready. All thoughts of concealment now appeared forgotten as the old soldier ran at full tilt towards the tractor. Charlie, however, was moving with much more caution and was intent on watching to see if the doctor still had ammunition for his firearm.

Following a lapse, during which the doctor continued struggling in an attempt to free himself, the man then recommenced firing in the general direction of Luc and the tractor. This act seemed one of complete desperation as the doctor's face was now contorted with what was presumably extreme pain.

Luc had selected neutral on the power shift change and, as the large machine ground to a halt, it seemed he was about to re-engage forward drive when bullets whined off the metalwork of the now stationary tractor. It was then also obvious from the intensity of this wilting rain of fire that Zin Bax was also armed. With the arrival of the next fusillade, Luc Tun slumped back in his seat, with blood oozing from his head.

"Those bastards have killed him," Charlie screamed, on reaching the Gurkhas side. "Quick, Boom, I need help getting him off that thing."

Sheltered from view by the bulky machine Charlie, with support from Boom, managed to slide Luc's lifeless body out from behind the controls.

While they were struggling with the Cambodian's limp form it seemed obvious that the concentration of bullets ricocheting off the engine canopy at regular intervals was an attempt to deter further use of the tractor.

"I would have expected them to be out of ammunition by now," Boom muttered to no one in particular, as they lowered Luc's body gently to the ground. Ignoring this and the mayhem of noise that was going on all around them, Charlie climbed back onto the tractor's seat and raised the bulldozer blade to its full height in an attempt to use it as a shield against incoming fire.

Calling down with some effort to overcome noise from both the engine and the alarming sound of small arms fire, Charlie told the old soldier that he was about to attempt what Luc had just failed to do. He also added,

"You should keep down behind cover. It will certainly not help our situation if you also get killed. Kate and the others will need all the help they can get if they are to make a safe passage back to Vietnam. "

Charlie did not hear Boom's reply as he had engaged forward selection on the power shift and opened the throttle to its full extent. He was now more determined than ever to not make the same mistake that Luc had made moments before.

Although operating blind because of the raised bulldozer blade, Charlie knew exactly where the Zil was located as he had mentally marked its position and the upright towering supports of the ferry link span gave him an accurate direction. He had also made a mental note that there was now a stretch of Armco behind the limousine, which he realised had been erected to prevent passenger cars from driving off the quayside.

When Charlie judged that he had reached a point where the bulldozer blade should be lowered, he saw that one arm from within the vehicle was still pointing a weapon in his general direction. It seemed, however, that the doctor had used all his ammunition, as the hand gun he'd been using was next placed on top of the vehicle and he was desperately still attempting to free his trapped leg. Showing little sign of fear, the man appeared to momentarily give up on his attempt and he next turned and then mouthed off something in Charlie's general direction, which could easily have been defiance or a last desperate threat. The sneer of contempt on the doctor's face certainly suggested that it was not a plea for mercy.

Oblivious to intimidation or reason, there was one thing now uppermost in Charlie's mind. He was remembering that Dr Chang Jin-Ming and his associate had violated the lives of many innocent would-be refugees. They had also now ended the life of a very brave and likeable Cambodian who had asked for nothing more than to live a peaceful life with his family. No matter what happened next, the big car and its occupants were going into the harbour, irrespective of the cost. Charlie's determination was such that he was also prepared to sacrifice Luc Tun's tractor if necessary.

On lining up the leading corner shoe of the bulldozer blade with the middle of the Zil's front fender, the impact when it came was barely felt. Agonisingly the Armco barrier held and he was aware that the large expensive limousine was being squeezed to an extent where its roof bowed upwards. The fact that the car was not being completely crushed only served to indicate the quality of metal and workmanship which had gone into its build.

"Maybe the thing is armoured," Charlie mentally speculated.

With more power applied, the tractor seemed to settle into its high flotation tyres and Charlie realised that something now had to give. Through tyre settlement the need for further traction was slowly transferred to forward motion and the first signs of winning the battle came with a high volume screeching sound as the Armco barrier stretched and then buckled outwards.

While wrenching the power shift lever to reverse as the limousine rolled off the outer edge, Charlie bit into his bottom lip. For agonising seconds it seemed that both he and the machine were destined to follow the Zil into the harbour. His decision not to jump clear was decided when he realised in those final seconds that forward motion had been arrested. With only millimetres to spare the tractor's front wheels teetered on the brink and its wide tyres slowly gained adhesion from the reinforced concrete.

A gasp of relief escaped from Charlie as he next realised that the quayside appeared to be retreating and the lumbering green machine was moving slowly away from what would certainly have been a watery grave.

Seconds later, and with a feeling of satisfaction, Charlie closed the throttle and brought the machine to a standstill, yards from where Boom was huddled over the figure of Luc Tun.

A very slight twitch from one of the Cambodian's legs was noticeable as Charlie wearily descended the tractor's metal steps.

"Is he alive?" There was disbelief in Charlie's voice as he once more regained stability from the same mother earth that Luc Tun had levelled only hours before.

"I tried to tell you that before you went careering off. The bullet probably ricocheted off his machine and was a spent force, before giving our friend here a hair parting which is surely going to change his appearance." There was now an all too familiar grin on Boom's face as he continued,

"He is thankfully a lucky fellow, although from the little I saw of him before this, he was never going to become famous through his good looks."

Responding next to Charlie's further anxious and persistent questions, the old Gurkha explained,

"He has stirred once or twice, and I don't think it will be long before he regains consciousness. My guess is that he is going to have one hell of a headache, though."

This brought a mixture of emotions for Charlie, who had himself so recently avoided what might have been a life-threatening incident. In realising that Luc was not dead, he now breathed much more easily. Lorna's daughter owed her life and a great deal more to this very likeable man and he was overjoyed to learn that Luc Tun had not after all been killed.

With a return to reality Charlie also realised that sentiment and indecision was something they could now ill afford in their current situation.

"Getting the hell off this island has to be our main priority, although it's obvious that we can't leave until we are sure that Luc is able to cope. Fortunately for us, I think the ferry had rounded the sea wall before Luc began his assault. Hopefully the noise will not have carried and with any luck the sound of firing will have been drowned out by the racket from Luc's tractor or, at the very least, contained within this enclosed area."

It then occurred to Charlie that Boom probably had no idea what had prompted the recent furore, and not for the first time he admired the old soldier's complete and unquestioning loyalty. Quickly explaining the reason for Luc Tun's action and his own attack on both the Zil and its occupants, Charlie next suggested,

"If you can take care of Luc for a few minutes more, I would like to go back and make sure the car has sunk and that the water is deep enough to cover it. Awkward questions will be asked of our friend here if the thing is still visible from the hard standing." Other than nodding both his agreement and acceptance Boom did not respond.

Still somewhat shaken from his moment of action and in something of a daze, Charlie made his way once more to the dockside, while thinking of how Kate would have reacted if he'd had to tell her that the man responsible for her freedom was dead.

Peering down, the first noticeable thing was large bubbles, which were erupting at regular intervals on the otherwise smooth surface of the dock.

"I imagine it sank instantly, as the windows were open and water would have poured in. Thank God it's not visible from here, although the bottom will have been disturbed when it sank and it might still be seen when the water clears."

Thoughts that he should be feeling a similar guilt to that which his previous killing in Cyprus had created, then crossed Charlie's mind. Instead he was now more than satisfied that it was he who had brought about the destruction of two evil men; both of whom had been responsible for the termination of a great many innocent people. That they had not, after all, ended the life of Luc Tun did not by any means alter his feelings. Charlie's only regret was that someone had not disposed of the doctor and his associate many years before, when countless lives might have been spared.

Some additional disturbance in the water brought his thoughts back to the present and he watched with astonishment as the lanky figure of General Zin Bax broke through and came to the surface. Aghast at what he was witnessing, Charlie realised that the man had somehow squeezed out through one of the car's open windows. Cursing with frustration, he turned from the dock and raced back to where Boom was helping Luc Tun regain a sitting position.

"That bastard is not going to cheat justice a second time," Charlie ranted, as the two men looked at him with uncomprehending astonishment.

"Is this the rapid fire lever?" Charlie asked, as he snatched Boom's machine pistol from where it was lying beside the two men.

"Yes, and there are only thirty rounds in the magazine, so use them sparingly." It was typical of the trust which had developed between them that Boom did not hesitate or question Charlie's need of his weapon.

A large open-sided workmanlike boat emerging from behind a dogleg in the sea wall coincided with the moment that Charlie reached the spot from where he had seen Zin Bax surfacing.

Four men, dressed in what he thought might be party uniforms, were looking steadily up at him. Their dress seemed out of keeping with any form of nautical or port-related activity, and Charlie decided there was something about their attitude which suggested that he was not immediately the centre of their attention.

Steering the boat in a purposeful direction, the four uniformed men maintained a course which would intercept with General Bax.

Charlie's earlier satisfaction now crumbled to one of despair, while believing the newcomers to be close associates of the general and who would after all aid his escape from the fate that he and Luc Tun had wished for him.

There was only a short distance left for Zin Bax to swim when the heavy boat gently nudged into him. Despite being within easy reach of some metal steps there was evident relief on the general's face as he turned onto his back and reached up to be helped aboard.

"The bloody man is not going to get his just deserts after all, and I don't think it will be in anyone's interest for me to slaughter four other men who may or may not have had involvement with the doctor's organisation."

While these thoughts crossed Charlie's mind, he next watched with macabre fascination as the general's expression changed from relief to fear.

A covering of water quickly disfigured the man's features as one of the larger individuals in the boat grasped Zin Bax's throat with both hands and then firmly held him beneath the surface.

Having never witnessed an act more deliberate or cold, Charlie watched with mesmerised interest as the submerged man thrashed and fought to break free from the other man's unbreakable grasp. It seemed as well that the recently arrived boat was sturdy and stable. Certainly a smaller, more flimsily built craft would have capsized with the ensuing struggle which was taking place.

Despite distortion from a covering film of water, resignation finally registered in the slowly weakening eyes and moments later a whoosh of air escaped from General Bax's rapidly deflating lungs. Some minutes then passed while the uniformed man in the boat maintained his grip and kept his victim's face beneath the surface.

Struggling to come to terms with the deliberate and coldblooded execution that he had just witnessed, Charlie quickly concluded this to be a fitting end for the man responsible for killing many others through asphyxiation.

Yet again Charlie realised that he should be feeling guilt for his responsibility in the disposal of two greed-driven and heartless individuals. Instead what he was now experiencing was a complete form of emptiness, together with an overwhelming loss of purpose.

Looking round for something on which to focus, Charlie desperately strove for a return to normality. What his attention came to rest on, however, was the figure of a corpse, floating face up with unfocused eyes staring at a cloudless sky.

Watching from the boat the powerfully-built individual responsible for Zin Bax's execution stood apart from his three companions, with legs spread wide to compensate for the heavy boat's continuing movement.

As Charlie's gaze settled on him, the man then did something quite unexpected. His right arm came up from his side and Charlie was convinced that he was about to be lined up in the sights of a weapon. Instinctively he also realised that any reaction from him with Boom's Uzi would be altogether too late.

Instead of the expected, the stocky erstwhile executioner first saluted and then followed this surprising gesture with a slow almost childlike wave of farewell.

The incongruity of this seemingly comical move had the effect of bringing Charlie back to the sense of reality for which he had been striving. Acting on impulse he returned the salute and the man who had denied him the opportunity of finishing Zin Bax smiled before repeating his goodbye wave.

Making his way back to where Boom and Luc were waiting, Charlie's mind was totally confused by the traumatic turn of events.

Convinced that the uniformed men somehow represented authority, he expected to feel the impact of a bullet at any minute or at the very least some verbal challenge which would halt him in his tracks. Every instinct warned him that the men in the boat were trifling with him and that he would simply not be allowed to walk away.

On reaching the spot where Boom was attending Luc Tun, Charlie was immediately encouraged by the wounded man's appearance. Despite a bloody face and a dazed expression, he responded to Charlie's questions with more clarity than should have been the case.

"I am okay; your friend has stopped the bleeding and also checked to see if I have concussion. When he gives up soldiering he might think of taking up nursing," Luc added with a grin.

"I have told him that we Cambodians have thick skulls, although I think his diagnosis of a pending headache is beginning to materialise. He has also explained that you have probably finished off what I failed to do? I am so pleased that you decided to come back instead of making good your escape."

An affirmative nod from Charlie, which indicated that two evil men had gone to a well-deserved and watery grave, brought a mixture of both relief and some regret to the Cambodian's face.

"When my head clears and it has sunk in that the world has truly been rid of those two maniacs, my gratitude will know no bounds. Thank you, Charlie. I am so grateful that you were able to cover for me."

"You are certainly a man of hidden talents, Sergeant. I was rather pre-occupied at the time, although from what I saw, it would seem that you also know your way around machinery. I was quite convinced that you were going over the sea wall and into the dock. I'm glad you didn't, as having to tell young Kate that we were unable to return you to her mother would have been a little difficult."

In a rare demonstration of bonhomie, Boom then grasped Charlie's hand who, in an attempt to hide his embarrassment, changed the subject and told them about the extraordinary thing that he had just witnessed.

"When I raced back with your weapon after that first look, it was because Zin Bax had somehow escaped from the car. I was seriously intent on finishing the job when four men appeared in a boat and one of them completed the task for me." Charlie next described in detail all that had happened. Luc, although still visibly shaken, was the first to react.

"My guess is that those men are from the Beijing State Secrecy Bureau. The mechanic friend I have who works here in the port told me a few days ago that he had heard in the offices that some Bureau people were nosing around asking questions. Those people are not normally spoken of, as they appear to pose uncertainty throughout the community." The bloodied man then struggled for a more comfortable position, before continuing,

"I also heard that the Guangdong Public Security Department are not at all happy with interference from this outside source."

None of this meant anything to either Boom or Charlie and their main concern was now centred on how Luc would cope with his injury. Both men realised that considerable time had passed since leaving their three companions with the imprisoned hydrofoil crew and they were anxious to be off. Sensing this, the Cambodian urged,

"You should not trouble yourselves with me. There is an excellent ambulance room here in the port and the nurse will dress my wound, after giving me something for this headache. When she asks how I injured myself, I will tell her that I got too close to the edge of the dock and struck my head on the controls while taking evasive action."

"I'm not sure that will sound too convincing, as it will take some imagination to accept that the bullet graze on your crown was caused by hitting your head against controls, although for the life of me I can't think of a more plausible explanation and it will at least explain why that section of Armco is damaged."

Saying this once more reminded Charlie of how close he had been to following the Zil into the water and he shuddered at the thought of being trapped beneath Luc Tun's tractor.

"Boom has told me where your bicycles are hidden and he has also described where I will find the inflatable that you came ashore in. When things have settled, I will borrow a truck and go out to the old iron works with my sons and collect both the boat and its engine."

Luc then told them that Kate had left her address with Lai Mee and that they would both be writing when the demise of Dr Chang Jin-Ming was recognised and threat from him removed.

"Now I really do think you should leave. Those men in that boat were probably surprised by your involvement and they were waving you off because they did not want the added complication of explaining your presence. They are known to be unpredictable people and could easily change their minds. So please don't delay any longer."

# Chapter Twenty Seven

Although anxious looks were very much in evidence from the waiting trio, there was certainly some relief expressed when Charlie and Boom returned to the hydrofoil.

When it was explained that the doctor and his associate Zin Bax were no more, and Charlie was in fact responsible for their deaths, looks of amazement eventually turned to utter relief on Kate's face. Bing and Bang then also expressed their surprise and satisfaction for the outcome.

"Coming to my rescue is not the only thing for which I shall now be in your debt, Charlie." A questioning look prompted Kate to explain.

"You will remember I recently vowed that whatever it took, I would strive to bring about the doctor's downfall. I was completely serious with my resolve, although it now seems you have taken that obligation from me, and Boom's description would indicate that the horrible individual suffered a great deal for the last remaining minutes of his miserable life. My appetite for vengeance has been satisfied and, but for a chance meeting on that London bound plane, it might never have happened. Thank you, Charlie. The doctor's elimination will be one less thing to trouble me in the months ahead, although it can never lessen the pain that I shall always feel for the loss of Molly and the guilt I will also suffer for the two men."

Concern for Luc Tun's head wound was then expressed and Charlie was hard-pressed to prevent the young woman from returning to offer help to her former rescuer.

"Luc was adamant that the port authority nurse would dress his wounds and that we should make good our getaway. Remember, Kate, getting word to the outside world is as important to Luc and Lai Mee as it is to you."

This attempt at persuasion worked and Kate then made her way up onto the small pilot deck. Bing and Bang were standing by to cast off and Charlie was about to follow Kate onto the bridge when the sound of angry cursing came down to him.

"Oh bugger, so much for my cockiness. The batteries are dead and I can't get a spark of life from the bloody engines."

"Surely not? It's only hours since they made their crossing and the generators would have pumped plenty of charge into the storage batteries," Charlie offered as he scrambled in beside her.

Thoughts of bringing Tommy Jung up from the saloon and forcing him to explain how the problem might be overcome were racing through Charlie's mind, when he remembered something from his early days of working with construction equipment.

"Has this thing got an isolater or master switch, do you think? And if so, have you turned it on?"

"Gosh, yes of course! How stupid of me to overlook something so fundamental! Thanks, Charlie." Kate gasped with obvious relief as she reached beneath the control panel. Whatever it was that she then manipulated immediately caused the instruments to light up.

"What a fool I am for panicking and overlooking something so essential, and even more so after boasting of all that I knew about hydrofoils."

Pressing a button on the control panel caused a familiar sound as the first starter motor engaged. Noise from the starboard engine then obliterated sound from the port engine as it also throbbed into life.

If Charlie had been impressed by Lorna's flying skills he was now equally surprised by her daughter's capability in piloting a large and powerful hydrofoil. Kate had asked him to stay with her on the small bridge and given him the task of keeping a lookout for channel marker buoys.

When the two Gurkhas had cast off, they had gone about and there was then a moment of concern as they approached the ferry terminal.

Luc Tun's tractor was standing where Charlie had left it, although there was no sign of Luc, fumes from the exhaust stack caused Charlie to realise that, in his haste to return to Boom, he had not stopped the engine.

"It can't be helped. I imagine Luc is over at the ambulance room having his wound dressed, and when he returns he will take care of it. The only harm done will be the waste of some fuel," Charlie consoled himself.

Two men were already using an acetylene cutting torch to strip away the damaged Armco barrier and a track-mounted crawler crane was in position with a very large cactus scrap handling grab dangling from its boom. This device was plunged into the dock as they slowly approached and it was then quickly retrieved. Following a third attempt, the grab operation appeared to succeed, as the Zil had been ensnared and was being lifted clear of the dock, with water cascading from it. Dr Chang Jin-Ming was then clearly seen dangling from the large vehicle with his leg still trapped in a badly distorted door frame.

Kate shuddered and Charlie was also sickened by this gruesome spectacle. The doctor's face was a deathly greyish white and his lips were drawn back in an expression which could only be interpreted as a last snarling attempt at expressing his final hatred and contempt for the world at large.

As the hydrofoil gathered way and moved slowly past this macabre salvage scene, Charlie recognised a collection of men standing on the quayside, all watching with interest. A hand from the noticeably larger one of this group gestured at Chang Jin-Ming's dangling body before pumping the air with his fist and then pointing at Charlie. This display of mimicry was concluded with hand clapping in a show which could only be interpreted as approval. Seconds later he issued the now familiar salute and Charlie, with a weak grin, acknowledged it.

"I have a strange feeling that those four individuals know a great deal more about us than we will ever know about them."

It was unlikely that the young woman had registered anything Charlie said as, in an attempt to clear her mind of the sights she had just passed through, Kate was concentrating on steering them out through an unfamiliar port.

They travelled slowly in a westerly direction until the channel widened. Kate then applied more power, the craft came up onto its foils and their speed increased dramatically.

Despite inexperience Charlie was very aware when they met open sea, as the waves assumed a pattern of long rolling combers through which their shallow foils sliced. It was at this point that he exhaled a deep sigh of both relief and disbelief; against all the odds Charlie now believed that he and the three old warriors had successfully carried off Kate's rescue.

Satisfied that they were at last on a heading for Hai Phong and safety, Charlie asked the Gurkhas to radio their success through to Lorna, who he knew would be anxiously waiting. A request was also made that a police presence should be available to take five seamen into custody, pending charges of being accessories to mass murder.

At certain intervals during their moonlit crossing one or other of the Gurkhas took turns to bring coffee and other small snacks up to the bridge. On each of these occasions they marvelled at the speed with which the Flying Dolphin skimmed across the surface. They also reported on the prisoners, who in the main were quiet. Tommy Jung, however, was suffering sore ribs, which had resulted from his making further attempts at bribing them.

There was a large crowd waiting on the hydrofoil berth at Hai Phong as Kate manoeuvred the craft alongside, and early morning sun glistened off the fuselage of Lorna's aircraft, which was also bobbing close to the wharf on a temporary mooring.

Watching with a mixture of interest and admiration as Kate applied deft touches to the throttles of the hydrofoil, it quickly became apparent that the temporary skipper was more in control of the vessel than she was of her emotions. Large tears sat on her cheeks and Charlie distinctly heard uncontrollable sobs coming from her.

Realising that Kate had lived through days in which she thought it unlikely that she would ever see her mother or Ruby again, Charlie thought it sensible to allow her space and the privacy of her thoughts while also hoping this distress might eventually help her to come to terms with all that she had recently experienced.

Bing and Bang once more accepted the role of deckhands and made passable attempts at casting mooring lines over the dockside samson posts.

Once the engines had been set to idle and then cut completely, Kate quickly made her way down from the pilot cabin and momentarily disappeared from view. Charlie did not attempt to follow, watching instead as she reappeared on deck and then raced across the outer wing to her mother's open arms.

From his vantage point Charlie looked on as Ruby joined their embrace, and he was not surprised at the emotion shown by all three women. Eventually, when it seemed they might never disentangle, Lorna broke free and appeared to be visually searching the crowded quayside.

It is possible that Charlie's complete absorption with a very attractive middle-aged woman had telepathically drawn her attention up to him. On seeing him Lorna's expression changed from one of concern to the most dazzling smile he had ever witnessed, and almost instantly she was beckoning for him to climb down and join her.

Charlie's exit from the craft was briefly delayed while waiting for Tommy Jung and his crew to be escorted off the vessel by two of the Gurkhas before being handed over to a waiting police presence.

"What were you doing, hiding yourself away up there when I so desperately needed you to be with me?" Lorna scolded, in a tone which was certainly not disapproval.

"Initially I thought you'd disappeared to avoid this," Lorna continued, while indicating the crush of people who were now surging around Kate. Some were brandishing reporter's notebooks while others were armed with cameras, and Charlie realised that the media had been alerted to Kate's rescue from abduction. He also understood that this was something she would welcome as, despite her preoccupation with a joyous family reunion, it would be an opportunity to reveal to the world's press the awful crimes that Dr. Chang's organisation had been guilty of. Charlie also knew Kate hoped the ensuing publicity would ensure it was unlikely that similar things would ever be perpetrated on unsuspecting and innocent people again.

It had been agreed with the three Gurkhas, during their night passage home, that their group would credit the Beijing State Secrecy Bureau with the doctor's final and dramatic end, by suggesting that resisting arrest had been his downfall.

It was also assumed that denial from the Chinese authorities would not be forthcoming and certainly not if the gory detail of Zin Bax's final elimination was not elaborated upon.

Kate, in particular, had strongly emphasised that Charlie should not be accredited with either death, as she thought the notoriety which would ensue from such an admission would be an encumbrance to his future life.

While these thoughts were being recalled, Lorna did something which further surprised Charlie. She turned him to her and, heedless of the people around them, took his hands in both of hers and gazed at him for what seemed an abnormally long period.

Feeling unsure as to what this out of character gesture was about to reveal, Charlie felt a moment of panic, believing that Lorna was about to issue some statement which he would regret.

"My dear, dear Charlie, had I been told when we met all those years ago in Birmingham that you would eventually have such a profound effect on my life, I would not have believed it. Saying thank you can never truly describe the gratitude that I feel for what you and those three brave Gurkhas have accomplished. I am deeply indebted to all four of you and always shall be."

Very much aware that their physical closeness was attracting attention, Charlie unsuccessfully attempted to divert Lorna from her discourse by being dismissive.

"No, please don't play down what the four of you have achieved." Lorna's shaking him to emphasise her sincerity lasted mere seconds before she continued, with a look of determination,

"Whatever it is that you have agreed to pay Boom and his men, I would like it doubled and the total amount is to come from my account." Lorna then pressed fingers to Charlie's lips, in an attempt to forestall the protest he was about to make.

"When we are married there will be no mine and yours. We will share everything and that includes money. For now though, making payment to those three brave and marvellous Gurkhas is something I very much want to do."

The finality of this was lost on Charlie as he was still absorbed with the opening words of Lorna's statement. His astonishment and happiness in response to this was also causing a choking sensation to rise in his throat.

"I hope you will accept that Kate's rescue has not prompted my presumption. You have made it clear on at least two occasions that you would like our relationship to be close and permanent. While we were in Kashmir I decided that was what I also wanted. Unfortunately unforeseen events intervened and the opportunity to express my acceptance and strong feelings for you was lost in the horror of coming to terms with what we both had to do."

This prompted a gasp of astonishment from somewhere and Charlie was unsure if it was Kate or Ruby that was responsible.

"Please, Charlie Greenwood. Will you marry me?" Swallowing hard and shaking his head, in an attempt to convince himself that he had not imagined the whole thing, a familiar voice then urged,

"Oh please say yes, Charlie. You will be just perfect as a dad and I have always so wanted one."

# Chapter Twenty Eight

Hanoi was not at all what Charlie was expecting, although he realised he should not be surprised that it had little in common with Ho Chi Min City, where he was now based.

Watching a photographer gaining pictorial footage of a wedding party on the steps of a large civic building reminded him of his own marriage to Lorna in the tiny chapel at Koggala. Charlie's own wedding ceremony still held both magical and unbelievable memories for him, with only a small number of family and friends attending. Bill Arthurs, together with Pauline and Charlie's cousin Yvonne, had travelled out together from England, with Bill agreeing to be Charlie's best man.

A new operations director had fortunately been engaged by the Mekong Express Company and, on satisfying herself that the man was reliable, Kate was also able to attend her mother's wedding, along with Ruby, who mostly now divided her time between Saigon and the hotel in Bournemouth.

Surprisingly Gongy elected to remain behind in Vietnam, where he had become a permanent fixture, and was these days noticeably less reticent. Kate's abduction, and the fate of Molly, whom the old engineer had admired, was probably responsible for his current change of temperament.

It now seemed a long time ago, and a great deal of water had certainly flowed under the bridge since the wedding. At Charlie's instigation he and Lorna built a house with a large wooden veranda which extended out over the waters of the Mekong Delta. Lorna, surprisingly, adapted to her new role as housewife and, when not preparing meals and generally fussing over Charlie, busied herself in a riverside garden which had been created for her. Charlie in turn slowly gained some knowledge of river fishing.

Ruby and Kate were their most frequent guests and Charlie's new work colleagues regularly visited them. This involvement created a very acceptable social life for the newly married couple and was in itself a discovered pleasure for the hitherto long established bachelor.

Grant Aid funding had been withdrawn abruptly from the harbour project in Colombo, and Charlie's company assumed he would be returning to their head office and his former role as a director of engineering.

When recovering from the shock of Lorna's marriage proposal, Charlie immediately decided that long spells of separation was not what he wanted from the marriage that he had always dreamed of, and he had not hesitated in tendering his resignation. The construction business was littered with broken marriages, mostly caused by absentee husbands engaged on contracts in out of the way and inhospitable places. There had been too many years of bachelorhood for Charlie to not now make every effort for his marriage to succeed.

Lorna had further surprised him by insisting that she would also devote her time to their new partnership, and that this would not be possible if she retained managerial responsibilities for Savage Air. She had also foreseen that inactivity would be a problem for Charlie, and when Kate offered him a position in her rapidly expanding ferry company, Lorna helped his decision by indicating that she would find relocating to Vietnam both challenging and exciting. Kate had, however, shown some concern with this arrangement, thinking that her mother might wish to become involved with the Mekong Express Company. This had so far not happened and Lorna's only business involvement was when she attended Savage Air's bi-monthly board meetings.

Life had changed dramatically for Charlie with his responsibility for the ferry company's infrastructure and shore based engineering projects. This new balance of involvement was intermingled with considerably more leisure time than previously enjoyed and it enabled both him and Lorna to settle to a life of domesticity which neither had previously experienced.

Despite regrets that there had been wasted years when they might have been together, Charlie could not now imagine a more perfect life. Occasionally he was haunted by memories of Kate's abduction and fears of failure which he had experienced leading up to her eventual rescue.

Tommy Jung's impending trial now rekindled those unpleasant memories and Charlie hoped a just verdict would be reached that might offer Kate some respite from the guilt he knew she still felt for the deaths of Molly and the two men. He had learned through an overheard conversation in the offices on Bang Dang jetty that a generous financial allowance had been arranged for Molly's aged parents and that both the taxi driver and office manager's dependants also received substantial financial support from the company.

It was as well that he had taken advice and brought warm clothing with him to Hanoi, as people and the city's architecture were not the only differences he was currently experiencing. Despite being forewarned, Charlie was now surprised by the icy wind which cut through the material of his winter coat as he walked past the Reunification Palace on his way to the Central Law Courts. Some weeks before, he and Kate had received a summons to appear for the prosecution to give evidence in the trial of Tommy Jung.

Dodging through the many motorcyclists and cyclists who bore down on him as he crossed a very busy road, Charlie was relieved to see his step-daughter waiting on the steps of the law court. A prior commitment necessitated Kate travelling up that morning and Charlie had been concerned that her flight might be delayed. As a key witness for the prosecution her absence or late arrival might, he realised, cause difficulties.

"I'm so relieved to find you already here. Have you made contact with anyone from the legal set-up yet?" Charlie questioned, after giving his recently acquired stepdaughter a very long and welcoming hug.

"Yes, and a clerk suggested that we should sit in the waiting area until we are called." Kate then went on to explain it was possible that Charlie would not now be required to give evidence. His look of surprise prompted further explanation.

"Tommy Jung's crew have turned state's evidence, or however it's described, and the evidence they will offer should negate a need for you to take the witness stand. The crew are obviously attempting to lighten their sentences and the clerk says it's certainly the case that Tommy is facing an additional charge of being an accessory to murder. The woman also informed me that the prosecutor is going to push strongly for the death penalty."

Kate's latter words were uttered in a tone of misgiving and Charlie realised that, despite the desire for a severe sentence, her abhorrence of taking another person's life was once more placing a heavy burden of guilt onto her young shoulders.

"This trial is going to be yet another unpleasant experience. When you are called to take the witness stand, you should try to remember what was done to Molly and the many other victims of that ghastly regime."

Before responding to this, Kate appeared lost in thought, until finally reiterating something which she had previously expressed.

"I shall never ever forget what took place in those showers. Since that awful day I have wanted nothing other than justice and that is more important to me than any sympathy I may now feel for Tommy Jung."

Kate's shiver was probably a reaction to those memories, although Charlie suggested they move off and find the waiting room when realising that the outside temperature might be contributing to her discomfort.

That they did not immediately recognise Luc Tun was understandable. When they had last seen him he had been dressed in work clothes. Now he was resplendent in a Western style suit. His hair and beard had also been trimmed for the occasion and a very noticeable scar ran across his forehead. On noticing this, Charlie realised that had the ricocheting bullet been millimetres lower, Luc might have lost sight in at least one of his eyes.

"Hello Kate, hello Charlie. I'm sorry I was unable to inform you that I was to attend the trial. Everything just happened so quickly. My understanding is that the Vietnamese authorities only obtained permission for me to give evidence at the eleventh hour and, as you might imagine, making arrangements for getting here absorbed a lot of time and paperwork."

More explanations may have been offered had Kate not then enveloped the Cambodian in her arms. When she finally released him, Luc was only just breathlessly able to answer some of her many questions regarding Lai Mee and the children.

Since being rescued and on returning to Ho Chi Min City, Kate had received regular correspondence from both Luc and Lai Mee. Those communications had, however, been written in what appeared to be couched terms and this seemed to indicate that the Cambodian couple were still wary of censorship.

"I think our update is now going to be put on hold," Kate announced, when she recognised the prosecution counsel's clerk making her way through the crowded waiting area to intercept them. Then much to the waiting trio's next surprise, the rather studious middle-aged legal executive informed them with some disdain that the defending counsel was requesting an adjournment to allow further time for fresh evidence to be submitted.

Colour drained from Kate's cheeks and Charlie realised that she feared a reprieve for her former hydrofoil skipper. On then learning from the clerk that there was to be a two hour adjournment, Charlie suggested,

"Why don't we take ourselves off and find someplace to have coffee? This justice building is certainly not furnished for comfort and it will be more pleasant to learn what has been happening to Lai Mee and Luc in a place where it's at least warm."

The small café they found close to the law courts had retained both its original French décor and atmosphere; coupled to this was the fact that it also served excellent coffee and croissants.

Luc's interest in Kate's wellbeing and the activities of her company at first dominated conversation, until Charlie managed to interrupt and tell him that he and Lorna had met up with Bing, Bang and Boom on their honeymoon excursion to Kashmir. When the description of this reunion was exhausted, Kate and Charlie were then able to ask questions which they had thus far not known the answers to.

"Did you manage to learn anything of those men who spared me the task of finishing off Zin Bax?" Charlie asked.

"Yes indeed. In fact they came out to the homestead to interrogate us the day after you left with the hydrofoil, and it was as I suggested while Boom was attending to this." Luc gingerly fingered the scar on his forehead.

"They are Beijing State Secrecy Bureau agents and they were on the island investigating irregularities that the Guangdong authorities were so obviously turning a blind eye to."

Kate, who had never before had the role of the State Secrecy agents fully explained, caused a brief flow to Luc's description of the Bureau men's visit to the homestead. When satisfied that she now had some understanding, the Cambodian turned back to Charlie.

"The large individual who carried out Zin Bax's execution was very obvious by his immense size. Frighteningly so in fact; the man has the appearance of a wrestler, or perhaps a weightlifter. Despite a rather overwhelming and imposing stature, the big man was obviously the senior member of the quartet. It was also obvious that he is an educated individual. When he discovered that we were Cambodians, he went so far as to ask if we would prefer our interrogation to be conducted in French. My response, I remember, was somewhat hesitant. I suppose I was still trying to come to terms with the shock of them turning up. It seems he mistook my hesitancy and assumed I had no passable understanding of Cantonese. The big man also suggested he had a reasonable grasp of English and if preferred we could use that language. He then actually surprised both of us by apologising for not being able to discuss our situation in Khmer. I like to think that I am a reasonably good judge of character and decided he was not simply showing off. Not only was I impressed by his obvious intelligence, it also occurred that despite what I knew him to be capable of, he appeared surprisingly mild-mannered and gentle." Charlie then thoughtfully agreed that from his brief experience, this seemed an unlikely characteristic.

Luc Tun appeared to mull this observation over before continuing with what had taken place.

"We were told that as the Bureau already had a presence on the island the agents were alerted to the fact that an unidentified aircraft had entered Chinese airspace and then been lost from radar. The big man explained that a surveillance screen was immediately put in place and that you and your three Gurkhas were easily spotted as you cycled into town. Although there was not a need for our visitors to offer lengthy explanations, they in fact suggested that they at first believed you to be an insurgent group from the nationalist island of Formosa. You will probably be aware that the nationalists and mainland authorities have been in a standoff situation since the days of Chiang Kai-shek. Probing one another's defences, the agents told us, is a fairly regular occurrence. Because of this, the bureau men decided not to intervene until they had discovered what it was that you were attempting. Their close surveillance then picked up on the fact that you eventually found and made contact with me. Initially they then believed me to be an undercover agent who had been planted out on the marshes by the nationalists. When Kate duly appeared on the scene, this caused further confusion in their ranks. They were already aware that there had been an extensive search made by the medical centre staff in an attempt to reapprehend a donor patient who had escaped by murdering one of the medical centre's employees. On piecing together the bits of information that they then had, the agents concluded Kate was in fact that missing patient and that I, the suspected nationalist, had been sheltering her. Realisation of this added further confusion to their thinking and they decided to wait and see what might develop."

When coffee and food was brought to the table it caused a further break to Luc's lengthy explanation.

"Watching you five climb up into the bowels of that gravel washing plant created some surprise and it eventually dawned on them that your interest was not at all subversive and was in fact the plight of the recently docked refugees. As this was also uppermost on their list of priorities for investigation, it reinforced their earlier decision to play the waiting game and see what might develop with your involvement."

Charlie, who had spent a great part of his life worrying about weight problems, was then aghast at the quantity of sugar which Luc Tun next spooned into his coffee.

"When the agents saw your two Gurkhas overpower crew from the hydrofoil they were finally convinced that you and they were sharing a common objective. It was at this point that they decided to let you continue to run with things and see what the outcome might be. Apparently they were disappointed that my attempt at pushing the Zil and its occupants into the dock failed, as they believed it would be left for them to deal with an embarrassment which was rapidly growing for the Chinese people. Your intervention was approved of and they were on their way to ensure that neither the doctor nor his accomplice escaped from the car when you once more appeared at the dockside. The bureau men laughingly suggested that they were relieved that you no longer had my bulldozer with which to create further damage and chaos. It seems they also have a sense of humour."

Luc paused, allowing Kate and Charlie sufficient time to absorb the extraordinary significance of what he had just related.

"Lai Mee and I had one awful fright when the agents turned up at the farm on the day after your departure." Searching for a handkerchief to wipe something from his eye then caused yet further delay.

"Now would probably be an appropriate time for me to explain that when we realised there was no immediate alternative other than to come clean, we explained that we were refugees who had escaped from the medical centre. We also described how we were given shelter by the former owner of the farm. In fact I even offered to take them to Lin Yen's grave and suggested it would be an easy task to exhume his body if they wished to determine that his death had not resulted from foul play. It had occurred to me during our questioning that possession of the homestead might appear suspicious and those men would conclude that we had murdered the old man simply to gain ownership of his property. Lai Mee was mortified by my proposal as she has come to revere the spirit of Lin Yen and felt very strongly that his remains should not be disturbed. Fortunately she kept those feelings to herself and the agents dismissed my offer as being unnecessary. The story of our escape they suggested was very convincing, particularly so as I had admitted to killing one of the medical centre employees in the shower block. They also told us that they quickly concluded that we were an honest couple who had simply fought to survive. At that stage I was beginning to feel things might turn out all right, although it was obvious that Lai Mee was still terrified by thoughts of the disastrous outcome for our family."

A waiter asking if they would like more coffee then intervened and when their cups had been once more replenished, Luc continued.

"Although Chang Jin-Ming believed that his operation on the island was secure, it seems at least one well-meaning citizen was brave enough to take his suspicions to a higher authority in Beijing. This unsubstantiated account was believed to have substance and an undercover agent was sent to the island, ostensibly to work as an artefacts expert in the local museum. This same plant quickly concluded that things were not as they should be and within days of his arrival, the main body of Bureau agents was dispatched to Haikou."

"So it is possible that had Charlie and his team not shown, I might eventually have been able to emerge from hiding?" Kate questioned.

Luc Tun shrugged in a way which suggested that he didn't know, although after consideration he suggested he thought it was as well that things had not been left to chance.

"It quickly became apparent that the agents' main interest was what Lai Mee and I had learned of Dr Chang Jin-Ming's activities. They questioned us very thoroughly on what we knew of the medical centre and also for details of our initial contact with the organisation that had led to our becoming a part of the vast victim chain. It seems many thousands were murdered in one way or another and if the organisation had not been stopped, more would almost certainly have perished. The location where we first made our approach to become illegal refugees was of special interest and I imagine the authorities have since been alerted in an attempt to apprehend those involved at the Phnom Penh end."

Kate was the next to interrupt by suggesting she hoped that all the active and guilty parties would eventually be brought to justice from wherever they were operating.

Charlie's immediate concern was for the outcome of Luc Tun and his family when it was discovered that they were living on the island as illegal immigrants.

"Surprisingly, the Bureau men were sympathetic. They quickly put us at ease by suggesting that they would recommend us for citizenship on the basis of our being both long established and law abiding. This was after I had tentatively asked if my admission to what had happened in the shower block might lead to my facing a murder charge. The lead agent said that in the aftermath of clearing up, one unidentified body was neither here nor there and my admission was being treated as self-defence by them and that no one outside their group would ever know what had truly taken place. In fact the big man went on to say that Lai Mee and I would be kept from the publicity which would almost certainly follow. I rather think now that had Tommy Jung's trial taken place back in China, I would not have been allowed to give evidence and the prosecuting lawyers would simply have relied on both of you. It is possible of course that they would also have called on your three Gurkha friends to give evidence."

Kate interrupted him again by saying that had he not rescued her and become involved, he and Lai Mee might have been left to live out happy lives with their children undisturbed.

Responding to this, Luc shook his head before going on to explain.

"It's okay. The good news is that not only were we able to rescue you, we have also now been given Chinese citizenship and everything has turned out just fine. I thought it unwise to write and give an account of everything that has happened as I suppose it will take time for us to understand that we are no longer living under the shadow of Dr Chang Jin-Ming's influence."

Luc's interruption was next caused by Kate expressing her feelings of relief and happiness.

"I suppose we would have considered ourselves lucky if the only punishment we received was to be sent back to Phnom Penh. Cambodia, however, holds nothing other than unpleasant memories for us and so rest assured, all is well that has ended well."

Luc went on to tell them he had also learned that most of the medical centre employees were sentenced to lengthy spells of hard labour and that the supervisors had been executed. The very best news the Cambodian had was kept until last, and he told them that the final shipment of refugees had been released by operatives from the Beijing State Secrecy department. It seemed that in the absence of Zin Bax, the senior medical staff, after carrying out their routine examinations, had hesitated in following through with the mass exterminations. Surprisingly it also transpired that the agents had found one single male candidate amongst the small intake who was occupying Kate and Lai Mee's special treatment cell. The refugees, after taking their showers, had then been left in limbo while waiting for General Bax to show. The eventual and somewhat confused outcome to this was that sadly, and despite their best endeavours to find an easier and safer life, the refugees were speedily repatriated to their countries of origin.

On realising that the three Gurkhas would be relieved to learn the shipment of people they had witnessed coming ashore had not suffered the fate of earlier refugees, Charlie assured Kate and Luc that he would pass this information onto Bing, Bang and Boom in Kathmandu at the first opportunity.

Tommy Jung's trial was concluded in six days. He was found guilty on the four main charges of trafficking in drugs and for being an accessory to the murder of Molly and the two men abducted with her.

Had sentencing been left with the Vietnamese authorities, Tommy Jung may have been condemned to two concurrent life sentences of imprisonment. As the sea captain was the holder of a Chinese passport, the decision was taken from the Vietnamese court and an extradition order to China ratified.

With the conclusion of the trial an air of sadness overshadowed the trio on their final evening together. The reason for this had nothing to do with the decision to extradite Tommy Jung, although they had by then learned that the death penalty would be enforced by the Beijing authorities.

Eventually it was Luc who suggested that this might be the last time that they would ever be together.

Kate's smiling response seemed at least out of keeping and certainly insensitive, although her next divulgence quickly reinforced Charlie's growing admiration and respect for his stepdaughter.

"You almost certainly will be seeing more of us than you might have imagined. On my last afternoon at the office, I was able to conclude agreement for a new ferry service. Subject to contract, our company will be operating a regular schedule between Haiphong and Hong Kong via Hainan Island and the port of Haikou. My aim is that we will be under way in the next six months and Charlie's input with the infrastructure will be one of the first things to begin." It was probably the look on Charlie's face which prompted her to add,

"It's okay, Charlie; you will be able to handle most of the work from home, with only occasional site visits. It's also possible that those visits will coincide with Mum's trips back to Koggala for board meetings."

While very aware of the surprise her announcement had created, Kate next turned to Luc Tun.

"I could ill afford the time that I have spent here at the trial, although avenging the deaths of Molly and the many other refugees was an absolute priority. Now, however, there is going to be much less time to get things rolling and we will need to put our skates on."

Luc was then about to say how much he admired her enterprise when Kate forestalled him.

"I have decided that I would like to offer Lai Mee a position at Haikou as I feel her linguistic skills will be a great asset to the company. With the boys both at school, is it possible that you might find someone to care for your daughter if Lai Mee is interested in taking on new responsibilities?"

An expression on Luc Tun's face mirrored Charlie's own astonishment, although it shouldn't have, as he had quickly learned that his wife was not a person to let the grass grow beneath her feet and he concluded that like mother, like daughter. Kate was proving to be something of a human dynamo.

In the weeks following Tommy Jung's trial, Charlie was at a peace within himself. Life with Lorna was every bit as good as he hoped it would be and his work involvement, although small by comparison to previous responsibilities, produced an enthusiasm which had certainly been lacking during his latter and somewhat tedious occupation.

Walking back into his office following a return trip from Haikou, Charlie's attention was drawn to a saddle sitting astride the back of a chair; this reminded him that it was now more than three years since he had purchased that same saddle at the auction rooms in Bedford.

It was also a reminder that he had left an altogether different life behind and that he had no regrets. The saddle was, in fact, one of the few items which he had shipped out when making his home in Vietnam.

It was also something of a coincidence that the saddle would be going with him and Lorna to Srinagar in the following weeks, when they would be revisiting Ali Baba. Charlie was looking forward to that reunion, not only with the livery stable owner but also the three Gurkhas, Bing, Bang and Boom, who would regularly escort them whenever he and Lorna returned to Kashmir.

The hacking saddle would be used exclusively on Tadger and Charlie had only future fulfilment to look forward to.

# Epilogue

Chantille Schmitt was not in the least bit interested in a brochure which had been handed to her by a salesman at the International Boat Show in Olympia. What was more to Chantille's liking was the fluted glass of chilled champagne she had been given when wandering onto the boat builder's stand.

Chantille's lack of enthusiasm was partly due to the fact that probate on her mother's estate had still to be finalised; mostly, though, it was because she had no desire to buy a yacht of any description. Spending time in rough seas, being constantly wet and coping with the foul smell from bilges was not something which Chantille could ever imagine enjoying. The exhibition featuring all manner of pleasure craft was merely an opportunity for her to observe the rich and famous, whose ranks she soon hoped to join.

"Gosh! Why would anyone who looks that stunning bother with boring old business?" This observation came from a female companion who Chantille had met in a London gay club three nights before. The girl was pretty, although Chantille was beginning to tire of her.

Looking across at a picture in the maritime and yachting magazine which had attracted the young blonde teenager's attention, Chantille read the title of the article, "Young Up and Coming Entrepreneur". The full page photograph displayed a very attractive young woman whose best features had obviously been captured by a skilled photographer who was keen to display his subject at her very best. Chantille liked attractive women and shared her companion's opinion that, if blessed with beauty, it was foolhardy not to use those gifts.

Chantille had lived most of her life in the shadow of her mother's success and because of this she might not have bothered reading the article, had her eyes not focused on reference to the Fan Chee Medical Institute.

Nancy Schmitt, Chantille's mother had been showered with accolades while retaining a prominent position in the competitive world of banking and commerce.

By comparison, Kate Savage was attributed with the development of a highly successful ferry company which was operating throughout South East Asia from a base in Ho Chi Min City.

It transpired that the Savage woman had rejected offers of a safe position in her family's business and instead used a legacy to purchase an ailing marine company.

"What an idiot," Chantille thought. "I shall certainly find better things to do with my inheritance." She watched the yacht salesman as he disengaged from yet another time-wasting stand visitor, who had held him in worthless conversation for some time.

"Will you allow me to freshen that glass for you, Miss Schmitt? When my colleagues have returned from lunch, I will then give you my undivided attention."

"Please, take your time. My friend and I are in no hurry and we are enjoying your generous hospitality." Privately Chantille thought the man a fool for clutching at straws; she had drifted into the Boat Show simply to kill time until the gay bars reopened.

"Mm, that is nice. If we stay here much longer, I shall get quite squiffy on that gorgeous man's delicious champagne, darling!" Chantille was annoyed by the remark. The young woman had spoken too loudly and she glanced irritably across at her.

Chantille's attention was then immediately drawn to a bare thigh and the sight of black silk, which she knew was the hem of one of the teenager's undergarments. Familiar stirrings sprang from deep in her belly and Chantille realised she would not be escaping from the girl's obvious attractions that night, despite an earlier resolve to do so.

In an attempt to distract her thoughts from pleasures of the flesh, Chantille turned her attention back to the magazine, hoping somewhat reluctantly to relieve herself from thoughts of the previous night's abandon.

Following a description of Kate Savage's successful achievements in a business which seemed out of keeping with the young woman's appearance, Chantille read that the up and coming female entrepreneur had been instrumental in bringing about the downfall of an infamous transplant surgeon, who had obtained donor organs for his hospital in China from an illegal people trafficking organisation.

The magazine article concluded that the current whereabouts of Dr. Chang Jin-Ming was unknown, and that the Fan Chee Medical Institute was no longer operating.

On turning back to the frontispiece, Chantille noted that the magazine print date was some thirty months earlier.

"Well, they've got that wrong," she murmured. Her blonde companion looked quizzically across at her, but failed to ask for an explanation.

The Fan Chee Institute might, in the report's opinion, no longer exist, but Chantille knew for certain that Dr. Chang's organisation was still functioning.

Chantille had always realised that her brother worshipped their mother, although she was amazed by his stupidity when insisting that Nancy have one of his kidneys when hers were failing. This opinion had to some extent been confirmed when Nancy's body rejected Helmut's organ.

When Aunt Sin-Lee and Chantille's mother then went off to the Fan Chee Institute for transplant operations, Chantille believed it was a risk that she would not have taken. In her opinion, being permanently disabled was preferable to risking surgery and the ultimate sacrifice. She had therefore not been surprised by her aunt's death when a replacement heart was rejected. Chantille had, however, felt cheated of her inheritance when her mother made a remarkable recovery.

When, after serious illness, Helmut's remaining kidney began to fail, Nancy had been beside herself with guilt, and she had then devoted all her time and energy in an attempt to find a replacement kidney for her son. Conventional routes produced nothing other than a number of devastating disappointments and so once more Nancy sought help from the Fan Chee Institute.

Perplexed by learning that Dr. Chang was no longer available, Nancy considered long and hard before agreeing that the doctor's son, Julian, could deputise for his father. Nancy's decision was not helped by also learning that the institute was no longer able to supply donor organs.

It had seemed to Chantille that her mother's decision to forfeit one of her own transplanted kidneys, in an attempt to prolong Helmut's life, was a desperate act of insanity, and in this instance transplant surgeons throughout both Europe and America had all agreed with that assumption. As a final last act of desperation Nancy had asked highly respected surgeons in Cuba to perform the operation; sadly, without exception they all agreed with previous advice, that the risk was far too high.

When both Nancy and Helmut died at the Fan Chee Institute within days of one another, Chantille had wasted little time in contacting her mother's legal adviser and from him she learned that she was to be the main beneficiary of her mother's considerable estate.

"Helmut and my mother were receiving treatment at the Fan Chee Institute less than nine months ago. This statement about its closure is a load of baloney," Chantille muttered to herself. She then put the magazine to one side and almost instantly forgot the article.

While the yacht salesman was engaged with yet another prospective client, Chantille led her companion discreetly from the stand. There were more interesting things to occupy her than thinking about the Fan Chee Institute.